MW00830533

Cassie's Miracle

by
Yvette Blake

www.YBlake.com

Skinny Brown Dog Media
www.SkinnyBrownDogMedia.com

Published by Skinny Brown Dog Media Atlanta, GA
www.skinnybrowndogmedia.com

Distributed by Skinny Brown Dog Media
Developmental Editing and Design by Eric G. Reid
Content Editing by Timothy Swiney
Cover Design by Skinny Brown Dog Media
Publisher's Cataloging-in-Publication Data Print

Cover Photo by Helena Taylor Photography
Copyright 2022 by Lena T. Photography. All Rights Reserved.
Cover Model: Shaina Raymond Kurth

eBook ISBN: 978-1-957506-21-0
Hardback ISBN: 978-1-957506-22-7
Paperback ISBN: 978-1-957506-23-4
Case Laminate ISBN: 978-1-95706-3-3

Dedication

I would like to dedicate this to my husband, Bruce Blake, who has been my hero since before we were married, over thirty years ago. Through the many years of balancing work-life and raising our children, he has been there for me, working alongside me, doing his best to be a good husband and father. And especially of late, he has shown an increased amount of love and support, believing in me and my dream of becoming a published author. Without him, "Cassie's Miracle" would not have been possible.

Acknowledgement

I would like to thank my family and friends who have been there with me from the beginning as I started my writing journey. And especially my Heavenly Father who inspired this series of "Cassie's Miracle" and lead me to those people who could help me accomplish this monumental feat. The list of friends and family would be too long to name here, but I want all of them to know it is because of each one of you that I believed I could achieve what I once thought to be impossible. Thank you from the bottom of my heart.

A special thanks to my mother, Marie Meng, who was my first reader and fan. She has always believed in me and whatever I have endeavored and has been an inspiration to me of what a wonderful mother and wife should be. Her time and talents have always been focused on her family and those she associates with, and we feel of her sincere love and support.

An overwhelming thanks to Peggy Jefferson. God put you in my path and me in yours so that we could become friends and look what a wonderful friendship it has become. You have been a blessing to me since the day I met you. I appreciate all your encouragement as a new writer as you took my work and added your expertise as a line editor. I couldn't have accomplished this without you, my kindred spirit.

A special thank to Shaina Raymond Kurth for your modeling services and being my Cassie for this cover.

And last but not least, a heartfelt thank you to Eric G. Reid and his team at Skinny Brown Dog Media. His skill as an editor/writing coach and publisher has helped me bring this work of fiction into reality. My dream of becoming a published author and putting my best work out to the world has been made possible due to your guidance. You brought out the best in me and my abilities. I'm grateful that God sent me to you right when I needed you. Bless you and your team for this beautiful masterpiece called, *Cassie's Miracle*.

Testimonials

"*Cassie's Miracle* is a heartwarming novel that takes you on a journey of loss, love, and finding true joy. Cozy up with this feel-good story of resilience, friendship, love, and kindness while you read about Cassie, Ed, and their friends and family. This should be a Hallmark movie!" ~Alyssa Hunter

"As an avid reader, I truly enjoyed Yvette Blake's historical fiction story, *Cassie's Big Move* and her first historical romance novel, *Cassie's Miracle*. Her writing is equal with many fine established authors. Definitely a 5-star rating!" ~Rita Mucci

"As Cassandra Black travels her own trail of tears from tragedy to romance, she discovers true friends and faithful families who support her with unflinching generosity. The "wild west" becomes Cassie's haven in the midst of deep sorrow, and the miracle of a healing heart. Yvette Blake weaves her story with compassion, courage, and humor, always painting a picture with rich detail underlined with an appreciation of old-fashioned American values." ~Peggy Jefferson

"*Cassie's Miracle* is a fresh and innovative take on the old west. The well-researched details offered interesting insight into this historical romance. I love that through-out the love story of Cassie and Edward, they both have to work through hatred and fear of the people who took those they most loved, to grow toward understanding and empathy—reminding me and giving me hope that I can overcome difficulties in own life. This story provides not only a historical fun romance but takes the reader through the characters struggles to work through the hardest trials people have to face. You find yourself cheering for them both and enjoying their journey. *Cassie's Miracle* is such an inspiring story, it gives a feeling of hope and peace, even amidst trials. A book definitely worth reading!" ~ D. Stansel

"I loved *Cassie's Miracle*. It kept me on the edge of my seat the whole way through. I'm a sucker for romance and the way this one unfolded was beautiful. I absolutely loved the happy ending. Can't wait for the rest of the series." ~Rhonda Floyd

x

Contents

Chapter 1
Missouri, May 1, 1869

Cassie lay curled in a ball, arms wrapped around her knees, shaking with fright in the wheat field behind her house. She didn't know how long she'd been there as she drifted in and out of consciousness. Her nightdress was torn and filthy, smeared with soot, dirt, and blood, evidence of her recent battle for life. Cassie was unrecognizable with her matted black hair, tear-streaked face, and bruised frame. Laying there in shock, Cassie's broken soul wished for the peace that death would bring. Squeezing her eyes shut, she tried to block out the horrific events of the night, as they flashed into her mind before she fell into unconsciousness again.

It had been a little after midnight when she awoke, dreading the thought of leaving the warm bed where her sister Charlotte lay sleeping soundly beside her. Cassie reluctantly sat up on the edge of the bed and slipped on her boots, not bothering to fasten them before she headed outside to the outhouse. As she tiptoed down the hall, passing the doors to her younger brothers and sister's rooms, she could hear her father's soft snoring, at the end of the hall. No one stirred as Cassie crept through the house, feeling her way as she went, being careful not to bump into the furniture. Reaching the dark kitchen, she felt for the lantern and lit it with the strike of a match. Quietly, Cassie went out the front door, closing it softly behind her, not wanting to disturb her sleeping family.

Max, their blue heeler, met her on the porch with a whimper. "Shh, Max. Go back to bed," she whispered, rubbing his furry head. Obediently, he went back to his favorite sleeping spot, curled up, and watched her momentarily before closing his eyes. Leaving the lantern hanging outside the house on the porch rail, Cassie hurried across the yard chilled by the cool night air, as she raced towards the outhouse, letting the door with the moon cut hole close behind her. Moments later, she heard the blood-curdling cry of attacking Indians.

Max barked ferociously as he stood guard at the bottom of the porch steps. The Indians' shrill cries intensified as the beating sound of horses' hooves became louder and louder as the Indians entered the yard. Cassie pulled the outhouse door shut tight and latched it, peeking out through the small crescent hole. In the lantern's yellow glow, she was able to see a group of war-painted braves as they approached the farmhouse. They were bare chested, wearing buckskin breeches, riding bareback as they circled in the yard with lifted bows strung and ready to release their arrows, aiming them towards the house. Max yelped and collapsed in the yard as an arrow pierced his heart, Max raised his head one last time before falling lifeless in the center of the yard. Cassie covered her mouth to hold in her scream, then ducked down, fearing the invaders would see her. A shock of terror ran through her body as she feared what they planned to do to her family and her.

Cassie heard gun shots ring out from her father's rifle. Cassie pushed herself into the corner of the outhouse trying to make herself as small as possible. Glass shattered and screams from her mother and two sisters cut through the night. Cassie heard the Indians crash through the front door of the house and she jumped involuntarily as more gunshots rang out. Her brothers must have joined in the fight. Helplessly, Cassie covered her ears, trying to shut out her family's screams as they fought for their lives.

Cassie sobbed as she prayed. "Dear God! Please help us!"

The sound of crashing furniture and the cries of the struggling family members inside the house fell silent. Cassie slowly removed her hands from her ears. She waited for some clue of who had survived the battle. A high-pitched yelp followed by exuberant screams went up as the Indians rejoiced at their victory. As she heard the sound of glass shattering and feet running just yards away from her hiding place, Cassie's terror increased, and her trembling body jumped. Cassie sank lower to the floor holding her breath, listening for anyone approaching the outhouse. Being drawn back into the horror of the moment, the smell of smoke reached her. Cassie peeked through a crack between the boards, and saw yellow flames leaping from within the house's open front door. Windows popped and shattered as the heat from the blaze grew inside the house. Cassie watched, hoping that somehow her family had miraculously survived and would soon escape the inferno that was now their home. Cassie waited in horror as the flames overtook the walls and roof of the home that had been lovingly constructed to protect them. The thick beams of the roof snapped and cracked as they burned, as the roof caved in and came crashing down. Black, torrid smoke began to fill the air, blocking her view of the burning farmhouse and her hopes of anyone surviving.

The smoke began to fill the outhouse burning her throat and choking her. How much longer could she stay hiding? Leaning forward, Cassie peered out a knot hole in the wall, seeing the Indians round up her family's horses that were in the corral along with her beloved horse,

Midnight, as he bucked and kicked, trying to escape the ropes he'd been lassoed with. Cassie restrained herself from screaming out to Midnight as he snorted and whinnied in fear. Flames and cinders spread from the barnyard, and the straw inside the barn caught fire as the other animals inside fled through the open barn doors, scattering into the dark woods. Cassie watched as the Indian party left, taking Midnight and the rest of the family's horses with them across the field behind the house, then disappeared into the thick trees.

More smoke seeped through the cracks of the small outhouse and Cassie knew if she stayed inside any longer it would soon become her coffin. Flames now licked the roof of the outhouse and the thick black smoke became so overpowering she couldn't breathe without coughing. Cassie had no choice but to lift the wooden latch and slowly open the door. Hunched over, and eyes stinging, she peered out, searching for any sign of movement. Covering her mouth and nose with the crook of her arm, she tried to silence the violent coughing that began to wrack her body. Cassie stumbled out, blindly trudging through the clouds of smoke as she made her way across the yard to the front of the fully engulfed farmhouse.

"Mama! Papa!" Cassie cried out in anguish. "No!" she wailed as the flames grew higher. "Charlotte! Mark! Nathan! Mary Jane!" she called out, hoping they would call back to her, but her family was silent. "It can't be!" She hysterically sobbed as her body shook, and her legs began to lose their strength. The scorching heat from the fiery inferno drove her stumbling away from the house back out into the yard, where she collapsed to the ground.

Cassie lay unconscious on the hard packed dirt; her breathing was so shallow she appeared to be dead. Cassie was roused from her stupor as she felt someone grab her by the arms and begin dragging her limp body. "What's happening?" she wondered in her dream state. "Where am I? How long have I been out?" These questions filled her mind as she tried to regain consciousness. "Was I too close to the fire? Are you taking me to safety?" she screamed in her mind.

When the dragging finally ceased, her arms were freed, and in her semi-consciousness, she tried to command her eyes to open. Her dark lashes fluttered, but her eyelids would not obey and remained closed. Cassie's freedom was only momentary, as she now felt the weight of someone pressing their body, hard against her. Pinning her down, and placing his large hand around her throat, he began choking her. Adrenaline shot through her veins as she tried to fill her lungs with air. Panicked, Cassie struggled with all her strength, kicking and hitting against the immovable weight, feeling as if she was having a nightmare. Desperately she forced herself awake. As her eyes briefly opened, she made out an Indian's face, so close to hers, she could feel his breath on her skin. Cassie began frantically clawing at the Indian's face that was marked with white war paint around his black piercing eyes. He gnashed his brilliant white teeth at her as he laughed wildly. That face would forever be burned into her mind. Cassie squeezed her eyes closed and tried to turn her head away from him, but he was too strong, she was unable to escape. Cassie felt the darkness close in on her as she fell into unconsciousness, and her body went limp as he finished his evil intent.

As Cassie slowly regained consciousness, she remained lying there as still as she could, with her eyes closed, not knowing if he was watching to see if she was still alive. Cassie listened for any sound of the attacker. Once convinced she was alone, she rolled on her side and slowly curled up into a ball, wishing death would come and take her away.

***

As morning dawned, black smoke hung in the sky, signaling to the neighbors a mile down the road, that something was horribly wrong at the Blacks' home. As Mr. Smith and his oldest son, Jacob, raced the wagon down the road to the Black property, they were horrified to see nearly nothing left of the Blacks' home, that had once stood proudly surrounded by the rich farmland.

"What do you think happened?" asked Jacob, staring at the charred remains of the home as timbers continued to burn amidst the white ash. Jacob coughed as the smoke burned his lungs and his eyes watered.

"I can't be sure," Mr. Smith said as he jumped down from the wagon to stand next to Jacob and began searching the property for clues as to what could have happened. "It doesn't look like anyone made it out alive," Mr. Smith added, shaking his head in disbelief at the rubble that had once been a grand home. His heart ached for his dear friends. As Mr. Smith searched the ground for more clues near the remains of the barn, he noticed the horses were gone from the corral. "Look here!" Mr. Smith motioned to Jacob and pointed to the tracks around the corral.

"What is it?" Jacob looked down to where his father was pointing in the soft dirt. They were odd tracks. The footprints weren't made by boots and the horses' hoof prints appeared to be made by unshod horses.

"Indians! These prints were made by moccasins," Mr. Smith declared, as anger built inside him. "Look for others," he said sharply, and Jacob scanned the loose dirt for more tracks.

Mr. Smith followed one set of prints that appeared to

have been dragging something. The trail led him into the wheat field. Mr. Smith noticed something white among the green stalks of wheat and ran towards it. Laying there among the spring wheat, was a young woman in a white nightdress. Mr. Smith knelt beside her, brushing away the black hair covering her scratched and bloodied face.

"Jacob!" he hollered. "I found someone! I think it's Cassie, she's alive!" Mr. Smith could barely recognize the Black's oldest daughter, Cassandra. "Bring the wagon," he yelled to Jacob as he carefully lifted Cassie. She blinked her eyes in the sunlight as she tried to come to.

Cradling Cassie securely in his arms, Mr. Smith repeatedly shook her. "Cassie, Cassie. Where are the others?"

"The Indians," she whispered, "killed them all. I was hiding…in the outhouse…" Her eyes closed as her head fell back, exposing the red marks around her neck.

Mr. Smith was shocked by the handprint on her throat as much as he was from her words. "What in the world? Indians! Have our friends been massacred?" he questioned with horror. He couldn't believe it. Just thinking the words made him sick to his stomach. And yet, here was the proof, all the footprints, the fire and Cassie. There was no other explanation. "Frank and Mary! Oh, and their poor children! Dead," he thought as the truth sank in.

Mr. Smith remembered stopping over earlier that spring when the Blacks were clearing the surrounding acres and was impressed by Mr. Black and his boys in their efforts to improve the property. Now, scanning the property as he walked through the field, there was nothing left but a pile of smoldering timbers and memories. The devastation was catastrophic, and to think that Cassie had survived. Cassie's appearance witnessed how barbaric it must have been. "How could they have been so brutal? This poor girl, so young and innocent. How did she manage to survive?"

Mr. Smith wondered as he looked at the bruising on her throat and face, tangled hair, and filthy nightdress.

Jacob pulled the wagon to a stop in the field and Mr. Smith gently placed Cassie in the back of the wagon, climbed in next to her, and held her as Jacob snapped the reins and drove the wagon home as quickly as he could.

As Jacob pulled the wagon into their yard, Mrs. Smith came running out of the house. "What's happened at the Blacks'?" she asked nervously, knowing fire on a farm was never a good thing. As she rounded the back of the wagon, she saw Mr. Smith was holding Mary's oldest daughter, Cassandra. "Oh, Lord no! What's happened?" Mrs. Smith's eyes pleaded for answers as Jacob climbed in back to help her husband lift Cassie out of the wagon.

Mr. Smith scowled and shook his head. "Cassie said it was an Indian attack. I think the family was all inside the house when the Indians came, except maybe her. Cassie had said something about hiding in the outhouse. I can't imagine how horrible it would have been for her to watch. I found her unconscious in the wheat field. She looks like she's been through a nightmare." Mr. Smith shared the rest of what he knew as he began to remove Cassie from the wagon. "The Indians must have set fire to the house while they were sleeping. There's no sign of anyone making it out alive, Ma. The house burned to the ground, with everyone inside it." Then the horror of what he was saying hit him. Grief-filled and eyes watering, he pulled the still unconscious Cassie closer to him, wanting to protect the dear girl from what had happened to her and her family.

"Dear God, no! Not Indians!" Mrs. Smith covered her mouth, trying to hold in her hysterical sobs.

"I have no idea how Cassie escaped from being killed. It looks like there was a struggle though. She's lucky to be alive, poor girl," he said. It sickened Mr. Smith as he imagined what it would be like if it had been one of his girls. He pushed the thought out of his mind as he carried Cassie into the house, her limp body easily cradled against his hardened frame.

"It's a miracle she survived. Yet maybe she wishes she hadn't," Mrs. Smith thought. "Put her in the girls' room." Mrs. Smith wiped away her tears as she rushed in front of them to the girls' bedroom and pulled down the blankets on the bed in the corner. Her heart was breaking at the loss. Mary and Frank had become their closest friends. With similar aged children, they had enjoyed spending time with one another, sharing meals and visiting while the children played. "And now they're gone…all but Cassie," she thought. Looking to her husband she asked, "Why would the Indians do such a thing?"

"I don't know, Ma. Maybe they were after the horses." Mr. Smith carefully placed Cassie on the bed. "I'll need to get to town as soon as possible," Mr. Smith said as he turned to see Jacob who'd entered the room brushing away his tears. Mr. Smith wished he'd been able to spare Jacob the harsh realities of the cruel world for just a little longer, feeling sixteen was too young to witness such things. The best Mr. Smith could think to do right now was to try to help Jacob feel useful. "Jacob, you go get Doctor Humphries."

Jacob nodded, then left the room to head to town.

Turning back to his wife, Mr. Smith put a hand on her shoulder. "Ma, I've got to let Sheriff Clark know what's happened," he said, and gave his wife a hug before leaving Cassie in her capable hands. "She'll be needing you more than anything right now." With a final squeeze he turned and left her with Cassie.

Mr. Smith rode the three miles into town as fast as his horse could go, anxious to get to the sheriff's office.

Reining his horse into a sliding stop, he jumped down and burst through the office door, shouting, "Sheriff, there's been an Indian attack out at the Blacks'! They've killed the family and stole their horses; they even burned the house and barn to the ground! Cassie barely survived. We've got to get a posse rounded up before they get away!"

"Hang on there, Mr. Smith." Sheriff Clark put up his hands trying to calm the man so he could get the story straight. "You say there's been an Indian attack?" The sheriff scowled. "That's the second one. They hit the Petersons last night. No one survived. Their neighbors found their home destroyed by fire and all their horses gone. The Petersons' neighbors discovered arrows in the burning timbers of the house. I just got back from there. Those poor people, they never made it out of their house."

"The same thing happened at the Blacks'. So come on, Sheriff. We have to hurry. They're puttin' miles between us. I know there's men in town who will help us hunt them down. Let's go!" Mr. Smith said with insistence. "They have to pay for what they did to our friends. If you'd seen what they did to Cassie, you'd be out for blood, too."

"Now Mr. Smith, I understand your wanting to get revenge, but we don't know anything. We can't go off half-cocked. Let's think about this," Sheriff Clark said as he paced in front of his desk. "Do you think the girl could tell us at least what they looked like? Maybe we can determine which tribe they're from." Sheriff Clark rubbed his stubbly chin as he thought of how he could track down the Indians. "Are they a renegade band, stealing horses and murdering the witnesses? Or is it a local tribe looking for revenge?" he wondered.

"Sheriff, I don't think she's in any condition to be questioned. Maybe my wife can get something from her, but she's in shock and pretty beat up. When I found her, I wasn't even sure she was alive."

"But we don't even know which way they headed." Sheriff Clark walked over to the wall where the map of the town hung. As he located the Peterson's home, he then traced his finger down the map to the Black's, circling a three-mile radius between the homes. "It's a huge area to search. They could be fifteen or twenty miles away by now and we don't even know which direction they've gone." The woods surrounding the homesteads to the south and west could've given the Indians cover as they headed into the mountains. Without a trail to follow, the Indians would be just as hard to find as a needle in a haystack.

Mr. Smith stood beside Sheriff Clark and looked over the map. Mr. Smith locating the Black's home, then pointed to an area marked as timberland. "There! That's where I saw their tracks heading off through the woods to the west of the Black's property. At least a dozen Indians, from the look of the tracks they left." Mr. Smith frowned, thinking of how he'd found Cassie in her blood-stained nightdress with bruising around her throat.

"Well, at least we know which way they went. Now we have a trail to follow. Can you get me any more information? It would really help." Sheriff Clark went to his gun cabinet and took out two of the shotguns and a handful of shells and set them on his desk and began packing his saddle bag with provisions. "Cassie's the only living witness. I'll have a posse gathered here in an hour," Sheriff Clark said, anxious to get moving.

"Thank you, Sheriff." Mr. Smith tipped his hat to him. "I'll go home and get my rifle and pack, and then I'll be back." Mr. Smith turned to go and paused in the doorway as Sheriff Clark buckled his holster onto his hip and removed the revolver to check the chamber. "Sheriff, they slaughtered my friends. I want them caught and hung." Mr.

Smith gritted his teeth and glared as he fumed. "I can only imagine what those Indians did to that poor girl. I want them to pay for what they did."

Sheriff Clark looked up at Mr. Smith, seeing how distraught he was. "We'll do what we can within the law, Mr. Smith. I understand how you feel, but we don't want an Indian uprising on our hands. We must handle this the right way. But I'll make sure they pay. Right now, I've got to send a telegram to the Indian agent and let him know what's happened. Once we catch them, they'll be dealt with accordingly."

"They don't deserve a trial!" Mr. Smith shouted over his shoulder as he went outside and swung up onto his horse. "Not if I have anything to say about it," he thought bitterly, determined to get justice one way or another. "I'll be back!" Mr. Smith yelled and kicked his horse into a gallop.

***

Jacob informed Mr. Smith on his return home that the doctor had arrived and was conducting his examination of Cassie. As Mr. Smith impatiently waited to talk to the doctor, he packed his saddle bags with ammunition, food and necessities for the next few days. The doctor emerged from the bedroom, walking slowly into the kitchen, with his shoulders drooping and a troubled look on his face. Mrs. Smith followed the doctor out of the bedroom and closed the door quietly behind her.

"How bad is it, Doc?" Mr. Smith asked, searching for answers.

"Well, to be honest, she's pretty bad off," said Doctor Humphries.

Mr. Smith had assumed as much. "Did she say anything, anything at all? We need to find out who did this. We're gathering a posse and any information would be helpful," Mr. Smith said hastily. Time was of the essence. He didn't know how much of a lead the Indians had, but he imagined it was significant. The posse would have to ride all day and night if they were going to catch up.

"Cassie's in shock and has taken quite a beating as well as sustained lung damage from the smoke." Doctor Humphries ran his hand over his face, unable to meet their eyes. "Someone's done the unthinkable to her," he said with disgust as he frowned and slowly shook his head. He hated thinking of how people could inflict such heinous cruelty on each other especially to someone so innocent. "After what Cassie has been through, I don't advise questioning her. I'm afraid it would push her deeper into shock. She needs to rest. I hope she can pull out of this. She's been through more than I think a girl her age can handle."

"I should go be with her," said Mrs. Smith, her heart breaking from the horrific news. "I'll clean her up, and let you know if she says anything." She went back into the bedroom and closed the door quietly behind her.

Mrs. Smith was a small, gentle woman with the heart of an angel and took great care to gently wash and change Cassie out of her blood-stained clothes. Mrs. Smith calmly talked to Cassie as only a mother knew how to do as she helped Cassie dress. Cassie's eyes were open, but she was utterly indifferent to all that was around her. She barely registered Mrs. Smith's instructions to help her get changed. Her movements were automatic, and her mind was stuck in a reverie where she could safely remain.

"Cassie dear, can you tell me what happened?" Mrs. Smith quietly asked as she gently pulled the nightdress over Cassie's head.

Cassie didn't respond. She couldn't.

"That's okay dear, you don't have to tell me. You're safe here. I'll take good care of you," Mrs. Smith said, trying to soothe Cassie with her soft words and gentle touch.

Cassie lay down and turned away from Mrs. Smith as she closed her eyes, still lost in the deep recesses of her mind.

"You rest, dear. I'll be here." Mrs. Smith pulled the covers over Cassie and tucked her in.

Mrs. Smith came out of the bedroom, her face showing deep sadness. "She's in no shape to be questioned. Go and do what you must, Pa. The poor dear is fighting an inner battle right now. Her pain isn't over, I'm afraid," Mrs. Smith said, unable to hold back the tears, as she began sobbing. "The poor child, her whole family's gone," she muttered as her husband came and hugged her.

Mr. Smith shook his head. "I'll go with the posse. You stay here, Ma, and do what you can for Cassie. She needs you," he said, gently rubbing her back.

"Mrs. Smith, try to get her to eat something, even a little broth will help. In time I think she'll come around. I'll come back tomorrow," Doctor Humphries said as he reached into his bag and brought out a small bottle. "Here's some sleeping powders she can take. It will help her rest and heal." He handed Mrs. Smith the bottle. "You can give her a teaspoon, but only when she really needs them."

"Thank you, Doctor," Mrs. Smith said, taking the powders. "Pa, you'd better get going, they'll be waiting for you." Setting the bottle on the table, she wrapped her arms around her husband and hugged him goodbye. "Be careful, dear, we don't need any more tragedy from this."

"I hope I won't be gone more than a day or two. I'll be home as soon as we've caught them," he said, kissing her on the forehead. "Jacob will be here, and the other children. They can manage the chores. You'll be safe, we'll make sure of it. My guess is those Indians are trying to get as far away as possible," he said, trying to comfort her. Mr. Smith didn't say it out loud, but he thought attacking innocent families while they slept was the most cowardly of all acts. "We're going to chase them down like the dogs they are. They will pay," he thought with disgust as he grabbed his gun and supplies and rushed out the door.

***

Mr. Smith was gone for five days. The posse followed the tracks as far as they could and finally lost them in the mountains. The trail had grown cold, and they were wandering aimlessly. So, with great reluctance, they called off the search and headed home. Sheriff Clark had sent word to neighboring counties about the Indian attacks. But, even after five days, there was still no signs of the Indians. It was if they had disappeared from off the face of the earth.

While Mr. Smith was gone, Mrs. Smith had spent hours sitting with Cassie as she drifted in and out of sleep, riddled with nightmares. Each time the nightmares came, Mrs. Smith tried to comfort Cassie, holding her hand and talking to her in a soothing voice until she dropped off to sleep with help from the sleeping powders. Over time she helped bring Cassie to some safe place in reality. When Cassie began processing the overwhelming loss of her family, the tears flowed, and her body shook uncontrollably, and Mrs. Smith would take Cassie in her arms and hold her until they subsided. It broke Mrs. Smith's heart to see her suffering. It was almost more than she could bear to watch.

In her grief, Cassie barely acknowledged the physical wounds and pain she had. The physical pain paled in comparison to the pain in her heart. Over the next week

15

she remained in bed unaware of the passing days. In time Cassie's stiff and aching muscles healed, the bruises disappeared, her lungs improved, and the coughing eased. Her body was healing but her mind was still in a state of shock and struggled to stay in the present. Without warning, Cassie's thoughts would wander back to that night, replaying every detail, over and over. Peace would only come as she fell asleep with the help of the sleeping powders, but only until the nightmare would jolt her awake again. Cassie was grateful for Mrs. Smith, each time she was there to comfort her until she was able to fall back to sleep.

One afternoon when Cassie seemed able to focus, Mrs. Smith asked Cassie if there was any family, she could send word to, letting them know what had happened.

"Just my mother's sister, Mabel Hartford and her husband. They're the only living relatives I have," Cassie answered numbly.

"Do you know where they live?"

"I think Aunt Mabel and Uncle George live in Cheyenne, Wyoming Territory. I haven't seen them in years." Cassie tried hard to think of what they had said about their life in Cheyenne and could only recall that they had started cattle ranching on a homestead not far from the newly constructed Union Pacific Railroad.

Right away, Mrs. Smith sent word by telegram to Cassie's aunt in Cheyenne, Wyoming Territory.

"Mabel Hartford regret to inform you of death of your sister and family, only Cassandra survived. Letter explains," the telegram stated.

As soon as Mabel received the telegram, she sent a response back. "Cassandra Black, so shocked and heartbroken. Come to Cheyenne as soon as possible Love Mabel," it read.

Mabel received the letter three days later and quickly

opened it.

May 5, 1869
Dear Mabel Hartford,

It is with a heavy heart that I inform you of a terrible Indian attack that resulted in the murders of your sister and her family. The only surviving member was Cassandra. The attack seemed to have happened while the family was sleeping. It was on the morning of May 1ˢᵗ when we discovered the smoke rising from the Black farm. When Mr. Smith arrived, he found the home and barn were a complete loss, burned to the ground, and not a living soul was in sight, including the livestock. On closer inspection, Mr. Smith discovered Cassie in the backfield in a terrible state. From what we can gather, Cassie was hiding in the outhouse and witnessed the Indians attacking. Sadly, when she came out of hiding, she was attacked by one of the Indians but was thankfully left alive, for whatever reason.

We have taken Cassie into our home, and she is slowly recovering under our care. The doctor believes she suffers from shock and was badly beaten, along with some lung damage, which has healed for the most part. We want you to know, that we will care for her as long as needed until she can travel. I'm sure you would want her there with you as soon as possible.

Mr. and Mrs. Black were dear friends of ours and we're grieving their loss. Our thoughts and

prayers are with you and your family and espe-
cially for Cassie.

A funeral for the family will be held here as
soon as Cassie is feeling better. We will send
word as more information comes.
Regretfully,
Mrs. Smith

Anxious to get word back to Mrs. Smith, Mabel immediately wrote a letter in response. Three days later, Mrs.
Smith picked up the letter from the post office and shared
the news with Cassie.

May 8, 1869
Dear Mrs. Smith,

It was a horrible shock to learn of my sister
and her family's deaths. I am greatly saddened by
the loss. Mary was my only living sister and I will
miss her immensely.

Thank you for taking care of our niece, Cas-
sandra. We pray continually for Cassandra's
speedy recovering. My husband and I are anxious
to be with her. We have no children of our own
and have more than sufficient means to care for
Cassandra. Funds will be wired to your bank to
help provide for Cassandra and enough for you
to purchase a train ticket when the time comes.
We would like Cassandra to come to Cheyenne
by train as soon as she is well enough to travel.
News is that The Union Pacific Railroad will be
open and running through Cheyenne, Wyoming

Territory, by the 10th of May. Please send word of any needs that Cassandra may have, and we will provide the funds to meet them. And please let Cassie know we love her and look forward to seeing her soon. Kindly give her our love. Our prayers are with you and your family, and especially Cassie during this difficult time.
Sincerely,
Mabel Hartford

***

Three weeks after the attack, they held the funeral for Cassie's family. Simple grave markers were made for each member and placed in the local cemetery, where they buried the few remains. Mr. and Mrs. Smith stood on either side of Cassie as she stood facing the reverend with the family markers between them. Cassie looked like an angel of grief in the simple black dress she wore. Her flowing ebony hair framed her face as her wide emerald eyes shimmered with tears. Cassie couldn't hold back the tears and let them spill down her smooth porcelain face. She stood with shoulders rolled forward, wrapping her arms around her waist with her eyes down cast. Mrs. Smith placed her arm around Cassie's small waist, hugging her close trying to comfort her, but Cassie still felt alone.

Many townspeople gathered at the graveside, including friends from school, as well as neighbors and congregation members. Even Cassie's betrothed, Bartholomew Clark, was in attendance.

Bartholomew, or Bart as he was most often called, stood with his family as he glanced at Cassie. Bart hadn't

19

seen Cassie since before the attack. He felt too uncomfortable and unsure of what to say to her. The last thing Bart wanted to do was say something that would upset her. For days, Bart had thought about what he should do but was unable to gather the courage to make the trip out of town to see her. Bart was uncertain of himself around Cassie even though he was the son of the most prominent businessman in town. Standing across from her now, he felt completely at a loss.

Bart's father was the owner of the largest mercantile in Jackson County, Missouri, where Bart stocked shelves and managed the books as he apprenticed alongside his father as he prepared to someday take over the mercantile. As much as Bart preferred working indoors due to his fair complexion which he'd inherited along with his red hair from his mother, Bart did enjoy the solitude of the back office and storerooms. He was frequently found there with a book or deep in thought. Every new book that his father bought for the mercantile, Bart would read first, ensuring it was worth the shelf space. As much as he loved reading, he loved learning more, and would have gone to college if it hadn't been for his father needing his help running the business. Bart's quiet demeanor and shyness used to make him feel inadequate in comparison to his classmates. But over the past three years, working alongside his father since graduation, he had become a man of some standing. Bart's position as a future merchant gave him enough self-confidence to start pursuing Cassie as a prospective wife.

Bart remembered first noticing Cassie as she rode her horse through town one day. Her self-assurance struck him as she casily smiled and openly greeted people on the street. Bart asked around and found out that Cassie had graduated from high school recently and was two years younger than him. From that moment on, he went out of his way to wait on her when she came into the mercantile. Cassie was polite but seemed to take no notice of Bart's interest in her. Bart decided he needed to be bold. That was the day he asked her father if he could take her for a buggy ride.

As the reverend read from the Bible standing in front of the gathered mourners, Cassie glanced up and saw Bart and looked away quickly as memories flooded her mind. Cassie remembered how Bart had first approached her father after church one Sunday and asked if Cassie could accompany him on a buggy ride that evening. Mr. Black looked at Cassie, waiting for her response after telling Bart it was up to her. Bart's question had taken her completely off guard and she answered, "Sure," before realizing what she'd said. That evening together, Bart had been very gentlemanly but was nervous and uneasy the whole ride. Cassie remembered Bart's trembling hands and how he prattled on and on about a book he had read and the new goods they were getting into the store. Cassie did her part keeping up her end of the conversation but found Bart quite dull. Although Cassie gave him no encouragement, Bart appeared to be unaware of her disinterest and must have felt encouraged by her silence because he asked her again the next week. Over time, Cassie rationalized that it was an acceptable courtship as Bart treated her with respect and was an intelligent man with means.

Only weeks later, without warning, Bart asked her father if he would give his blessing for her hand in marriage, explaining how he would provide for her all that she could ever want. Mr. Black had given his blessing without hesitation. Cassie was eighteen years old, and her father believed Bart to be a very good match for her.

When Bart finally found the courage to ask her to marry him one evening, it was done so with a quivering voice and shaking hands. Cassie was unsure how to respond. She

21

had respect for him but felt nothing in the way of love for him.

Bart's proposal was more of a sales pitch as he asked Cassie to marry him. He told her he would build her a beautiful home and give her whatever she needed and would never want for the luxuries of life. He informed her of his plan to take over the mercantile one day, securing their futures as the elite in the small town. Then Bart concluded by saying, "Cassie, you would make me so happy if you would do me the honor of being my wife." When Cassie didn't answer, he added, "Your father gives his blessing, and I believe this to be a perfect arrangement. You're everything I've ever wanted in a wife, and I'm as good a prospect as any girl could want in a husband. We would have the best of everything, you'll see. What more could you ask for?" Bart asked, trying to reason with her.

Bart's words hadn't been what Cassie had dreamed a marriage proposal to be like. She'd always imagined her future husband taking her into his arms, kissing her while professing his love for her. This man would promise to always be by her side, to care for her in sickness and health, for richer or poorer, forever, and ever. On the other hand, Bart's proposal had felt like a business transaction and Cassie was too shocked to think clearly.

When she finally answered him, Cassie asked, "Could you let me think about it? It is, after all, a very important decision to make." That was not the answer Bart was hoping for. But he agreed to give her some time to see reason.

Cassie spent the next week thinking about Bart's proposal. It wasn't like she had never had suitors. She'd had plenty of beaus before, but they were just silly schoolboys. Cassie had never had serious feelings for any of them, much less thoughts of marrying any one of them. Cassie felt torn. "Maybe it's enough to be suitably matched. Many marriages are arranged and find happiness." And so, with the encouragement of her family, she accepted his proposal. The day she told Bart yes, was the first and only time that Bart ever showed her any physical affection. Overcome with excitement, he quickly hugged her and then released her just as quickly in embarrassment. Bart again promised to make her the most envied woman in town, and that she would never go without anything. Bart was beaming as he left her that day, but Cassie was less excited as the reality of her decision of spending a lifetime with Bartholomew Clark as her husband sank in. "It could be nice," she reasoned with herself. "Having the best of everything won't be bad either. He is, after all, a respected man and will be a kind husband." Cassie had always been practical and optimistic above everything else and could find satisfaction and happiness in almost any situation. She decided she could settle into the role as wife of a merchant and find happiness in her role of wife and someday mother.

Bart and Cassie set the date to be married the next April. Little did they know that three weeks later the Indians would attack her family farm, changing everything in her life all in one night.

Bart had heard about the tragedy at the Black's along with the others in town. He was saddened to hear the news, but relieved to hear Cassie had survived. Bart's mother told him she'd heard that Cassie was badly beaten and in shock and wasn't taking visitors for a while. So, as the weeks went by, Bart waited while he frequently asked around for word of how she was doing. The reverend told Bart that Cassie was improving and was beginning to help with chores at the Smith's home. Bart became hopeful that he would soon see her. Then one day, while crouching down, stocking new shirts on the shelves in the mercantile, Bart had overheard the town's biggest busybodies, Mrs. Cook and Mrs. Rogers, talking about Cassie.

"Well, I heard something about Cassie Black." Mrs. Cook paused long enough to look around to make sure they were alone. Before going on, not seeing Bart hidden, she continued, "I heard Miss Black is putting a burden on the Smith's finances. You know they have six children of their own already. And now with her to provide for, I don't know how they will ever manage," Mrs. Cook said in a loud whisper.

"Oh my, that's just not right. She should go live with relatives. The Smiths can't be expected to take her in," Mrs. Rogers said while they stood shoulder to shoulder, heads together, pretending to look at the bolts of fabric.

Bart's mind raced. "Maybe I should marry Cassie sooner," he thought. He stayed still, straining to hear Mrs. Cook's words as she whispered quietly.

"Wasn't that Clark boy going to marry her?" Mrs. Cook paused to look around the store for Mr. Clark and his son. She continued, "I doubt he'll want to marry her now, not after what happened to her." Mrs. Cook raised her eyebrows, giving her friend a knowing look.

Bart wondered what she meant but didn't have to wonder long.

Mrs. Rogers gasped in shock. "You mean…she was defiled by one of those savages?" Mrs. Rogers' mouth dropped open when Mrs. Cook whispered, yes. "No one will want to marry her now."

Bart's heart pounded almost out of his chest as their words sank in. Full of rage from the women's filthy gossip, he abruptly stood and walked away, hearing them gasp, as they realized they had been overheard. Bart chose to dismiss the rumor as just that, unable to imagine such a terrible thing happening to Cassie.

Slowly, Cassie realized that the funeral service was

over, and she couldn't even recall what was said. She was sure the preacher had shared some comforting words as friends and neighbors looked on with sad faces, pitying her. One by one the mourners solemnly left the graveside, but not before passing the family's sole survivor and offering soft condolences and tender touches. Cassie nodded in acknowledgement and tried to speak, but nothing would come out except more tears.

Mr. and Mrs. Smith excused themselves, telling Cassie they would allow her a moment alone to say her last goodbyes, and walked back to the wagon. Cassie stood alone, facing the six crosses bearing the names of each of her family members. Cassie remembered when they had moved to Jackson County, Missouri. Her parents had wanted to raise their five children away from the big city of Springfield, in a small farming community. Her father loved living far out of town where it was quiet and peaceful, a perfect place to raise two growing boys and the three spirited girls. As a family, they had worked hard to put in crops, build a beautiful home, and a large barn, for their many horses and animals. They had been happy and felt safe in their secluded home.

Cassie whispered her last goodbyes to her family and wiped the endless trail of tears from her face, about to leave and join the Smiths when she looked up and saw Bart approaching her. She paused as he stepped in front of her in his black Sunday suit with his head hung low holding his black bowler hat. Bart shifted his weight nervously from one foot to the other on the thick sod surrounding the fresh graves, waiting for some sign that he could speak.

Bart cleared his throat. "I'm so sorry for your loss, Cassie. I wish there was something I could do or say to help you," he said as he kept his eyes downcast, glancing up only momentarily to see her look away. Bart twisted the brim of his hat between his hands. "I hear you're leaving in a few weeks to go live with your aunt and uncle in Cheyenne."

"Yes, I am." Cassie looked up just long enough to see Bart was unable to meet her eyes. Her heart was broken, and her world crushed. How could she tell him what had happened to her? Cassie felt ashamed and dejected, full of guilt.

Cassie's quietness panicked Bart, and he hurried to fill in the silence. "A year is a long time to not see each other." Bart suddenly doubted his conviction to marry her. "I would understand if you changed your mind and didn't want to come back and marry me. If you wanted to call off the wedding, I would understand," he said, hoping he was wrong.

There it was. The truth she had known all along. "That must be why he didn't come to see me," she thought. "He doesn't want to marry me anymore. Somehow, he must know what the Indian did to me." Cassie didn't want his pity. Without looking up she said softly, "Yes, I think calling off the agreement would be for the best." Cassie resolutely turned and looking forward, walked towards the Smiths, suddenly feeling numb inside. How could she ever be worthy of any husband, she was tarnished goods. Deep down, Cassie was relieved she was leaving town, glad to never have to face Bart again, her once future husband. Now she knew for certain, Bart would never want her as a wife, no one would. Soon she would leave all the memories and pain behind. Cassie was satisfied with this new plan.

Bart stood there stunned. Things had not gone as he had thought they would. "But perhaps it is for the best. She definitely doesn't seem herself," he thought as she walked away, looking smaller in her modest black dress. Bart hardly recognized her. Cassie was gaunt and hollow-looking.

The girl he once knew was gone. Even Cassie's carefree, cheerful spirit that he had once reveled in was missing.

As the days passed, Cassie was able to do more around the Smith house. She spent time helping with meals and laundry that seemed never to end in a family of eight. As much as Cassie tried to help, she continued to feel poorly. Since the attack she had no appetite for food, even the look of it repulsed her. Cassie tried to force herself to eat at meals, but it was difficult. And on top of that, now she was often nauseated.

Cooking became a struggle for Cassie. The smell of certain foods would frequently send her running to the outhouse to relieve the nausea. Cassie decided to put on a strong exterior and not let anyone know she was ill. But her pallor and weight loss were becoming more and more apparent to everyone. Even the skirts that fit Cassie a few weeks ago now hung loosely on her already small frame.

Only at night when everyone was asleep, would Cassie let the tears come as she thought of her family.

Cassie thought of her dear mother, Mary, only thirty-eight years old, when her life was cut short. Mary was a kind and loving person who always found a way to make whomever she was with, feel important. Mary was blessed with a gift for knowing who needed help and what needed done to help them. Among her mother's many talents, was her gift for natural healing, giving herbs and remedies to the sick and injured. Cassie had learned the best herbs to use for most health issues by watching her mother. Her mother was a great teacher of the healing arts, having learned it from her mother. Cassie frequently had the opportunity to accompany her mother on visits to people's homes. There, Cassie learned how to treat wounds as well as comfort and console patients. Cassie's favorite memories were when she was allowed to go along and assist with the delivery of babies. Sickness and blood didn't bother Cassie, and she felt a deep longing to help care for people in their time of need, just as her mother had. Now, Cassie would never be able to assist her mother again.

Charlotte, was her sister and best friend, being only two years younger, and they were as close as twins. She couldn't remember a time when Charlotte wasn't with her. They shared a bed since the time they were little, whispering late into the night until their parents would scold them to go to sleep. The two of them were frequently seen walking arm in arm on their way to town, excitedly talking about school and boys or whatever secret excited them at the time. They shared everything with each other; the happy and the sad. Oh, how Cassie wanted to tell Charlotte all that had happened since that night of terror. "Charlotte, you were my best friend. How will I ever get along without you?" she thought, and tears sprang forth as they soaked her pillow.

How she missed the heroics of her brother Mark, four years younger but always acting like a big brother. Mark was always her protector as if it was his responsibility to defend her. Mark was tall and strong and did the work of a man. Cassie's father had raised his sons to work hard from a very young age.

Nathan, four years younger than Mark, was tall for his age and had the strength of a much older boy. A few times, Nathan had gotten in trouble for fighting at school. But it was because Nathan was defending the little kids who were being picked on. Quickly he had become known for his strength and fighting skills. Nathan worked beside his brother and his father as an equal. Cassie knew he must have fought the Indians with all his strength. He wouldn't have gone down without a fight, it was not his nature.

Mary Jane was a smaller version of Cassie. Like Cassie, Mary Jane was carefree and high spirited. Both had black hair that they got from their father except Mary Jane had brown eyes. Mary Jane was doted on as the baby of the family and got plenty of attention from all of them. Mary Jane could do no wrong in their eyes, and was a complete joy to have around, with her giggling and active imagination.

Cassie had always seen her father as invincible. Pa was capable of doing anything he set his mind to. He would have been devastated to know his farm had been sold. Cassie's father had planned and saved so long to get his family this place. Maybe he would have been glad knowing the money made from selling what remained of the farm had left a good inheritance for his daughter.

With a little of the money, Cassie paid for new clothes, accessories, and a trunk she would need of for the journey. Aunt Mabel had wired the money to her for the train ticket, and the money her parents had saved in the bank was used to pay for the grave markers and to pay off their store bills. With the family debts settled, the rest transferred to the bank in Cheyenne to provide for her when or if the need arose.

It had been five weeks since the attack and Cassie couldn't wait to be leaving on the Saturday morning train. All she wanted to do was leave this place with its painful memories and the rumors. Even the memory of her horse, Midnight, was hurtful. The two of them would race across the countryside as Cassie would feel uplifted and carefree. She loved galloping full speed through the fields feeling as one with her horse. It felt as if she was flying free as a bird. Cassie tried to imagine herself riding Midnight as she lay there that last night in the Smith home. She thought of how her hair would blow back in the wind as she leaned forward in the saddle, light as a feather, letting Midnight race. But, imaging it didn't feel the same, it wasn't real, it was only a memory. Cassie cried hot angry tears as her heart broke, thinking of all she had lost. On top of losing her family and her home, losing Midnight was just another reminder that she was completely alone in the world. Everything she loved and held dear to her was gone.

Chapter 2
Journey by Train

It was still dark outside as Cassie awoke Saturday morning and began dressing for the trip to Cheyenne. The last of her new clothes were carefully folded and placed in the large leather trunk, then closed and latched securely as she finished packing for the journey. Nearly all of Cassie's belongings for her new life were inside that trunk. Taking her last two items, Cassie opened the small floral carpet bag on the bed and placed her comb and brush inside with her nightdress and toiletries. Soon she and her luggage would travel across the country over hundreds of miles leaving Missouri far behind her. Mrs. Smith came into the bedroom and placed a small bundle of food she'd prepared into Cassie's handbag, giving her one last gift of kindness.

"It's time, Cassie," Mrs. Smith said in a gentle voice, her heart aching, knowing they were soon to part.

"I'm almost ready," Cassie said softly as she sat in front of the small mirror and placed her light blue hat slightly forward on her head. Mrs. Smith stepped behind her and took the hat pin from Cassie and carefully used it to secure the hat through her upswept hair. Cassie smiled slightly at her reflection, thinking she looked pretty in her white blouse and hat with her dark hair.

While Cassie put on her jacket, Jacob and Mr. Smith came into the bedroom and took the trunk and carpet bag and carried them out and loaded them into the back of the wagon. Picking up her drawstring purse and hand-bag, Cassie followed Mrs. Smith out to the yard where the Smith children were gathered and paused to say her last goodbyes.

Cassie faced Mrs. Smith, the small motherly woman who had cared for her over the past month and hugged her tightly. "Goodbye, I'll never forget what you did for me. Ma and Pa would be so grateful to know how well you took care of me. I'll write you as soon as I get there, I promise. Thank you again for everything." Cassie tried to hold back her tears as she pulled away and looked into Mrs. Smith's soft blue eyes one last time.

"Dear child, no thank you is needed." Mrs. Smith held Cassie by the arms and gave them a tender squeeze. "It was our pleasure to have you in our home as long as we did. You and your family have been our closest friends and we'd do anything for you. We wish you the best, dear. Please write often. We want to know all about Cheyenne and your new home. We'll be praying for you." Mrs. Smith leaned in and kissed Cassie on the cheek, then pulled her close and hugged her one last time. "God speed, Cassie," she whispered.

The tears began as they finally pulled away from each other, knowing it was time for Cassie to be going. More tears filled Cassie's eyes as she hugged each of the Smith children, starting at the youngest. June and Ruthie cried, not wanting their new big sister to go away. Next, she hugged Scott and Roy, who tried to act big and hide their tears. Then Betsy hugged Cassie as she told her she would miss having an older sister to talk to, then began to sob as Cassie moved to hug Jacob. Jacob had always liked Cassie and Charlotte. They were fun to talk to and play games with whenever their families got together. But over the past two years of being neighbors, Jacob began to have feelings for Charlotte and hoped she would one day see him as more than just a friend. Jacob had kept his feelings for Charlotte to himself and never let anyone know how he had fallen for her. After the Indian attack, in which Charlotte was killed, it had been hard keeping his feelings of a broken heart from everyone as he mourned the loss of his secret sweetheart. When Cassie came to live with them, Jacob began to think of Cassie as more of an older sister, but still felt embarrassed at being hugged by a pretty girl. Before she turned to go, Cassie thanked the family one last time for being so kind to her, and then with Jacob's help, climbed into the wagon and sat down beside Mr. Smith. Even after she thought she had walled up her heart against feeling anything, Cassie had come to feel close to this family and she couldn't deny she loved them. They had taken her in and cared for her as one of their own. Living with them this past month had gotten her through the roughest days of her life. Cassie turned back and waved goodbye as the wagon pulled away. As she watched, Mrs. Smith hugged Jacob and buried her head in Jacob's shoulder as she cried. Cassie turned to face the road ahead and straightened her shoulders with silent tears streaming down her face.

***

The wagon pulled into town just before sunrise, driving down the main road toward the train station. Cassie looked around at the growing farm town, making some last mental notes. There was the dress shop and hat boutique that had the prettiest things to wear and the tannery where she'd picked out her first saddle. Further down the street was the church that she had attended with her family.

All these places and memories would be filed away in the back of her mind to be revisited when she was ready. As the wagon neared the middle of town, they passed the old school building where she attended the last two years of school, then the post office and lastly, the mercantile. The mercantile was a memory she would definitely put away in the very back of her mind.

***

The train platform was crowded with bustling people and luggage waiting to be loaded into the big black train. Steam blew out of the engine as it prepared to begin the next leg of its journey. Cassie waited on the platform beside her luggage while Mr. Smith went inside the small train station to get the ticket. Mr. Smith returned to Cassie, as he searched the platform for a black-suited porter who could tag and stow her trunk.

"Here's your ticket," Mr. Smith said as he handed Cassie the stiff printed card, stamped for passage to Cheyenne, in Wyoming Territory. Mr. Smith wished Cassie had an escort to take her to Cheyenne. But finances were too tight to pay for one, so the least he could do was make her trip a little more comfortable. "The ticket for the trip was seventy-five dollars, but I chipped in a little extra for the sleeping car."

"Oh, Mr. Smith, you shouldn't have. That was so kind of you." Cassie had grown to think of Mr. Smith as someone she could count on to look out for her, just as an uncle would. Mr. Smith had won a special place in her heart following the attack, and she still felt his sincere concern for her safety.

Mr. Smith shook his head and rubbed the back of his neck as he hoped he was doing enough to help her get to her aunt and uncle safely. "Stay on the train the whole trip and you'll be fine. The money you have left can be spent for meals in the dining car.

Once Mr. Smith located a porter, Cassie's carpetbag was taken and stowed away in the sleeping car, while her trunk was tagged and taken to the freight car with the other passengers' trunks. Cassie was in awe of the train and the depot. Only a month ago their town had celebrated the monumental completion of the Transcontinental Railroad as the last spike was driven, connecting the east with the west in one continuous track. And now she was about to ride on the historical railroad and embark on a journey of her own. This would be an exciting adventure, and a new beginning as Cassie had never ridden on a train before or traveled more than a few hundred miles in her whole life. The black train cars stretched out along the platform and down the track, each car having a purpose. Closest were the first-class passenger cars, the sleeping cars and the dining cars. Further down the line were more passenger cars for those in coach, the mail car and freight cars at the very end, and lastly the caboose. Cassie nervously held her small drawstring purse and handbag and thought of what lay ahead. In just a few more minutes she would embark on a trip that would take her through four territories over the next three days.

The conductor walked the platform as he blew his whistle and called out, "All aboard!" "All aboard!"

"Thank you, Mr. Smith, for taking me in and watching over me. I can't tell you how much it has meant to me." Cassie gave him a quick hug before the tears could collect and hurried to board the train.

"Goodbye Cassie! God speed!" Mr. Smith waved and said a small prayer that Cassie would continue to be in the palm of His hand.

As Cassie found herself a seat in the first-class car, she felt small and more alone than she had in a month. She was leaving behind all she knew, her once betrothed, her friends, and her family's homestead.

Cassie sat proudly in her new light blue traveling dress, with a button-up shirtwaist jacket that matched the Grimaldi skirt, and white linen blouse with lace collar made specifically to her measurements, that complimented her tiny waist and curves. With her smooth black hair up in a twist under her matching blue hat, she appeared slightly older than she was. Cassie's outfit was complete with her white gloves. Cassie never saw the sense of wearing gloves, and rarely did, except for at church or the occasional town social. Mrs. Smith had insisted that Cassie be dressed as a lady, and that included gloves, now that she was going to be traveling. Cassie sat tall and tried to remain calm in her seat. But the excitement of the journey was building.

Admiring the new leather and woodwork of the armrests, Cassie ran her hand over the cushioned seat. Everything smelled new and looked very plush.

As the train began to pull away from the station Cassie glanced out the window. "Goodbye forever," she thought.

Buildings, homes and fields of green extended across the blue horizon. The view rushed by her as the train picked up speed, traveling much faster than she ever traveled before. Cassie watched out the window for a long time. As the buildings diminished, so did her interest. Cassie took the book out of her handbag, opened it and began to read. It was going to be hours before the first stop, and she didn't feel much like talking to anyone. The book was not keeping her attention and with the rocking motion of the train, she was soon lulled into a light sleep. Not long after closing her eyes Cassie began dreaming. It was the usual nightmare, and she awoke with a start. Cassie opened her eyes and looked around. Across the aisle her eyes were met with a warm smile from the woman sitting near her.

"Are you OK?" asked the woman.

Cassie quickly straightened herself and cleared her throat. "Oh, yes. I must have dozed off," she said, covering her mouth as she yawned.

"I was worried. You didn't seem to be having a very good dream," continued the woman. "My name is Madeline, Madeline MacRea." She reached out her gloved hand to Cassie across the aisle.

With only a moment's hesitation, Cassie came to her senses and responded in kind, and shook Madeline's hand. "Hello, my name is Cassandra Black. Most people call me Cassie. Nice to meet you."

Madeline gave her a warm smile. "Where are you traveling to, Cassie?"

"I'm going to Cheyenne, to live with my aunt." Cassie, trying to be polite, quickly asked, "And where are you going?"

Madeline was a nice-looking woman with brown hair and eyes that matched and was happy to be asked. "How nice, I've never been that far west. I'm going to stay with my sister in North Platte, in Nebraska Territory. She is close to delivering her third baby and needs someone to help with her two small children while she's on bed rest. Her husband is such a dear but doesn't know his way around a kitchen, poor man. Thankfully, my four children are old enough to take care of things so I can come and help my sister until she and the baby are healthy. Is that why you're going to visit your aunt?" Madeline asked.

Cassie didn't want to give the details, so she answered with the most simple and unemotional reply she could muster. "No, I lost my home and family in a fire last month. My aunt is my only living relative. I'm going to live with her and my uncle in Cheyenne."

"Oh no, my dear child, I am so sorry to hear that. I hope you're doing OK." She paused, "Oh, of course you're not OK. I'm sure you are still suffering, and now traveling all alone." Madeline reached across and took Cassie's hand and said sympathetically, "Dear, I'll be your traveling companion as far as I go and help you with whatever you need."

Cassie felt a fondness for this sweet woman, lifting the corners of her mouth slightly, trying to smile back at her. Cassie steeled herself before her emotions came to the surface, for fear she would not be able to stop crying once she started. "Thank you," was all she could manage at the moment.

And that was enough for Madeline, the mother in her took over and she was now determined to see that this sweet girl would be taken care of. Madeline let go of Cassie's hand and sat back in her seat. Madeline knew instinctively that Cassie didn't want to talk about the incident and decided to give her some time to compose herself. Instead, she turned her attention to her bag where she had stashed some yarn and began to busy herself with some crocheting. Cassie watched as Madeline's hands moved effortlessly, building what looked like the beginnings of a baby blanket.

Cassie was not usually patient enough to complete a large project like a blanket but was very intrigued. "What is that you're making?"

Madeline looked up. "I'm making a baby blanket, for the new baby," she explained as she worked the hook in and out of the row, adding more loops of yarn to it. The cream-colored yarn Madeline was working with soon took the shape of another row of beautiful scallops.

Cassie leaned over to investigate. "Will you show me how you make that stitch? I know the basic stitches, but

I've never seen that design before."

Madeline moved her things from the place beside her and said, "Sure, come on over and sit beside me and I'll teach you."

Cassie moved to sit beside Madeline and watched and listened to the instructions as the row took shape. After a minute or two, Madeline encouraged Cassie to take over and practice. Cassie tried to decline, not wanting to ruin the blanket, but Madeline insisted and explained she could always unravel the stitches if she made a mistake. Cassie took the partial blanket and crochet hook in her hand and strung the yarn through her fingers and began slowly making the stitches. Madeline carefully repeated the instructions as Cassie worked until she had the proper technique. Madeline encouraged Cassie to continue for a few more rows to get the pattern memorized for future use.

Cassie's hands worked as she concentrated on the stitch to get the proper count and tension correct, welcoming the distraction. Cassie was a quick study; the stitches were a near perfect match to the ones Madeline had made. Seeing Cassie enjoying herself, Madeline commented on how wonderful she was doing and encouraged her to continue as long as she liked. Madeline pulled out a book and began reading quietly as Cassie continued to crochet. The time seemed to pass quickly to Cassie as she now had a project to keep her fingers busy and her mind occupied. Cassie felt relaxed and content as she worked the soft yarn. It had been a long time since she had done something like this, and it felt good to be creating something again, especially for a sweet newborn.

"Would you mind accompanying me to the dining car?" Madeline asked, after some time had passed. "It's almost lunch time and I could use a break to stretch my legs."

"I think that's a splendid idea," said Cassie. "I'm more

than ready." Cassie smiled at Madeline as she gathered up the crocheted yarn and handed it back to her to stow away in her bag. Leaving their bags in their seats, they took their purses and headed to the front of the car and through the doors to the dining car ahead of them.

The dining car was already partially filled with passengers with the same idea, some ordering and others eating what appeared to be a decent lunch. Madeline and Cassie settled at a small table sitting closest to the windows so they could look out at the beautiful passing countryside as they dined. The waiter took their orders of beef stew and corn bread with coffee. It tasted delicious. Even with Cassie's nausea, she was able to enjoy it.

They concluded their lunch with tea and apple pie. Completely satisfied, they took their leave of the dining car and returned to their seats.

"You know, I just had a wonderful idea. I think you should buy yourself some yarn at the next town, so you can make a blanket while you're on the trip," Madeline suggested.

"Oh, what a wonderful idea. I think I'll do just that." Cassie began looking forward to the next big town, watching out the window for the first hint of civilization in the wide expanse of green.

As the train passed small streams and rivers, groves of trees, and deep ravines under bridges of steel track and mighty beams, they made small talk about all of the things they saw. All the while, Madeline was careful not to bring up topics she thought would upset Cassie. After some time, Madeline took over crocheting and Cassie began reading her book again. Later that afternoon, both of them decided to go to the sleeping car and take a short nap before the evening meal. The sleeping cars were past the dining cars, near the engine. They wove their way through the aisles, occasionally moving to the side as other passengers came through going back to their seats from the other cars. As they came upon mothers with their children, they politely gave them the opportunity to pass. And just as politely, the gentlemen they encountered gave way for Madeline and Cassie to pass. The families and women Cassie greeted with ease, but she found it most difficult with the various men they passed, only meeting their eyes briefly then quickly looking away as she blushed uncomfortably. Although she couldn't meet the gaze of the men they passed, she noted out of the corner of her eye, many turning to stared after her. One of the cars they passed through was full of finely dressed men sitting around playing cards and smoking as they laughed loudly, making her feel even more uncomfortable. Cassie noted all the fancy suits and hats they wore, while all the other men were dressed in less intimidating traveling clothes. Each man they passed, whether dressed like they were going to an opera or a trip to town, politely tipped his hat and greeted her with a "How do you do?" or "Good-day." Cassie forced herself to glance up, to respond in kind. She became more self-conscious as their eyes stayed on her too long or turned to watch her pass. Finally, making it to the sleeping car and with the help of the porter who set up her sleeping berth, she settled in for some much-needed rest. Cassie heard mothers with small children nearby, attempting to settle them for naps as well. Hushed whispers and whimpers were heard as the curtains were drawn, hiding them from her as Cassie sat on the soft mattress and removed her jacket. As Cassie lay down on the bed across from Madeline on the opposite side of the aisle, an elderly couple passed, holding hands, making her smile at their love for one another. Cassie sleepily smiled at Madeline, then drew the heavy curtains in front of her sleeping berth and quickly fell asleep.

Cassie was awakened by Madeline as the sun was setting lower in the sky and long shadows stretched out across the prairie. Supper was going to be served soon and Cassie and Madeline wished to clean up a little in the washroom before going back to the dining car. In the privacy of the two-foot washroom located at the end of the sleeping car, Cassie was able to comb her hair and secure the stray hairs that had escaped while she slept. She washed her face and hands with the cold water, then gathered her belongings and followed Madeline back to the dining car.

Cassie grew uneasy as the men who'd moved their card game to the dining car became more intoxicated as the day wore on. Glances continued to be made her way, even though she was not in their direct line of sight.

Madeline smiled at Cassie and tried to ease the situation. "You know, they're just noticing the prettiest girl on the train. You can hardly blame them for staring," Madeline said, trying to compliment her.

Cassie's usual confidence was gone, she felt vulnerable and repulsed by the forwardness of these strangers. Cassie smiled slightly and tried to calm herself. She had never felt this uncomfortable around gentlemen before, but then again, it had been a month since she had been around this many people at once.

Madeline could tell that Cassie was unsettled and continued to try and distract her by telling a humorous story. Cassie smiled as she chuckled at the quippy tale and moments later the menus were brought, and they made their selections. This time they had ham and bean soup with rolls. Madeline had coffee and Cassie took tea, hoping the tea would help settle her stomach which was becoming upset with the constant swaying motion of the train.

Madeline eyes widened in awe as she looked out the window. "Oh, would you look at that! What a magnificent sunset!"

Cassie marveled with equal awe at the vibrant sunset. "My goodness, the sky looks like it's on fire with the orange sunbeams shining through those wispy clouds."

Soon their food came, and they ate as rapidly as they could, noticing the dining car was becoming crowded with more hungry people waiting to eat.

After paying their tab, they went back to the passenger car and took their seats. Both were content to sit quietly and look out the windows and watch the shadows lengthen across the prairie as the grass swayed in the wind, looking like waves across a great ocean. The darkening hills in the distance reminded Cassie of a beautiful oil painting, with rich shades of blue, deep green tones and brilliant red and orange sunbeams as the sun dipped below the mountains. The evening sky was emerging, as they moved west with light blue where the sun had set and falling behind them, the darker blue in the eastern horizon.

As Cassie stared out the window, she began daydreaming, remembering the warm summer nights with her family sitting on the porch after supper. While she and Charlotte would be working on needlepoints for their future dowries, Ma would be working on a sewing project as well. Pa would be reading the newspaper as he sat in his favorite chair. And the family would be pleasantly distracted by Mark and Nathan's antics as they chased Mary Jane around the yard playing tag or hide-and-seek.

Oh, how she missed her family. It seemed like a lifetime ago since they were all together, and yet at other times, she could almost believe that nothing had happened and that everything was as it was before the Indian attack that night.

As evening turned to night, Cassie and Madeline took their belongings and headed to the sleeping cars again. One last trip was made to the washroom before Cassie pulled the heavy curtains closed behind her as she changed into her nightdress. Cassie was glad for the time alone even though she enjoyed Madeline's company. Cassie was weary of trying to be attentive and smile when she still felt ill and wanted to cry sometimes.

Madeline had taken the sleeping area across the aisle from Cassie, and both wished each other a goodnight through the curtains before retiring. Cassie lay down on the small pillow and pulled up the sheet. Immediately, she noticed how stuffy the small sleeping compartment was and unlatched the window to lower it, allowing some cool air to blow inside. She lay back down and finally able to relax, began to think of all that had happened that day. Today was June 5th, the day Cassie had said goodbye to the hometown she would probably never see again. Tears began to stream down her cheeks as she closed her eyes and cried silently, wishing she hadn't had to say goodbye to all she had known and loved. Slowly, the rhythmic rocking of the train lulled Cassie into a peaceful sleep.

***

Cassie awoke to the noise of rowdy children and bustling people getting ready for the day. Sunshine streamed through a crack in the thick curtains over the window she'd closed in the middle of the night. Yawning and stretching her stiff muscles, Cassie sat up and rubbed her eyes. "At least sleeping makes the time go by quicker," she thought. "I wonder how far we've traveled."

Cassie hurried to dress behind the curtains, not wanting Madeline to have to wait for her much longer. When she finally opened the curtains, she found that Madeline was already dressed and gone. Looking up and down the car, Cassie noticed Madeline coming out of the wash-room, slowly moving towards her as Madeline maneuvered around the people crowding in the aisles.

"Good morning, Madeline." Cassie smiled as Madeline approached. She stopped once again to let an older man pass before she finally reached Cassie's bed.

Madeline smiled in return and asked, "How did you sleep?"

"I slept very well," Cassie said honestly. "I'm sorry for sleeping so late. I'll be ready in just a few minutes." Then Cassie chuckled, seeing the line of people at the washroom door. "That is, if I can get to the washroom." Gathering her toiletries, Cassie got in line and patiently waited her turn for the washroom. At last, her turn came, and she was able to enter. Hastily, closing the door behind her, she washed her face and hands and combed her messy hair into a neat twist and secured it high on her head. Finishing up, Cassie put on her hat, and waist coat, buttoning it up, and then attempted to smooth the wrinkles out of her skirt, which proved to be futile. As she turned to leave, she caught her reflection in the mirror and noticed her green eyes were sparkling and her cheeks had a little more color. Even the dark circles under her eyes were less noticeable this morning. Emerging from the washroom, she joined Madeline and together they headed to the dining car for breakfast.

Tea with toast was the most Cassie dared to eat that morning but wished she could be like Madeline and en-joy the griddle cakes, eggs, ham, and coffee, that looked so scrumptious as she watched Madeline eat every morsel. Completely satisfied with their morning meal, they went back to the passenger car and found two empty seats that sat facing one another beside a window.

Soon, Madeline spotted a porter walking by. "Excuse

me, sir. Could you tell me when the next town is coming up?"

"Yes, ma'am," the smartly dressed porter answered and nodded, withdrawing the train schedule he carried in his pocket and looked it over. "The next stop is Marysville, in Kansas Territory. We should be arriving in about an hour."

"Could you tell me how long we'll be stopped there?" Madeline asked, then turned and smiled at Cassie, hoping for good news.

"We'll only be there for thirty minutes. No more, no less, ma'am. That's how long it takes to refuel the train and give the passengers time to get to the eating houses before we leave. We must keep the train on schedule."

"We understand, thank you, sir," Madeline said to the dark-skinned gentleman who tipped his hat and resumed his walk down the aisle. "That should be enough time for us to get to the local mercantile, Cassie." Madeline grinned, pleased with the information they had received.

"Perfect, I can't wait." Cassie smiled and gave Madeline's hand an affirmative squeeze.

Now, feeling more excited than before, both women watched out the window as farmhouses and fields of wheat and corn grew in frequency as they approached the next town. Not only were they looking forward to shopping in a new town, but both were looking forward to being off the train for the first time in a day. Before they knew it, the train was slowing. The engineer blew the train's whistle, signaling that it would soon come to a stop at the next town. The wheels of the iron giant squealed as the conductor pulled on the brakes, grinding metal against metal. With one final jolt the train came to an abrupt stop, lurching the passengers forward slightly and blew out its final breath in a white cloud of steam as it hissed from within.

Cassie and Madeline gathered their purses and handbags and moved to the door, exiting down the steps onto the platform.

Madeline stopped to ask a young woman selling flowers at the depot, "Pardon me, miss. Would you happen to know which way to the nearest mercantile?"

"Yes. It's down the end of the block here," she said as she pointed north, "then take a right and two more blocks, it'll be on the right. Yost's Mercantile, you can't miss it."

Madeline thanked the young woman and Cassie and Madeline hurried down the boardwalk along the street, then took a right at the corner, passing various businesses until they found the shop named "Yost's Mercantile and Dry Goods." Entering the opened double doors, they breathed in the aroma of coffee beans, leather, spices and all sorts of wonderful smells as they paused momentarily letting their eyes adjust from the bright sunny day to the dim interior of the building. With a little guidance from the proprietor, Cassie was able to find the sewing section and chose a few balls of pink yarn that she thought was very pretty and a crochet hook. Wasting no time, Madeline and Cassie walked back to the train with only minutes to spare.

A few passengers had left the train and not returned, having ended their journey, and others were boarding for the first time. Cassie and Madeline watched as the new first-class passengers took their belongings to the sleeping car, then returned and found seats in the passenger car. Many of the men that had stepped off the train made a stop at the local tavern, as Cassie could tell from their overly loud and crude behavior as they called out to passing ladies and laughed when the women blushed.

Madeline and Cassie avoided the men and took their seats in a different car, then settled in for the next leg of their journey. Cassie immediately took out the new pink yarn and began crocheting her blanket, even before the

47

train pulled out of the station. She heard the train conductor blow his whistle and heard him shouting, "All aboard!" Within minutes the train lurched forward as the steam hissed and the iron wheels squealed on the rails as it gained momentum, inching forward slowly at first and then increasing in speed. They were on their way and soon the familiar ba-bump, ba-bump, ba-bump was felt again as it rolled over the rails. Glancing up between stitches, Cassie watched as the scenery out the windows moved by quickly, and they left the new city behind. With the town out of sight, they now saw rolling hills of prairie grass, lines of trees along small streams, and an occasional farmhouse on the distance

By evening they would be into Nebraska Territory. And by morning they would be halfway to Cheyenne.

Madeline took out her book and began reading. As time passed, Madeline and Cassie became weary of sitting and took turns walking up and down the aisle, stretching their legs. Walking through the aisles of passengers and the individual cars took only a little time but was an adventure. All the new faces that had arrived at the last stop made Cassie wonder, "Where are they going? Why are they traveling there?" It was amusing to imagine each person with a new adventure they were about to embark on.

Not only was Cassie's mind intrigued by the other travelers, but her eye was also drawn to the plush furnishings of each car and each short walk she found small details as she passed through, that she hadn't noticed before. When Cassie had first stepped on the train, she had immediately noticed the rich dark wood doors and trim, the burgundy velvet on the chairs, and the heavy curtains around the sleeping compartments. Now she noted the raised pattern on the doorknobs, the gold paisley print of the wallpaper and the gold ropes and tassels on the curtains. In the dining cars, Cassie loved the starched white linens on the tables and beautiful gas lamps and sconces on the walls and ceilings that gave the appearance of dining in a fine restaurant.

The porters' immaculate black suits and white linen shirts added an air of luxury to the experience. Cassie had noticed that the porters were all black men, well-groomed and always polite and helpful. They served them at meals, acting as waiters as well as pulling down the sleeping compartments and fixing the beds for the passengers. At night, the porters kept watch at the end of the sleeping cars, standing guard and helping anyone who may need assistance. Cassie was grateful for them and their assistance. They seemed to take good care of the passengers with whatever they needed.

It had been well worth the money Mr. Smith had paid for the sleeping car with her first-class ticket, and on-board dining, which served three square meals a day, unlike the passenger cars at the end of the train where the coach seats were without luxuries. Those passengers, mostly immigrants who were traveling to the West, would be seated on hard wooden benches, unable to lay down and rest as comfortably as she was able to. One hundred dollars and seven days by train, was quite a savings, compared to the one thousand dollars and months spent on a wagon trail to travel from the East Coast all the way to California. Thankfully, the frequent stops for the train to take on water, freight, and mail at small towns gave passengers a chance to eat at the eating houses and take care of necessities. Unfortunately, this was their only break from the confined quarters of the coach seating.

Weary of sitting and ready for a chance to stand and stretch her legs, Cassie stood with the others as the train slowed and pulled up to a quaint town. The passengers hurried off the train for the eating houses or gathered their belongings and ended their journey while making room for new travelers to board.

The mid-day meal was soon to be served, and Cassie and Madeline headed to the cars to where the washroom was, waited their turns to use the facilities, and cleaned up for dinner. Cassie's appetite was much improved, and she was looking forward to a good meal. It was a pleasant experience, having someone wait on you and eat on fine linen and beautiful dishes with polished silverware. Growing up in a big family never afforded her the luxury of such a treat, but Cassie would, however, trade it all in a heartbeat for everything to be back to how it was before the attack.

A kind porter welcomed them and promptly sat them in the corner with a great view of the whole dining car. Businessmen and wealthy families filed in and were seated quickly, ready to feast on the train cuisine.

The kitchen was serving fried buffalo steaks and boiled potatoes with buffalo country gravy. Biscuits were served on the side with butter and honey and coffee, tea, milk or water to drink. Cassie didn't feel up to the heavy steak so decided on biscuits covered in the buffalo country gravy and coffee. Madeline was excited to try the buffalo steak and gravy, so ordered that and the potatoes with gravy as well. The biscuits were delicious with the light peppered cream gravy with buffalo cracklings mixed in, perfect for her upset stomach. Visiting as they ate passed the time pleasantly. Dinner concluded with scones and coffee for dessert. They finished and thanked the porter for a delicious meal and stood to take their leave.

When they returned to their seats in the passenger car, they settled for the evening with books to read. Cassie wondered how much longer until Madeline would be leaving her. Madeline determined it would be mid-morning the next day when they would arrive in North Platte and Madeline would leave. Cassie would miss her new-found friend. The time together had passed pleasantly. She glanced out the window of the train, admiring the beautiful gentle hills and countryside as the sun set again on another day on her journey to her new home. Questions filled her mind. "What will it be like, living in Cheyenne? Will I be able to call it home? Will I make new friends?" So many unknowns awaited her. Cassie closed her eyes and thought a silent prayer of hope. Hope for a new beginning with peace and happiness. Cassie opened her eyes and glanced up at Madeline and smiled.

Madeline asked, "Are you getting excited to finally be to your aunt's?"

"Yes, and a little nervous as well." Cassie looked down at her folded hands in her lap. "I hope I find a friend as nice as you in Cheyenne. I feel as if you are one of my closest friends, almost like a sister."

Madeline reached across and took Cassie's hands and as Cassie looked up, Madeline looked her in the eyes and smiled warmly. "I feel the same way, Cassie," as she squeezed Cassie's hands. "You're as dear to me as my own sister." With sincerity, she added, "And if you ever need anything, I will be there for you just as I am for her."

Cassie couldn't stop it, a tear rolled down her cheek and as she looked down, it dropped into her lap. She swallowed the lump in her throat and tried to keep control of her emotions. "Thank you so much, Madeline, that means the world to me," Cassie whispered.

Madeline released Cassie's hand gently and sat back in her seat. "We should exchange addresses so we can write to each other. I can give you mine and once you get to your aunt's and find out what yours is, you can send it along with your letter. I want to hear how you're getting along. And with my sister's new baby coming, I will have something more interesting to write about than dishes and laundry." Madeline chuckled lightly at the jesting.

That made Cassie smile, thinking of a sweet little baby coming into the world with an aunt and family to love and care for it. What a joyful time it would be in that home. "Yes, you'll have to write to me and tell me all about the baby!" Cassie was feeling the excitement. "You'll have to tell me if it's a girl or boy and who it looks like. I want to hear it all!"

The darkness outside filled the vastness and the swaying of the train was making it hard for Cassie to keep her eyes open. The lamps of the car cast a warm yellow glow and the books they were reading were not holding their attention and sleep was all they could think about. They both closed their books.

"Well, I'm ready for sleep," Madeline said. "I think we should go get settled for the night. Tomorrow will be a busy day for the both of us."

Back in the sleeping car, they pulled the curtains closed and changed into their night clothes and lay down on their beds.

"See you in the morning, Cassie. Sleep well," said Madeline behind the curtains.

"Good night, Madeline," Cassie replied through the curtain as she lay back to pull up the covers and close her eyes. Cassie didn't have time to even think before she drifted off to sleep. Her body was becoming accustomed to the sway of the train and fell immediately into a deep sleep. As she slept, Cassie dreamed of a bumpy wagon ride into town with her family. Traveling down the road, Cassie laughed cheerfully with Charlotte over some joke she'd told and watched her parents smile back at them, wondering what was so funny. Soon Mark, Nathan and Mary Jane also joined in the laughter. Looking around at her family, Cassie smiled, and her heart soared to see them so happy. It was glorious to be with her family, safe and sound as if nothing had ever happened. When Cassie awoke, she was crying tears of joy and heartache. "How can one be happy and sad at the same time?" she wondered. But that was what she felt. Cassie was sure in her heart that they were in heaven, happily together. Her heart ached for it to last and never change. "Oh, how I miss you all," Cassie thought as she sat up and wiped the tears from her eyes. She looked around, seeing the sun outside her window and realized she had slept the whole night through. She could hear people around her getting ready for the day. Today was her last day with Madeline and she didn't want to miss a second.

Madeline had gotten to the washroom and was back to packing up her things when Cassie opened the curtains. "Good morning, Madeline! You are up-and-at-'em early today!" Cassie said cheerfully to Madeline's back as she was putting away her toiletries.

Madeline turned around smiling, "And good morning to you, sleepy head! You must have slept well."

Cassie had to admit that she had. "I'll be ready in a few minutes so we can go and eat." Cassie gathered her toiletries and went to wash up.

Cassie had tea and toast again for breakfast as she continued to feel nauseated in the morning. The dining car windows allowed her a gorgeous view of the morning sun rising over the green sodden hills. Platte River was in the distance lined with large poplar trees. In a few hours they would be to Platte Valley. Suddenly Cassie caught sight of hundreds of majestic buffalo, scattered on the plains along both sides of the train. Her eyes widened, observing the thick herd of buffalo on both sides. Within moments, the buffalo began moving, slow at first then began running away from the train, kicking up dust as they went.

Cassie's head jerked back toward the sound of gunfire. Another round of multiple gunshots rang out from the train car behind them. The sound made her ears ring and she instinctively covered them as she watched. One after another, buffalo collapsed in clouds of dust as the two-thousand-pound beasts dropped to the ground.

"What's happening!" Cassie cried out in panic as the rest of the dining car occupants all jumped out of their seats to see what all the commotion was.

"They're killing the buffalo!" someone shouted. Gasps and murmurings were heard everywhere.

"Why would they kill them?" Cassie thought in horror.

Madeline was alarmed at the carnage. The train came almost to a stop as the firing of guns continued. There were hundreds of buffalo falling to the ground in billows of dust. Cassie had never seen such brutality and her stomach lurched. "OH NO!" she thought. Cassie turned and dashed down the aisle and out the back door of the train car. She leaned over the rails as her breakfast evacuated, but her stomach wasn't done, and she continued to heave. Cassie was having a hard time catching her breath as the last of her meal came up. Finally, she stopped and sank down to the metal grating, shaking and pale. Gingerly she wiped her mouth with her hand and looked up in surprise when she heard a man's voice.

"Sorry you had to see that, little missy. Not everyone has the stomach for the Wild West, that's why they call it wild!" The rugged man reached out and handed her his handkerchief. "Keep it."

Cassie nodded her head as she took his handkerchief and wiped her hands and mouth. As gruff as he appeared in his cowboy hat, buckskin jacket with fringe, his eyes were kind and his smile wide between his moustache and full beard. He looked like a real mountain man. Cassie remembered seeing him quite a few times over the past few days, sitting in the center of the group of businessmen telling stories. She'd specifically noticed how the men had all been intrigued by him and would only leave his attention to glance her way as she passed. Cassie assumed this man had been a part of the shooting of the buffalo.

The mountain man reached out his hand again and helped Cassie to her feet, holding her steady for a second then released her as she held onto the railing. "My name is William Cody, but my friends call me Bill, Buffalo Bill. And now I guess you can see why," he said smiling as he motioned toward the lifeless beasts strewn across the prairie. "What's your name, little lady?"

"Cassandra," she muttered as she turned away, looking out the other side of the train at the rolling hills covered in grass and large brown mounds of fur.

"Nice to meet you, Cassandra!" he boomed and tipped his hat to her as she looked up at him with disgust.

Cassie could tell he was quite proud of himself by the beaming smile on his face, but it infuriated her to see his destruction of such majestic creatures. "What a waste of life." Cassie smirked. "Thank you for your kindness, but I don't see why this slaughter was necessary!" she spat the words.

Bill chuckled, "Ma'am, I do what I'm paid to do and don't question what they call it," he stated honestly.

Cassie recovered enough to turn back toward the car entrance. "Good day!" she said curtly and opened the door to go inside. "And thank you again for the handkerchief."

"My pleasure, miss. Good day!" Bill stepped aside as he tipped his hat.

"Oh!" Cassie exclaimed, nearly running into Madeline as she entered.

"Cassie! There you are! I was so shocked by what was going on, I didn't see you leave. I was just coming to look for you."

Madeline put her arms around Cassie and they both broke down in tears.

"It's the most shameful thing I've ever seen," Madeline sobbed through her tears.

The train lurched forward, unbalancing them slightly as it picked up speed, slowly leaving behind the hundreds of beasts on the prairie. Madeline and Cassie returned to their seats and tried to settle their nerves.

"While I was outside being sick, I met a man named Buffalo Bill who offered me his handkerchief," Cassie explained as Madeline's eyes widened.

Madeline looked back toward the door where Cassie had entered and leaned forward whispering, "I heard tales of a man who was such a great marksman that he could take down a buffalo with one single shot while galloping on his horse. His name's Buffalo Bill. He's known for supplying the army with buffalo meat during the war. That has to be the same man!" Madeline said with astonishment.

"Well, whoever he is, it's still a horrible thing to do. I wonder if that's what all those men were doing on the train; maybe they were coming out West to hunt," Cassie wondered out loud. "Except, I wouldn't call this hunting, it's more like a slaughter. No sport in sitting in a train and shooting from a window as the animal is grazing," she said with disgust.

"I know the railroad doesn't like the buffalo, since they tear up the tracks. I also heard that the Army is trying to kill all the buffalo as a way to get rid of the Indians. They say, 'Every buffalo killed is an Indian dead.' I guess they really are trying to kill them all, the buffalo I mean," Madeline said in amazement.

Cassie went a shade paler at the word "Indian," and her hands started shaking. "Well, I guess some good will come of it then." Cassie excused herself and left to go to the washroom.

In the washroom she splashed water on her face and washed her hands. What had come over her? Cassie had never spoken so bluntly about her feelings towards the Indians. It wasn't that she hated all Indians, just the ones that had killed her family and took away everything she loved and knew. She knew better than to hate a whole people just because of the acts of some. Cassie didn't want to hate. She had always been taught that it is better to forgive, but it was easier said than done. Cassie didn't want to become a bitter, hateful person. She wanted her cheerful, bubbly self back. Cassie dried her face and looked in the mirror. Her reflection was pale with dark circles under her eyes and the green in them looked dull, the sparkle was gone. Cassie's long black hair pulled up in a twist was held fast with pins, and she hardly recognized her reflection. "Who are you now? Huh? Are you still in there?" she asked herself. Maybe she would never be the same, she had changed already. But over time, she hoped she would return to herself. Closing her eyes, she whispered a prayer of pleading. "Dear Father in Heaven, please help me. Help me find peace and forgive those who have hurt me and my family. And give me courage to go on. Help me start this new life with hope. Guide my path back to Thee, that I may see my family again. In Jesus' name. Amen." Cassie took a deep breath and opened her eyes, wiped away the tears and gave herself a small smile.

Madeline had followed Cassie to the sleeping car where the washroom was and sat on the edge of the bed that she had used for two nights, as she waited for Cassie to come out.

As Cassie came out, she saw Madeline, and came to sit down beside her. "I'm so sorry for my comment earlier. I don't know what came over me, I don't feel that way," Cassie said, feeling ashamed.

Madeline waited for Cassie to look into her eyes. "Do you trust me?" she asked.

Cassie slowly nodded her head.

"You know you can tell me anything, right?" Madeline asked sincerely and waited for Cassie to nod again. "I noticed how pale you got when I mentioned the Indians. Do you want to talk about it?" she asked.

Cassie trusted Madeline. "Should I tell her," She wondered? "Maybe unburdening myself would help with the pain." She took a deep breath and started slowly, telling Madeline about the night trip to the outhouse. Cassie paused, as the lump in her throat choked her, much like the smoke did that night. Beginning again, she proceeded to tell Madeline about the sounds she'd heard and the longer she talked the easier it was to let it all pour out. Madeline moved to sit closer to Cassie and put her arm around her shoulders as Cassie wept. She briefly told her about being dragged away into the field and the Indian who held her down, smothering and hurting her, then leaving her for dead. Cassie described the loss of her home to the fire and then being taken in by the neighbors, finally explaining the funeral and her fiancé breaking off the engagement. Cassie let the tears roll down her cheeks unchecked. Madeline reached in her small bag and handed her a clean handkerchief.

"There, there, dear. You let it all out. It isn't good to hold it all in. You need to grieve. It's been a horrible ordeal that you've been through, and I can only imagine how you must feel. Bless your heart, my dear. You can lean on me. I'm here for you. I know we must part soon, but I'll write to you and keep you in my prayers. You are my kindred spirit. I love you as my own sister," Madeline said.

Cassie took some deep breaths and wiped her tears, then slowly looked up at Madeline. "Thank you for listening. I don't know why I told you all that. I hardly know you. But I feel close to you and it was just the right time, I guess. I haven't talked about that night to anyone. I have only been able to cry, and never been able to explain the details. I guess this morning's incident brought my feelings to the surface. I never realized how much I was holding in. And I didn't realize my hate was so strong for the Indians who attacked us. At first, I was just in shock and afraid. Now I am feeling something different." Cassie looked down at her hands in her lap. "I don't want to feel hate," she said truthfully.

Madeline reassured her, giving her hands a gentle pat. "It is understandable for you to go through different emotions as you are working through what's happened. It's hard to feel peace, I'm sure. But it will come, in time. You will always miss your family, because you love them. But you will build a new life just as good as the one you have left behind. Cassie, mark my words; the Lord will bless you with joy and happiness again! You are a strong, special young woman with the world at your feet. Your life is just beginning on a new path." Madeline gave her shoulders a squeeze and placed a gentle kiss on her cheek. "Now, I must be leaving the train in the next hour, so let's spend it well. How about we eat the candy that I bought and have some tea and biscuits? That should settle your stomach. You need some sugar in your system," Madeline said smiling as she stood and took Cassie's hand.

Together they went to the dining car and asked for tea and biscuits and ate the hard candy. Licorice was one of Cassie's favorites, which she knew helped with nausea, so it was a blessing to have the treat. Cassie quickly felt better and relaxed with a deep sigh. She felt the weight on her shoulders lighten and was able to sit a little taller, feeling hopeful.

Madeline and Cassie drank their tea and ate the biscuits and made conversation about the beautiful lush green valley as the trees and farmland came into view. The porter walked through announcing that Platte Valley was the next stop in about fifteen minutes and those departing needed to gather their belongings. Madeline and Cassie exchanged looks of sadness. All too soon, Madeline would be leaving.

By the time they had gone back to the sleeping car and gathered their overnight bags and settled back into the passenger car, it was time to say their goodbyes.

Cassie followed Madeline off the train to help her locate Madeline's trunk. Madeline spotted her bother-in-law.

"Welcome, Madeline," said the tall man greeting his sister-in-law with a big hug.

"Matthew, this is my good friend, Cassie," Madeline said as she turned to Cassie.

Matthew tipped his hat to Cassie and quickly excused himself as he located the trunk and managed to get it dragged off to his wagon. Madeline apologized for him, "He isn't much for talking, he's shy around strangers. But he's a good man, a hard worker and loves my sister beyond measure. My sister is no doubt in bed resting, unable to ride in the bouncy wagon. Matthew's determined she follow the doctor's strict instructions," Madeline explained.

Madeline faced Cassie and took her in her arms in a long hug. Trying not to cry, the two of them held each other, sharing their last moments together. They felt like sisters parting. "Take care of yourself, Cassie! Write to me as soon as you can and tell me all about your new home!" Madeline chuckled, trying to keep the topic light. "And I want to hear everything about the handsome young men there, too!" Madeline kissed Cassie on the cheek and whispered, "You're my sister forever." Then turned and grabbed her bag and walked away before she broke down and cried.

Cassie was left standing there, too choked up to respond, as she watched her kindred spirit leave her. Tears rolled down her cheeks, and as she wiped them away, was jolted back into action when the conductor shouted, "All aboard!"

Cassie returned to the passenger car and sat alone near the window and tried to see if she could spot her friend driving out of town to her real sister's home. Looking up and down the platform and streets, there was no sign of Madeline. Cassie wondered if she would ever see Madeline again as the train wheels squealed and spun on the tracks gaining momentum, slowly moving forward and rolling out of the town of North Platte.

"Goodbye, my dearest friend," she whispered.

Cassie sat daydreaming for a while, then slowly came back to her surroundings and picked up the pink yarn and crochet hook from her bag and resumed her crocheting on the baby blanket. "Perhaps if Madeline's sister has a girl, I can send the blanket to her." That thought brightened her spirits as she continued to imagine a newborn baby wrapped in the delicate pink blanket, being snuggled by her mama as she drifted off to sleep.

It would be another eight hours before Cassie would arrive in Cheyenne. Her aunt and uncle were expecting her at the train depot around six thirty PM. As long as there were no delays she would be in her new home by evening. Cassie was getting excited to finally be off the train and together with family.

By lunch time she had made some real progress on the baby blanket. The passengers around her were beginning to stand and move to the dining car. Cassie placed her partial blanket in her bag and followed the others.

Cassie sat alone at first, until the porter sat a young married couple across from her. She smiled as they introduced themselves.

"We're the Davenport's, Emma and Paul Davenport. Come from Georgia to move out West, California is our last stop," the man explained.

"Hi, I'm Cassandra, I'm from Missouri and on my way to Cheyenne. So nice to meet you both," Cassie said as she shook their hands.

"Are you traveling alone?" asked Emma, looking around for clues of a husband.

"Yes, this last stretch. I made a friend that was with me for most of the trip, she got off at Platte Valley this morning," explained Cassie.

They stopped visiting for a moment as the porter came back and asked for their orders. Everyone chose the ham and cheese sandwich with potato salad. The food was delicious as usual, and they enjoyed each other's company as they ate. When there was a pause in the conversation, they would look out the train window and enjoy the view. The terrain was miles and miles of grassy hills with the Platte River in the distance surrounded by wooded areas along its banks, occasionally opening up to show the rushing water as a ribbon of blue through the green blanket of grass and trees.

Once her meal was eaten, Cassie politely excused herself and returned to the passenger car after a stop at the washroom. Moving around in the train helped keep her legs and back from aching from the long hours of sitting. Cassie was becoming increasingly anxious for her journey to be over.

Cassie returned to the passenger car and found a spot

in a back corner to sit alone. She leaned back and closed her eyes to try to take a nap. No sooner had she closed her eyes did she hear a familiar voice.

"Are you feeling any better, little missy?"

Cassie opened her eyes to see Buffalo Bill standing in the aisle looking at her and gave him a half smile. "Yes, I am, thank you."

"It was Cassandra, right?" Bill asked smiling back at her.

"Yes, it is." Cassie was surprised that he remembered and blushed slightly.

"You ran off so quickly I wasn't sure you were OK. But I see that the color has returned to your cheeks," he remarked.

At that, Cassie felt her cheeks burn hotter.

"Yes, you do appear to be doing much better." He grinned broadly as he saw the rising color in her cheeks. "Again, I apologize for this morning. I really hate to see such a pretty young thing have to witness 'the hunt.' If there's anything I can do to make it up to you, just name it. I've spent so many years hunting and have become so accustomed to it; I forget that not everyone has the stomach for it," he said kindly.

Cassie really did believe that he meant what he said. A mountain man must deal with killing on a daily basis. Even though she grew up on a farm, she always hated the killing part. Her dad and brothers did the butchering, and once cleaned she and her mother did the cooking. Cassie was thankful for that. She had rarely even held a gun and didn't think she would ever be able to shoot one, especially to kill something. In a way, she was impressed that he would seek her out to see if she was alright. Buffalo Bill seemed to be a decent man, not as callused and rough as she had first thought. "Well, I am doing better. Thank you for asking,"

Cassie said and looked down shyly.

Bill tipped his hat. "Just doin' what's gentlemanly. You enjoy the rest of your trip, Miss Cassandra, and I honestly do regret having upset you," he said as he smiled, turned, and walked out of the car to return to where the men had congregated to play cards, drink and tell stories.

Cassie let out a long slow breath; she felt embarrassed to have attention on herself. She felt her cheeks flush again as some passengers turned their heads to look at her and whisper about the conversation they had overheard. Cassie turned her head toward the window and pretended that she hadn't seen them staring at her. Eventually, everyone went back to their own business, and she relaxed and closed her eyes. This time she was able to fall asleep. A few hours passed and she awoke to the afternoon sun. The train car was very warm, and she felt woozy. Cassie fanned herself but finally got out of her seat to walk to the back of the train and go outside to get a bit of fresh air. Outside was much better and felt very refreshing. She could smell the grass and trees, and the breeze from the moving train was cooling her down. Cassie held onto the railing and looked out at the countryside. In a few more hours she would be at her new home. She lingered there for quite some time, dreading returning to the stuffy car with the warm bodies that were becoming smelly from the long journey. Cassie was longing for a bath herself. Maybe in the morning after she got settled, she would ask to be able to take a bath. She wanted to wash her hair badly and change into some different clothes.

Cassie could only imagine what her aunt's house would be like. Most likely very quiet with just the two of them, having no children running around. It would definitely be different. In her home and the Smith home there had always been young children making noise and commotion.

Soon it was time for dinner and then the porter was calling out that the next stop was Cheyenne. Cassie retrieved her overnight bag and organized her things, making sure she didn't forget anything. Cheyenne was coming into view, and she could see buildings in the distance where the center of town was. They were on the edge of town where the train depot was located. "Cheyenne!" she thought with excitement. The train blew its whistle, alerting all that it was pulling into town. Cassie was sure her aunt and uncle were waiting for her. Cassie hoped she would recognize them; it had been years since she had seen them. She took a deep breath and stood as the train pulled into the station and screeched to a halt, steam blowing out as it rested from its journey, just long enough to refuel, load and unload its various passengers and cargo.

"Here at last!" she thought.

Chapter 3
Cheyenne

The train station was bustling with people coming and going, with crowds on the platform exchanging welcomes and goodbyes. Cassie nervously looked around for Aunt Mabel and Uncle George, but before she even saw them, she heard someone calling out her name.

"Cassie! Cassie!" Mabel called out as she broke through the throngs of people with her arms outstretched.

Before Cassie could respond, a petite curvy woman with greying brown hair, looking like Cassie's mother, rushed forward and took her into her arms. Cassie couldn't hold back the tears, feeling the weight of the past month pour out of her. Aunt Mabel held her tightly as she let her own tears fall as she clung to the last piece of her sister that was left, feeling a great wave of grief wash over her. The two of them stood silent in the midst of surrounding commotion, feeling alone in their own world of shared sorrow for the moment.

George stood back, watching, with a lump in his throat. He was a kind, hard-working man and protective of all that he loved. His tall stature had allowed him to see Cassie above the flock of bodies and had pointed her out to his lovely wife. Together George and Mabel had created a wonderful home outside of town and were both happy to finally have someone to share it with. They had always wanted a large family, but sadly, Mabel was never able to carry their babies to full term. But now, George and Mabel had their niece to care for. It was a terrible way to have gained a child, but they would make sure she was as happy and loved as if their own daughter.

George cleared his throat. "I'm sorry to have to cut in and break up this wonderful reunion, my dears," George said with a chuckle, "but, we have to get Cassie's trunk off the train before it pulls out. And if we want to get home before dark, we should get going."

The two women loosened their embrace and looked up at him, laughing through their tears, and his heart swelled to near bursting.

"Welcome home, Cassie!" Uncle George said tenderly as he took them both into his long and loving arms, which made his chin tremble with emotion. George cleared his throat again and pulled away quickly as he smiled. "Come on. Let's get your bags and trunk loaded, my dear!"

Arm in arm, Cassie and Aunt Mabel walked behind Uncle George to the freight car and waited as the porter retrieved the trunk for them. Singlehandedly, Uncle George carried the trunk to the wagon as Cassie and Mabel followed close behind. Sliding the trunk into the back of the wagon, along with Cassie's carpetbag, he then assisted her up to take her seat between him and his wife.

"Well, let's get you home!" said Uncle George as he clucked to the horses to get them going.

Cassie sat back and took in the town's layout as they followed the road running along the train tracks, then turned right, heading toward the main road through the center of town. Right away she noticed how close all the buildings were built, with nary a space between them as they lined the dusty street. Cassie turned her head back and forth trying to take the whole town in. They immediately passed two grand hotels facing one another.

"Those two buildings are the Cheyenne and Interocean Hotels," Aunt Mabel said pointing to each one. "I'm sure it's hard to believe that all the way out here, we have such luxuries. But these two hotels have accommodations fine enough to appease the wealthiest travelers from back East and even Europe," Aunt Mabel proudly explained.

Uncle George drove slowly past saloons, dance halls, dress shops, and other establishments, then further down the street, the sheriff's office and jail. Cassie could see at the very end of the street sat two churches, one on each side. As they passed another of the many saloons, a tinny sounding player piano was heard playing the familiar parlor tune of "Camptown Races," drawing her attention as the saloon door burst open. Two drunken men emerged, and boisterously called out to her and waved as two scantily clad saloon girls giggled and pulled them back inside. Cassie blushed and quickly looked away.

Aunt Mabel saw Cassie's embarrassment and tried to explain. "It's a drawback of living in such a fast-growing city, along with the railroad men came the vices they have. This isn't the most civilized place at times. But we only come into town twice a week for church and supplies," she said as she squeezed Cassie's shoulders. Mabel pointed toward the sheriff's office as they passed it. "Thank heavens for Sheriff Havoc. Since he came to town, the town has settled down substantially."

"Sheriff Havoc?" Cassie puzzled. "What an odd name."

"I guess it is. I believe his ancestors emigrated here from Germany or Sweden. I suppose it's sort of ironic that his name is exactly what he put an end to in Cheyenne," Aunt Mabel said with a chuckle. "All the same, I don't want you in town without a chaperone. You are a beautiful young woman with too many wild men around," she said with a warm smile and another squeeze.

Cassie smiled weakly in response and tried to take heed of what Aunt Mabel was saying. The railroad town was so different from the sleepy farming town she was used to. This place had an energy about it, raw and wild among the scattered signs of structure and civilization. Only sparse grass and dwarfed trees grew where vigilant hands or leaky rain barrels and troughs watered them. A gust of wind stirred up a small cloud of dust, whirling it across the parched earth where it wasn't hard-packed. Further down the road, almost out of town, were large homes built as ostentatious as ones she'd seen in the big city of Springfield, Missouri. It was obvious quite a few wealthy individuals lived in Cheyenne. Many of the two-story mansions had fenced yards with a few flowers and small trees around the perimeters. Cassie's mouth fell open in awe when Aunt Mabel pointed out that the street was called "Millionaire Row," where eight millionaires lived.

"Where'd they get all their money?" Cassie asked.

Uncle George explained that some had made their money as he had, raising and selling cattle, and the others were investors from the East who made their fortune from the hotels, dance halls and saloons they owned.

Cheyenne was so unlike any place Cassie had ever seen, and she hoped that she would come to love it as much as she had the contrastingly quiet town in Jackson County, Missouri.

Turning left off the main road they passed by smaller homes, cabins, and shanties and were soon headed out to the open countryside. The two-track road lead across prairie grass toward low hills in the distance that ran along a large stream, lined with trees and bushes.

"That must be where Aunt Mabel and Uncle George have their cattle ranch," Cassie thought with a twinge of

69

excitement and apprehension.

It took about thirty minutes to get into the hills where the grass was thick and green, and trees dotted the hillsides. The stream they had been following was called Crow Creek and ran past the ranch, they told her.

"I would love to go for a ride and explore this place," she thought as they drove on.

Uncle George turned off the road, down a lengthy lane where the trees pressed in, shading them as they went. The rutted grass road curved and opened up to a clearing where their well-cared for home sat nestled inside a grove of timbers. The thick trees along the back side of the homestead protected the house from the wind and winter storms. The single-story dwelling, with newly whitewashed plank board siding and full-length porch, greeted her. Green shutters framed each of the windows, where the morning sunshine could filter in. Flower boxes hung under the windows, displaying pink, red and yellow flowers. There was a well and a clothesline to the right of the home. Further on to the right was the garden with small plants growing in straight rows and then the large barn with the corral and chicken coop. And lastly her eyes were drawn back to the steps up to the porch where dark pink delphinium bushes were in full bloom, looking so beautiful and inviting.

"Welcome home, Cassie!" exclaimed Aunt Mabel gleefully, giving Cassie's shoulders a hug.

"We hope you'll be happy here. It has been a good home to us these past few years," said Uncle George proudly.

Cassie smiled back at their loving faces as her heart filled with gratitude. "Thank you."

Seeing the weariness on Cassie's face, Mabel suggested, "I'm sure you're exhausted from your trip and want to wash up and get to bed as soon as possible. We'll have your bath ready for you in no time."

As soon as Uncle George brought the wagon to a stop, they climbed down. Aunt Mabel took the carpetbag from the back and Cassie by the hand, leading her up the steps with Uncle George following closely behind with her trunk.

Aunt Mabel opened the door and let Cassie step inside and allowed her a moment to take it all in. The open living area was large and inviting, with a rock fireplace on the far wall, surrounded by a three-piece parlor set, and a rocking chair in the corner. To her left was the kitchen area, with a big black cook stove and an up-to-date sink with a water pump. And in the center of the kitchen was a table covered with a white tablecloth.

"It's so pretty," Cassie declared, gazing around the cozy ranch house.

"Thank you, dear. This way is your room, Cassie." Aunt Mabel motioned to the right.

Cassie followed Uncle George into the bedroom as he placed her trunk under the window and stood with Aunt Mabel and watched Cassie as she surveyed the room. Aunt Mabel smiled at Cassie's obvious pleasure. Her wide eyes and open mouth were all the couple needed as reward for their efforts in creating a special place for her.

In the center of the white bedroom was a large oak bed covered with a pink patchwork quilt. She never had a room to herself before, much less her own bureau and matching chest of drawers. Each item in the room had been carefully chosen and placed with loving care, including the framed oil painting of roses that hung above the bed.

About to burst with excitement, Cassie exclaimed, "OH! Thank you so much! I've never seen such a beautiful room! It's more than I could ever want, and better than I deserve! Thank you both so much!" she said giving them each a beaming smile.

"Darling, we're so pleased to have you here and want you to have everything you need and all you deserve," explained Aunt Mabel, grinning broadly.

"We're so glad that you're happy with your room! We had such a fun time getting it ready for you." Uncle George removed his hat and backed out of the room. "I'll let you put away your belongings while I go get the water heating for your bath. The water should be ready by the time you're unpacked," explained Uncle George. "I'll leave you two ladies to it," he said and closed the door.

Cassie smiled and unbuttoned her jacket, removed it, and placed it on the back of the chair, then opened her carpet bag and began taking out her night clothes and toiletries that she had used on the train. She placed the small silver hand mirror, brush and hair combs on the dressing table where a white runner lay, embroidered with pink flowers. She opened the chest of drawers and placed her night dress and underclothes in them while Aunt Mabel opened the trunk and began removing the dresses and hung them in the bureau along with her long wool winter coat. Cassie's belongings were finally tucked away as she noted the sun setting behind the trees through the open curtains. The rose painted lamps on the nightstands were lit and cast a soft amber glow in the bedroom that she thought was fit for a princess.

Uncle George peeked in and smiled pleasingly. "Your bath awaits, my dear!" He was proud of the home he had built and took pleasure in showing her all that he could provide for his family.

Cassie smiled and thanked him, gathered her clean clothes and toiletries and followed him across the living area to the door in the back corner of the kitchen. Inside the storage room a lamp illuminated the large cast iron tub full of steaming water. Beside that was a chair for her to sit on and undress. A small window behind the tub was draped with heavy curtains, allowing her complete privacy.

Clearing his throat, he backed toward the kitchen door. "Take your time and enjoy." Uncle George excused himself and closed the door behind him.

Cassie smiled at how thoughtful Uncle George was by getting everything ready, even setting out towels on the bench beside the cast-iron tub for her. Her aunt and uncle had done so much for her already, with her own room, completely furnished and decorated so beautifully. It made her feel overwhelmed with gratitude for their love and concern for her.

Cassie could hear the couple's muffled conversation as things were being moved in the kitchen. She began to undress, excited to get in the tub. The days on the train had been hot at times and wearing the same clothes three days in a row had left her feeling grimy. She carefully dipped into the warm water, not wanting to get a drop of it on the wood floor and allowed herself to relax and soak. Eventually, she began washing hair and body until she felt squeaky clean. Rubbing dry, she dressed in the comfortable house dress she had chosen. Thoroughly brushing the tangles out of her damp hair, she decided to leave it down so it could finish drying before braiding it. Gathering up the wet towels and her dirty clothes, she left the room.

"There, do you feel better?" Aunt Mabel asked as she emerged.

"Oh yes! Much better, thank you!" exclaimed Cassie. "Where would you like me to put my dirty clothes?" The room was fully aglow with lamps, as dusk had descended into night.

"Here let me take them, I have a tub of wash soaking

right now, I'll add yours and we can wash them tomorrow." Aunt Mabel took the dirty clothes from her. "I made you something to eat. Just some hot biscuits and warm milk before bed."

"Thank you, Aunt Mabel," Cassie said, smelling the warm biscuits fresh out of the oven.

"Here, come and sit down, Cassie," Uncle George said as he motioned to one of the chairs in front of the hearth where a small fire was now burning.

Cassie sat in the cushioned chair as Aunt Mabel brought over a plate of golden-brown biscuits with melting butter and a large glass of milk and set them down on the table beside the lamp and the family Bible.

"The warm milk should help you sleep," explained Mabel.

Cassie thanked her and picked up a powdered biscuit and took a bite. It was flaky and buttery, just like her mama used to make. She ate and drank slowly as she watched the dancing flames of the small fire that popped and crackled cheerily. She was quiet, as Aunt Mabel and Uncle George talked about their preparations for her arrival and all the fun they had painting and picking out the furniture and decorations. Cassie smiled and tried to focus on their stories as she began to feel the exhaustion of the day seeping in. The warm milk was working its magic and she was struggling to keep her eyes open as she stared into the fire.

Aunt Mabel reached out and put a hand on Cassie's shoulder, drawing Cassie's gaze back to her. "My dear child, you must be tuckered out. Don't let us keep you up. There will be plenty of time to talk in the days to come."

"Yes, don't let us keep you from sleep. You've had a long trip," Uncle George said as he folded his newspaper and laid it on the table beside his chair.

"You're right, I should get to bed. If you'll excuse me,

I'll see you both in the morning," Cassie said as she yawned.

Uncle George and Aunt Mabel stood and gave Cassie a hug and kiss goodnight and told her again how happy they were to have her with them. She thanked them again for taking her in and for the beautiful room and left them for the night.

Alone in her room, Cassie closed the door, pulled the curtains closed, and changed into her nightgown. She quickly brushed and braided her hair, then kneeled beside her bed on the braided rug and thanked the Lord for the safe journey and for her wonderful aunt and uncle and their generosity. She quickly closed her prayer before she fell asleep on her knees and climbed into the soft bed and blew out the lamp. Her head barely hit the fluffy pillow before she was sound asleep.

***

Cassie slept late into the morning and stretched and yawned before fully realizing where she was. She smiled and lay still, looking around the room, observing it in the morning sunlight streaming through the lace curtains. She heard familiar noises in the kitchen as pans rattled and smells of breakfast permeated the room. Her stomach grumbled hungrily; it was time to get up. Cassie made her bed, then sat down at the dressing table in front of the mirror and took her hair out of the braid and brushed it until it was shiny and smooth, then braided it again. She dressed in the simple light green house dress she had worn briefly the night before and pinned on her apron. Satisfied with her appearance, she came out of her room to behold her aunt standing at the stove, looking so much like her ma that it made her heart skip a beat before she registered it fully. The strong smell of bacon, eggs, and coffee brought her back to reality. Uncle George sat at the table reading the Bible and looked up, beckoning her to come and sit down beside him. She smiled and obliged.

"Did you sleep well?" he asked.

Before Cassie could answer, Aunt Mabel turned from the stove. "Oh Cassie! Good, you're up!" she bubbled excitedly.

"Good morning!" Cassie answered, feeling the cheerfulness touch her heart. "Yes Uncle, I did sleep well."

Mabel noted Cassie's smiling eyes and color in her cheeks, she looked well rested and appeared happy. Aunt Mabel came and stood beside Cassie, leaned over, hugged her shoulders and kissed the top of her head. "It's so good to have you here, I can't tell you how much we are already enjoying it! We were pretty lonely with just the two of us, but that's in the past. You are such a blessing to us!" Aunt Mabel kissed her head again and released her to go dish up the food and bring it to the table.

Uncle George reached over and patted Cassie's hand as it rested on the table. "It will take some time getting used to us, I'm sure. But we're patient and hope eventually this will feel like home. Just don't let us scare you with all our love and attention. We've been saving it up for years, and you're now the lucky recipient!" he said as he laughed, making crinkles by his joyful eyes.

Cassie smiled at his teasing and felt their sincerity. "I already feel loved beyond measure; you both are most dear to me. As for feeling at home, you're right, I'm sure it will just take a little time. I already feel better than I have in a long time," she said, with a tightness in her throat. Just being with her aunt, who looked and sounded like an older version of her mother, brought her great comfort.

Aunt Mabel set the food on the table and sat down for

the prayer. Following the blessing, she encouraged Cassie, "Eat up, the day is wasting and there are many wonderful things I want to show you," Aunt Mabel said with a twinkle in her eye.

Cassie ate as quickly as she could, smiling weakly as they glanced at her occasionally.

Uncle George excused himself and headed out to do more chores on the large ranch, then he paused at the front door, turned and gave Cassie some last words of advice. "Don't let her wear you out, Cassie. Mabel loves hard work and forgets not everyone is built as tough as she is!" He winked at them and left, closing the door behind him.

Aunt Mabel broke out in laughter at his teasing and Cassie joined in as Mabel waved him off. "Oh, that old goat!" Mabel teased as she laughed.

Cassie began cleaning off the table and asked Aunt Mabel where things were kept so she could wash the dishes. Mabel was happy to show her around the kitchen, then sent Cassie to the wood box for more wood to heat water for washing.

It was hard to believe that three days had passed since she had first left Missouri. Cassie thought of how her new life was beginning in her new home with some of the same daily rituals she had done for most of her life and it helped comfort her. She was grateful for the chores that would keep her mind busy. After the breakfast dishes were clean and put away, Cassie added more water to the large kettles and set them to heat for the wash tubs lined up outside on long benches next to the house. Together, her and Aunt Mabel worked, washing and hanging the clothes as they chatted about different things.

Suddenly, Cassie became overcome with nausea and excused herself before running around to the back of the house. She came back a few minutes later, looking pale and exhausted. Cassie apologized to her aunt for the interruption as she began hanging the clothes again. But Aunt Mabel could see that she was not feeling well and sent her in to lay down and rest for a while. She tried to argue, but Aunt Mabel was persistent, and she finally gave in and went inside. Cassie fell asleep quickly and awoke a few hours later, feeling much better. When she discovered that the house was empty, she went outside and found her aunt in the garden, pulling weeds.

Cassie startled Mabel, as she approached. "Oh, Cassie dear, you're awake! I hope you feel better." Aunt Mabel stood up, brushing the dirt from her hands.

"Much better, thank you. I didn't realize how exhausted I was. I must have slept for hours. I'm sorry I left you alone to do the chores." Cassie stood at the garden's edge looking for a place to start weeding.

"It's not your fault dear, you're worn out from the trip and that's understandable. I'm about to go in and make dinner if you would like some?" Aunt Mabel brushed the dirt from off her apron as she stepped over the rows of young plants, leaving the garden.

"I'd like that. But let me make it while you take a break. I'm feeling much better, really." Cassie reassured her with a smile.

"We'll do it together." Mabel slipped her arm through Cassie's and they went inside to wash up and make the noon meal.

Dinner was ready when Uncle George came in from working with the animals and commented on how tasty everything was. As they finished up, Uncle George offered to take Cassie for a horse ride.

Cassie was thrilled at the opportunity to see the countryside and the "family business." She clapped her hands and responded, "Oh yes! I would love that, more than anything!"

Cassie missed riding through the fields on her horse, Midnight, immensely. What a wonderful treat it would be, to go riding on this beautiful June day.

Out in the corral, Uncle George saddled up Ginger, one of the mares that was used for herding cattle, then helped lift Cassie up onto the horse, as Aunt Mabel stood by.

"George, dear, she wasn't feeling very well this morning, please take it easy." Mabel's hands wringed nervously, unsure if it was such a good idea. It was George and Mabel's responsibility to keep Cassie safe and Mabel worried that something might happen to her.

"I'll be careful," reassured Cassie as she situated her skirt and took the reins from Uncle George, grinning ear to ear.

"I won't let anything happen to her, Mabel, dear." George mounted his horse and led the way out of the corral down to the creek that ran behind the house.

Cassie followed George through the trees along a worn path as she kept to the shade. The tall grass and wildflowers tempted the horses to grab a mouthful every few minutes. Cassie loosened the reins and allowed Ginger the pleasure of grabbing a mouthful, patting Ginger's neck. Ginger was a beautiful red bay, with a shiny black mane and tail. Ginger kept picking up her pace, seeming to be almost as excited as Cassie about being on the open plains. Uncle George could hear behind him and hurried his horse along to give them space. As they came to a clearing, George slowed to let Cassie come up beside him. Together, side by side they headed toward a gentle incline, were miles and miles of grassy plains were dotted with grazing cattle.

Uncle George pointed to the cattle. "Our herd is mixed in with other herds on the open range until fall, then we'll have a roundup and sort them all out. Some will go to market and the spring calves will be branded. We started with around 150 head of cattle, but our herd has nearly doubled the size in the past two years. Last fall, we sent a third of them to market and kept the rest, to grow the herd.

Cassie listened intently as Uncle George explained further.

"I'm not a big rancher, there are other ranch owners who have much larger herds. Last year I was told that there are over thirty thousand head spread out over the one hundred miles surrounding Cheyenne, and even more when the cattle drives arrived from Texas in the fall."

"How do you do it all?" she asked, astounded at the number of cattle to sort.

"Oh, I don't do it alone. I hire ranch hands and local cowboys to help with the roundup in the spring and fall. It's busy during roundup, but for the most part, the cattle ranch is self-sufficient. It's a prosperous endeavor to be a cattle rancher in Cheyenne these days," Uncle George said proudly.

Cassie had a new appreciation for Uncle George as she rode beside him, thinking of his success and hard work. Before her lay miles and miles of thick grass and low hills. As they turned back toward the homestead, Cassie noted the grove of trees hiding their own piece of heaven from the world. She looked up at the clear blue sky and felt the sun on her face. Today's ride made her feel so free. She smiled and asked, "May I ride her back to the ranch in a trot? I'm a good rider and will be careful."

Uncle George nodded his head. "Just don't let Aunt Mabel see you doing anything but walking the horse, or I'll have some explaining to do." His mouth spread into a cheerful grin as he teased Cassie with his warning.

"I promise!" Cassie patted Ginger's neck. "Are you

ready for some fun?" she whispered into Ginger's ear that twitched with wonder. Cassie secured the reins tightly in her hands, nudged the horse forward and kicked a little harder in the stirrups and got Ginger into a good gallop. The wind blew her bonnet back off her head, threatening to loosen her hair from its braid. Cassie leaned forward to be able to move smoothly with the horse. Down the gentle slope of soft grassy earth, they flew. She looked over her shoulder and caught sight of her uncle. Cassie smiled and kept going until the ground leveled out where she passed some cattle that had been grazing. The cattle closest to her moved off, some of them running a few yards before they resumed eating. Cassie reached the road that ran past the homestead and slowed the horse to a walk.

"This must be the road that heads back towards home," she thought. "How funny…already I'm thinking of it as home." Cassie slowed and let Uncle George catch up as they neared the lane that ran through the grove of trees that hid the homestead.

"You really can handle a horse, Cassie!" Uncle George shouted as he neared her. "I haven't seen many women ride as smoothly as you. You're a natural horse woman," he said beaming as he came up beside her.

Cassie smiled at him. "Thank you for taking me riding."

"My pleasure," Uncle George said tipping his hat to her.

Cassie's love and appreciation for him grew even more that day as they traveled down the long lane through the shady trees. Aunt Mabel came out of the house and met them at the gate, opening it for them as they rode through, then closed it behind them. Cassie dismounted with Uncle George's help, not because she needed his help but because it was the polite thing to do. Cassie patted Ginger's neck as she nuzzled Cassie's shoulder.

"How was the ride?" Mabel watched Cassie and George with pride as she stood by the gate.

Cassie handed Uncle George the reins and ran to Aunt Mabel and gave her a big hug. "It was the best ride ever! Ginger is a wonderful horse! I loved the wide openness of the prairie and even the wind. Oh, and the pretty cattle, there are so many!" Cassie chattered on and on, explaining all the beauty she had enjoyed, but was careful to leave out the part about her galloping home. Talking excitedly, the women left the corral arm in arm.

Half-way across the yard, Cassie shouted over her shoulder, "Thanks again, Uncle George!"

Uncle George grinned and hollered back, "Any time, Cassie, any time!"

That afternoon Aunt Mabel and Cassie finished the laundry, ironed the clothes and put them away. Mabel found it much easier with Cassie's help and a lot more enjoyable. Her company had made the time fly by.

That night while sitting in front of the fireplace, Cassie began composing her first letter to Madeline. She wanted it to be ready to take with her when her aunt and uncle went into town on Thursday. Cassie had decided to go to the bank as well to take out a small amount of money to purchase a riding dress.

***

The next day started bright and early. Cassie awoke before sun-up and dressed in her house dress, ready to help with chores. Today would be mending day, along with all the other daily chores that needed done. She didn't want to be a burden in any way and determined to do her part. The only thing that kept nagging her was how tired and nauseated she was. Cassie had hoped the motion sickness from the train ride would be wearing off. Aunt Mabel would start worrying if she continued to act sickly. Usually by afternoon she would be feeling better, but not today. She ate only a small amount at dinner and was barely able to keep it down.

That afternoon as they sat on the red velvet chairs, Aunt Mabel worked on mending stockings, while Cassie worked her crocheting. Mabel was delighted to see the project Cassie had started.

"I declare! Aren't you talented! I've never seen such a pretty pattern. And what a beautiful color of yarn," exclaimed Aunt Mabel.

"I learned the stitch from my friend Madeline while on the train. I planned on making a baby blanket to send to her sister who's expecting soon. Well, that is if it is a girl and if I get it done by then," Cassie said as she crocheted.

After supper, Cassie finished her letter to Madeline, enclosing her address and described all the new things that had happened. She asked about Madeline's sister and closed with a sincere wish for Madeline and her family to be happy and healthy. Cassie missed Madeline and wished she could be here. She doubted that would ever happen, but she wished.

Thursday morning after breakfast and chores, George went to get the wagon hitched for their ride into town, while Mabel readied a list of goods and supplies she needed.

"Cassie is there anything you need to pick up in town?" Aunt Mabel asked.

"I would like to stop at the post office and the bank if we could?" asked Cassie.

"We go to the post office every week and the bank is

83

right next to it, so we can do both. George will be going to the feed store and saddle shop for supplies while we do our shopping, so we can all be done around the same time," said Aunt Mabel.

Cassie had put on her next best dress for the trip into town, a light blue cotton skirt with a white blouse and blue jacket, and her blue hat to match. Her hair was brushed and twisted up and held with a comb and pins. Cassie looked more grown up this way, her curves accentuated by her tiny waist. Uncle George smiled when she came out to the wagon.

"Mabel, it looks like I might need to bring my rifle to fight off the young lads today with Cassie coming along. I doubt they've ever seen such a pretty girl," George exclaimed and chuckled in his jolly way.

Cassie's cheeks blushed and she looked away shyly. Uncle George assisted her into the wagon and then his wife. "Oh, George stop teasing her, you're embarrassing her," said Mabel with a grin.

The trip into town was pleasant, and Cassie appreciated the difference that coming into town from this direction offered. The tall buildings were all that seemed to stand still in the bustling town. There was so much going on around them as they entered the center of town.

As the postmaster took Cassie's letter, he recognized her name, and exclaimed, "OH! Yesterday I got a telegram for you. Just a minute, I'll get it." He turned around and sorted through a small stack of telegrams as Cassie and Mabel exchanged looks of surprise.

"Who would be sending me a telegram?" Cassie wondered.

"Oh, here it is!" He pulled out the half sheet of paper. "Cassandra Black?" he asked.

"Yes, that's me! I wonder who could be sending me a

telegram?" Cassie asked her aunt in bewilderment.

The postmaster handed Cassie the telegram. "Cassie Black, your horse came home. Sending him by train. Arriving in Cheyenne Sunday at 3 pm. Mr. Smith."

Cassie couldn't believe her eyes. She was overcome with joy and looked at her aunt in astonishment. "My horse, Midnight, escaped from the Indians and found his way back to our farm! The Smiths are shipping Midnight here. He'll arrive on Sunday!" she exclaimed, clasping her hands together, then without warning, she hugged her aunt as tears streamed down her exuberant face.

"My land! I've never heard of such a miraculous thing! That must be some horse!" exclaimed the postmaster, overhearing the news.

"You're truly being blessed, my dear!" said Aunt Mabel with a squeeze before releasing her. "Sunday we'll be in town for church services and can pick him up afterwards," she continued. "We'll go to the bank and then find George and tell him the good news."

Suddenly, Cassie wanted to share the news with Madeline and asked the postmaster for the letter back so she could add the good news. He handed the letter back to her and she quickly wrote the exciting news and resealed the letter, handing it back to him. The postmaster was smiling and wished them a good day as they left.

At the bank, the teller was able to confirm the deposit had been received and she would be able to withdraw money at any time. Cassie withdrew enough for a riding dress and a little extra for her purse. This was a new place, and she wasn't sure what she might need and she didn't want her aunt and uncle to feel like they had to provide her with everything. She placed the bills in her purse and left with her aunt to go down to the next block where Uncle George would be getting feed for the animals.

Cassie and Mabel walked arm in arm down the board-walk past various store fronts, as people bustled every-where, coming in and out of the stores with their purchas-es. And the street was filled with riders and wagons in a hurry. Cassie was getting open looks from young men as they passed by, and she quickened her pace as she kept her eyes ahead and tried not to make eye contact.

Cassie and Mabel entered the feed shop and found George had already been and gone. Together they went back outside and down the block to the saddle and tack shop. Inside, Cassie spotted Uncle George's head above the aisles of tall shelves and hurried over to tell him the amazing news.

"I declare, girl! That's the best news I have ever heard!" Uncle George said in astonishment. Suddenly, an idea came to him. "This means you'll be needing a saddle. I've had my eye on this one over here. It's a very suitable sad-dle for your size." He walked to the end of an aisle where the saddles were displayed. As she followed the smell of leather grew thicker in the air. "This one here!" he said as he pointed it out. "It's marked thirty dollars, but I'm good friends with the owner, and I know I can get a better deal," he whispered to Cassie. "I'll be right back."

Uncle George went to the counter and began discuss-ing the price of the saddle with the owner. He was able to strike a deal with the owner, for thirty dollars he could get the saddle with a new bridle and for another two dollars a saddle blanket.

Cassie and Mabel stood back while the men finished their business, then followed them outside as the new saddle and the other items purchased were packed up and placed in the wagon. Cassie, overcome with gratitude, thanked her uncle and reached up on her tip toes and hugged him around the neck and gave him a kiss on the cheek.

Uncle George blushed at the attention. "Aww shucks, it was nothin'. I'm happy to do it for my only niece. Come on, let's get the rest of your shopping done and get home," he declared, trying to change the subject.

It was Cassie's turn to smile at causing him to blush. Uncle George cleared his throat and helped them into the wagon to drive over to the general mercantile. As he dropped them off, he told them he would drive over to the railroad station to find out the details about the freight train that Midnight would be on.

Cassie and Aunt Mabel went inside the mercantile and purchased flour, sugar, lard, salt, kerosene and coffee. The clerk said he would gather the goods and have them ready in a box when they were done with their other shopping.

Their last stop for the day was at the dress shop next door. There Cassie found a stylish full split skirt of golden buckskin with brown buttons down the front flap on each side, with a matching vest. She tried on the skirt and vest with her white blouse and was impressed with the exquisite feel of the soft suede. Aunt Mabel loved the fit and color as well and encouraged Cassie to purchase them, offering to buy her a matching hat. She tried to protest but her aunt wouldn't take no for an answer. A small wide brimmed Stetson cowboy hat made of similar-colored leather was Aunt Mabel's gift. Cassie imagined she would look very fashionable in her new Western wear. Her clothing purchases were placed in a flat box and the hat in a hat box, then handed to the women.

Finished shopping, they met Uncle George at the mercantile where he was loading the box of dried goods and the can of kerosene.

"Did you find everything you wanted?" asked Uncle George seeing the boxes.

"Yes!" Cassie smiled broadly.

"Let's get home for supper before wc waste away from hunger," teased Aunt Mabel. She had noticed how slender Cassie was when she tried on the new dress and her motherly instincts kicked in, wanting to fatten her up a bit.

Cassie and George laughed as they climbed into the wagon. George had never known his wife to refuse someone a meal. Where Mabel was, food was always being prepared and offered. It was her talent and Christ-like gift, to feed the hungry and comfort the weak in spirit. George smiled at Mabel lovingly as he turned the wagon around and headed towards home.

On the way home, Cassie couldn't stop thinking about Midnight and the amazing day she was having. Then it occurred to her. She would give it all away, the clothes, Midnight, and the beautiful bedroom just to have her family back. Suddenly, she began to feel guilty for being happy about the nice things she had been given and to have Midnight back. Cassie fell quiet and stared off into the distance, thinking.

"What's wrong Cassie? You look so sad. Aren't you happy?" asked Aunt Mabel as she saw the change in Cassie's countenance.

Cassie blinked a few times as she processed the words her aunt had asked her. She didn't want to seem ungrateful and quickly responded. "Oh yes! I'm happy, and so thankful for everything you have given me. I love my room and new clothes and now Midnight has been found. But I feel bad that I am happy. I can't explain it. It doesn't make sense when I say it out loud," she said looking down at her hands in her lap, feeling ashamed about her good fortune.

"My dear child. No one expects you to be sad forever. You've had many sad days and will feel that way at times, I'm sure. But you're allowed to have happiness too. You will never forget what you've lost, but that doesn't mean you need to be sad continually. And most certainly you shouldn't feel guilty about being happy. You can see the rainbow even though it's still raining. Please enjoy the moment and feel happy. Today's been a very good day. Let it be just that!" Aunt Mabel said as she patted Cassie's hands and gave them a squeeze.

"Thank you, Aunt Mabel, I'll try," Cassie said, finally looking up, and gave her a small smile. She loved her Aunt Mabel so much for trying to help her understand.

"I can't wait for you to show me what you got at the dress shop!" George said, trying to change the subject.

Cassie smiled at the thought of her uncle caring about a dress and began to laugh lightly, as they both joined in with her.

"That's my girl!" said Uncle George as he continued to laugh.

"Come Sunday, after church and the church picnic we'll pick up your horse. It'll be another great day. You'll see," said Aunt Mabel joyfully, squeezing Cassie around the shoulders.

Chapter 4
Church Picnic

Sunday morning Cassie awoke with mixed feelings. Normally, she enjoyed church, with its inspiring sermons and uplifting music. But this Sunday would be different. Cassie was apprehensive about all the new faces that would be staring at her, wondering who she was and why she was there. She knew all too well how girls and women gossiped about each other, especially the newcomer. Then feeling a surge of excitement, she imagined how wonderful it would be to be reunited with Midnight, her long-time friend, the only piece of her old life that was left.

Cassie put on her Sunday best dress and evaluated her reflection in the mirror. The tiny waist of the full gathered skirt with pale blue flower print complimented her figure. Pulling back part of her ebony hair, she tied it with a matching blue ribbon, letting the rest fall over her shoulders. Lastly, she buttoned her polished black shoes and headed outside to meet Uncle George and Aunt Mabel.

They were dressed in their finest as well. Uncle George looked very distinguished in his dark brown wool suit with a black ribbon necktie, his tall frame topped off with a brown bowler hat. His dark brown curly hair with a touch of grey at the sideburns was carefully smoothed back. Aunt Mabel was wearing a handsome sage green cotton dress that looked pretty with her brown eyes and hair. A small cameo broach ornamented the high collar. Her greying brown hair was pulled back and tied neatly into a knot at the nape of her neck.

Uncle George had harnessed the horses to the canopy-covered two-seated surrey and helped the ladies climb in. Aunt Mabel had placed her freshly baked cinnamon rolls in a basket for the church picnic and handed them to Cassie to set in the back seat beside her.

As they drove into town, Cassie wondered if there were going to be girls her age at church. Since her arrival she had seen very few young women and guessed they spent most of their time at home doing chores, like her. Entering the much quieter town, Cassie noticed the people who were slowly moving towards the entrance of the church. Uncle George pulled to a stop and tied up the horses and explained as he helped the women out of the surrey, that the Sabbath morning was the only time that the saloons and dance halls were closed. Instead of the usual noise of the street, the soothing sound of the organ playing a familiar hymn floated out of the open chapel doors.

"Good morning, Reverend Gather," George and Mabel said as they shook the hand of the black robed pastor at the top of the stairs.

"Welcome Brother and Sister Hartford. And who do we have here?" Reverend Gather kindly asked as he turned to Cassie to shake her hand.

"This is our niece, Cassandra Black. She has come to live with us, since she lost her family about a month ago." George gently put his hand on Cassie's shoulder, showing his support for her through this trying time.

Cassie had an immediate thought, "There, it's out. Short and to the point." Cassie smiled weakly at the pastor.

"I'm so sorry to hear that, child. God bless you and keep you. I hope you find peace and happiness here. You definitely have wonderful relatives. None are better than the Hartford's. Go with God, dear," Reverend Gather said sympathetically as he smiled at Cassie and her aunt and uncle, then finally released her hand.

"Thank you, Pastor." And Cassie followed her aunt and uncle into the church.

A couple of women entering the church behind her had overheard what Uncle George had said and began whispering as they took their seats. It was warm in the chapel and Cassie began feeling nauseated almost immediately. As she sat waiting for the service to begin, she could hear the whispers, "Oh the poor dear. She doesn't look well. I wonder what happened to her family?"

With the opening song, the gossiping was silenced. Cassie fanned herself with her program like many of the women in the chapel. As the heat increased and her nausea continued, Cassie hoped she would not have to leave as the meeting seemed to drag on. She couldn't wait to get out and tried to concentrate on the reverend's words. Once the worship service was closed, she became trapped as so many well-meaning people who wanted to meet the newcomer intercepted her as she tried to make it down the aisle.

Once free and outside, Cassie quickly stepped into the surrey and breathed a sigh of relief. She'd made it through the whole service without being sick. Grateful for the breeze that always seemed to be in Cheyenne, she relaxed. In the shade of the surrey, they drove a little ways out of town to a neighboring property.

The homestead's yard was set up with long tables of flat boards a-top sawhorses covered with tablecloths and filled with food that the families had brought to share. Small children ran around playing and chasing each other as the mothers and young women set up the food and a few men brought out the roasted pig. Reverend Gather said the blessing over the gathering. Cassie tried not to make eye contact with those who would most definitely ask her questions as she fixed a small plate.

Cassie politely excused herself to find a shady place to sit far away from the noisy people. Aunt Mabel and Uncle George stayed at a table with their neighbors as they ate. They understood how Cassie must be feeling and allowed her to settle in with the congregation at her own pace.

Cassie sat in the tall cool grass and took a few bites of her dinner while she watched the people cheerfully visiting and mingling. In the far corner of the yard there was a group of young men and women sitting apart, who would glance her way occasionally; Cassie suspected they were probably talking about her right that minute. She didn't care, let them talk, she wasn't interested in making friends right then.

Overwhelmed with fatigue, Cassie lay back with her hands resting on her stomach and looked up into the tree, watching the leaves flutter in the breeze. She didn't realize she had fallen asleep until she felt someone patting her hand. Cassie slowly opened her eyes as she realized there was a man kneeling beside her and holding her hand. Her eyes focused on a sandy blond-haired man with a neatly trimmed mustache.

"Are you OK, miss?" he asked in a deep soothing bass voice.

Cassie saw concern in his sea green eyes.

When she went to prop herself up, he realized he was still holding her delicate hand and released it, feeling embarrassed. "Sorry, I was worried you were ill when I saw you laying here. I was just making sure you were OK," he said, trying to explain his actions.

Before she could answer he continued, "Sheriff Havoc, at your service, miss," as he smiled and tipped his hat.

"I'm Cassandra Black, George and Mabel Hartford's niece," she said smiling and reached out her right hand as she sat up.

Sheriff Havoc took her hand gently and kept his eyes on hers. "It's a pleasure to meet you, Cass. I'd heard that George and Mabel had a relative coming to live with them," he said. "But I hadn't heard that it was a beautiful young woman," he thought as he continued to smile at her.

Cassie smiled warmly, noticing that he had shortened her name to Cass, and not Cassie as most people called her and didn't want to correct him. She tried to explain, "It was so hot and crowded, and this seemed like such a nice spot in the shade. It was so peaceful and cool, I must've fallen asleep," she said timidly. "How embarrassing," she thought as the heat rose in her cheeks.

"If you would be up for it, I know of an even prettier spot, just a short walk from here. It's very peaceful and much cooler there," he offered.

"That sounds very nice." Cassie looked over at her aunt and uncle who were watching her.

Sheriff Havoc waved to them. "George, would it be all right if I took Cass for a walk?" he asked in a raised voice.

Uncle George waved, giving Sheriff Havoc the OK. They'd never heard of Sheriff Havoc even entering a saloon except for keeping the peace. Sheriff Havoc was known as an honorable man, and a faithful Christian.

Cassie really wanted to get away from the prying eyes and smiled up at Sheriff Havoc, grateful for the offer. He extended his hand to her and helped her up.

"There's a trail that leads to a stream just a little way away," he said, releasing her hand. "If you please." He motioned in the direction they were to go, letting her go first.

Cassie began walking, then slowed, to allow Sheriff

Havoc to walk beside her, still keeping some space between them. She glanced out corner of her eye to observe Sheriff Havoc. He was much taller than her, at least by a head, about the same height as her uncle. Sheriff Havoc had on a well-worn cowboy hat and a leather vest over his white cotton shirt. He wasn't wearing his sheriff's badge or gun, she noticed.

As they walked along the path, Cassie took in the tall green grass and wildflowers in full bloom. A cool breeze rustled the leaves of the tall trees. She could smell the clean scent of pine from the pine trees they passed. The trail declined slightly and within a few minutes she heard the rush of water from the stream beyond. Cassie noticed how at ease Sheriff Havoc was as he made polite conversation.

"So, where are you from?" Sheriff Havoc asked as they walked.

"I'm from Missouri," Cassie said without emotion. She figured he knew about her reason for moving to Cheyenne and didn't give any further explanation. "So how long have you lived here in Cheyenne?" she asked quickly.

"Oh, about two years now. I came here as a favor to my friend, Mayor Hook, who needed help to restore law and order after the railroad was built. He knew I had some experience that would come in handy." Sheriff Havoc grinned to himself, remembering the wild unruly town and all the things he and the good townspeople had accomplished since then.

As they reached the stream bank, Cassie noticed the clear water had cooled the air around them. In the middle there were a few large rocks that the water flowed over, making a babbling sound. She noticed Sheriff Havoc as he stood watching her. He looked pleased.

"Thank you for bringing me here. You're right, this is a lovely spot, and much cooler." Cassie stepped closer to the water's edge.

Sheriff Havoc smiled. "I'm so glad you like it. I come here to think once in a while."

Cassie became thoughtful as she watched the water move the tall grass along the banks.

"Here, come and sit down." Sheriff Havoc motioned to a fallen tree. He was intrigued by her. All these years he'd been in Cheyenne, he'd never felt drawn to a woman. He couldn't put his finger on it. Why did he feel so drawn to Cassie? Sheriff Havoc wanted nothing more than to protect her from the world and whatever pain she was feeling. He wanted to help her, but how? He didn't know what she was carrying inside, but he knew it was heavy…he sensed it. Sheriff Havoc understood her somehow. Little did she know he was also carrying a heart full of pain.

"Thank you," she said, and sat quietly enjoying the sounds of chirping birds and buzzing insects.

After a moment had passed, Sheriff Havoc broke the silence. "You're lucky to have such a nice family to come and live with. I've known George and Mabel ever since I arrived in Cheyenne. They're good people. Come to think of it, they were the first ones to have me out to their place for dinner after I moved here." He rubbed his strong jaw as he thought back to that day.

Cassie looked up at him, standing in a relaxed stance, as he placed his hands in his pockets. "Maybe we should have you to supper again soon," Cassie said, then realized it sounded very forward of her and chided herself. "Oh, good grief! What must he think of me?"

Sheriff Havoc quickly answered as she blushed, "I'd be most appreciative to eat a home cooked meal. My cooking leaves a lot to be desired and the company would be even more appreciated." It was his turn to feel self-conscious. Why did he feel the need to tell her every detail of his personal life? He didn't feel like he needed to be guarded with her. He trusted her with whatever he told her. He didn't feel judged. Usually, he was very private. He frequently blended into the background, trying not to be noticed. Sheriff Havoc could command respect by his demeanor when he needed to, but usually kept to himself.

"Well, we'd better get back before people start talking. I don't want you to get a tainted reputation because of me. The busybodies will be having a hay-day with us walking off together," he said chuckling.

Cassie really didn't care what people thought about her. She already felt like damaged goods and didn't care if people spread rumors about her. But she didn't want Sheriff Havoc's reputation to be ruined. He was a well-respected law man and seemed to be an honorable gentleman. Cassie stood and brushed the wrinkles out of her dress. "Yes, we'd better get going. I don't want you to get in trouble," she said, laughing lightly. It felt good to laugh, it had been a very long time.

Sheriff Havoc offered his hand to help her up the bank. She took it and he pulled her up to stand next to him. Cassie made the mistake of looking up at him which almost took her breath away. Her heart was pounding, and butterflies fluttered in her stomach as she felt her cheeks become hot and flushed. She looked down quickly and stepped past him as he placed his hand gently on her lower back to guide her. She felt his light touch and her heart skipped a beat again. She was relieved he couldn't see her cheeks deepen in color as she blushed even more.

Sheriff Havoc surprised himself for being so bold as to touch her. His heart was pounding so loud he was sure she could hear it. "What's happening to me?" he wondered. As Cassie walked slightly in front of him, he noticed how tiny her waist was. She was a mature woman, with curves in all the right places. Her beautiful long hair blew back with the breeze reminding him of flowing black silk. He wanted to touch it to find out if it was as soft as it looked but resisted.

Cassie slowed to let him come up beside her. "Would you tell me your first name?" she asked. "You know mine, but I don't know yours."

"It's Edward, but before I was sheriff most people called me Ed. My ma calls me Eddie. But you can call me whatever you want," he explained, regretting that he'd told her what his mother had called him. "Can't you just give her a simple answer, must you keep telling her everything?" he wondered.

Cassie smiled up at him. "I like the name Edward. I'll only call you Ed when we're alone…I mean if we're alone," she cleared her throat as she blushed. "I mean, I don't want people to get the wrong idea. After all, you're the sheriff and should be called so…out of respect."

Sheriff Havoc smiled at her, loving the way she'd said his name. His heart raced. He hadn't heard his name spoken by a woman in many years.

"I would love that. And may I call you Cass?" he asked sincerely.

Cassie's heart was pounding as he said her name. "Most people call me Cassie, short for Cassandra, but I like the even shorter version. But only you may call me Cass," she said smiling up at him again as they walked side by side.

"Cass it is then!" he said, smiling at her, and almost lost his footing.

Ed and Cassie broke through the trees to the sounds of parents hollering to their children trying to round them up to head home, as others laughed and chatted animatedly.

"What time is it?" Cassie asked.

Ed reached into his vest pocket and took out his watch and opened it. "It's half past two. I'm sorry, did I keep you too long?"

"Oh, no, no. I was just wondering. We need to go back into town and pick up my horse at the train depot. I received a telegram a few days ago saying he'd come back home after being lost. He'll be on the three o'clock train."

Ed and Cassie walked up to George and Mabel as they were gathering up their things. "I'm sorry for taking her away for so long," Ed said as he tipped his hat to them.

George and Mabel smiled at each other. "We weren't worried even for a minute. But we'd better get going if we're going to make it into town in time to pick up your horse, Cassie," George said, helping his wife with the empty picnic basket.

Ed walked them over to the surrey and assisted Cassie into the back seat while George assisted Mabel in, before he climbed up.

"Goodbye, and thanks again for the nice walk," Cassie said with a smile towards Ed.

"It was my great pleasure, Cass," said Ed, smiling back at her.

"Good seeing you again, Sheriff," said George, taking the reins and releasing the brake.

Before they started to pull away Cassie leaned forward and quietly asked Aunt Mabel if she could invite the sheriff to supper sometime.

Aunt Mabel smiled at Cassie and turned back. "Sheriff Havoc, it's been a long time since we've had you to supper. How about joining us this Thursday?"

Ed smiled broadly. "You bet. I'd be happy to join you."

"Until Thursday then, Sheriff!" George called out to Ed, then clucked to the horses. "Giddy up!"

Cassie smiled and waved, thanking Ed again for the

nice time, and turned around before she blushed again.

Ed stood there as they pulled away, watching Cassie's hair blow in the wind as his heart went with her.

Cassie's face flushed as she thought about their walk, his touch and his deep soothing voice. What was she thinking? He would never want her once he knew the truth about her. But her heart kept racing as she remembered the way Ed called her Cass. No one had ever called her Cass before, and it felt special. She felt like someone new, not the damaged girl from Missouri. Cassie felt safe and protected around Ed. Was it the fact that he was the sheriff? No, it was something more, she wasn't sure yet what it was. Well, maybe she would figure it out on Thursday. Oh, my goodness, how bold she'd been to ask her aunt to have him to supper. What must they think of her? Oh well, they seemed pleased to ask him. Maybe they liked Sheriff Havoc as much as she did. There, she admitted it, she liked him, and Cassie smiled to herself.

As they pulled up to the train depot, Cassie snapped out of her thoughts about Ed. She looked around to see the train hadn't pulled in yet.

Uncle George tied up the horses and went into the train station to ask if the train was going to be on time. He came back moments later saying it was expected any minute. And sure enough, it was right on schedule. The train blew its whistle as it pulled into town and the brakes screeched as steam blew from its engine and finally came to rest. Uncle George, Aunt Mabel and Cassie stepped back to let the passengers off and waited for the conductor to open the double doors of the stock car. A ramp was pulled up to the iron barred doors to allow the animals to be brought out. As they stood to the side of the cattle car, a man led her beautiful horse to the door. Cassie watched as Midnight was brought down the ramp. Not wanting to startle him, she remained quiet. Midnight had been through a lot on the train ride over, she assumed.

Cassie called out his name, "Midnight!" The black stallion recognized her voice, turned towards her lifting his head, and whinnied in response. She ran up to him and took his head in her hands as he nuzzled her with his muzzle. She put her forehead on his and talked quietly as the tears flowed.

"Oh, Midnight, I've missed you so much. I'm so sorry. Did they hurt you?" Tears streamed down Cassie's cheeks, remembering that night. "It's ok, you're safe, and I'll never let you go again." She raised up and kissed him on his forehead.

Midnight began prancing in place, excited to see his friend, the girl who loved him. It was a glorious day. All those watching couldn't help but feel emotional about the reunion of the young woman with her horse.

Uncle George spoke up, "I think we'd better move away from here so they can get the other animals off."

Cassie took the lead and walked Midnight to the surrey. There she turned and wrapped her arms around Midnight's neck and held him tight as he whinnied again.

Mabel started crying and George wrapped his arm around her to comfort her. These were tears of joy and sadness for having lost so much. Mabel had cried over the loss of her sister for weeks leading up to Cassie coming to live with them. Mabel hadn't talked about the attack yet with Cassie, afraid it would be too painful. But watching Cassie reunited with her horse, was very emotional. Mabel was full of gratitude that the good Lord had given Cassie this one thing for her to hold onto, something physical. George and Mabel tried to give Cassie all she would want; plenty of love, and a comfortable home. But they still felt like she was unhappy. Oh, Cassie didn't let on to them that she was unhappy, or so she thought. But they could see it in her face when she sat quietly, thinking no one was watching her. Today was the first hint that she was showing signs of healing. The look on Cassie's face as she emerged with Sheriff Havoc was simple happiness, the smile had reached her eyes, and they were sparkling. And now Midnight was back, a miracle, just for Cassie. There was no other explanation. Mabel said a prayer in her heart of thanksgiving, smiled and looked up at George as he smiled back at her. The unspoken bond they had; George knew his wife was rejoicing as he was for this blessing. Cassie's happiness was all they wanted.

George was getting choked up and cleared his throat and pulled himself together. "Cassie, we should get going. Let's tie Midnight to the back of the rig to lead him home."

Cassie released her horse and patted his neck as she led him over to the back of the rig and tied him to it. Midnight would follow her anywhere. He wasn't about to let her out of his sight. Cassie shouldn't have been surprised that he'd escaped. As a colt he'd bonded with her and trusted her completely. As he grew, he was very aware of how small she was and was careful not to step on her. Even as a yearling, he would patiently let her use his mane to climb up, he hardly felt her there. Midnight had instinctively known how to get back to the farm, and nothing would keep him from her. So, when she tied him to the surrey, he went willingly. Together with their newest family member, Midnight, they headed home.

Chapter 5
Edward Havoc

Ed helped clean up the church picnic and headed home in a daze. His thoughts kept coming back to Cassie. He was feeling something he hadn't in over two years. In all that time, he'd shielded his heart, not wanting to ever feel anything for another woman again. But Cassie swept in and penetrated his armor. There had been other women who'd tried, and Ed had been polite and side-stepped the advances. But Cassie wasn't even trying to get his attention when she gained access to his heart. Every time Ed thought about Cassie it felt like his heart skipped a beat.

"This is foolishness!" Ed thought as he rode home from the picnic. "What could she ever see in me? I'm a broken man." He couldn't reconcile that he already felt something for Cassie, something that he hadn't thought possible.

Ed's thoughts drifted back to Mary Elizabeth Sanders, his childhood sweetheart. He had met Mary at grammar school in Kansas. Mary had always been a blonde beauty, who was spontaneous and playful and stood out in a crowd. When the boys teased her, she easily turned it around by teasing them back and pulled some wonderfully good-natured pranks on them. What attracted Ed the most was her bubbly energy. Mary was the type of person that always seemed to be the center of attention, and Ed was the shy reserved tall thin boy in the back of the crowd. As they got older, Mary had searched him out and was somehow able to draw him out of his shell. When alone, Ed was comfortable joking around with Mary, telling her funny stories and witty phrases, wanting to hear her contagious laugh. They could banter back and forth, laughing for hours. Ed and Mary began courting the last years of school and made plans to marry and start a family as soon as they graduated. Then in April of 1861, the Civil War broke out.

Ed with his pa and brothers signed up to go to war for the Union. Ed had always been a good shot and years of hard farm work had toughened him up. These were the things that would keep him alive on the battlefield. That, and the sure will to live. The thought of coming home to Mary was what kept him going in the darkest, coldest and loneliest nights of war. Mary's letters were his lifeline. During their time apart, Ed read them over and over until they were almost worn out. Ed returned home after four years in the war without his brothers and his pa, and often questioned why he had survived and not them. He felt guilty about that, he was no better than they were. But home he came, feeling broken. Over the next year, Mary was the one who pulled him back together and made him feel like living again.

Ed and Mary were married on June 16th of 1866. "Exactly three years ago this Wednesday," he thought.

The wedding was held on a beautiful Friday morning. The grass and flowers were in full bloom and Ed could almost forget the war he had left a year earlier. Mary was beautiful, with her long blonde hair in ringlets pulled up and adorned with flowers. Ed's ma was so happy that day. She had been so heartbroken to lose her husband and two sons, but that day she gained a daughter, and soon she hoped a grandchild.

Ed and Mary had settled a few miles out of town on a farm growing corn, as most families did in Kansas. Soon Mary learned that they were expecting, and when she told him, Ed was ecstatic. His first child would be born mid-summer the next year. Ed worked harder than ever building Mary a good home, he wanted to give her everything possible. The winter came and went, and both of them worked hard to keep the farm running well. In order to afford the seed, they needed that spring, Ed took a job as deputy in town. His military leadership experience served him well as a lawman. Word spread that Ed had been a major in the war at only twenty-three years old, which was quite an accomplishment. Being the town deputy meant he was away from the farm for long spells during the day and sometimes at night. In March, a band of Indians in the area were harassing the newer settlers, especially the ones farther out of town, and trying to force them off the land. Often, Ed would be out at night scouting for the band of Indians and worrying about his wife at home. Mary wouldn't listen to him when he begged her to come stay closer in town with his ma until the unrest settled down.

One night he was hunting down a man who'd broken into a livery stable and stolen a horse. They had found the man hiding in a cave about ten miles away from town. As Ed was coming home that next morning, he became concerned as he noticed fresh horse tracks around his place and didn't see any smoke coming out of the chimney like usual. Approaching the homestead, he saw the front door was wide open. In a panic, Ed jumped off his horse and ran into the house. Mary was laying limp on the floor, pale as a ghost. Ed ran to her, lifted her, and carried her to the bed. She was barely breathing. He didn't want to leave her, but she needed a doctor. There was blood coming from under her skirt, and he worried that the baby was coming too early. Ed covered Mary with blankets and quickly built a fire, then jumped on his horse and rode into town to get the doctor. Together they raced back to the house. She was no better when they arrived. The doctor gave her some smelling salts that aroused her slightly. In her fragile state she told of the Indians that broke through the front door in the night and dragged her out of bed and threatened to kill her if she didn't give them what they wanted. The Indians took the rifles and the knives and warned her to leave and never come back before they hit her on the head. That was all she was able to remember. Mary began to cry as she placed her hand across the motionless baby inside her. Without warning her body began to cramp and contract. The doctor told Mary she had to push and that there was nothing that could be done for the pain until after the baby was delivered. Exhausted from the night of terror and the hours of pushing, the baby was finally born and Mary sank into unconsciousness. On the bed lay a lifeless, tiny baby girl. Within minutes, Mary's spirit withdrew from her body, leaving this world and Ed behind, joining her baby girl.

Sitting at the bedside, watching the love of his life leave him sent Ed into shock. His grief turned to rage that he blamed himself for not being there, and God for not saving his Mary.

Everything was gone now. There was nothing left for Ed; he didn't care if he lived. His only motive to live was revenge. Ed became a machine, not eating or sleeping, only searching day and night for the Indians that took his wife and child from him. Months of searching led him nowhere. His mother and friends pitied him. Everywhere he went people would politely ask how he was doing out of respect. Everything reminded him of Mary and that she was gone and never would be with him again.

His chance to escape the memory of what happened to him came when he was asked by a friend to come out west to Cheyenne, Wyoming Territory, and help regain order in town. Ed's mother, being concerned about his state of mind, begged him to stay with her in Kansas. Ed had become bitter and angry and wasn't thinking clearly in his grief. But he knew one thing, he was ready to escape the constant reminder of his loss and get on the stagecoach for Cheyenne, Wyoming Territory.

Cheyenne was being overrun with railroad workers and the tent city that followed. The city had grown from 150 residents to over 4,000 overnight. The saloons and dance halls brought in all sorts of ruffians and scoundrels. Thieving and murdering were common occurrences. It wasn't a safe place to live, and the way Ed was feeling, this was perfect for him. It took him and a group of townsmen to band together and round up the worst of the troublemakers. He wasn't proud of the fact that some of the worst had been hung as a warning to the others, but as a show of strength, they had gotten the job done and the town became a more civilized place.

Ed's anger and rage were worn out after all the fighting with the worst scum imaginable. Softening some, he chose to associate with the church going folk of the community and met some very respectable men, one of which was George Hartford.

George and Mabel were some of the first people who'd invited Ed to their home for dinner and the best news was, they weren't trying to set him up with a young woman. The women of the community were frequently trying to match Ed up with their daughters or granddaughters and he wasn't interested. He never planned to marry again. His heart was broken. In time, Ed found his purpose by serving his community and the good people of Cheyenne. He was determined that the innocent wouldn't suffer at the hands of anyone. He eventually stopped blaming God for the loss of his wife and daughter and reconciled that the Indians would be punished in God's timing. The one person he couldn't forgive was himself. In Mary's honor he would keep her memory alive and his loyalty to her and never remarry. Ed had never told anyone in Cheyenne about his wife and daughter. He preferred to keep that private. Eventually the town folk learned to respect his wishes to remain a bachelor, imagining he had his own reasons. But it did pain so many of the women to see such a good man go to waste. The less honorable women in town still tried to get his attention, but Ed was always polite and very clear that he was not interested.

And then there was Cassie. Ed felt drawn to her. He had overheard the people at church talking about how she had lost her family. It was clear by the way she walked and her pale complexion that she was carrying the weight of the world on her shoulders. Cassie was frail and needed his protection and it was in his nature to want to protect her. Or was that all he wanted? Well, he wasn't going to figure it out today. When he arrived home, he decided he would simply put her out of his mind. Besides, he would see her again on Thursday and try and figure it out then.

That night Ed awoke in a cold sweat brought on by a far too familiar dream. In this dream, Mary was being held by Indians, screaming for help as he raced his horse as fast as he could to save her, but never got there in time. The nightmare ended the same way, with Mary on the floor, pale and bleeding followed by the screams as she gave birth to the lifeless infant. "Oh Mary, if only I'd gotten there in time," he cried out.

The next few days passed slowly and Ed longed for Thursday to come so he could see Cassie again.

Wednesday, on his way out of town he thought of an excuse to stop by the Hartford's place, hoping to see Cassie. His mind began rehearsing what he would say as he turned down their lane to their home. Feeling nervous, anticipation rose in him at the thought of seeing her. Oh, how he hoped he would see her.

Ed wasn't disappointed, as he rode into the yard and spotted Cassie from a distance, watching her move as her slender figure bent forward, her ebony hair shining in the sunlight as she worked in the garden. Seeing her sent a thrill through him. Ed smiled to himself and tried to calm his shaking hands.

Cassie stood in the garden and quickly dusted off her apron and hands as something up the road caught her eye. She recognized the man on horseback coming towards her was Ed. Cassie pushed her stray hair back with her hand, trying not to put dirt on her face. "Oh my! I must look a sight!" She smiled nervously as she walked out of the garden to meet their guest.

Ed noticed the way her face was glowing from the heat of the morning as she walked towards him.

"Howdy, Cass!"

Cassie blushed deeply. "Good morning!"

Ed spotted Mabel coming out of the house and George emerging from the barn. He swung down easily and led his horse into the yard to meet them. He kept his eyes on Cassie for as long as he dared before turning to greet George.

"Good morning! How are you all doing this fine day?" Ed asked, as he shook George's hand, then Mabel's. As he took Cassie's hand he was struck by her beauty. "You're looking well this morning," he thought. Her face was colored not only with a little dirt but crimson cheeks and rosy-pink lips. And there was a sparkle in her emerald eyes the moment she smiled.

"Yes, I'm doing well, thank you," Cassie replied as she felt moisture at her temples and brushed it away with her shirt sleeve as Ed looked away.

George already had a pretty good idea but asked all the same. "Sheriff, what brings you out today?"

"I was on my way past your place on town business and thought I should ask when you'd like me to come for supper Thursday." Ed adjusted his hat, trying to appear relaxed. He could face the most dangerous men with nerves of steel but was rattled with the thought of how obvious his intentions must seem to George and Mabel.

"We eat about six o'clock if that works for you, Sheriff." Mabel looked at George and smiled knowingly. "We understand how busy you are, but you're welcome to come earlier and visit for a while if you like."

"I may just do that." This was going better than he'd imagined. "If you don't mind, may I water my horse before I go?" Ed asked. "It's going to be a hot day and I still have a ways to travel."

"We'll do you one better; take your horse to the trough by the corral while Cassie and I get some cold drinks," offered Mabel.

"Sounds mighty nice, thank you, ma'am," Ed said tipping his hat and turned, walking with George leading his horse to the trough.

Cassie followed Aunt Mabel into the house while the men watered Ed's horse. Aunt Mabel and Cassie soon emerged with glasses of cold buttermilk to find Uncle George and Ed talking as they sat in the shade on the porch.

"He's some beauty, Cass!" praised Ed. "What do you call him?"

Cassie smiled as she handed Ed a glass. "His name's

Midnight. I got him for my twelfth birthday. My pa knew how much I loved to ride and made a deal with a neighbor. I started working with Midnight as soon as we got him. He took to the saddle very easily." Cassie fell silent as she realized she was the only one doing all the talking. Stepping back shyly, she went and sat next to Aunt Mabel to drink her buttermilk, occasionally glancing up from under her hooded lashes to watch Ed.

Ed was content to listen to Cassie talk about anything as he tipped his glass up and emptied it.

George chimed in, "Cassie's done quite a good job training him. He's getting along with my other horses very well. As a matter of fact, Midnight's taken a shining to Ginger. It's like love at first sight. The two of them are constantly together." George chuckled as he pointed towards the corral where the black stallion stood next to Ginger.

Everyone laughed and Cassie blushed. Ed could see Cassie was uncomfortable and changed the subject. "George, I must get going. Thank you for the cold drink, ma'am. But I really should be on my way. I need to get to Horse Creek and check on some suspicious activity." Ed stood and put his hat on.

"Oh, what's going on up there?" George stood, looking at Sheriff Havoc with concern. Horse Creek was only eight miles away.

"Someone's been 'squatting' up that way. I want to find out what their intentions are. If they plan to settle here, they need to get the proper paperwork. Otherwise, they need to get moving." It wasn't uncommon for people traveling west to "squat" on someone's land unknowingly. Or worse, "squatting" on public grazing lands, diverting water and trying to take over grazing lands without going through the proper legal process of paying a small fee. The Homesteading Act of 1862 stated that if a man worked hard, broke the land, planted crops and established a dwelling for five years, the 160 acres of land was his free and clear. It was a great opportunity for settlers, but it was a real problem for the local cattle ranchers. Mainly because it took away the free grazing land for their herds. Ed knew he needed to check it out before disputes arose. Although he could've sent one of his deputies to investigate, the road to Horse Creek passed the Hartford homestead. So, Ed decided he'd go instead, allowing him a good excuse to stop and see Cassie.

"I would go with you if I wasn't already behind in my chores, but maybe Cassie could go with you? She hasn't had a chance to ride Midnight since he got here. The ride would do them both some good," George suggested, smiling at Cassie. "Unless you feel like it would be unsafe, Sheriff."

"Oh, she's welcome to come. I don't expect to find any trouble." Ed rested his hand on the belt of his holstered pistol. "I'm certain it's just weary travelers. But if they're still there I'll be giving them a warning to either make a claim or move on." Ed tried to keep his voice even as he spoke, although he was elated about the prospect of spending more time with Cassie. "She'll be safe, I'll take good care of her," Ed reassured George and Mabel.

"I'd like to go, but I'm not sure Aunt Mabel can spare me today." Cassie looked to Aunt Mabel for her answer.

"Yes Cassie, you can go. I can finish the gardening. You'll be back in a few hours. Go ahead and change while Uncle George gets your horse saddled."

"I'll be out shortly. I won't keep you waiting." Cassie rushed inside to change. "What a day this has turned out to be!" she thought. Cassie was finally able to go riding, and with Ed. Cassie put on her riding skirt and buttoned her new vest over her white blouse and pulled on her boots.

She sat in front of the mirror and adjusted her cowboy hat over her French braided hair. There wasn't time to fuss, she looked closely and saw a smudge of dirt on her cheek; embarrassed, she wiped it off, realizing it had been there since she'd left the garden. Cassie blushed in humiliation. "Oh!" She rubbed both sides to make sure her face was clean. "It will have to do."

Cassie emerged from the house and was greeted at the steps by Ed and Uncle George with Midnight saddled and watered. Ed's broad smile said it all as Cassie wondered what Ed would think of her new riding clothes.

Ed cleared his throat. "Looks like we're ready to go!"

Uncle George assisted Cassie onto Midnight and handed her the reins as Ed mounted his horse and turned toward the road. Cassie patted Midnight's neck as her spirits lifted. "Let's go, Midnight." Midnight followed the gentle pressure on his withers and Cassie caught up with Ed as he slowed to ride side by side.

"You look like you know what you're doing," he mentioned casually. "And you make it look good too," he thought as he grinned.

Cassie felt like he was teasing her. She would show him what a good rider she was before the day was through. But right now, in front of her Aunt Mabel, she would ride like a lady.

They rode along quietly, enjoying each other's company when Ed suddenly remembered something Cassie had mentioned. "You said you got Midnight on your birthday. When's your birthday?" He'd already done the math and knew she would be turning nineteen.

"June sixteenth," she said, glancing over at him.

"You mean today?" he asked, looking at her for confirmation.

"Oh!" she exclaimed and blushed. "So much has happened this past week I forgot what the date was. I guess to-day!" Cassie chuckled lightly. "How embarrassing to have forgotten my own birthday. What must he think of me?"

"Well, happy birthday, Cass!" Ed was surprised by the date, and thought, "Three years ago, today was my wedding." He gave her a sincere smile.

"Thank you, Ed! Just don't mention it to my aunt and uncle, all right? I don't want them to feel bad. I'm sure they don't even know today is my birthday. Besides, they've already given me so much. This is the best present I could have asked for. I get to ride Midnight and I thought that would never happen again!" Her heart rejoiced over her miracle as she stroked Midnight's mane.

"Well, I guess it worked out pretty well. My present to you, I mean. And I didn't even know it was your birthday." Ed laughed.

Cassie laughed with him, loving the sound of his deep bass laugh. She wanted to make him laugh all the more, just to hear it. Suddenly she kicked her horse and bolted forward, shouting, "Race you!" as she took off sprinting into a full gallop.

Ed was surprised, but quick to follow. "Come on, Major!" he shouted as he kicked his horse into action. "Don't let her get away from us!"

Cassie glanced over as Ed closed in on them. "Go Midnight!" She kicked harder and leaned forward. This time she would show Ed how she could really fly! Cassie loosened the reins and let Midnight stretch out his neck as she pumped her legs with each stride. Cassie rode with only her weight in the stirrups, her body suspended above the saddle and laughed as she flew down the road! She hadn't had this much fun in forever. Midnight gave her all his pent-up energy. Midnight and Cassie's hearts soared as they raced free.

Ed did his best to catch her and marveled at Cassie's grace and speed. She was an experienced rider, and what a beautiful sight it was to watch Cassie and Midnight move as one. He let her stay in the lead, wanting to watch her, and stay close.

After a mile or so, Cassie slowed and looked back to see if Ed was still there. Sure enough, he was about fifty yards behind her.

Ed rode up beside her, as she laughed. Was she laughing at him, or because she was happy to be riding? He couldn't tell, but either way he liked it. Cassie's laugh sounded like music to him, bubbly and playful.

"Wow, you gave me a run for my money!" he exclaimed, a little breathless. They slowed to a trot, cooling the horses as they went.

Cassie smiled at him. "That felt wonderful!" She patted Midnight on the neck. "Good job, Midnight! You hear that? We gave him a run for his money!" She laughed again.

"Well, you came to the right place, woman! An experienced horsewoman like you fits perfectly in this Wild West cowboy town of Cheyenne. I think you'd give anyone here a run for their money!" Ed hadn't seen this kind of riding from a woman in his whole life. Cassie had talent and could easily learn how to herd cattle and possibly rope, if she had a mind to. He wouldn't suggest it. Cutting and herding cattle is dangerous work, especially if a bull decided to charge. No, he didn't want her to be in danger. But she could do it, if needed. "I'm honestly impressed. I've never seen anyone ride as well as you, and most certainly never seen a woman ride that well."

Cassie was flattered to have impressed him but was sure Aunt Mabel and Uncle George wouldn't like her riding like that. She'd shown Uncle George she was a safe rider but hadn't let on that she could actually race. Cassie feared they would be worried that she would get hurt and not let her ride. But she felt she could be herself in front of Ed.

"Thank you, Ed! It's a great compliment coming from you." Cassie gave him a pleasing smile.

"You're welcome, and I mean it."

"Would you do me a favor and not tell Aunt and Uncle that I raced Midnight? I'm afraid they will worry needlessly about me. They think I'm fragile and will break. But I've grown up riding. In time they will see I'm a capable rider. But for now, could we just keep it between us?" she asked.

"Cass, I'll not say a word as long as you promise to be careful," he added.

"I knew I could trust you," she smiled. "Thank you."

Cassie wondered how much longer before they reached Horse Creek. She rode along content to go as far as they needed, not wanting the time to end. They traveled on the dusty road heading more northward for almost an hour as they talked, enjoying the time getting to know one another.

Ed told her about being the oldest of two brothers and two sisters, and he told her about living in Kansas and what a shock it was when he first saw Cheyenne.

Cassie agreed that Wyoming was different than her life back in Missouri. In Missouri the heavily forested hills made it difficult to travel except what had been cleared away. The flatter farmlands flourished there due to the muggy climate and was so vibrantly green it almost hurt your eyes. Cassie admitted she could appreciate the beauty here in Cheyenne as well. The rolling plains were dry and breezy, covered with hearty prairie grasses as far as her eyes could see. Wyoming made her feel free and she imagined riding for miles across the open expanse with nothing to stop her.

Ed led them off the road to the west. Cassie could see a line of trees, breaking the expanse of wind-blown prairie grass. "That must be Horse Creek," she thought with anticipation.

Together they galloped across the stretch of open space until they reached the poplar trees. Riding along the banks of the stream shaded by quaking aspen and choke-cherry bushes, the lush knee-high grass brushed the dust from their boots. They stopped their horses at the stream to drink. Ed swung down and helped Cassie from her horse, which she was thankful for, as it'd been a long time since she'd ridden that hard and her legs were feeling shaky. Ed offered his canteen to her after filling it in the crystal-clear water and she took a long refreshing drink of the cold water then handed it back, thanking him.

"This stream must be from a mountain runoff, it's so cold," she guessed. "The water in Missouri was never this cold in the summer," she thought.

"It is. All the streams here come from the mountain snowpack," Ed explained. "I don't see any sign of squatters here, maybe a little further down the stream," he said and took a long drink from the canteen, wiping the moisture from his lips with the back of his hand. "Would you like to rest for a minute before we head back? I doubt a wagon could get much further than this, since the bank gets much steeper downstream."

Cassie sat down on a fallen log while they let the horses drink water and graze along the bank. Taking off her hat, she tipped her head back letting the wind blow through her hair and across her face, cooling it some. The shade was greatly appreciated.

Ed placed his hat on the log and went to the stream to wet the bandana he had around his neck. He wrung it out and came back, handing it to Cassie to wipe the dust off her face. She thanked him and took the bandana, performing a sweep of her face, imagining how she must look from all the dust.

Trying not to stare, Ed watched as she tipped her head back and wiped down her slender neck. Feeling cleaner, Cassie handed the bandana back to Ed and thanked him as she pulled her hair back and replaced her hat. Ed took the bandana and walked down to the stream and washed his face and neck in the creek, then tied it back around his neck.

Cassie envied how easily it had been for Ed to clean his face and wet his hair in the stream, thinking how good it would feel to get more of herself in the cool water.

Ed refilled the canteen and offered it to Cassie again as she noted what a gentleman he was, thinking of her needs before his own. She drank until her thirst was thoroughly quenched, then handed it back and thanked him with a smile.

It was time to move on. Ed and Cassie led the horses up the riverbank. As Ed helped Cassie back on her horse, he was surprised at how petite she was. She could fit right under his chin. Ed mounted his horse and led the way down the stream a little further. The only sign of the "squatters" being there was an old campfire and trampled down brush. It must have been where they'd camped, and their animals had bedded. Ed figured the "squatters" had moved on and was not concerned.

"Well, we can head back now. The problem solved itself," Ed assured her.

"That's good. It seems we've been gone a while. I don't want Aunt Mabel and Uncle George to worry." Cassie was also becoming hungry and feeling exhausted. This had been the most activity she'd had in months. She knew she would be sore the next few days but didn't care.

Ed could see she was weary when she fell silent and appeared thoughtful. He was glad they had an easy ride to the ranch. Maybe he'd been wrong in allowing her to come along. Ed worried about her.

The ride back was relaxing, and Cassie felt at peace. Her mind was replaying memories of home and her family. This time thinking about her family didn't cause her as much pain as usual. It had been good to get away and have time to talk to someone whom she felt comfortable enough to say anything They took their time enjoying the view and letting the horses set the pace. As they neared the ranch the horses picked up speed, anxious to get another drink of water and some hay. Cassie offered to let Ed go on his way as they came to her lane, but he felt it wouldn't be proper. As they entered the yard, George and Mabel came out to greet them.

"Did you have fun?" Uncle George asked Cassie as he helped her down.

"I had a wonderful time! Thank you for letting me go with Ed, I mean Sheriff Havoc," she said, quickly correcting herself. "I think Midnight enjoyed it as much as I did." Cassie patted his neck as he nuzzled her.

"Cassie is quite the horsewoman, George! She did very well for herself today," Ed said, complimenting her without giving too much away about her expert riding skills.

"That she is, Ed!" George agreed as he winked at Cassie, keeping her secret too.

"Well, I best be getting on. Thanks for accompanying me, Cass! It was quite enjoyable." Ed turned his horse and looked back. "Until tomorrow…and happy birthday, Cass!" he shouted as he rode off smiling.

"Oh, that tease! He wasn't supposed to say anything," she thought with a smile as she watched him ride away.

Slowly she turned to face Aunt Mabel and Uncle George and smiled sheepishly as they looked at her in astonishment.

"Well, Cassie dear, happy birthday!" Aunt Mabel gave her a quick hug and kiss on the cheek. "I guess we should go in and eat your birthday supper and cake now. So much for the surprise! You go change and wash up while Uncle George takes care of Midnight and I set the food on," Aunt Mabel said, smiling broadly.

"So, they hadn't forgotten." Cassie hugged Aunt Mabel back. "You didn't forget, but I did! I only remembered when Sheriff Havoc asked me when my birthday was," Cassie said as she followed Aunt Mabel into the house. She noticed the table was set, and the house smelled of mouth-watering food. Cassie's stomach growled. "I'll wash up, it'll only take a minute." Cassie hastened to the washroom behind the kitchen to give her face and hands a good scrubbing.

The birthday celebration was just right. Aunt Mabel's delicious meal of chicken and dumplings completely satisfied Cassie, as did the chocolate cake. Uncle George and Aunt Mabel sang "Happy Birthday" to her as she blew out the candles, making a wish for continued happiness.

While Cassie lay in bed, it was hard not to reminisce about her past birthdays. Cassie felt sad as she missed her family, but she was very grateful for what she had.

Chapter 6
Supper

Thursday evening, Ed showed up right on time as the sun was lowering in the sky, making long shadows in the yard. The house's windows were open, letting the cool breeze blow through the kitchen, sending delicious smells out to greet Ed as he tied his horse to the railing.

Cassie had changed into one of her nicer everyday dresses and brushed her hair until it shined. Her heart pounded as she opened the door and invited Ed in with a timid smile. She had to hide her hands behind her back because they were shaking with excitement as Ed stepped through the entry.

"How are you this evening, Cassie?" Ed asked as he removed his hat and hung it on a peg by the door.

"I'm very well, thank you, Sheriff Havoc. And what's that you have there?" Cassie asked, smiling with a twinkle in her eye, teasing him as she observed the guitar he was carrying.

Ed grinned at her. "Well, I thought I would play some music and see if I could get the cats to howl tonight," he teased.

Cassie laughed in her bubbly voice, "Set your guitar here while we eat. Then, after supper you can play to your heart's content." She hoped he would play for a long time; she loved music, especially from a guitar. "Hmm, Ed's a man of many talents," she mused.

Aunt Mabel turned from the stove. "Welcome, Sheriff

Havoc, right on time. Won't you come and sit down?" Mabel pulled out a chair next to Cassie's.

George came inside from his chores. "Sheriff, good to see you. How are things?" George hung up his hat and walked over to shake his hand.

"I can't complain. It's been a good week so far," Ed said with a smile. "Is there anything I can do to help?" he asked as Mabel and Cassie set the dishes of food on the table.

"This is the last of it, we're ready. Go ahead and have a seat," Mabel encouraged. Ed and George took their seats, followed by Mabel and Cassie sitting beside them.

Cassie took Uncle George's hand for the blessing and blushed as she took Ed's to close the circle. The warmth of his hand made her whole body feel flushed. She quickly released his hand once the blessing was over. Cassie tried to keep her eyes on everything but Ed, afraid she would blush again.

"So, George, how are the cattle doing?" Ed asked as he handed Cassie the bowl of vegetables. They glanced at each other as their hands touched.

"They seem to be doing well this year," George said, watching from the corner of his eye as the two of them exchanged looks.

Ed was distracted and wasn't listening to what George had said and took a second to respond. "Oh, that's nice," he said as he slowly registered what George had said.

Mabel stood and went to the stove, removing the second batch of freshly baked biscuits, and brought the pan over, offering everyone another helping.

"This all sure is delicious, ma'am. I especially love these biscuits. You're a wonderful cook," Ed said as he took a bite.

"Actually, Sheriff, I didn't make the biscuits…Cassie

did," Mabel said smiling at Cassie. "She's a very good cook and a great help in the kitchen."

"Oh! Is that so? Then compliments to you, Cass!" Ed smiled at her and took another biscuit from the plate.

"Thank you," Cassie said softly and smiled as the heat in her cheeks returned.

"It's the same recipe my ma used to use, and Aunt Mabel uses too. So, they would've tasted just the same, if she had made them," Cassie explained humbly.

"Well, if I'm not mistaken, it takes some skill even if the recipe is the same. I know mine never turn out this well, and I use the same recipe my ma uses, and hers are wonderful," said Ed as he chuckled.

"I guess so," said Cassie, accepting the compliment. "How does he do that? Making me feel like I'm better than I am."

Cassie searched for something say to turn the attention away from herself. "Oh, I was going to ask you about your guitar. How long have you been playing?" Cassie took a small bite of biscuit and chewed carefully, trying to be ladylike as he gave her his full attention.

"My ma started teaching when I was about five years old. I was very guarded and withdrawn as a child and my ma could tell I loved music. My ma's the best thing that's ever happened to me," said Ed thoughtfully.

Cassie cleared her throat. "Oh, so playing most of your life then. You must be very good," she surmised with delight.

"I'm fair enough. The guitar is my ma's. She gave it to me when I left for Cheyenne, hoping I would play often, to remind me of home. Truthfully, it's been quite a while since I've played. I'm pretty rusty right now." It was Ed's turn to be humble. It was true that he hadn't played in a long time, but recently Ed had felt like playing music again.

He figured he would try it out on Cassie. Ed really wanted to see her smile and hoped his music would do the trick.

"Come on, I'm sure you're just being modest, I'll bet you're really good," encouraged Cassie, teasing him a little.

"I hope I don't disappoint you," Ed chuckled. "I may never live it down."

They all laughed with him, assuming he was joking.

They finished supper, cleared the table and washed the dishes together, handing dishes back and forth as they talked.

"We can have pie after we've heard Ed play his guitar," said Mabel,

"Maybe we should go out on the porch where it's cooler," suggested George, leading the way. No one argued as he opened the front door.

They all settled on the porch where a gentle breeze blew. George and Mabel took the chairs near the railing, leaving the bench against the house for Ed and Cassie to share. Ed sat down and began tuning his guitar. Cassie focused on his nimble fingers moving smoothly over the strings. Cassie had always wanted to learn how to play the guitar but never had the opportunity.

Ed cleared his throat. "Hmmm, let's see." He pondered for a moment until a song came to him. "Oh, I have one I think you might like!" He began the folk song, *Buffalo Gal,* tapping the toe of his boot to keep time. Ed's deep bass voice ticked off the words just as quickly as his fingers picked over the strings.

"As I was walking down the street,
Down the street, down the street,
A pretty little gal I chanced to meet,
Oh, she was sweet to me!

Buffalo Gal, won't you come out tonight?
Come out tonight, come out tonight?
And dance by the light of the moon?

I'd like to make this gal my wife
Gal my wife, gal my wife
I'd make her happy all her life
If she would marry me!

Buffalo Gal won't you come out tonight,
Come out tonight, come out tonight.
Buffalo Gal won't you come out tonight,
And dance by the light of the moon?"

Everyone's toes tapped, and hands clapped to the beat. The jolly tune brought smiles to their faces as they reveled in Ed's musical talent. Ed fumbled only a few times, smiled and laughed as he played the last chord. George, Mabel and Cassie cheered and clapped heartily.

"My goodness, your ma must be proud!" Mabel put her hand to her heart as it pounded in excitement.

"Bravo maestro!" George praised as he clapped again.

Cassie was overcome with approval. "You were being modest. You play extremely well, Ed, and have an exceptional singing voice."

"Thank you. I'm a little rusty though," Ed said self-consciously. "But yes, Ma would be proud." Ed appreciated their compliments, especially Cassie's. He relaxed his broad shoulders and flexed his fingers, loosening them up a bit.

"Please play us another song!" begged Cassie abandoning all restraint. "I love music!"

Cassie's bright smile and twinkling eyes reflected adoration back to Ed. In the moment Ed would have done anything Cassie asked just to keep that smile on her face.

125

Ed winked at her, causing Cassie to blush and look away demurely. "OK, here's one you may like." Ed began singing, "*Yellow Rose of Texas*".

George, Mabel and Cassie joined in by clapping as they felt the tempo course through their bodies.

Ed looked at Cassie as he sang in his low voice, "No other fellow loves her as half as much as me!"

Cassie felt her face flush and fanned herself as if the heat outside was getting to her.

Ed continued playing and smiled as he finished. They clapped energetically as another song came to mind and he began again. This time Ed encouraged them to sing with him, "'*I'll Fly Away*.' You know the words."

Cassie had sung this song many times in church; it was one of her favorites. Mabel sang alto and Cassie soprano with Ed singing bass and George tenor. They harmonized beautifully as they sang with conviction and clapped for each other when they finished. Ed adored the sound of Cassie's singing. Her voice was sweet like honey, and he wanted to hear it again. Ed took up the tune, "*Dixie*", as he swept his thumb and fingers smoothly over the tense guitar strings. The ballad's tune floated softly under his deep soothing voice.

> *"Oh, I wish I was in the land of cotton,*
> *Old times there are not forgotten,*
> *Look away, Look away,*
> *Look away Dixie Land."*

Ed's singing was deeply moving. He nodded to Cassie and whispered, "Sing with me."

Quietly at first, Cassie joined in on the next line. Encouraged by his smile, her voice grew in volume.

> *"In Dixie Land, where I was born in,*

Early one frosty mornin',
Look away, look away,
Look away Dixie Land."

Harmonizing, Ed and Cassie watched each other to stay on tempo.

"Oh, I wish I was in Dixie,
Hooray! Hooray!
In Dixie Land I'll take my stand,
To live and die in Dixie.
Away, away, away down south in Dixie.

With one kiss she'd marry 'Will the Weaver'.
But Willum was a slight deceiver.
Look away! Look away!
Look away! Dixie Land!"

Ed and Cassie continued singing the heartfelt words as George and Mabel enjoyed the harmony floating through the evening air.

"But when he put his arm around 'er,
He smiled as fierce as a forty pounder.
Look away! Look away! Look away Dixie Land!

Oh, I wish I was in Dixie,
Hooray! Hooray!
In Dixie Land I'll take my stand,
To live and die in Dixie.
Away, away, away down south in Dixie."

Ed and Cassie drew out the last note, earning themselves a hearty applause from George and Mabel. Ed stood and took Cassie's hand to stand with him and take a bow to their audience. They laughed as George and Mabel clapped and Cassie blushed at the attention. Cassie reached out and put her hand lightly on Ed's arm as she continued to laugh with him. Her touch melted his heart like snow on a spring day. Ed didn't want her touch to end. He wanted his heart to be filled with her warmth forever. Ed glanced down momentarily at her delicate hand before Cassie realized what she'd done and slowly pulled it away, then sat back down.

Ed had a grand idea. "I'll sing you one last song…for your birthday, Cass. I think you'll like it; it reminds me of you." He smiled sweetly.

Ed began the romantic ballad, "*Beautiful Dreamer*".

Recognizing the song immediately, Cassie sighed and smiled dreamily as he began serenading her, completely forgetting her aunt and uncle were there.

"Beautiful Dreamer, Wake unto me,
Starlight and dewdrops are waiting for thee;
Sounds of the rude world, heard in the day,
Lull'd by the moonlight have all pass'd away!

Beautiful dreamer, queen of my song,
List while I woo thee with soft melody;
Gone are the cares of life's busy throng,
Beautiful dreamer awake unto me!
Beautiful dreamer, awake unto me!

Beautiful dreamer, beam on my heart,
E'en as the morn on the streamlet and sea;
Then will all the clouds of sorrow depart,
Beautiful dreamer, awake unto me!
Beautiful dreamer, awake unto me!"

Cassie's eyes were sparkling, and a tear streamed down her cheek. She swept it away as she sighed. "Oh Ed, that's my favorite song. How did you know?" She tilted her head, puzzling. "How could he know my heart?"

"A lucky guess. I'm glad you liked it." He was moved by her tenderness. He'd seen the tear that had fallen down her smooth cheek and hoped it was a tear of joy. Ed knew music could elicit deep emotions, triggering memories, sometimes even painful ones. It'd been difficult for him to play that song, being one of his wife's favorites too, but was delighted it had pleased Cassie.

"I haven't heard it in forever." Cassie's voice caught. "I forgot how much I loved it. That was the best birthday present I've ever gotten. Thank you so much!" Impulsively she kissed him on the cheek. Cassie realized the instant she'd done it, that her enthusiasm had gotten away from her. She sat back and looked down at her hands. "Sorry, I don't know what came over me." Cassie chuckled nervously.

"Wow, if I'd known that was all I needed to do to get a kiss from a pretty woman, I would've done it long ago! Just think of all the kisses I could've had, George!" Ed said, trying to ease her embarrassment.

Uncle George chuckled and then Aunt Mabel and Ed and eventually Cassie joined in the laughter, blushing from his compliment about her looks.

Aunt Mabel spoke up, saving Cassie from the awkward silence that followed their laughter. "Cassie, would you be a dear and help me dish up the pie. We'll be right back," she said as they excused themselves.

Inside they dished up slices of apple pie and poured milk into glasses to bring out to the men. Mabel and Cassie joined them on the porch, lit by a lamp in the house, casting a warm glow through the window. Crickets started chirping and the moon began rising in the eastern sky.

It would be night soon, but Ed didn't mind. As he finished his pie and milk, he thanked his host and hostesses. "I can't tell you how much I've enjoyed tonight! The food was perfect and the company even better. Thanks again for inviting me," Ed said cheerfully.

"We can't thank you enough for the music you shared with us, Sheriff Havoc. You're welcome to come back any time," encouraged Mabel. "George, would you help me into the house with these dishes." Mabel winked at George and slightly motioned with her head toward the door.

George caught the hint. "Oh, yes, yes of course. I would love to help you, dear!" George took some of the dishes from her and said goodnight to Sheriff Havoc.

Cassie tried to help, but Uncle George resisted, "No no. We've got them. You take your time and say goodnight. We'll have them washed and put up before you get inside." The two partners in crime left the young couple alone.

Ed stood and took his guitar in one hand and helped Cassie stand with his other hand. Once she was standing, he didn't let go.

Cassie felt butterflies fluttering in her stomach. She could hardly breathe. It wasn't the first time a man had held her hand, but Ed's felt so different, as his strong man-sized hand gently cradled hers. Ed turned and walked into the yard, bringing her with him.

"I'm so happy, Cass," Ed started slowly. "I really enjoy spending time with you. I hope you feel the same way."

"I've enjoyed our time together too. I've never met anyone like you," Cassie said, feeling breathless. She took a deep breath and went on. "I've never wanted to know someone as much as I want to get to know you. I feel like I could talk to you forever and never tire." Cassie looked up at him. It was hard to see his face in the faint light, but she could make out a smile and what she thought was a tear in his eye.

"Cass, I feel the same way." His eyes searched hers as she tipped her head back. "I've felt like a drowning man for so long, and you've given me the ability to breathe again. I don't know how you've done it. But I'm so grateful. Cass, I want to learn all there is to know about you." Ed paused, gathering his courage. "Sunday I'd like to take you on a horse ride to my favorite spot." He rushed on. "We can talk more then. I should get going so you can go inside." Ed glanced toward the house. "Would you join me?" he asked, feeling his heart nearly pound out of his chest.

"Yes, I'd love to. What time should we leave?" asked Cassie.

"We'll need a little time to get there and back before supper. How about two o'clock?" Ed asked, trying to hold in his excitement.

"Yes, that'll be fine. I'm sure Uncle George will give his approval. You seem to have won them over some time ago," Cassie said, smiling.

Ed smiled at that remark. "Well then, goodnight, Cass."

Ed leaned down and kissed her on the cheek. His soft lips and moustache brushed her cheek, making a lasting impression on her heart. Releasing her hand, he turned and walked to the corral, untied his horse, swung up and rode off down the drive into the darkness.

Cassie stood there watching him go, astonished by what had just happened. "Wow! What a night!" She was bubbling with excitement. Cassie wished her sister, Charlotte, was there so she could run and tell her the exciting details of her evening. Cassie had so much running through her mind. "What in the world are you doing? But he really likes me. Does he really know you? Would he still like you if he knew what happened? Never-mind! I'm happy and maybe

131

I'll never tell him. Besides, who knows where this will go? You barely know him. Maybe it won't last. But oh, I hope it does!"

Cassie slowly looked at the large rising moon and stars in the dark sky and folded her arms around her waist. "Dear God in Heaven, I want to be happy again, really happy, like tonight. I don't want this to end. Please help me do the right thing. I care for him so much. Ed's a good man and I don't ever want to hurt him. He deserves the truth. But how do I tell him? Will he understand? Will he still want to be with me? Please give me the strength to do the right thing. In Jesus' name. Amen," she silently prayed, then turned and walked back to the house.

Inside Uncle George and Aunt Mabel were heading to bed. Cassie smiled at them and gave them each a hug and kiss goodnight and excused herself to go to her room.

Once in her room, Cassie lay on her bed and closed her eyes, replaying the evening over in her mind, imagining the conversation she would have had with Charlotte if she were there. "Oh Charlotte, Ed is so wonderful. You should've seen him at supper. He found out I was the one who'd made the biscuits and complimented me on what a good cook I was, then proceeded to eat four of them!" Cassie laughed quietly to herself. "And later when he played 'Beautiful Dreamer' on his guitar to me. I've never loved a song as much as I did then. You would've loved his rich deep voice, it made my heart flutter and my head swim, it was so romantic." Cassie swooned. "I was so overwhelmed that I kissed him. Just on the cheek, but still. You know me, in all my life I've never been so impulsive. OK, OK, I'll admit I'm free-spirited and spontaneous in private but I'm always proper and ladylike in public…until tonight." Cassie rolled her eyes. "I was so mortified by what I'd done, and in front of Aunt Mabel and Uncle George, no less. But

Ed saved me by making a joke about himself and soon everyone was laughing about him. What a sweetheart! Later when Aunt Mabel and Uncle George went inside, Ed held my hand! Can you believe it? Oh my goodness, my heart was beating so wildly. I felt so wonderful I didn't want it to end. It's embarrassing to mention, but I've never felt this strong of an attraction for someone before. Oh, and he said he wants to spend more time with me and learn everything about me and that's exactly how I feel about him. Every time we talk, I learn something more I love about him. And it seems like he feels the same way. You'll never guess what happened when he was about to leave. Ed kissed me!! Not on the lips. That would have been inappropriate, but sweetly, on the cheek. Ed's an honorable man, concerned with my reputation, and such a gentleman." Cassie giggled as she imagined her father telling her and Charlotte to settle down and go to sleep, as he had so many times in the past. She lay quietly with a peaceful smile on her face and suddenly remembered something.

"OH! I forgot to ask Aunt Mabel and Uncle George about the Sunday ride. I'll have to ask them tomorrow." Cassie changed into her night dress, then braided her hair and climbed into bed, planning to dream about Ed.

***

Ed left Cassie quickly, feeling he'd let himself get carried away. He didn't want to be disloyal to his wife's memory. He cared for Cassie and wanted her to be happy. Wasn't that love? Was he in love with Cassie? How could he have fallen in love so quickly? How had she gotten into his heart so easily? There used to be a hard shell protecting his heart. Yet Cassie had melted it with her look, her touch,

133

her laugh, her song, and her kiss. There was nothing to do for Ed but move forward. It was like she had cast a spell over him, and he was powerless to do anything but follow her. That was it! She was magic! Cassie had to be some sort of enchantress who'd cast a spell on him. Ed chuckled to himself. At least that's how it felt. He knew she was only a young woman, and an amazing one at that. And for whatever reason they'd come together. Ed needed Cassie and hopefully she needed him. Maybe they would need each other forever.

That night Ed lay in bed and thought about Cassie, and all that had happened since she'd arrived in Cheyenne and came into his life. "Mary, would you mind if I was to fall in love again? I know you'd like her. Cassie's a special woman. Please, let me love her fully. I'll always love you and our daughter. I'm lonely and want to feel loved again. I miss you so much, Mary; Cassie has helped fill the emptiness. Please let me know," Ed begged, then closed his eyes and fell asleep.

Late in the night Ed dreamed of his wife, Mary. This time not pale and dying. No, this time she was healthy and happy. Mary was holding the hand of a little girl with long blonde hair. Their white robes flowed out behind them as they walked through a meadow of wildflowers towards him. Mary and the little girl stopped a little ways away with the sun shining brightly around them and smiled at him. Ed wanted to go to them, but he couldn't move. Mary spoke softly, "Edward, I will always love you. I want you to be happy. I want you to love again. Make Cassie as happy as you've made me." When he tried to speak, the lump in his throat made it impossible. Mary and the little girl, whom he knew was his daughter, smiled at him. Tears of joy blurred his eyes, as his heart almost burst with love. The vision became bright as the sun, and Ed awoke with tears streaming down his cheeks and the morning sun shining on his face. Ed lay there in peace, reveling in his dream. Oh, how he wanted that dream to never end. Ed knew in his heart that Mary and his daughter were angels in heaven, whole and happy. And Mary had set him free, given him permission to love again. Ed would never forget that dream. Maybe one day he would tell Cassie about it, he thought.

Chapter 7
Waiting

The next morning Cassie awoke to the cheerful sound of birds chirping in the trees outside her window. Throwing back the covers she jumped out of bed and parted the curtains to watch the dark horizon turn a vibrant fuchsia. Cassie sighed and smiled to herself as the sun peeked above the hills causing the trees' dewy leaves to sparkle like crystals. Pulling back the curtains even further, she opened the window and breathed in the fresh smell of damp earth. "What a glorious day!" she thought as she began to dress. Nearly floating, she headed out of her room to start her chores before breakfast.

"Good morning!" Cassie said brightly as she joined her aunt and uncle in the kitchen.

"Good morning, Cassie!" they answered cheerfully.

"You look positively radiant this morning," Aunt Mabel commented as she took down the coffee beans and put some in the grinder.

"I wonder why?" teased Uncle George, as he winked at Cassie.

"I don't know what you're talking about," Cassie replied playfully, shrugging as she took the egg basket from the kitchen counter and headed outside to the chicken coop. Cassie turned in the doorway and announced, "Ed asked me to go riding with him on Sunday at two o'clock. I said yes! I hope that's all right?"

"That sounds fine to me. I get a feeling we're going to be seeing a lot of him from now on," George teased with a toothy grin as he filled the wood box with kindling.

Cassie smiled broadly and turned back around and headed outside, closing the door behind her without a word of rebuttal.

"Mabel, I think we'll be having Sheriff Havoc over for supper more often," George said to his wife as she filled the kettle with water, and he lit the fire in the cookstove.

"Well, can you blame him? Cassie's a wonderful young woman. He's lucky to have met her and she could have done worse. He's the most respectable, trustworthy bachelor in the county. And you're the most respectable, unavailable man in the county," Mabel said smiling. "They will make a cute couple, almost as cute as us!" Mabel stopped what she was doing and wrapped her arms around George's waist, peering lovingly up at him.

George loved his wife more and more every day. It was hard to believe they'd been married twenty-nine years. Mabel looked more attractive today than the day they were married. She was beautiful then, and over the years she grew even more lovely to him. She was his rock, his everything. How she ever put up with him, he would never know. He could be messy and uncultured at times and she tolerated it with patience. She'd always stood by him no matter what or where his ambitious ideas led them, even when they'd moved away from her only family to start the cattle ranch. It'd been a crazy idea, with high risks, in a wild untamed country. They'd sold their farm in Missouri and came to Cheyenne. Mabel worked just as hard as he did, helping to make the ranch what it was. He had only one wish, to keep Mabel smiling. George looked down into the gentle sable eyes he knew better than his own and smiled softly.

137

"You're right! We make a very cute couple. You, my dear, are adorable. And I love you more than ever!" George said with a lump in his throat. He kissed her forehead and hugged her tightly.

"I love you too, my darling man." Mabel rested her head on his chest and squeezed him back. "Let's get this day started before it's over." As he leaned down, she gave him a quick kiss before she turned and sauntered toward the pantry door with a spring in her step, looking over her shoulder as she shrugged and laughed playfully.

George chuckled at his wife's antics, smiled, shaking his head, and left to start his chores.

Throughout the day, Cassie caught herself humming little bits of "Beautiful Dreamer." She didn't realize it at first until Uncle George started laughing at her; chuckling to herself, she waved it off and continued humming as she worked. She felt happy and lighthearted and couldn't help the song in her heart.

That evening she decided to write a letter to Madeline.

June 18, 1869
Dearest Madeline,

I hope this letter finds you well. So much has happened since I last wrote. Midnight arrived safely on the train, and oh what a marvelous reunion we had. I missed him so much. It was a miracle, no doubt about it. I've been blessed.

That same day I met a very nice man. I was at a church picnic, when he came over to me. His name is Edward Havoc, and happens to be the very respectable Sheriff of Cheyenne. He came here about two years ago to help clear out the ruffians that followed the railroad. People call him Sheriff Havoc, but he asked me to call him Ed. I think he's around twenty-six or twenty-seven years old. He told me he had two younger brothers that died in the war along with his father, and has a mother and two younger sisters still living back in Kansas.

A few days after our first meeting he came by the house on his way out to Horse Creek to check on some "squatters." Uncle George offered to have me accompany Ed. It was the first chance I'd had to ride Midnight since his arrival. It was so much fun to race Midnight with Ed. He said he had never seen a woman ride so well. He is so complimentary. And you should have seen the look on Ed's face when he saw me in my new riding skirt and cowboy hat. I could tell he thought I looked very nice. We had a wonderful time getting to know each other. It was the happiest I've felt since coming to Cheyenne.

Ed's a very handsome man. He has sandy blonde hair with a darker blonde mustache, and dark sage eyes. He's at least a head taller than me, trim but well-muscled, with broad shoulders and a rugged exterior. I'm sure he comes across as someone not to mess with, but anyone who really knows him would say he's polite, well spoken, and a perfect gentleman. That's how he is with me, very kind and gentle and his soft deep voice is very soothing when he talks.

Ed came to supper last night, and when he found out that I'd made the biscuits he compli-

mented me on how delicious they were and then proceeded to eat two more. His way of constantly making me blush makes me feel like I'm something special.

After dinner Ed played his guitar, and somehow got me to sing "Dixie" with him. He sings very well too. It was so much fun to sing our favorite songs. When he sang "Beautiful Dreamer" to me for my birthday, it brought tears to my eyes and before I knew what I was doing, I thanked him with a kiss on the cheek, right in front of my aunt and uncle! I could've died of embarrassment when I realized what I'd done. But Ed saved me by making a joke about himself and everyone started laughing at him and instead of me.

You won't believe what happened after my aunt and uncle went inside the house and left us on the porch alone. Ed held my hand! And as I was trying to recover from that, he told me how much he would like to spend time getting to know me. Before he left, he kissed me on the cheek. I feel very embarrassed telling you that, but I might burst with excitement if I don't tell someone. And I trust you. Besides, you told me you wanted to know everything.

I'd hoped it was the train ride making me motion sick. But I'm still feeling ill every morning, and sometimes through the day. I'm beginning to suspect it's something else. I haven't seen a doctor about it yet, maybe he can give me some medicine to feel better. I just hope it isn't anything *serious.*

Ed and I are going to go riding again this Sunday. He has a special place he wants to take me to. I'll tell you how it goes. I need to find a way to tell him what happened to me the night of the attack. Ed deserves to know before this goes any further. I really do care about him and want him to know. He's a good man and deserves the best. Wish me luck!

Write to me as soon as you can and let me know how everything is going there. I pray for you and your family daily.
Your Dearest Friend,
Cassie

***

That Saturday, Uncle George and Aunt Mabel were going on their weekly trip to town and invited Cassie to come along. They would've never forced her to go but Uncle George didn't feel comfortable leaving her alone. Cassie was excited at the chance to go to town so she could mail the letter she'd written to Madeline and would maybe even receive a letter from her. Mostly she hoped she would get a chance to see Ed. She hadn't stopped thinking about him and found it hard to stay focused on anything, as her mind would wander back to him and what he might be doing.

While Uncle George was at the feed store placing an order, Cassie asked Aunt Mabel if she could stop into the doctor's office for a moment, as she was having dizzy spells and nausea and wondered if there was something the doctor could give her. Cassie didn't mention to Aunt Mabel how she was still losing weight and feeling exhausted at times. Aunt Mabel agreed it was an excellent idea and confessed she'd been worried about Cassie since she'd come. It was settled; when Uncle George came out, they would tell him they were going to see the doctor while he made another stop at the gun smithery. Uncle George agreed and turned the team toward the doctor's office.

As they drove down the road, they passed the Sheriff's office; Uncle George noticed Ed walking down the boardwalk and immediately pulled the surrey over. Sheriff Havoc waved as he spotted them.

"Ho there!" George said, pulling the horses to a stop. "Sheriff Havoc!"

"Howdy, folks!" Sheriff Havoc briskly walked up to the rig and shook George's hand vigorously.

"I hear you'd like to take Cassie on a ride Sunday after church. I told her it sounded like a fine idea. And I'm wondering if you'd like to come to supper afterwards?" George asked.

"Thank you, George. Yes, I'd love to join you for supper. As a matter of fact, I think I'd like to have a picnic lunch with Cassie at the pond," Ed said to George as he smiled at Cassie.

"Sounds like fun. I can pack the picnic if you'd like," offered Aunt Mabel.

"No thank you, ma'am, that's very nice of you to offer but I have it all planned. Cassie, would it be all right if I came and got you a little earlier? Maybe around one thirty, so we can eat sooner? I don't want you to go hungry," he offered politely.

"Yes, that should be fine. We'll be home from church around noon and that will give me time to get ready," Cassie said beaming. "And I'll bake some cookies," Cassie volunteered eagerly.

"Sounds delicious. I can't wait!" Ed backed away, grinning from ear to ear. "Until then, Mr. and Mrs. Hartford, Cassie. Good day." He tipped his hat and left them to go to his office. Before entering he turned and took one last look at Cassie and waved goodbye.

Cassie waved and smiled brightly back at him. She was so excited for Sunday to come. She could hardly wait. Today she had gotten to see Ed and that was more than she'd expected and everything she'd hoped for.

Uncle George stopped at the doctor's office and helped Cassie and Mabel down, then drove off while they went inside. The doctor said he'd be able to see Cassie right away and Cassie asked if Aunt Mabel would wait for her while she went in alone. Aunt Mabel was happy to oblige and took a seat in the waiting room as Cassie followed the doctor back to his examination room.

"I'm Dr. Ward, nice to meet you." He shook her hand gently as he closed the door to the exam room and gestured for her to sit.

"Nice to meet you as well, I'm Cassandra Black." She went to the examination table, stepped up and sat down.

"Are you new in town? I've never met you before and believe me I would remember. I don't forget a face." Dr. Ward pulled open a file cabinet drawer and withdrew a new folder, opened it and wrote her name on the top edge, recording it in her medical chart.

"I just moved here about two weeks ago to live with my aunt and uncle, Mabel and George Hartford," she explained as she watched him scribble something quickly in her chart.

"That's nice." Dr. Ward paused, but she didn't explain further. "So, what is it that brings you to see me today?" He pulled up a chair and sat across from her.

Cassie clasped her shaking hands, trying to settle herself. "I've been having a lot of nausea and dizziness that doesn't seem to be getting any better. It's been going on for about six weeks. I don't have much of an appetite and I'm experiencing fatigue that isn't common for me," explained Cassie with concern on her face.

"Why don't you tell me what was going on about the time it started?" Dr. Ward wrote her symptoms down in his notes.

Cassie took a deep breath and began her story. "Well, around the first of May my family and I were attacked by a band of Indians." She looked down at her hands and proceeded to tell him all that had happened that night. Coming to the end of her story she quickly added, "It's probably just part of the shock. But I thought I should make sure. I would hate to get my aunt and uncle sick if it's something contagious," Cassie explained.

Doctor Ward was a good listener and sat silently thinking for a few minutes. "That sounds like quite an ordeal, Miss Black. What you've been through may explain some of your symptoms. Have you tried anything that's helped with the nausea?" he asked as he wrote more notes.

"I used to work with my mother as an assistant when she would make house calls. She was a midwife and a nurse, of sorts. She would've prescribed ginger, chamomile, or peppermint tea, and that's helped some. The nausea usually goes away as the day goes on, so I don't always think about it. Unless I happen to smell something unpleasant, or see something distasteful, then it's worse."

"Like what, for example?" he asked.

"Like when they killed all those buffalo on our train trip here. That made me violently ill," she recalled. "Or when I'm cooking raw meat, the smell is almost revolting. I'm convinced it's gone sour, but I know it hasn't."

"Hmm, I'm starting to understand. When would you say your last cycle was?" asked Dr. Ward as he pushed his glasses up his nose and waited for her to answer, pencil in hand.

Cassie gazed up to the ceiling as she pondered on his question. "Oh, let me think, it's been quite a while. I guess it would have been the middle of April. Yes, the middle of April." She watched him write the date in the chart. "I hadn't realized that it'd been that long. I really don't remember those first days very well," she muttered on, "and I guess it just slipped my mind with the move."

"I'll need to examine you to be certain, but could you possibly be pregnant?" he asked thoughtfully.

Cassie felt the room spin, and a deafening ringing filled her ears as the room went dark. Moments later she heard the doctor's calm voice telling her to open her eyes, and then the most awful ammonia smell filled her nostrils. Cassie gasped at the pungent odor and turned her face away, still unable to open her eyes. She knew that smell, she'd used it a few times when working with her mother; it was smelling salts. Cassie was laying on the doctor's examination table when her heavy eyelids fluttered open.

"I'm sorry dear, the idea must come as a shock to you. Do you think it's possible that it happened during the attack?" Dr. Ward asked gently.

Cassie turned her head away from his concerned look, as tears streamed down her face. "Yes, it's possible. I was examined by the doctor after the attack and can't recall what he said but I knew the Indian had done horrible things to me," Cassie said numbly.

"I'm so sorry to hear that. You've already been through so much, but I must do an examination, to be certain. I'm truly sorry for having to put you through this," Dr. Ward said sympathetically.

As soon as he was done with the examination, Dr. Ward confirmed she was indeed pregnant. He said she was about seven weeks along based on his calculations and the time of her attack. The baby would be due around the end of January or first of February. "I'm so sorry. Is there's anything I can do to help you?"

Cassie sat there in a daze. "Please don't say anything to my aunt. I'll tell her in time. I won't have to if I lose the baby. I don't want my aunt to know until we're certain that I won't lose it. Can we tell her I have something else for now? Please," she pleaded. "I heard of something called vertigo, it has similar symptoms. I could tell her I have that and follow up with you in a month to make sure it's getting better. Please!" Cassie begged as her heart sank into the pit of her stomach. She couldn't imagine what her aunt and uncle would think once they found out. Certainly, they would be ashamed that their niece was expecting an Indian's child.

"It's against my better judgement. But all right, if you want to tell her in your own time, then I won't interfere. But you must follow up with me in a month. I want to make sure you aren't losing any more weight. You're already too thin. I'll encourage her to make you ginger tea and let you take rests through the day. You need your strength. Wearing yourself out is only going to make your symptoms worse. Try having a dry biscuit before getting up in the morning and take your time eating. Drink plenty of water. You don't want to get dehydrated in this heat, which promises to get worse as summer comes," Dr. Ward instructed. He was sorry to see such a pretty young woman in her situation and wished there was more he could do to help. He put his hand on Cassie's shoulder as he opened the office door and followed her out to the waiting room.

"Don't worry, Mrs. Hartford. Cassie will be feeling better in time. I gave her some instructions to follow. If you'll help her, she should start feeling better soon," he said with a reassuring smile. "But just to make sure, I want to see her again in a month. Will you be sure and bring her?" he implored Mabel.

"Yes, Dr. Ward, I most certainly will. So, what's the matter with her, Doc?" Aunt Mabel looked concerned.

"I'll let Cassandra tell you. Have a good day." Dr. Ward left them and closed his office door.

Cassie gave Aunt Mabel a small smile. "I have vertigo, probably from the attack and made worse by the train ride. Dr. Ward says it should get better soon and gave me a list of things to try. He wrote them down," Cassie said, handing Aunt Mabel the list.

"Oh good, then it's nothing serious. I'm so relieved," Aunt Mabel said as she gave Cassie's shoulders a squeeze and opened the door. Mabel could tell something was off. Cassie had changed from the time she'd gone into the doctor's office and when she'd emerged. It was evident that her joy was gone. The grave look in her eyes made Mabel wonder if there was something Cassie wasn't telling her. Whatever it was she would do her best to make sure Cassie followed the doctor's instructions. Mabel's heart ached to help Cassie. Slipping her arm through Cassie's, Mabel gave her a reassuring smile.

After leaving the doctor's office, they walked arm in arm down the sunny boardwalk to the post office to mail their letters. Cassie found she had received a letter from Madeline and another from Bartholomew Clark. "What in the world! Why would Bart write to me now?"

Aunt Mabel asked Cassie who Bartholomew Clark was when she saw how shocked Cassie looked. Cassie brushed it off, explaining that he was a friend from school and had written to her unexpectedly, and nothing more.

147

Cassie tucked Bart's letter away to read in private. As Uncle George and Aunt Mabel discussed Cassie's diagnosis, she become engrossed in the letter from Madeline.

Madeline had written about her sister. "The baby is due in about three weeks unless she delivers sooner," she wrote. She told of the lovely weather in Platte Valley and expressed how glad she was that Cassie had a good place to live and a nice family to take care of her. She wished Cassie well and would await more news. She closed with, "Your Dear Friend, Madeline. P.S. You forgot to mention the young men, please send news." Cassie smiled at that and knew Madeline would enjoy the letter she had just mailed.

Cassie was anxious to get supper over with so she could go to her room and read the letter from Bart in private. With the dishes done, Cassie excused herself to go to bed early, telling them she was tired and wanted to be rested up for tomorrow. Cassie changed into her night dress and got into bed, before opening the letter from Bart.

June 15, 1869
My Dear Cassie,

I hope this letter finds you well. I've been doing a lot of thinking since you left. I realize I should've made an effort to keep you here. It was a mistake to let you go. I thought I was giving you time to grieve but I should've been there for you at your side, supporting you in your time of need. Will you forgive me and give me a second chance? I want to marry you, if you're willing. I know you're living with your aunt and uncle. But if you would come back we could be married right away. I know you'd be happy here. I'd take

148

good care of you and build you a house that we could fill with as many children as you wish. Cassie, you haven't left my thoughts. If you will have me, you will never want for anything. Please consider my offer and let me know what you think.
Sincerely,
Bart

Cassie didn't want Bart; she didn't love him, and he'd never expressed his love to her. She didn't want a loveless marriage. The truth was, they were barely even friends. She knew Bart wasn't right for her, especially now that she was pregnant. He would want nothing to do with her once he found out. She would write to him later, letting him know she was not interested in ever going back and especially not interested in him.

The tears flowed as she thought about what she was going to do now. How would she tell her aunt and uncle? How could she tell Ed? Telling him would ruin everything; she was certain of it. Finally, she blew out the lamp; exhausted from the day, she drifted off into a restless sleep.

That night, she dreamed of the Indian attacking her. His white teeth and war paint stark against his dark face, laughing ruthlessly as she fought to get away. Sitting up, she gasped for breath, her heart pounding in panic, her face wet with tears. Frantically looking around the room she realized where she was and lay back down and pulled the covers up under her chin as she shivered with fright and began to cry. She cried for a long time before finally falling asleep again.

***

Ed was so excited for Sunday to come; he could hardly sleep. He'd planned to talk to George before church and ask if he could take Cassie on a picnic. It had been a pleasant surprise to see Cassie in town that day. Now that he knew he was free to pursue Cassie, he was giddy with joy. He replayed over and over the things they'd talked about, the way she moved, how she sounded when she laughed, talked and sang. He made a mental note of the way her hair lay on her shoulders and framed her delicate face, and how her emerald green eyes sparkled when she was emotional or excited. He wanted to know everything about her. Ed rolled over in bed, and closed his eyes, determined to dream about her.

Chapter 8
Sunday Picnic with Ed

Sunday morning Cassie awoke to a quiet knock at her door as Aunt Mabel slowly opened it and peeked in. "Cassie dear, I hate to wake you. But I thought you'd like some tea and toast before you got dressed. I read the list of things the doctor suggested, and this was at the top. Take your time, and when you feel better you can come out for breakfast." Aunt Mabel set the tray on the bedside table. "We already did all the morning chores, so no need to hurry for that. It's been taken care of."

"Oh, thank you so much, Aunt Mabel, but you really didn't have to do that," Cassie said apologetically. "And I can help with breakfast, just let me get dressed. I'm really not that sick." Cassie sat up in bed and saw the hurt in Mabel's eyes, and immediately felt her eyes well up with tears, and gave her a loving smile. "Aunt Mabel, I'm sorry. I appreciate you helping me. I love you. Thank you for taking such good care of me."

Aunt Mabel's face brightened, and she leaned over and kissed Cassie on the top of the head. "Cassie my dear, it's my pleasure to care for you as my own. I love you so much, I hope you know," she said, placing her work-worn hand on Cassie's cheek. "And your Uncle George loves you too. Just remember we're here for you, no matter what," her voice shook with emotion as she stood to leave, closing the door behind her.

As the room brightened with sunlight, dawning a new day, Cassie sat in bed and made the decision then and there, she would be happy. She would find joy in even this situation. She had survived worse. So, she finished her tea and toast, and climbed out of bed to say her morning prayers with a heart full of gratitude.

Cassie dressed, braided her hair and went to eat breakfast with her aunt and uncle. Having something in her stomach before getting up was much better, and she was able to eat oatmeal and a boiled egg without difficulty.

With breakfast finished, Cassie set about making her favorite batch of oatmeal cookies as Aunt Mabel cleaned up the morning dishes. As the cookies baked Cassie set her hair in a twist and changed into her Sunday dress. Uncle George and Aunt Mabel were ready and waiting for her in the surrey as she set the last batch of cookies out to cool. She apologized for delaying their departure and climbed in back. Aunt Mabel and Uncle George reassured her that they would still make it to church in time. Relieved, Cassie relaxed and let her mind daydream of Ed as they drove into town. It only seemed a short while before they arrived at the church.

Cassie spotted Ed as he confidently walked down the street towards them. He was dressed in a handsome brown suit, starched white shirt, and a black ribbon tie. He tipped his hat, smiled and waved, walking briskly to the surrey to greet them.

"Good morning to you all! Don't you ladies look lovely today," Ed said as he helped Cassie down.

"Good morning, Sheriff!" Uncle George and Aunt Mabel said cheerfully as they stepped down from the rig.

Cassie smiled. "Good morning to you too. You look mighty handsome as well," Cassie said, and blushed as she realized it sounded very forward of her.

"Thank you, Cass!" Ed's mustache raised at the corners as he accepted the compliment. He'd never seen her in the powder blue traveling dress with matching hat. How attractive she looked with her dark hair piled high on her head, exposing her slender neck just above the white collar of her blouse. Ed took Cassie's arm and wrapped it through his and walked her into the church.

Ignoring the wondering eyes, they walked arm in arm down the aisle and found an empty pew up front and sat down together. Ed and Cassie shared the hymnal as they sang the opening hymn, making sideways glances at one another as they harmonized. When Cassie closed the hymnal their fingers touched, sending sparks through her. Occasionally they would glance at one another through the sermon, sharing a warm smile as they tried to listen to what the pastor said. They were too consumed with each other to notice anything else. Every now and then someone would turn to get a better look at the young woman who was sitting next to Sheriff Havoc. Cassie, upon noticing their stares, would grin their way, sending them an unspoken message. Gossip was flying even before the service was over. Cassie was confident sitting next to Ed, a well-known honorable man in the community.

As soon as the worship service was over, Ed gently guided Cassie out of the church, keeping his hand on her lower back. As they got to the door, he took her arm and led her through the huddle of parishioners in the doorway. Outside he assisted her into Uncle George's rig and said he would be out to the ranch to get her in an hour. Ed had to go home to get some things ready before the picnic and bid her farewell until then.

Cassie was excited and a little apprehensive about the picnic. As she changed into her riding clothes and took her hair down to brush out with long even strokes, she argued back and forth with herself, if she should tell Ed her secret. She pulled back half of her hair and tied a red ribbon around it, letting the rest cascade over her shoulders. It was almost time to leave, and she still hadn't reached a decision. Hurrying to finish getting ready, she put the decision out of her mind and focused on wrapping the cookies in a cloth and packing them snuggly inside a tin.

Ed arrived promptly at one thirty, wearing a new tan shirt under his leather vest and red bandana. He'd carefully prepared sandwiches and other food he'd packed in his saddlebag and tied a blanket roll to his saddle. "Good afternoon," he greeted George and Cassie as they emerged from the house.

"Good to see you again, Sheriff," George said, coming out to shake his hand.

"Hello, Ed!" Cassie stepped off the porch carrying the tin of cookies.

"Cass, are you ready to go?" he asked, grinning at the sight of her in the freshly pressed white linen blouse and soft leather vest and skirt.

"Yes, I'm ready. Could you put these cookies in my saddlebag?" she asked as she handed Ed the tin.

"I'd be happy to, Cass. Did you forget something?" he asked looking down at her free-flowing hair, admiring its shine.

"I don't think so." She honestly couldn't think of what she'd forgotten.

"Cassie! You forgot your hat!" Aunt Mabel shouted as she rushed out of the house. "You two have a good time and be back for supper. Supper will be ready by seven o'clock, so don't be late," she said, stepping back up the porch next to Uncle George.

Cassie thanked Aunt Mabel, then grinned at Ed, laughing lightly. "Oh, my hat." She put it on and adjusted it carefully as he watched. "There we go, now I'm ready."

Ed reached over and tipped the brim of her hat up slightly so he could see her eyes. "There, now the picture is perfect," he said as he winked at her, making her blush and turn her gaze away. "Can I help you up?" he asked as she went to mount Midnight.

Ed placed his hands around her waist and boosted her up as she placed her foot in the stirrup and swung her other leg over the saddle. "Thank you," she said, breathing fast as her heart raced from his touch. Cassie looked towards the house again and waved to her aunt and uncle as they stood in the doorway. "See you later!" Turning Midnight, she followed Ed out of the yard and down the lane.

Ed slowed and let her catch up as they walked their horses down the lane through the trees and turned south onto the main road, following it back towards town.

"So, where is this place you're taking me?" Cassie asked curiously.

"It's a surprise!" Ed's mustache twitched mischievously at the corners.

Cassie smiled in delight as the suspense grew inside her. Midnight seemed to sense her excitement, and his ears perked forward, then snorted and nickered in response to Major's playful whinnying.

Instead of following the bend in the road that led into town, Ed turned off heading southwest. A few miles later they crossed over the railroad tracks and traveled another mile or so into the trees. As they rode single file along what appeared to be a deer trail, Cassie followed Ed closely, not wanting to lose sight of him in the thicket of white-barked quaking aspen. Holding onto her hat, she ducked her head to avoid being slapped in the face by the low hanging branches. She became thankful for her sturdy riding skirt, that would have been snagged and torn by the thick underbrush and saplings, had it not been made of leather.

The deer trail gradually descended and leveled out as it opened to a beautiful meadow of flourishing grasses and wildflowers. At the heart of the glade was a large pond with cattails lining the edge. Ed rode into the meadow, then dismounted to tie his horse to a low branch of a large tree and waited for Cassie. Ed reached up to help Cassie, taking her by the waist and letting her slide down slowly so she didn't lose her balance on the soft earth.

Already flushed by the long ride and Ed's attention, Cassie became even more flushed as she turned around facing him, looking up into his eyes, standing only inches from him. He smiled, cleared his throat and slowly took the reins from her, sending chills through her as his fingers brushed hers. Ed seemed to leave her speechless with every touch.

Cassie recovered her composure, and walked to the water's edge, taking it all in. "This is such a beautiful place. It could be the Garden of Eden." She appreciated the secluded grove of trees where birds chirped and butterflies flitted from flower to flower, blooming along the clear pool of water. "What's this place called?" she asked, her eyes wide with wonder as she turned to Ed.

"Clearwater Pond. Pretty, isn't it?" Ed came to stand beside her, putting his hands in his pockets, taking deep breaths of the fragrant air.

"Pretty doesn't even come close to describing it." Pausing to find the right words, she went on, "It's simply… enchanting, like a mystical forest in a fairy tale!" She truly felt as if she was standing in a magical sanctuary, protected from the outside world.

Ed smiled, pleased knowing he had made the right decision to share his special place with her. "I'm glad you like it. Not many people know about this place. As you noticed, it's difficult to get to."

"It's like a dream," Cassie said as her heart soared. "Thank you for bringing me here."

Ed looked her in the eyes and smiled. "It's my pleasure." His stomach growled pulling him back into action. "I think under that granddaddy of a tree, would be a nice spot for our picnic," he said, pointing to a maple tree with far reaching limbs hanging over the meadow and water's edge. "Plenty of shade there."

"It looks perfect," she said and followed him back to the horses.

Ed untied the blanket from his horse's saddle and spread it out under the old maple's canopy. Cassie smoothed the blanket over the tall green grass and laid out the food Ed had packed. He had brought ham and cheese sandwiches wrapped in paper, apple tarts he'd bought at the hotel bakery the day before, and milk. Cassie complimented him on how everything tasted, "just right."

When they finished with their meal, they decided to take a stroll around the pond and explore.

"The pond is fed from a spring here on the west side and flows out there," Ed explained, pointing south to a small stream snaking through the trees.

So many of the flowers and berry bushes she had never seen before. Little black tailed chipmunks ran in and out of the many bushes and yellow birds chattered above them. Curious about each new thing, Cassie pointed to this and that, quizzing Ed, then listened intently as he taught her about the wildlife and plants in the area.

"You're so smart," Cassie declared.

"Oh, not really. I just know a whole lot about nothing," Ed quipped.

Cassie chuckled at his teasing. "Well, I think you know a whole lot about almost everything." She smiled warmly as she studied Ed's handsome profile, his intelligent sage green eyes, the crinkles around the edges of his eyes when he laughed, his long straight nose above his carefully trimmed moustache and full relaxed lips that pressed together when he set his square jaw. "He's so handsome and yet so modest, always downplaying his talents. Doesn't he know how wonderful he is?" "How did you know all of this?" She opened her arm in front of her indicating the whole area.

"I suppose I love learning new things. What I didn't know, I figured out. My ma and pa were both teachers. They said I had a thirst for knowledge and starved for attention. I would sit for hours learning everything they would teach me. That's how I learned to read and write and play the guitar at such a young age. I owe so much to my parents, especially my ma. Because of her I have a great love of reading," Ed explained as he took her hand to help her step over a fallen tree, then reluctantly released it once safely over.

Stopping to rest on a rock in the shade beside the water, Ed continued to talk about his mother and his childhood years. Cassie enjoyed listening to his stories and how he adored his mother. The afternoon was quickly becoming hot, and Cassie longed to dip her feet into the cool water just inches away. Knowing she should behave like a lady, she kept her shoes and stockings on. As she stared down into the clear water, she began to think of her own mother.

Ed stopped talking, realizing he had dominated the conversation, and patiently waited for Cassie to express her thoughts.

Cassie smiled and slowly began to speak of her mother for the first time since her death. "I learned the healing arts from my ma," she said in a shaky voice.

"Oh, you did," Ed responded with great interest, prodding her to continue as he smoothed his moustache with his thumb and forefinger.

Cassie felt his reassurance and found strength to go on. "Yes, my ma was a midwife and healer, although she never went to any formal schooling; she was taught midwifery by my grandma. I used to go with her on house calls, to help with bandages and even some deliveries," Cassie's voice caught as she remembered her ma.

"That's a very good skill to have," Ed said, seeing her delicate lips turn down at the corners, and her small chin quivered as she tried to control her emotions. He wanted to reach out and take her hand, but instead smiled compassionately. Cassie closed her eyes, took a deep breath and opened them again, continuing her story.

"Over time I got to be pretty good at knowing what plants to put on certain injuries and what herbs worked best for which ailments. My mother taught me how to cook, keep house, sew, and how to be a good wife and mother. I'll always be grateful for the things she taught me; it made me who I am today. I just wish she was here," Cassie said with a teary smile. She appreciated Ed's thoughtfulness; it felt good to talk about her mother. Sweeping the tear away, she redirected the conversation. "Of course, I've always wanted to learn to play the guitar. Maybe you could teach me some time."

"I would love to teach you to play the guitar. I will teach you all I know, and that goes for everything." Ed tilted his head and smiled. "It might take a whole day," he jokcd.

Cassie laughed as she shook her head in unbelief. "What a tease!"

Together they stood and continued their talk as they walked around the pond, discovering all sorts of new things about each other. The more they talked the more they felt they'd known each other all their lives, they had so much in common. Both loved reading and writing, but neither cared much for math, although proficient at it. Talking about the places they loved the most, they revealed they loved the mountains and all bodies of water, oceans, lakes, ponds, rivers, and streams. Their favorite foods were very similar as well, which happened to include their love of peaches. The excitement grew as they discovered they both loved the same sorts of music and complimented each other on their singing voices. Ed was embarrassed to reveal that he had a way with animals. He laughed when he told of a wild tomcat he'd tamed on their farm as a teenage boy. Cassie found it amazing that such a tough guy could have such a soft spot for a kitten. The longer they talked, the more amazed they were at how similar their likes and dislikes were.

"How could two people from different places be so similar?" she wondered.

Needing to rest, Cassie sat back down under the maple tree. Feeling relaxed, she put her hat aside and lay back on the blanket to looked up at the tall tree. "Look how big those leaves are, the ones on top are huge," she said as she breathed a deep sigh. "It's so peaceful here watching the leaves flutter and branches sway in the breeze." She felt very serene in this tranquil place with Ed.

Ed watched her lying in the shade of the tree, looking as heavenly as an angel, resting with her ebony hair spilling around her. Little wisps of it curled around her face tempting him to brush them gently away. She breathed in deeply as a smile subtly lifted the corners of her perfect lips.

Ed smiled and lay down next to her. He watched through the leaves the clouds sweep across the azure sky as he marveled at all he had learned about Cassie today. Time stretched on in silence, and Ed began to wonder if

Cassie was asleep or just thinking; either way he didn't want to disturb her.

As if pulled by some unseen force, Ed took his hand from behind his head and lay it next to hers. Little by little he moved it closer and closer until he was softly touching the edge of her hand. He waited and listened for her reaction, but her breathing remained deep and even and her face relaxed. She didn't make a move when their fingers touched; his touch sent warm waves through her body, nearly taking her breath away. Minutes passed before he became bold and gently placed his hand over hers, wrapping his manly fingers around her dainty hand. He closed his eyes, relishing the feel of her warm hand within his. Sensing Cassie, Ed opened his eyes to see her staring at him. Sadness filled her eyes as a tear ran down her cheek. It startled him, and he sat upright. "What have I done?" he thought in panic.

Before she could speak Ed jumped to his feet. "Cass, I'm so sorry. I didn't mean to upset you." Shocked and confused; he'd assumed she would welcome the touch of his hand. "She must've misunderstood my intentions," he thought. "I would never want to hurt you. I would just as soon cut off my own arm than take advantage of you. I'm so sorry." He begged her forgiveness as his heart twisted in pain.

Cassie's eyes softened as she realized what her actions must have portrayed to him. She reached her hand out to him. "Ed, come here." She patted the spot beside her. "Please, sit down," she urged. "You aren't the reason I'm upset. You did nothing wrong." Cassie took his hand and guided him down to sit facing her. She needed him to understand. In her tenderest voice, she said, "Ed, you are the dearest man I've ever known. You've shown me nothing but respect, and I know you'd never do anything to hurt me." Cassie placed a hand on his arm, hoping her touch would convince him. "And I would never want to hurt you either," she said, managing a reassuring smile.

Ed searched her eyes, seeing only truth and kindness there. "The only way you could hurt me, Cass, would be if you were to tell me you never wanted to see me again." He paused and swallowed hard. "That would kill me," Ed said with certainty.

Cassie was stunned and stared wide-eyed at him. "Does he really mean that?" she thought. "Maybe he won't feel the same way after I tell him." She decided then and there he had to be told the truth. Taking a few deep breaths, she gathered her courage. "Ed, I need to tell you something," she began timidly. "Something that may change the way you feel about me." She blinked back tears as she stared across the pond, choosing her words carefully. "You may have already heard gossip about me. But you deserve the truth. That's why I want to tell you everything that happened before I came here."

He waited silently for the words she was so hesitant to tell him. He squeezed her hand, not wanting to let go.

Cassie looked down at his thumb that was tenderly stroking the back of her hand. "It was the first of May when the Indians attacked," she paused to gain control of her voice. "I was leaving the outhouse when I heard the Indians approach. I locked the outhouse door and hid inside; afraid I would be found. The front door was beaten down and the Indians entered the house. I still hear the screams from my mother and sisters as Pa shouted for them to take cover." Her emerald eyes reflected the anguish of it all.

Ed thought he understood completely. "I can imagine," he empathized.

"I huddled on the floor of the outhouse shaking in

terror, trying to stifle my family's cries by covering my ears. I was horrified of what they were doing to my family and what they would do to me if I was found. Things grew silent and the triumphant war cries of the savages went up and sent chills down my spine. I wept alone in the outhouse thinking of what terrible things my family suffered before they died." She grimaced as she looked skyward, blinking back the tears. "Then they set fire to the house, circling it as it burned, riding and whooping, sometimes coming so close to the outhouse I was sure I was doomed." She glanced mournfully towards the horses. "The last thing I heard were the screams of our horses as they pulled them away." She paused, tears streaming down her face.

"Oh Cass, I'm so sorry." Ed pulled her into his arms and stroked her hair as she wept against his chest. He wanted to protect her and take away all her pain. It killed him to know she'd suffered so much.

"That's not all," she murmured between sobs.

"Oh," was all he could say as his heart sank further. "Oh, my goodness. Hadn't she suffered enough already?"

"Choking from the smoke that now filled the air, I ran across the yard trying to escape the scorching fire. I must have passed out because when I came to, I could feel I was being dragged by my arms. My mind was fuzzy, and I wondered if I'd gotten too close to the fire, and someone was dragging me to safety. I struggled to open my swollen eyes. That's when I recognized I was in the field behind the house. I wasn't being rescued." Cassie tucked her head down and squeezed her eyes shut tightly. Her words grew quieter, as if saying them would make the nightmare more real. "I tried to sit up and then I saw the Indian. He was on top of me, pinning me to the ground, his hand choking me so I couldn't breathe. I tried to fight him…" She shook her head and clenched her fists around his shirt. "But he

163

was too strong. I will never forget that face looking down, laughing at me as I struggled to get away."

Ed felt her panic and fear take over her body as if she was fighting the Indian again. "Dear God, give her strength to move past this," Ed thoughtfully prayed as he pulled her closer, clinging to her as if her life depended on it.

"When I passed out, the Indian did things to me... unspeakable things." Cassie cringed. "Then left me for dead," she stated coldly.

"I would've hunted him down and made him suffer for what he did to you!" Ed thought with renewed hate towards the Indians. "Now two women I love have been hurt by those Indians!"

Cassie continued telling of the horror she endured. "When I awoke, I knew what he'd done. I wanted to die." Her body shook with sobs as Ed cradled her. "Those Indians took everything from me, my family, my home... and my purity." With that word she released all the pent-up emotions and let the tears flow. The worst of the truth was still to be told.

Ed tried to remain calm as he clenched and unclenched his jaw, pushing aside his anger to comfort Cassie. "Oh, my dear Cass," he said, his heart was breaking for her. "I'm here, and I'll never let them hurt you again. I swear, I'd die for you," Ed murmured against her hair, the ache almost bringing him to tears.

"You won't say that when you find out the worst of it," she confessed in shame, "I'm pregnant."

Her weeping was shattering his heart. But her secret didn't surprise him, he'd suspected as much. He'd noticed how sick she was, and at some level knew. She was pure and innocent, and he intuitively longed to protect and save her from her plight. Ed held her closer and soothed her. "Shh, it's going to be all right, Cass. I'm here now. You don't have to be afraid anymore. I won't let anyone ever hurt you again," he said, swearing an oath in his heart and yearning to express his feelings for her. "I love you, Cass, and that means all of you," he confessed. "This baby is part of you and that means I will love the baby too," he assured her in his soothing bass voice.

Cassie began to settle, sniffling as Ed continued to hold her, stroking her hair as he rocked her. He'd said he loved her. He'd said he would love the baby too. She couldn't believe her ears. It was some kind of miracle. Her mind was reeling.

Ed pulled a handkerchief from his pocket and handed it to her. She wiped her eyes and nose. "Thank you," she whispered.

Ed loosened his arms and pulled back so he could look her in the eyes, but she couldn't seem to face him. So, he tenderly lifted her chin with his finger, bringing her face up, but still she kept her eyes veiled by her long dark lashes. "Cass, look at me," he said with gentle firmness, and waited for her to meet his tender gaze.

Slowly she looked up into his teary eyes, amazed by his compassionate response.

"I understand your loss and pain. I'm going to tell you something that I've never shared with anyone here. I was married once." He swallowed hard against the tightness in his throat.

Her eyes widened at his statement and she waited patiently for him to continue.

"It was two years ago, we were expecting, my wife was about six months along when Indians attacked her in our home." He paused when he saw the startled look in Cassie's eyes. He hurried on, "I was working in town and didn't know. By the time I got home it was too late to help her," he said and looked away, not wanting to see the sympathy in her eyes. "She died after giving birth to our daughter." His mouth turned down and his chin shook as he fought to control his feelings.

Cassie's heart ached for him. He was carrying such a heavy burden; one he'd kept a secret for so long.

"Cass, I loved her so much. My heart broke that day, and I didn't want to live without her. Her death is the reason I am here, I wanted to escape her memory." He tipped his head down and pursed his lips. "I never thought I could love again. I didn't want to ever love again," he admitted, and then slowly brought his head up and gazed into Cassie's eyes. "That is, until I met you." A slow smile lifted the corners of his moustache. "You've changed me, you broke down the wall around my heart and filled it with overflowing love." Ed tenderly placed his hand on her cheek. "And you didn't even know you were doing it. You were just being you. Can't you see, Cass? I was meant to meet you. You are the one for me and I am the one for you. You healed me, and I will heal you," he said with increased enthusiasm. "I love you, Cass, and I will till the day I die." He leaned in to kiss her softly on the lips as tears streamed down her face. He cradled her head as their lips connected, not wanting it to ever end. Reluctantly he withdrew and gently wiped the tears from her cheeks as a joyful smile spread across her face.

Ed's tender kiss had her heart pounding, head spinning and breathing ragged. When she regained herself, she admitted, "Oh Ed, I love you too!" Her heart swelled with love for him. "Do you know how happy you've made me? I, I was so worried," she stammered. Her eyes were pleading for mercy. "Yesterday when I found out I was pregnant, I wasn't sure you'd ever want to see me again. I hope you don't think I would ever deceive you. I felt you deserved the truth. I just wasn't sure how I would tell you.

166

And now you know…" Her voice trailed off, unable to match the incredible words she'd heard him say moments ago. Wanting to give him an opportunity to back out, she offered, "Still, I would understand if later when you've had time to think, you came to realize you didn't want me. I wouldn't blame you," she said, looking down dejectedly. She didn't feel worthy of any man's love, much less someone as special as Ed.

"Cass! I said what I said, and I am a man that stands by what I say. Do you understand?" asked Ed, studying her openly as he gently gripped her arms.

She hesitated. "Yes, I guess so," she said lamely as the tears collected.

"Thank you." His voice became more insistent, "I want to keep seeing you. Do you hear me?" He rushed on, "Cass, I love you, and as a matter of fact, I want to marry you!" he said gleefully.

She looked up at him in disbelief. Overcome with excitement she sat up on her knees, wrapping her arms around his neck with such force she almost tumbled over with him. "Oh Ed! Really?" She squeezed him tightly as he chuckled.

"Well, if you'll have me. Yes, I will marry you!" He encircled her tiny frame, lifting her knees slightly off the ground.

"Oh, Ed!" This time Cassie cried tears of joy. How had this miracle happened? Her heart had been empty, but now it was full of love. She thought she was ruined, and no one would ever want her, let alone love her, and yet she had found love and acceptance.

Ed released her and stood up, pulling her with him. "We should get you home. They'll have supper ready and waiting for us." He leaned down and kissed her lovingly on the forehead.

167

As his lips touched, she closed her eyes, feeling as if he'd kissed her soul. It was the most intense thing she had ever felt. She wrapped her arms around his waist and pressed her head against his chest. "Thank you, Ed, for loving and accepting me and the baby. I love you so much!" she said in almost a whisper.

"Thank you for allowing me to love you, Cass. I truly never thought I would again," he said, softly resting his cheek on the top of her head, breathing in her intoxicating scent.

Moments passed and they slowly released each other, both flushed and smiling. Then slowly gathering up their picnic blanket and leftovers, they packed the saddlebags and prepared to leave.

"Do you think we should tell your aunt and uncle about the wedding tonight?" asked Ed as he took her into his arms again, grinning broadly.

Cassie smiled back warmly, sliding her hands up his arms to rest on his shoulders. She blushed slightly, as she thought about being married to Ed. "I think maybe we should wait a little while. They don't even know I'm pregnant. I should tell them first and then we can share the wonderful news," she said, feeling hesitant and excited all at once. How could she tell Uncle George and Aunt Mabel? It had been hard enough to tell Ed. And yet it had turned out better than she could have imagined.

Ed could hardly contain himself. He wanted to shout the wedding news from the roof tops. "OK, but soon, or I will bust! And I don't want to wait to marry you. As far as I'm concerned, if you're going to be my wife, and I'm going to be the baby's father, I want everyone to think it's mine." Overjoyed, he wrapped his arms around her, picked her up and swung her around before setting her back on the ground.

Cassie was nearly bursting with joy and excitement. "Yes, yes! Soon, I will tell them!" she said breathlessly as she laughed, still secure in his embrace. "And then you can ask my uncle for my hand in marriage, and we can be married as soon as possible," she said with sparkling eyes and flushed cheeks.

With a quick kiss on the cheek, he released her. "Good enough! Now let's go!" he said with a huge smile as he lifted Cassie to mount her horse. Oh, how he loved to lift her. She was his to have and to hold, and soon, forever.

They rode back to the ranch, and when they were able to ride side by side, they did so holding hands. So many thoughts filled each of their minds, thinking about all the things they had shared with each other.

As they came into view of the house, with a reassuring squeeze, Ed released Cassie's hand. It would be hard to keep the smiles off their faces during supper, but they would try. As soon as they were in the yard, they were greeted by Uncle George and Aunt Mabel, who'd been watching for the couple to arrive.

"Oh good, you're back! Supper's ready. Did you have a good time?" asked Aunt Mabel as she came down the porch steps.

"Yes! It was lovely!" Cassie said, her eyes gleaming with happiness.

"That's wonderful! I'm glad you had fun," Aunt Mabel said, noting the radiant glow on Cassie's face.

"Here, let me take the horses, while you two go wash up," offered Uncle George, as he took the reins from Cassie as Ed came to help her down. The grins and looks they gave each other did not go unnoticed. George tried to hide his own grin as Ed eased Cassie down. "I see Midnight and Major had a good time as well; maybe not as much fun as you two did, from the looks of it," Uncle George said, teasing them.

Cassie and Ed both looked at Uncle George and started laughing. They couldn't wipe the smiles off their faces as they headed in to wash up, passing Aunt Mabel on the steps, offering compliments on how wonderful supper smelled.

Ed and Cassie left their hats by the front door and went to the washroom behind the kitchen, all the while beaming at each other. How in the world were they going to keep their secret when it was written all over their faces? It was obvious that they were joyfully hiding something. Ed snuck a quick kiss to Cassie's cheek while her hands were busy with the soap.

Cassie whispered, "You'd best behave, mister," as she quietly laughed. Ed poured the rinse water over her hands and handed her the towel, all while trying not to laugh at her mock scolding.

"Who's going to stop me?" teased Ed as he wrapped his arms around her and pulled her in for another kiss on the cheek. She pushed gently away from him. His arms firmly held her in place, causing her to blush and giggle with excitement, fearing they would be caught.

"Ed!" she whispered as she smiled coyly. "You big tease. Quick, Uncle George is coming to wash!" She heard the front door close and heavy footsteps walking through the kitchen.

Stealing one more quick kiss on the other cheek, he released her just in time for her to almost run into George coming through the door.

"It's all yours, Uncle George. We're all done," she said stifling a laugh. All his kisses were making her giddy with delight. She'd never dreamed that Ed was so playful and found herself feeling the same way and never wanted it to end.

Supper was very pleasant, a roast beef with new potatoes, carrots and peas from the garden. Mabel had opened a jar of applesauce for dessert that went well with the oatmeal cookies that never got eaten on the picnic.

Ed and Cassie offered to do the dishes while George and Mabel relaxed on the porch, feeling it only fair since Mabel had done all the work to prepare supper.

While Cassie washed and Ed rinsed, they took every opportunity to stand close and touch hands as they passed the dishes back and forth to each other. Cassie mischievously decided to get Ed back for his teasing earlier and splashed him with soap and water on "accident."

"Oops!" she said giggling.

Ed gave her a sideways glance and scooped up a mound of bubbles in his hand and slowly brought it towards her face.

Cassie backed up, "Ed! NO!" She squealed in delight as he wrapped his arm around behind her and held her as he deposited the soap suds on her cheeks and chin. Laughing as she squirmed, he kissed her nose. She tried to push him away as he held her and she giggled even more.

"What's going on in here?" Aunt Mabel peeked through the front door to see what all the ruckus was about. She smiled as she saw Ed release Cassie, as they both continued to laugh in embarrassment at being caught horsing around and embracing.

"Sorry, Ma'am! Cass here got some soap on her face, and I was just going to help her get it off," said Ed, grinning ear to ear as he handed Cassie a towel to wipe off the suds.

"Cassie, are you all right, dear?" asked Aunt Mabel with an even bigger smile.

"Yes, I'm fine! Just teaching Ed here how to wash dishes with plenty of soap. I guess I got carried away and got some on me too," Cassie said, looking from Aunt Mabel to Ed with a huge smile.

"Well, when you're done, come out and enjoy the cool air. It's a beautiful night and there's no sense spending it inside in a hot kitchen any longer than necessary." Aunt Mabel turned and went back outside, closing the door behind her.

As soon as the door closed, they both broke out quietly laughing until their sides hurt, eventually catching their breaths, and slowly calming down with an occasional uncontainable laugh.

"I should be heading home, Cass," Ed admitted finally, when he could speak without laughing. He took her hands and held them. "I want to say goodnight to you in here, in private." His eyes looked intently into hers. "Will you please tell them soon? I love you and want to marry you and spend every second of the day with you. Please, tell them," pleaded Ed, his sea green eyes beginning to mist up.

"All right, I will soon. Just let me find the right time and I'll let you know how it goes," she said resolutely. "I think it's going to be harder to tell them than it was telling you. What if they're embarrassed or ashamed of me?" she worried out loud. "Maybe I won't have to tell them. What if I miscarry? It could happen," she said, looking down at his chest, unable to meet his eyes as she said the words.

"Please don't wish that, Cass. I want you to carry this baby and deliver it when it's your time. If they love you as I do, and I know they do, they will accept and love the baby too. You don't know them very well, but they're the most accepting and loving people I know. I think you misjudge them. Just give them a chance, please. You don't need to worry so much about this. It will all work out as it was meant to be. You and I, starting a family together in love, is every reason to be happy. Just remember that." Ed took her gently in his arms and kissed her softly on the lips "Goodnight, my beautiful dreamer," he said as he released her.

"Goodnight, Ed, and thank you for everything. I love you," she said, a little breathless from his kiss.

He smiled as he walked to the door, took his hat and placed it on his head. "I'll see you in a few days. Tell them before then, please? I want to take you to the church dance on Saturday. Will you go with me?" he asked spontaneously.

"That sounds wonderful. All right, I'll see you in a few days then. Goodnight, my love," she said, repeating the sentiment.

Ed closed the door behind him and tipped his hat to Mabel and George. "Goodnight and thank you for the wonderful supper," he said and quickly added, "Oh, I asked Cassie to the church dance on Saturday, and she said she would go with me if that's ok with you. Until then!" he said, and briskly descended the porch steps.

"Goodnight, Sheriff!" George and Mabel said as Ed turned and walked to his horse, mounted and rode off down the lane in the dusky night.

Cassie came out and said goodnight to her aunt and uncle, kissing them each on the cheek, and retired to her room. Finally, alone, she thought about all that had happened that day. She was bubbling over with excitement as she sat down at her dressing table and wrote two letters. The first one was quickly written to Bart.

June 20, 1869
Dear Bart

   I am sorry to tell you that I will not be returning to Missouri. I have no desire to marry a man

I do not love. Please move on with your life and find someone more to your fitting.
Sincerely,
Cassie

Her next letter was to Madeline.

June 20, 1869
Dearest Madeline,

I have exciting news. I'm engaged! Well, officially no one knows but Ed and me. He asked me to marry him today after I told him about everything that had happened during the attack. I even told him the most shocking news. I'm pregnant. It came as a shock to me when I found out Saturday at the Doctor's office. As you know I have not been feeling well since the Indian attack. As it turns out there was a good reason why I have been feeling poorly. I will be having a baby in the end of January or first of February. I was devastated, and still am quite upset about being pregnant. But when I told Ed, he confessed his love for me, and told me he wants to marry me regardless. He wants to be a father to the baby and wants to be married soon. Possibly within weeks. I will have to tell my aunt and uncle soon. I dread having to disappoint and shame them. Ed says that if they love me as he does, they will accept me and the baby with love. I believe him when he says he will love me and the baby. I guess I should have faith that my aunt and uncle will too.

I'm going to go to the church dance on Saturday with Ed. He wants to ask Uncle George for my hand in marriage. I'm very happy. I love him. I never knew I could feel this way about someone. I think about him all the time. He says the sweetest things. He even kissed me. Now I'm feeling embarrassed, mentioning it. But I'm so excited I had to tell you.

I will write to you again soon, and let you know when the wedding is. Oh, my goodness, that sounds so wonderful! I'm getting married!

I hope you are all well there. Please write back soon.

Your Dearest Friend,
Cassie

Cassie sealed the letters, climbed into bed and blew out the lamp. She lay there awake, replaying all the words and feelings she had experienced that day, and said a silent prayer of thanks for the man that Ed was and for the miracle of love that was healing their broken hearts. She closed her eyes and fell into a peaceful sleep.

Chapter 9
Church Dance

The next few days passed quickly, with chores and a spontaneous trip into town on Tuesday to mail some letters and pick up supplies. Cassie had gone along, hoping to see Ed, but was disappointed. She was even bold enough to go to the sheriff's office and check if Ed was there. But Vic, the deputy, told her the sheriff was out of town for a few days, following up on one of the cases they were investigating, and should be back in a few days. Cassie left, feeling a little depressed. It was just a few days, she told herself, but in her heart, it seemed like a long time not to see Ed.

George and Mabel had waited for her in the rig outside the post office and met her to go inside together.

"Did you get to see him?" Mabel asked, but could tell by her expression she hadn't.

"No, he's out of town on a case. He'll be back in a few days," she said.

More disappointment followed with the news that no letters had come for Cassie yet. She hoped by the end of the week she would hear back from Madeline. Cassie handed the letters to the postmaster, one to Bart and one to Madeline. The Postmaster reassured her that they would get them by Thursday or Friday at the latest. She hoped after this letter she would no longer hear from Bart, putting that part of her life behind her for good.

176

Back home, Cassie tried to keep busy, but often found herself thinking of Ed, missing him more all the time. She continued to repeat his words in her head over and over. He'd said he loved me and wanted to marry me. Or was it just a dream? No, it was real. Her dreams had never been so amazing. More than ever she longed to hear him say her name again and tell her how much he missed her.

During the day there were plenty of chores to keep her mind occupied, but in the evenings, she found it harder not to miss Ed. Most evenings she spent time crocheting, making the blanket for the baby. As she crocheted, she began thinking of the coming infant. Would it be a girl or a boy? Would it look like her or would it look more Indian? It most certainly would be born with black hair. She guessed its skin wouldn't be completely white, more light brown or olive; possibly no one would ever guess that the baby was part Indian. Her cheekbones were high, and her skin an olive complexion; the baby would look like her, even if it had other Indian features. With the wedding being so soon, no one would even suspect it wasn't Ed's baby, she told herself. They would just think the baby had come early. As Cassie thought, she began to feel more accepting of the baby. She concluded that she would love the baby too. Just as Ed had said he would love the baby as his own. Being the oldest, she had loved helping take care of her baby brothers and sisters and loved babies in general. But this was now her baby, although it was going to be part Indian, she couldn't hold hatred against her baby for what the Indians did. This baby was completely innocent and pure, deserving all the love a mother and father could give it. Slowly, Cassie came to see that although the circumstances that had gotten her to this point were horrible, she could eventually find joy and happiness in spite of it. Or so she hoped. It was still hard to feel completely happy while being an unwed pregnant woman. She assumed that's why Ed had suggested getting married so fast.

Cassie still dreaded telling her aunt and uncle about the coming baby. Maybe it would be best to tell them on Sunday after church. Possibly, they would be feeling much more Christlike then. Hadn't Christ shown great compassion on the woman taken in sin? Besides, Saturday was the church dance, and she didn't want to spoil it for them. Yes, she would let them enjoy the church dance and tell them the next day. Then later, Ed could come over for supper and talk to Uncle George. There, she'd figured it all out. She couldn't wait to tell Ed her plan, hopefully on Thursday when he returned.

All day Thursday, Cassie kept watching for Ed to ride down the lane. Finally, she was rewarded for her efforts. He showed up a little after supper, dismounted and tied Major to the corral fence as she came out of the house. Ed turned and opened his arms to hug her as she ran across the yard to greet him.

"Oh Ed, I've missed you. You've been gone for so long, thank heavens you're back. I stopped in to see you at your office and your deputy said you'd be gone for a few days," she excitedly rambled on as she kept her arms wrapped around him, looking up into his happy face.

"I would've come out on Tuesday and told you I was leaving, but there just wasn't time. I had to go to Laramie to question witnesses about a theft here in Cheyenne. It turns out the stolen goods were taken to Laramie and sold. The two witnesses I interviewed will be coming here to testify against the thief when the circuit judge comes to town in a few weeks. It took some work to track them down, but it was worth it. Although, I missed you the whole time," he said tenderly as he squeezed her and kissed her on the forehead, aware that George and Mabel could be watching.

Cassie smiled lovingly up at him, pleased that he had missed her just as much as she had missed him. "There's so much I want to tell you!" Suddenly she couldn't wait to share with him everything she'd been thinking about and planning.

"Oh! What have you been doing while I've been away?" he cheerfully asked, releasing her from his embrace and placing his hand on her back, guiding her towards the porch. "Let's go sit down, and you can tell me all about it while I rest. I couldn't go another day without seeing you, so I've been riding all day to get back and I'm a little tuckered out," he said with a light chuckle. The fifty miles in the saddle had been arduous but his desire to see her had outweighed his discomfort. At last, he was where he wanted to be.

"Oh Ed!" Deep concern showed on her face as she stared up incredulously at him. She felt somehow responsible for his condition and chided herself inwardly for only thinking of herself, by willing him back. "Of course he's worn out after riding all day," she thought. "You should head straight home to get some rest," she said in a motherly voice, now seeing the exhaustion on his face.

"What? And deprive me from seeing you? Not a chance! And you can't tell me you wouldn't be disappointed had I not stopped by tonight," he said, trying to tease as he sat down heavily on the bench, leaning his back against the house.

"Oh, absolutely I would have been disappointed, but I would've understood. You have to take care of yourself, Ed. You look completely done in. Have you even had supper yet?" she asked with concern as she placed a hand on his arm.

"No, but I'm all right. I'm too tired to eat. You're all I need right now," he said, giving her a sweet smile and reaching his hand out to her.

"Come in the house and rest while I fix you some supper. You can close your eyes and relax while you wait," she insisted, taking his hand and pulling him up, guiding him into the house.

"Guess who came to visit!" announced Cassie as they entered, knowing full well they were aware of his arrival and had been polite enough to give them some time alone. "Ed just got back from Laramie, and I've offered to fix some supper for him."

"Good evening, Sheriff!" Mabel said, looking up from her book and smiling as she noticed Ed hanging up his hat.

"Hello Ed, good to see you back! Come on in and sit here and put your feet up," George said, motioning to the red velvet parlor chair and footstool. "Mabel and I were just doing some reading. Think we'll let you two catch up while we go sit out on the porch." He knew the two of them would have things to talk about. George said, "Come on, Mabel, let's give these young folks some privacy." George stood from his chair and took Mabel by the hand and helped her up.

"Glad you made it back safely. You two enjoy yourselves. Cassie will make sure you're taken care of. We'll catch up with you another time," Mabel said as she passed, patting Ed on the arm. "George wants to be alone with me," she teased, winking at Ed, laughing at her own joke.

"Thank you both, good to see you too," Ed responded with a slow smile. Reaching the sitting area, Ed sank into the cushioned chair and plopped his feet up on the stool. Groaning, he settled his aching back against the seat and closed his eyes, breathing out a sigh of relief.

"I'll just be a minute," Cassie said patting his shoulder, and he nodded slightly.

In the kitchen she rummaged around fixing him a sandwich with the left-over meat from supper, adding thick slices of cheese to the hefty slices of bread and butter. Filling a large glass of milk, she brought the plate of food out to Ed, only to discover he had drifted off into a sound sleep. Setting the food down on the side table, she sat across from him, watching him sleep. Studying his face, she noted his blond hair had been recently cut. His tanned rugged face, although thin, was defined by his straight nose, chiseled jaw and cleft chin. She admired his well-manicured mustache and full lips, thinking him very handsome. Relaxed as he was, he even appeared quite dashing. Cassie felt very lucky to have met and fallen in love with such a wonderful man, who also happened to be so good-looking. Cassie couldn't help herself; she reached out and placed her hand on top of his as it rested on the arm of the chair. She gently stroked the tan skin over his brawny hand. His strong but gentle hand remained relaxed as she traced the back and down each long finger.

Ed awoke and slowly opened his eyes as he felt Cassie's soft touch. He watched her as she studied his hand. He loved her delicate fingers stroking his sensitive skin and sat still, quietly watching. Grinning, he smoothly turned his hand over and grasped her hand in his.

Cassie looked up in surprise and smiled bashfully at him. She was caught. He held onto her hand and brought it slowly up to his lips and kissed it gently as her heart beat wildly, hardly able to catch her breath.

"Um, your supper's ready," she said self-consciously, nodding toward the plate of food on the table beside him.

"Hmm, oh. Yes, thank you for making me supper," he said, releasing her hand with another kiss, and winked. "You treat me like a king, and soon you will be my queen," he said smiling.

"Oh, Ed, you're so sweet, you make me blush with

your romantic words and kisses. It's no wonder I can't stop thinking about you," she said, feeling her cheeks color deeply.

Ed picked up the sandwich and took a mouthful. "Mmm, this is the best sandwich I have ever had, especially since it was made by my favorite gal."

"You tease. It's just a regular sandwich, made by a regular gal," she laughed.

"You're anything but regular, Cass. You're special in every way," he said, taking a long drink of milk.

"Oh Ed! Stop, you're going to make me blush again," she said, flushing a deeper red.

"Good, that's the way I like you best, rosy cheeks and sparkling eyes," he smiled again, taking another big bite. He paused as he chewed and swallowed, then continued, "My life's goal is to see you as my blushing bride!"

Cassie giggled. "Ed, you are adorable! Never change, all right?" she asked, loving him more and more all the time. Puzzling, she mused, "How did I get so lucky? I think you're the best thing to ever happen to me." Her heart swelled with gratitude and affection for him.

"And you are a gift straight from heaven! You healed up this broken heart without even trying. You are a miracle, Cass. A pure and simple miracle," he said, suddenly becoming very serious. He took her hand and gave it a sympathetic squeeze. "Have you told them yet?"

"No, not yet. But I have a plan. I'll tell them after church, on Sunday. Then you can come to supper and talk to Uncle George." Her face shined brightly with joy. Just thinking about it gave her goose bumps. "I can't believe we could be married in as short as a week or two. It's so exciting!"

"Yes, the sooner the better. I can't wait to be your husband," he said, kissing her fingers. "And the father of your

182

baby." He gave her hand another tender squeeze.

Cassie's face crimsoned and she smiled modestly. "Shh, not so loud, it's supposed to be a secret," she warned with a light laugh.

Ed laughed with her. Oh, how she filled his heart with joy, just to hear her bubbly laugh and see her eyes sparkle. He couldn't wait to make her his wife. Soon, very soon. He was even looking forward to the church dance that Saturday. The thought of holding and spinning Cass around the dance floor was enough to get his blood pumping.

"Shall I come and get you for the church dance or do you want to come into town with your aunt and uncle and meet me there? I will of course be your escort and make sure you have a wonderful time," he boasted with a broad grin.

"I can come into town with my aunt and uncle and you can meet me there. What time does it start?" she asked, suddenly thinking of a hundred things she would need to do to prepare for it.

"It starts at seven o'clock. I can meet you a few minutes before that, all right? I will walk you in, and we will dance the night away." Ed wanted to talk to her more but instead yawned as fatigue plagued him. "I really must get going home now, Cass. Thank you again for the delicious meal." He leaned forward and gently kissed her lips. "Goodnight, Cass, my beautiful dreamer." He stood up slowly, walked to the door and put on his Stetson, then turned back to wink at her as she stood to follow him.

"Goodnight, King Edward, my love!" She playfully grinned as he touched the brim of his hat.

"G'night, my fair maiden," he said in a deeply exaggerated drawl as he tipped his head.

Ed left, closing the door behind him, saying goodnight

to George and Mabel on the porch. He walked across the darkened yard, untied Major, climbed on and rode away.

Cassie lay back in the chair and closed her eyes. "How in the world is a girl supposed to sleep after that! My heart is pounding so hard I can hardly catch my breath," she thought in delight. Every second with Ed had been simply wonderful. And soon she would be his for always.

Saturday afternoon she took special care to bathe and wash her hair, fixing it into curls that spilled over her shoulders and down her back. Sitting at her dressing table, she placed two silver combs, one on each side, to hold some of the sable curls above her ears. Looking into the mirror she appreciated the finished results. Carefully she dressed in her ivory gown of lacey skirts and gathered hem held up in sections with small bows, showing off the layers of petticoats of ivory lace. The tiny waist of the fitted bodice was tied with a sage-green sash in the back. The neckline was cut in a slight v, with the sleeves off the shoulders, as was the latest style. Trimming the top edge was a wide ruffled lace that formed the sleeves of the gown. It was a gown she had never worn before and was thankful to Mrs. Smith, who had convinced her to purchase it. She twirled around in front of the mirror in her room to make sure everything was laying right. Finally, she took the matching shawl and wrapped it over her arms at the elbows and emerged from her room.

"Oh Cassie!" declared Aunt Mabel, dressed in her Sunday best. "You look so beautiful!"

"Thank you! I wasn't able to tie the bow very well. Will you do the honors?" Cassie turned her back toward her aunt.

Mabel was adjusting the bow as Uncle George came into the house, dressed in his Sunday suit. "Mercy me! You'll stop Ed in his tracks! Might even knock him out cold from just the sight of you," he said with a good-natured chuckle, feigning a blow to the face.

Both women laughed at his tomfoolery and Cassie thanked him for his compliment.

"Now, let's get this belle to the ball!" George's eyes twinkled with excitement. "Quick! Before the carriage turns back into a pumpkin!" he said, laughing even more as he came over and kissed Mabel on the cheek. "Mabel dear, you look beautiful, as usual."

Everyone loaded into the surrey to drive to town. Cassie threw a light blanket over her skirt to keep it clean and George drove slowly to avoid dusting their finest apparel. They arrived at the Town Hall where the dance was being held about ten minutes before seven. George tied up the horses and helped Mabel down and then Cassie.

"Cassie, we'll meet you inside. We need to help set up the punch and cookies before everyone arrives," said Aunt Mabel, as she had spotted Ed and knew he would be escorting Cassie in shortly.

Cassie straightened her dress and looked for Ed. Sure enough, there he was, standing on the steps of the Town Hall, looking right at her. His smile was one of pure delight. He was wearing his brown suit and white shirt with the black tie. He looked very charming. She waved and smiled back at him as he walked down the steps towards her.

"My, my, my, don't you look beautiful tonight!" exclaimed Ed as he approached her, shaking his head in dismay. "You get lovelier every time I see you," he said with delighted appraisal.

"Why, thank you, Ed." Cassie's cheeks blushed from the compliment he'd given her. "You look very dashing tonight as well!"

Ed offered his arm to her, "Shall we?" She wrapped

her arm though his, resting her hand on his arm.

"Yes, we shall," she answered, smiling up at him, feeling the heat rise in her cheeks. This was her first function with Ed as her escort and she knew all eyes would be on them as they entered.

Together they climbed the wide staircase to where a spacious room accommodated the band and hundreds of dancers. Ed and Cassie paused in the doorway, scanning the crowded hall for Uncle George and Aunt Mabel. They glanced around the room, where elegantly dressed men and women were chatting and laughing with old and new acquaintances. A group of people congregated near the back of the room around a long table filled with refreshments and a silver punch bowl. The tall windows had been thrown open to allow a cool breeze to blow through. The iron sconces on the white walls and the iron chandelier in the center of the room cast an amber glow across the polished floor as dusk approached. It was magical, as if they'd entered a fairytale-like castle ballroom.

Uncle George and Aunt Mabel were mingling with their friends when they, along with many others, saw them arrive. Ed and Cassie were clearly the most handsome couple there, perfectly complementing each other. Cassie's ivory dress flattered her petite hourglass figure and dark flowing hair, as she stood beside Ed's tall masculine frame in his chestnut brown suit and blond hair. Or maybe it was the way they were glowing as they looked lovingly at one another; anyone seeing them could tell they were in love.

Couples hurried to the dance floor as the band started playing the familiar jig, "Old Brown Jug." Jovial conversations and laughter of mingling friends gave the atmosphere a festive mood.

Ed smiled warmly at Cassie. "Would you care for a drink before we start dancing?" His mouth had gone dry the second he'd seen her standing outside. She was remarkable in every way and made his heart race.

"That sounds wonderful," Cassie said, feeling heated from the warmth of the room and all the eyes looking their way.

Ed led her through the finely dressed guests to the refreshment table, nodding and greeting people randomly. Ed was well-known and had many acquaintances but few close friends in town. Once Ed and Cassie made it to the refreshment table, he carefully ladled her a glass of fruit punch and handed it to her and then filled one for himself. Slowly they sipped the sugary concoction as they watched the other couples around the room. The church had done a good job announcing the event and it appeared to have brought out even those not of their fold.

As Cassie finished her punch, the first few chords of "Buffalo Gal" began and young men scrambled to find a partner.

Cassie's eyes lit up. "Oh, let's dance!" she exclaimed. "I do so love this song. Now more than ever since you played it for me!"

How could Ed resist her enthusiasm? "Then let's go, my 'Buffalo Gal'!" Taking her glass and setting it down, he led her to the dance floor. Ed took her by the hand and around the waist and began the two-step. Together, they practically leapt around the floor. Cassie was light on her feet as was Ed, and they pranced around the room like two antelope, bounding harmoniously between duos. They laughed, feeling the toe tapping beat flow through their bodies as they weaved in and out of the dancers.

"I want to make this gal my wife, gal my wife, gal my wife. I'd make her happy all her life, if she would marry me…" Ed sang, just loud enough so she could hear. It spread a huge smile on her face and made her laugh even more.

They joined the crowd in showing their approval of the band with hearty clapping and even some boisterous whistles from a rowdier bunch of gents in the back. Ed turned toward the noise, and with a steely glance from their sheriff, the boys settled and sheepishly tipped their heads towards him in acknowledgement of his unspoken words.

The next song, "I've Been Working on the Railroad," resounded through the hall. The slightly slower tune mellowed the more spirited men, but only by a measure. Pairs two-stepped to the beat as nearly everyone joined in singing.

Ed and Cassie were having a wonderful time dancing and singing among the energetic patrons. Then Ed began whistling the last chorus, causing Cassie to laugh in delight. By the end of the song, they were both shaking with laughter.

Cassie fanned herself with her hand, finding it hard to catch her breath. The exertion of dancing and laughter had her heart pounding. Many of the women in the stuffy room were using fans to cool themselves and Cassie wished she had one as well. The cool evening breeze did little to relieve the heat of many bodies crowding and dancing in the upstairs room. But Cassie and Ed danced on, not letting the warm summer day detour them from the opportunity of a good time.

The room calmed with the playing of "Yellow Rose of Texas" and then another two-step to the tune of "Big Rock Candy Mountain."

Cassie smiled as she held onto Ed's arm, grateful for the short pause before the band resumed. They followed others to the refreshment table and waited their turn for another drink. The punch and cookies refreshed them a little as they visited with George and Mabel and exchanged pleasantries with other familiar faces.

The next song was their song, "Beautiful Dreamer." Ed took Cassie into his arms again and waltzed with her around the floor. Softly he sang the desires of his heart to her. Cassie's emerald eyes stared up at him, sparkling in the lamp light as darkness descended. The soft melody transported them to a world all their own. Cassie's heart soared as Ed serenaded her whilst twirling and gliding her around the room.

Ed wanted to tell Cassie how much he loved her and never wanted to be apart from her. His emotions ran deeply with each word he sang. "Beautiful Dreamer, queen of my song, list while I woo thee, with soft melody…" He pulled her slightly closer, loving the feel of her moving with him as one. "Beautiful Dreamer awaken to me…." His voice held out the last note then leaned forward and whispered in her ear, "I love you, Cass!"

Cassie's breath caught in her throat at his words. She gave him a dreamy look as he straightened and took her hand.

"Let's go get some fresh air," Ed suggested with a squeeze of her fingers.

"Please," was all she could muster. Her head was spinning, and her heart was racing wildly.

They left the hall and walked out to the boardwalk along the street, away from the noise of the band. A slight breeze was blowing as they walked.

Cassie took a deep breath of the fresh air. "That was so much fun. I was starting to get dizzy." Using her hand, she fanned herself. "Maybe it was the heat, or maybe it was just you, taking my breath away!" she said with a small grin and sparkling eyes, as she teased him.

He smiled in response, pleased with the effect his words had had on her.

Becoming more serious, she reached her hand up to touch his cheek. "I can't wait to be your wife! It's all I think about, and all I want," she said lovingly as she gazed up into his eyes.

"Cass, you are my one and only desire!" Secluded by the darkness of the night on the boardwalk, Ed wrapped his arms around her waist and leaned down to kiss her tenderly on the lips.

"Cassie! Cassie!" a voice called out, "Cassie!"

Cassie pulled away and turned to see who was calling her name. A silhouette of a man ambled towards them. "Cassie?" the figure from the dark asked in confirmation.

"Yes?" she answered apprehensively, wondering who would be calling her name.

Ed stood beside her with his arm still around her waist. "Who wants to know?" Ed insisted. "Show yourself!"

Out of the shadows of the night the man stepped into view. "Cassie! I thought it was you! It's me, Bart!" he said with exhilaration on his face, until he saw the expression on Ed's. "Um, hello. I'm Bartholomew Clark. I'm a good friend of Cassie's, as a matter of fact we were even engaged," Bart said, reaching his hand out to Ed cautiously. "Nice to meet you."

"Sheriff Havoc," Ed said sternly, exaggerating the sheriff part, then gripped Bart's hand in a firm handshake. Ed immediately noted Bart's weaker handshake and released his hand quickly.

Bart was a little shocked as he registered Ed's title and that Cassie was with him. Bart had seen a beautiful girl in a white gown come out of the Town Hall, and then realized it was Cassie. She was being led down the walk toward the street with her arm through another man's. Bart rejoiced at having found her. Crossing the street to go to her, he'd almost stumbled when he witnessed them embrace and kiss. Bart never had the chance to kiss her while they were courting, and his face flushed with anger as Bart thought about it. Now even more, he was glad he'd added the part about being engaged.

Ed's face reddened, as realization sunk in. Cassie had been engaged to be married to this man. Ed looked at Cassie for some sort of explanation.

Cassie went white as a ghost. "Bart! What are you doing here? How…" The world began spinning and her eyes went black. Ed felt Cassie collapsing and his reflexes took over and caught her, sweeping her up into his strong arms in an instant, never letting her reach the ground. Cassie limp body weighed much less than her skirts, he guessed, as he gathered her up and let her head fall against his chest. He cradled her as he carried her to a long bench outside the Town Hall and set her on it, supporting her still.

Sitting beside her, he tried to wake her. "Cass! Cass! Come on, wake up, Cass!" Ed gently patted her cheek as her eyelids began to flutter, as she took a deep breath. The color began returning to her lips and cheeks as she opened her eyes. The dim light shone down on her, like an angel, just fallen from heaven. "Luckily, I caught the angel," he thought.

Dazed, she asked, "What happened?" Looking around, she blinked as she tried to focus her eyes. She registered the concern on Ed's face, and felt his strong arm supporting her as his other hand rested on her cheek. Straightening up, she smiled weakly at him as he steadied her.

"You fainted, darling. Are you all right?" Ed looked from Cassie with tenderness to Bart with scrutiny.

"Oh Cassie, I'm so sorry I scared you," Bart said apologetically. How could he have known she would react this way?

Cassie looked up at Bart where he stood behind Ed.

"Why is Bart here in Cheyenne? Why?" She couldn't find her voice as the questions filled her mind. "What will Ed think of me? How could he? He'll ruin everything!"

"Sheriff Havoc, was it? Can I talk to Cassie alone for a minute? I'd like to explain a few things to her in private," Bart asked kindly, feeling horrible for making her faint. Cassie had been ill when she left, maybe she still was. "I should have waited for her letter in response before I came," he thought as he chastised himself for being so foolish. Spontaneity was not in his nature, and this was exactly why. He may have blown his only chance with her now.

Ed was not about to let this stranger upset Cassie further, and was about to tell him to "go to hell." But luckily his manners were still intact. "It's not up to me," Ed said curtly. "It's up to Cass." He brushed a curl from her forehead. "Cass? I'll make him go away if you want me to," he said with determination in his voice.

"No, Ed. It's all right. Give me just a few minutes alone with him. He's fine. I was just surprised to see him here, that's all. Really, I'm feeling better now," Cassie said, trying to reassure him.

"All right, Cass. But I'll be standing right over there where I can see you. I'll give you two some time alone." Ed stood, straightening to his full height right in front of Bart, and glared at him. "I'll not have you upsetting her again," he threatened, and Bart nodded in agreement. Slowly Ed walked a little ways off toward the horses and wagons along the boardwalk and stopped within sight of the two, now sitting together on the bench. Ed's blood began to boil. "Who is this man? And what did he mean, 'engaged'? Why didn't she tell me? I can't believe she would keep this from me. Not after all we've shared with each other. Maybe I don't know her as well as I thought. There has to be an explanation, and it better be a good one!" he thought as he fumed.

As soon as Ed was out of earshot, Cassie started in with her questions, her temper flaring. She was humiliated and angry. "Bart! What in heaven's name are you doing here?" she asked in a biting tone. Based on the letter she'd gotten a few days earlier, she thought she knew the answer, but wanted to hear his explanation.

"Cassie, I'm sorry I surprised you like this. I wrote to you as soon as I'd realized what a mistake I'd made in letting you go. But I couldn't wait for your response." He looked down, studying his hands nervously, noting how unsettled he felt around her. With determination he pushed through his uneasiness to say what he'd come to say. "I, I decided to come here to talk to you in person. I want you to come back to Missouri with me and get married. I know you think you have to live with your aunt and uncle now that your family's gone, but there's another option."

Cassie's heart stabbed with pain at the mention of her family and swallowed back her tears.

"There's nothing here for you. I know you couldn't be happy in this awful place. Who could?" He looked around at the stark buildings and barren ground. "But you don't have to stay." He realized he was rambling. None of this was turning out how he'd planned. He paused, watching for a glimmer of hope, for some sign that she was interested. When she didn't reply right away, he pressed her further. "Please, come back and marry me."

Cassie's heart was still aching from his comment about her family and her mind took a moment to grasp what he was saying. But as her frustration with him grew, the ache gave way to her anger. "Look, Bart, I wrote you a letter days ago," she said sharply. "If you had stayed in Missouri, you'd have gotten my answer by now. I'm sorry you made the trip, but I am happy here." Taking a deep breath, she tried to soften her tone as she watched his crestfallen face. "I have a new life, and I'm planning to marry Ed…Sheriff Havoc," she said, looking over where Ed stood and smiled. "I really wish you had waited for my letter. I don't want to marry you, and I'm sorry you came all this way just to find that out," she said, gently putting a hand on his arm, hoping to ease his despondence.

Ed saw her gesture and stiffened, ready to make a move if Bart so much as moved to touch her.

Bart stared back at her in disbelief. "Are you seriously considering staying here, when you have the opportunity to come back with me? You'd be making a terrible mistake," his voice increasing in volume with his desperation. "I'm the best chance you have for a good life. Not here in this desolate town with this cowboy," he said with disgust, motioning towards Ed incredulously. "How can she turn me down, she's acting like a fool," he thought in frustration. "You don't understand, I went against my parents' wishes; used my own money to buy my ticket and just spent three days on a train to get here. Doesn't that mean anything to you?" he asked, getting a little frustrated. He'd only just arrived, left his bags at the hotel, and went looking for her right away. While inquiring about how to get to the Hartford ranch, a local boy informed him that they were most likely attending the church dance. Bart's hopes soared as he walked the blocks toward the Town Hall, imagining what it would be like to finally see her again. Would she gratefully thank him for coming to rescue her from her misery, possibly fall into his arms and kiss him? He'd hoped so.

"I'm so sorry, Bart, really I am. But I'm happy here, and I'm going to marry Ed. Please understand, I've moved on with my life. I don't ever want to go back, not with you or anyone else," she said with conviction.

"You're acting insane, you don't realize what you're saying, what you're giving up." The sparks in her wild eyes seemed to confirm what he had just accused her of. Bart put his hands up, softened his voice and tried to calm her. "Look, I can see you're upset and need some time to think about it. I'm staying at the Cheyenne Hotel for a few days and can come and see you tomorrow. We'll talk then." Bart planned to bring her back with him as his fiancé and wasn't going to let her get away so easily this time.

Her words had an edge of coolness, "No, Bart. My mind is made up. I don't need time to think, and I'm not going to sit here and listen to you tell me that I'm crazy and that I'm making a mistake. You're wrong! I'm as happy as I've ever been, and I'm in love with Ed, not you!" The words rang true as she said them. "I've never been in love with you. Now please go! Go back to Missouri, where you belong!" she said, now furious.

Bart stood abruptly, red-faced with humiliation and anger. "You will get what you deserve then, Cassie. Good luck with 'him'!" he said with sarcasm. "I hope it works out as well as you think it will!" he thundered as he stormed away. Unfortunately, the way out to the street meant walking past Ed. Bart brushed past him mumbling under his breath, "Good luck with her!"

Ed clearly heard what he'd said but didn't respond, instead he let him pass, tipping his hat as he hid the grin on his face. It was apparent that Bart was fuming mad from whatever Cassie had said and he decided not to provoke him further.

Ed walked back to Cassie and sat down beside her, noticing her rosy cheeks and clamped lips. "Are you ok?" he asked as he put his arm around her shoulders and pulled her to him.

195

Resting her head against his shoulder she let out a sigh. "Yes, I'm just angry. He had no right coming here. I would have told you, but Bart and I were only engaged a short time. I gave in to Bart's proposal after my father gave his consent, thinking it was an acceptable arrangement. I never loved him but thought that maybe with time I would grow fond of him. Two weeks after our engagement, was the Indian attack." She bit her lip as the familiar sadness tugged at her heart. "I didn't see him until weeks later at my family's funeral. He suggested we call off the engagement as I stood watching them bury my family. I was sad at first, that he didn't want me, thinking he must have known what had happened to me during the attack. So, I agreed to end the engagement. Now, I fully realize what a mistake it would have been," she said, calming. She had realized she yearned for something more than just an arrangement, she wanted love. Tenderly Cassie turned to face Ed and took his hands. "I would never have been happy with him, because you were meant for me." She looked deep into Ed's green eyes, her voice shaky with emotion. "I was supposed to fall in love with you, I know that. I've never felt love like this before, and it's all for you, Ed. And with all my heart, body and soul I feel your love for me, and it's the most glorious feeling in the world. I want to spend the rest of my life with you. Can you manage that?" she asked with a radiant smile and glistening eyes.

"Oh, Cass. It's my one desire above all else to have you in my life forever, and I will cherish you every day of my life," he said and took her face in his hands, leaned in and kissed her tenderly. Slowly, he pulled back. "I love you so much, Cass. I promise, if you will be my wife, I will make you happy all your life," he said, feeling his heartstrings being pulled as a joy-filled tear slipped from his eye.

"I know you will." Cassie wrapped her arms around his

neck and hugged him tightly as she whispered, "Ed, you're all I need…want…and love."

Ed held her close, breathing in her sweet scent, making a mental memory to cherish forever. "And you're all I need…want…and love, Cass," he whispered soulfully as his heart hammered in his chest.

"There you are!" exclaimed Uncle George, causing them to pull apart suddenly. "You've been gone so long that Mabel sent me to find you. She was worried something had happened to you, Cassie. But I see you're in good hands," said Uncle George, chuckling deep in his throat as they blushed.

"We were just about to come back inside," Cassie said, looking from Uncle George to Ed, smiling mischievously. "Weren't we, Ed?"

Ed grinned. "Yes, we were just saying, we should go back inside and dance a little longer before it's over."

"Then I'll see you inside," Uncle George said, turning to go back inside as he chuckled softly to himself.

Ed took Cassie's hand and helped her up, leading her back to the dance. The stuffy room took a minute to get used to again as they entered and followed Uncle George to where Aunt Mabel was waiting.

"Oh, Cassie dear. I was so worried. Are you all right?" she asked, taking Cassie's hands, and noted the color in her cheeks. "When I didn't see you dancing, I was sure you had gotten sick."

"I'm just fine, Aunt Mabel. I just needed some air," she said, fanning herself with her hand. "It was stifling in here, but I feel much better now."

Once they'd taken a few minutes to reassure Aunt Mabel that Cassie was all right, they took the dance floor again. But not without a warning from Aunt Mabel for Cassie to take it easy.

Cassie and Ed danced for the next hour or so, taking breaks to mingle and introduce Cassie to the townsfolk. Although Ed didn't like to draw attention to himself, he was a person that everyone liked. Everyone he called by name received a warm greeting along with questions about their family and how they were doing. As sheriff, Ed had made it his priority to know the people of his town. Cassie figured that keeping the peace meant there were those on the wrong side of the law who probably hated him.

As the night drifted on, the crowd diminished. Many people had to get home to feed their stock and others had a long ways to go. George and Mabel were helping clean up the table of refreshments, when a man came running into the hall looking for Sheriff Havoc. George pointed over to where Ed was standing next to Cassie.

The man rushed up to him. "Sheriff Havoc!" he said trying to catch his breath. "We need you to come to the Happy Day Saloon quick! There's a young man there causing problems. He's drunk and trying to start a fight with some of the local cowboys. They're giving him some of his own medicine, but he won't let up. He's some red-headed city boy and drunk as a skunk. I couldn't find Vic, so I came here looking for you. He's going to get hurt real bad if it comes to blows," he explained with urgency.

"Oh no! You don't suppose it's Bart, do you?" Cassie began to think this was all her fault. Bart wasn't one for drinking, but she knew people do crazy things when they're hurt and angry.

"I'd better go. Sorry, Cass, I'll see you tomorrow at church." Ed rushed out of the room, following the man.

"What was that all about?" asked Aunt Mabel as she came up to Cassie.

"I'll tell you on the way home," said Cassie. "It's a long story."

Chapter 10

Bart

Bart walked back towards his hotel in a rage. "How could she reject me?" he thought. Bart was used to getting what he wanted. He was well respected and came from money and a good family. "What more could she want? Any girl would be lucky to have me for a husband." But Bart didn't want any girl. He wanted Cassie. Passing the noisy saloons, Bart found himself impulsively deciding to go into one. "What does she see in this God-forsaken place?" Standing in the doorway, Bart let his eyes adjust to the hazy, smoke-filled saloon. In the center of the musty room was a table of rowdy cowboys playing cards, cheered on by several scantily clad saloon girls, shamelessly flirting with the men while serving glasses brimming with golden brown liquid. "These cowboys and dirt farmers are all roughnecks! Not a civilized person here!" Bart thought in his anger as he approached the bar.

"What'll ya' have?" asked the bartender, busy drying shot glasses behind the counter lined with various sized bottles.

Bart didn't know what to order; he'd never been in a saloon before. "Give me whatever you got!" he growled at the bartender.

The sweaty potbellied man filled him a mug from a keg against the back wall and slid it to him. The foam sloshed onto the smooth counter as Bart pulled a coin out of his pocket and slapped it onto the bar. Grabbing his drink and still raging, he walked to an empty table in a dark corner of the saloon. Guzzling the first drink, he returned to the bar and ordered another. A heavily rouged blonde woman brought his next two drinks to the table, each time being sure to lean down provocatively as she placed the drinks in front of him. Bart ignored her obvious advances while tossing a coin on the table.

The wench winked at him. "You just let me know if you need anything else, honey." She sauntered away to serve her next prospect, who openly welcomed her brazen advances.

Bart replayed Cassie's words in his mind as he sat drinking alone at the edge of the crowd. The more he drank, the less his heart ached, and the angrier he became.

The cowboys playing poker at a nearby table whooped and hollered as the man wearing the blue bandana won the pot. The winner gleefully pulled the piles of coins and cash toward his side of the table as the loser threw down his last two cards. Exuberantly the men slapped the lucky player on the back as they chanted for the victor to buy a round of drinks in celebration. "Drinks for me and my friends!" the victor shouted, waving a few bills from the pile in the air.

Bart was in no mood for such ruckus. He looked up and hollered, "Hey! Keep it down, you bunch of redneck hillbillies!"

"Who you callin' red? Red!" replied one of the men at the poker table as the other men from surrounding tables laughed.

The "red" comment didn't go over well as Bart was very sensitive about his red hair. Drunk, angry and now insulted, Bart's face flamed with rage as shouted above the laughter. "You bunch of Mary's, that's who! You all smell like you've been sleeping with the…cows." Bart had never been so blatantly rude, but then again, he'd never been this mad or drunk before.

The players laughed and returned to drinking their beer. It was late, and everyone was feeling tired after their long day of work on the local ranches. That is, all but one.

That one, was the spunky blond-haired wrangler who was known for letting his mouth run ahead of his better judgement. "Keep your opinions to yourself, city boy. You wouldn't know a hard day's work if it kicked you in the ass. Then again, it's hard to kick yourself in the ass when you are one!"

This time the men kept their heads down allowing their hats to cover their amused expressions as they snickered. The room of onlookers watched to see what would happen next.

"Come on over here and let me show you how hard I can kick your ass!" yelled Bart, eager to release his anger on someone.

"Man, I don't think you want to find out what it feels like to hit the floor flat on your back. But I'm willing to make it happen if that's what you want," he challenged as he kicked his chair back with a loud scraping sound and stood up, adjusting his hat and planting his feet wide apart with his chin jutted out stubbornly.

Bart rose to his feet with difficulty as he felt the room tip a little. "You talk big for a little fellow!" Bart said, towering over the cowboy's short stocky build. "You think your cowboy hat makes you look bigger and tougher, huh? It doesn't! You're still a short piece of cow crap," provoked Bart, wanting a fight.

That was all it took to set off the short, tough-talking cowboy. "You're asking for it now. It's about time someone took you down a notch. And it's my pleasure to do it!"

"Now boys!" shouted the bartender. "This has gone far enough! If you're gonna fight, then take it outside! Or I'm gonna get the sheriff!"

Glaring fiercely at the bartender, Bart hissed, "OH! By all means, get the sheriff! I would love to meet the sheriff!" his voice thick with sarcasm. "Again!"

The bartender turned to a man sitting close by. "Run and get the sheriff. Check the jail, and if he's not there you'll find him at the dance."

The young man grabbed his hat and took off.

"There, he's gone for the sheriff. So, you'd better cool down and leave on your own accord, while you still can!" the bartender warned, trying to stall the fight.

"I'm not goin' anywhere until I've had my say!" Bart slurred as he swayed a little. "This little cowpie was thinkin' he could take me on. I'd like to see him try!" Bart challenged.

The agitated cowboy lunged towards Bart, taking the first swing. Bart was an experienced fighter and dodged the first swing but caught the second one square in the gut, throwing him back a few steps. Being drunk was not in his favor. Bart gasped as the wind was knocked out of him. He resisted the urge to vomit while the cowboy chuckled.

"See? Thought you could get the better of me. You've got no idea who you're dealing with, Mister," the cowboy declared as he turned to walk away, feeling the fight had been won.

Bart's anger compounded. He was not about to be beaten by a short hick, cow-smelling cowhand. Rushing forward, he hit the cowboy in the back of the head with a hard-right hook. The cowboy stumbled forward, catching himself against a table. Men scooted back away from the fight, not wanting to get in the middle of it.

"Get him, Clancy!" someone shouted.

Clancy's head was now throbbing as he blinked the stars out of his eyes. He turned around, his eyes blazing. Clancy was going to show this red-headed city slicker what it was like to come toe to toe with a work-hardened stockman.

Clancy charged forward, ramming Bart in the stomach with his rock-hard shoulder, plowing him back and sending them both to the floor. Bart hit the floor hard, his back pinned flat against the filthy floorboards with Clancy's thick hands pushing against his shoulders. Using his long arms to hold Clancy back, Bart was able to keep from getting hit in the face, but his ribs took a few solid blows. Bart pulled up his legs and pushed with all his might, bucking Clancy over his head. Clancy lay stunned by the throw but only for a second before he sprang to his feet. Bart was a bit slower at getting off the ground and took another hit as Clancy charged him again. Bart swung his fists trying to beat him off as Clancy made contact with Bart's face.

"That's enough!" Sheriff Havoc's deep bass voice boomed as he walked through the door. "Break it up, you two, before someone gets seriously hurt!" Sheriff Havoc rushed over and pulled Clancy up by the back of the shirt and threw him off Bart.

"He started it!" shouted Clancy. "He was askin' for it! Kept eggin' us on. I was just defending myself, and my buddies here!" Clancy jerked his head toward his friends. Clancy's temper had gotten the best of him again and now he was faced with spending time in jail. He couldn't afford to spend time in a jail cell. Work started early in the morning, and he didn't want to lose his job. "Please, Sheriff! This guy comes in here and picks a fight with me for no good reason," Clancy pleaded.

"I understand. Let's talk about this in my office so we can get to the bottom of it," Sheriff Havoc said, extending his hand to help Bart off the floor.

"No thanks!" seethed Bart. "I don't need your help!" Resenting the man who was now trying to help him up off the floor, Bart refused the gesture and teetered as he pushed himself to his feet and dusted off his clothes as he replaced his hat.

"Come on, let's go." Sheriff Havoc took Clancy and Bart by the arm and forcefully led them out of the saloon. Clancy and Bart knew better then to resist and allowed themselves to be roughly taken outside. Ed seeing no sense in further force once outside, released them and herded them towards the jail, staying close enough to make sure they didn't start fighting again.

A few blocks down the road, suddenly Bart leaned over a railing and vomited. Patiently, Clancy and Sheriff Havoc waited for Bart until he stood upright.

Clancy gingerly rubbed the back of his head and licked his bloodied lip. Clancy's cheek was also swelling where he had either collided with the floor or Bart's fist. "Man, he has a good arm. Never woulda' guessed a city kid could fight like that. Especially a gangly redhead," Clancy thought and then fumed, thinking, "Jerk, I hope I don't lose my job because of him."

"Right here." Sheriff Havoc pointed to the jailhouse, and they let him pass to open the door. The young men followed him inside and stood silent as he lit a lamp, then each sat down in the two chairs opposite the desk at his gesture. "I don't want to assume I know what happened. So why don't I hear from each of you, and I'll decide what's to be done," he said, taking a seat behind his desk.

"My pals and I were minding our own business playing a good game of cards when this city slicker came in and started giving us lip. At first, we all laughed, and I gave it right back to him. Then he kept lipping off after we asked him to stop. Sheriff, it was like he was looking for a fight. He kept spurnin' me about my height and sayin' I smelled like cows. So, I showed him up close how I smelled." Clancy did his best to contain the smile that threatened to get him in further trouble. "Honest to goodness, Shcriff, he wouldn't stop harassing me," Clancy's voice became serious and his eyes pleading. "I can't get locked up. I got a good job and I need to be there before sunup. Please Sheriff, it wasn't my fault, if he hadn't come into the bar this would have never happened!" Clancy said, pointing at Bart.

Sheriff Havoc knew Clancy well. He was a local cowboy, hard-working, although a misguided young man known for fighting. But Sheriff Havoc knew Clancy wasn't dangerous, he was just a guy with something to prove all the time. Sheriff Havoc could see what had happened but wanted to be fair. "OK, Bart. Let's hear it. What happened?"

Bart didn't feel like engaging his rival. "Like he said. I was asking for it. I wanted a fight, and he was available. End of story," Bart said bluntly while avoiding looking at the sheriff. Bart despised Sheriff Havoc for taking away his last chance with Cassie. It irked him to no end, that he also just-so-happened to be the local law. All Bart wanted was to do was get out of this horrible place as soon as possible.

"Hmm, I think I understand. So, you decided to harass the local boys. Bart, you really know how to pick 'em," he said, trying to keep a straight face. "He literally picked the most wonderful woman to pursue and the toughest fellows in town to pick a fight with," Ed thought amusingly. It was clear that Bart had left Cassie in a huff, then tried out the local drink, which led him to take out his anger on the first person that would fight back. Ed couldn't blame him, really. He'd have felt the same way if the boot had been on the other foot. He felt bad for Bart, but he couldn't let these young men think they could go around fighting. Suddenly Ed had a grand idea.

"Boys, you need time to cool off and sober up. I'm going to have to lock you up for the night. It's for your own good, Clancy. I'll let you out in time so you can get to work. The last thing this town needs is a man like you without work and too much time on your hands. 'Idleness is the devil's workshop.' Bart, in the morning you will leave on the first train back to where you came from. Understand?" Ed asked as he looked for confirmation.

"Yes sir," they said.

Sheriff Havoc stood and took the cell keys off a peg and unlocked a cell in the back corner. "All right, you two, in you go." There was only one cot in the cell. "Get cozy, you're going to be together all night. It's your choice to get along or not." The two young men slowly entered the cell and Sheriff Havoc shut the door and locked it behind them. "Goodnight, boys. See you in the morning. I trust the two of you will still be here when I get back." Sheriff Havoc went to his desk and penned a note to Vic, explaining why the boys were in jail, and that he would return in the morning to let them out. Leaving the lamp on, Sheriff Havoc closed the door, locking it behind him. Briskly he walked back to the Town Hall to get his horse and went to make sure that Cassie made it home safely. The moon was high in the sky, and the stars were bright, lighting the night.

In the distance, Ed spotted the Hartford surrey and galloped to meet up with them as they turned down the lane to their house. "Hello to the wagon!" he hollered from a little way back, not wanting to startle them.

Cassie had heard the horse coming down the road behind them and hoped it was Ed. And she wasn't disappointed. Her heart leapt when she heard Ed's familiar voice and turned to see him come up beside her.

206

Cassie's smile was Ed's reward for everything he had been through that night. The moonlight illuminated her face and the stars shone like diamonds in her eyes. She looked like an angel in her ivory dress with lace shawl over her bare shoulders, and her dark hair spilling down her back in long curls.

George smiled. "Well, hello, Sheriff! Nice of you to escort us home!"

"My pleasure," Ed said as he cleared his voice. "Umm George, I was actually wanting to say a proper goodnight to Cassie, if I may." Addressing Cassie, Ed quickly asked, "Cassie, would you walk with me? I have some things I'd like to talk to you about."

"I'd be happy to," Cassie said with a smile.

"Whoa!" Uncle George slowed the horses and stopped the surrey.

"Thank you, George, I'll see her the rest of the way." Ed jumped down from Major, holding the reins with one hand, and reached out to assist Cassie to step out of the surrey. "Good night, Mr. and Mrs. Hartford," Ed said, as they pulled away

Ed, still holding Cassie's hand, smiled down at her. "I couldn't wait to talk to you until tomorrow."

"I'm so glad! I didn't want the night to end, especially like that," Cassie said, squeezing his hand. "So, tell me what happened?"

They walked slowly hand in hand down the moonlit tree-lined lane, as Ed explained. "It was Bart; he went to a saloon and got drunk and picked a fight with one of the local cowboys."

Cassie looked up at him in dismay.

Before she could ask, Ed continued, "He's OK, I got there and broke up the fight before either one got hurt. The two of them are in a jail cell for the night cooling off.

I'll let them out in the morning. I'm sending Bart home on the next train."

"Then he's all right?" Cassie asked, feeling partly responsible.

"Nothing more than a bruised ego, and he had that before he got into the fight, Cass. He's fine. It's not your fault." Ed saw her look away sadly as she shivered. "Are you cold?"

"Just a little, but I'm almost home. I feel bad that Bart came all the way here for nothing. If Bart had waited for my letter, he would have known my feelings," Cassie said as Ed placed his jacket around her shoulders.

"Here, I can't have my favorite beauty catching a chill," he said, keeping his arm around her shoulders and pulling her close against his side. She fit perfectly under his arm. Cassie wrapped her arm around his waist and leaned her head into his shoulder.

Smiling up at him she whispered, "You always make me feel so safe, and beautiful, and loved. Ed, you're everything I've ever wanted. You know that? I couldn't have dreamed of a more perfect man than you," she said.

"Aww, Cass. I'm not perfect, I have my faults. I can't think of any right now, but I have them," he said with a light chuckle. Pausing, he turned towards her, taking her by the shoulders. "Cass, you are the most perfect person I know. I don't want anyone but you. You're a dream, and I never want to wake up." Placing his hands on her face, he gently guided her to his lips and kissed her sweetly. When he pulled away, they were both breathless and smiling. Carefully, he brushed a single curl off her shoulder. Oh, how he loved her.

Cassie felt warm all over. Her heart was drumming, and her knees felt weak. "I'd better get inside; they'll be getting worried," she said reluctantly. "I'll tell them tomorrow, you know, about the baby. Then you can come to dinner and find some time to talk to Uncle George. All right?" Her heart ached to be with him forever.

"Sure, but I want to get married next Saturday. Would that be all right with you?" Ed hoped he wasn't pushing too hard. But by his calculations, she would be over two months pregnant by then and he wanted everyone to believe he was the father.

"That would be perfect. I don't need anything fancy, just you and me. And Aunt Mabel and Uncle George. Oh yeah, and the preacher," she said with a chuckle. "Otherwise, I don't care about anything else." She smiled as excitement built inside her.

Ed walked with her the rest of the way up to the doorstep. "Goodnight, my beautiful dreamer, my one and only." Kissing her quickly, he left and climbed up on his horse.

"Goodnight, my Prince Edward!" she said, watching him ride away.

Cassie entered the house in a daze, practically floating off the ground. She said a quick goodnight to her aunt and uncle and went to her room.

"Tonight would have been the most magical night of my life if only Bart hadn't shown up. He should have waited for my letter. He almost ruined everything between Ed and me. It was clear that Ed wasn't happy finding out about me being engaged to Bart. How could I have overlooked telling him? Bart was in my past. A part of my life I wanted to forget. I can see how it must have looked to Ed. Oh, what a mess! And then to have Bart go and get into a fight. How could Bart behave like that? Just because he didn't get what he wanted. The audacity of him!" she thought in frustration.

Cassie hung up her gown and petticoats in the wardrobe, then slipped on her nightdress and sat at the dressing table to brush out her hair. As she braided her hair, she thought of the romantic way Ed had danced with her and kissed her outside the Town Hall. Looking into the mirror, she noticed her eyes were a brilliant green in the lamplight and sparkling with excitement and her cheeks were pink and flushed. She smiled; Ed had put that glow in her face. He was the reason for her happiness. There was a look of joy and peace where there had once been sadness and despair.

As she said her prayers, her heart softened, and she asked for a blessing on Bart, that he would find his own path to happiness. Then she prayed for strength to tell her aunt and uncle about the baby. She closed her prayers with gratitude for Edward and their love, as well as her aunt and uncle for their love and generosity. She slipped into bed, blew out the lamp and relaxed as her mind replayed the dance and the kiss they had shared. She fell asleep to "Beautiful Dreamer" playing in her head.

Ed smiled the whole ride home. It had been a beautiful night. He was sure Vic would be back at the jail soon and make sure the boys were watched. Ed hummed a little, then blurted out, "You know, Major, I'm the luckiest man alive. Can you believe it? Two perfect women in a lifetime." The horse whinnied in response and Ed continued. "They're both so different, and yet each unique and beautiful in their own way. I could never have imagined that someone as lovely as Cass could love me. I know you might not realize it, but Cass is an angel, an angel straight from heaven. She was falling and I caught her! I caught an angel, Major!" Ed said with a chuckle. The horse moved his ears back, listening, then whinnied again. "That's right Major, I'm going to marry an angel," Ed declared with a smile.

Ed got home and headed straight for bed. He had an early morning; he had to get Bart and Clancy out of jail before dawn.

***

Meanwhile, back at the jail cell, Bart and Clancy were sitting on opposite ends of a small cot in a stifling hot room. The tension was as thick as the air between them. Bart groaned, feeling sick all over; his face was throbbing, and his stomach was rolling. All he wanted to do was sleep. His eye was swelling shut and his jaw felt broken. Clancy was in no better shape. The back of his head had a huge lump on it giving him a splitting headache, and his lip was swollen to twice its normal size.

Finally, Clancy couldn't stand the silence any longer. "You know, you could have just minded your own business and we wouldn't be in this mess! It's all your fault. If I get fired because of you, I'll kick your ass all the way back to wherever you came from!" he declared in frustration.

"Not to worry. I'm leaving for Missouri as soon as I get out of this place. I have nothing to stay for now," Bart said with reproach.

"Why'd you come to Cheyenne, anyways?" Clancy asked, curiosity getting the better of him.

"Only a crazy person would come here on purpose. This is as close to hell as I ever want to get. I'm getting out of here as soon as I can." Bart shifted uncomfortably on the cot, trying to stay as far away from Clancy as possible.

"Spill the beans! Why did you come to 'hell' then?" Clancy asked impatiently.

"For a girl, stupid! Okay! For a girl!" Bart shouted in frustration.

"OH! Now, that makes a lot of sense!" Clancy slapped his thigh, pleased with the answer. "I'd go to hell and back for a beautiful girl too! Is she beautiful?"

"Of course, she's beautiful. No one would come here for anything less than a beautiful girl." Bart touched his jaw gingerly and winced. "Except maybe you! You're here for the cows! Stupid hick!" he spat bitterly.

Clancy ignored Bart's last comment and instead shot back his reasoning. "You're right! I came here for the cattle. I'm going to make enough money to buy me a ranch and become a wealthy cattle rancher. That way I can have my pick of the girls! You know, Cheyenne has ten men to every woman. You have to get ahead of the pack to get a good one. I've been all through the country, from Texas to Wyoming, and have seen quite a few beauties along the way. I would love to be married one day, but I have nothing to offer right now," he said dejectedly as he removed his hat and twisted the brim in his hands.

"Well, I have plenty to offer! My father owns the most successful mercantile in Jackson County, Missouri, and I'm going to take it over one day. I already have enough money set aside to buy any girl the best house in town," Bart said proudly. "But I only wanted Cassie. I had her, too! I proposed, and she accepted. We were going to be married next spring, but then some Indians attacked and killed her family. She was really beat up, and in shock for a long time. With all her family gone, she had to move here to live with her aunt and uncle." Bart didn't know why he was telling a stranger all this. But it didn't seem to matter anymore. He was leaving anyways.

"Wow! That's horrible!" Clancy stared at Bart in amazement. He'd heard similar stories about the Indians raiding and killing whole families. But to actually talk to someone who knew a survivor of an attack made it real. "The poor girl. Wow, her whole family wiped out! How did she manage to survive?" Clancy asked, becoming more interested in Bart's story.

"I don't really know all the details, but I heard that she was hiding in the outhouse when they came and was later found in the field behind the house, all beaten up and in shock. I never did get to really talk to her again after that. At the funeral, I did try to for a minute. But I'm terrible with words, and I didn't know what to say to her," Bart confessed.

"Hmm, you had plenty of good words to say tonight. Maybe it's just hard for you to talk to her," Clancy reasoned as he stood and paced the cell. His back was aching where he'd hit the floor.

"Yah, I'm better at talking to guys. Girls really get me tongue-tied, especially Cassie." Bart pulled his watch out of his vest pocket and checked the time. It wasn't even ten o'clock yet. He sighed deeply. It was going to be a long night.

"Wait! What's her name? Cassie? Do you mean George and Mabel Hartford's niece, Cassie?" Clancy wondered out loud.

Just then the door was being unlocked and in walked Vic. They sat wide-eyed watching the door open and a medium-sized man stepped through the threshold. His expression at seeing them was less than enthusiastic.

"Oh great, I get to babysit. I was hoping for a quiet night so I could catch up on some shut-eye," complained Deputy Vic as he ambled over to the desk and saw the note from Sheriff Havoc. "Ugh, you guys better be quiet so I can sleep, or I'll make sure you stay locked up another day," he said gruffly. He'd been in a bad mood most of the day; his first assignment hadn't been a pleasant one, following up on a fight between neighbors over water. Then he'd gotten summoned to check on a dead cow and ended up missing his supper; he was ready for the day to be over. He

213

placed his hat on the desk and went to the other cell, sat down, and took off his boots and lay back on the cot and was snoring within minutes.

"I guess that's Vic." Bart thumbed toward the other cell. "And yah, her name is Cassie. I'm not sure of their first names but I think their last name is Hartford." Bart glared at him with his one good eye. "What of it?" he asked peevishly.

"Wow! You really know how to pick 'em. She's gotta be the prettiest gal in Cheyenne. I saw her a few weeks ago at the church picnic, and she's somethin' else. With her long black hair and green eyes, she captured my attention, and that's not even mentioning her shapely figure," he said. "And she said 'yes' to marrying you?" he asked in astonishment. "No wonder you came after her, I would have never let her out of my sight." Clancy sat back on the cot and pulled up his leg to rest his elbow on it.

"Yah, that was my first mistake. I should have asked her if we could move up the date. Instead, I gave her the option to break off the engagement. I took the coward's way out and gave her an open door, and she took it. I regretted my decision almost immediately," he said sadly.

"You sure did mess up. Cassie's seeing the sheriff now, on a regular basis, and that's saying something since he has never taken a shinin' to any girl. And he's had plenty of opportunities, let me tell you. Sorry to say, he found your shiny lost penny and picked it up," Clancy said matter-of-factly, not meaning to be rude. "Your loss."

"You don't think I know that!" Bart whispered angrily, slightly louder than he intended, and Vic grunted and turned over.

"Shhh!" hissed Clancy. "I just meant, it's too late now. She's taken, by none other than the honorable Sheriff Havoc." He raised his eyebrows as he glanced over at Vic

214

and whispered, "Even those of us who've gotten on his bad side think he's more than fair. He's been the most eligible bachelor for over two years, and not one single girl was able to keep him interested." He shook his head slowly. "And then, Cassie shows up, looking so harmless and innocent. We all watched it happen that day at the church picnic. Once he made his move, the rest of us fellows realized we had lost our chance. Sorry to say, those are the breaks," Clancy tried to explain.

"Yeah, well, I saw her first. It took all I had to ask her out for a buggy ride. My tongue was always tied around her, and when it wasn't, I just rambled on and on, trying to sound interesting. I could tell she wasn't that interested in me. But I figured she would get to know me and come to love me like I loved her. There's no other girl compared to her. At first when I asked her to marry me, she wasn't sure. But in time she did say yes. And then the Indians attacked her and her family and everything changed."

"Wow, I really do feel sorry for you. I thought I had it hard. All through school I was too shy to talk to the girls, being short and all. I didn't think any girl would want to be with a guy like me. Being here in the West, driving cattle, gave me a sense of pride. I ain't so shy any more, and I feel like I'm not as short as I used to be. And then you come along and bring back all those old feelings again," said Clancy.

"Yeah, you are hard as nails. I'm not usually so easily taken down. But then again, I've never been drunk before." Bart ran his fingers through his shock of curly red hair as he thought back to his younger years. "When I was in school the kids used to tease me because of my red hair. It really got to me. Once I figured out no one else was going to stand up for me, I decided I had to. I wasn't good with words and witty come backs, but I was good with my fists. That didn't do me any good with the girls as far as I know. Eventually I became known as the hot-headed red head with a mean right hook." Bart rubbed his fist where the knuckles were red and swollen. "Kind of like tonight," Bart said, chuckling a little.

Vic coughed, grunted, and turned over in a huff. "Hey, you guys, shut up," he said sleepily.

They sat quietly for a few minutes until they heard his breathing change and knew he was asleep again.

"Well, now I can understand why you were looking for a fight. I would've acted the same way if I'd come all the way to the middle of nowhere for my gal, only to find out she's with another guy when I got there. And come to find out the other guy just happened to be the sheriff. Not like you can hit the sheriff," Clancy said, chuckling quietly. "Life just isn't fair, is it?"

"It never is." Bart looked away, feeling his throat tighten with emotion. All his hopes and dreams had been crushed in one blow. "I tried to talk some sense into Cassie tonight. But now I realize she really did look happy when I saw her coming out of the Town Hall. I watched them hug and then kiss. Oh man, that about killed me," Bart said with a pang in his heart. "All I wanted to do was run up to the guy and punch him in the face for touching her. But when I went up to them, and saw her up close, she acted as if she'd seen a ghost. That's about the time he introduced himself as the sheriff and she fainted. I feel terrible for frightening her so badly. When she finally came to, Sheriff Havoc gave me a chance to talk to her and I tried to convince her to come back with me and told her we'd get married right away. Unfortunately, I was too late. She was pretty adamant that she was staying here and going to marry the sheriff," Bart explained with bitterness.

"Wow, she said that!" Clancy mused, "So, the rumors

are true. I heard that they looked like they were getting pretty friendly with each other, but that's news!" Clancy couldn't wait to tell all his friends.

Vic grunted again, turned over and resumed snoring after a spell.

"Yeah, she said she loved him, and he loved her and that was all she ever wanted. Good grief, I thought she understood how I felt. If that's all she wanted, I would have told her. That is, if I could have gotten the words out," Bart said, staring through the bars of the cell.

"I get it. I'm the same way. But that seems to be what the girls like; to be told they're pretty and how much you love them. At least that's what I hear. I tell you, if I get the chance, I'll tell the next pretty girl I see, that she's beautiful, and that I love her, and see how it works out." Laughing in spite of himself he continued, "At this point, what do I have to lose?"

Bart couldn't help but laugh as he imagined a short cowboy going up to a pretty girl and saying, "Hey, you sure are pretty. I love you. Want to get married?" Bart tried to keep quiet as he laughed, then moaned as pain shot through his bruised and swollen face. He stifled his laughter as he spoke. "I would love to see you try! And if it works, I'll do the same."

Clancy thought about it and realized it would sound pretty funny as an opening line and started laughing too. Laughing seemed to make his head hurt worse, but he couldn't help it.

"You know, you aren't such a bad guy after all," Clancy said. "You really are a good fighter, even drunk. I would hate to go up against you sober," he said, rubbing the back of his head. Even his knuckles were bruising and swelling.

"You aren't so bad either. I am sorry I said all those things. I'm not usually rude. I was just mad, and that wasn't your fault," Bart said sincerely.

"Hey, no hard feelings, really. I don't mind a good fist fight once in a while. Keeps me sane," Clancy said, grinning the best he could with a fat lip.

Vic's head popped up. "Look fellows! I'm glad you're all kissin' and makin' up. But can you keep it down? Good grief!" Vic grumped as his head dropped heavily on the pillow, sending the two of them into hysterics.

They tried to stifle their laughter, but Bart was still a little drunk and couldn't stop, which made Clancy laugh even harder.

"Oh, for the love of all that is holy!" Vic grabbed the pillow and put it over his head in exasperation, sending them into a peal of laughter.

The two boys continued to whisper and laugh through most of the night, as they told stories and shared their views on life.

Just before dawn, Clancy had a great idea. "Hey, you know what? I have a cousin that lives here. She's a little older, twenty-one I think, but I know you'd like her." He rushed on, "She's a teacher here at the school. She reads a lot and is kind of shy, but once she warms up to you, you can't get her to stop talking. I think she's really smart, and funny in her own way. Her name is Bea. I could introduce you to her before you go home. Maybe you two would hit it off," he said excitedly.

"Well, I love to read, and I'm almost twenty-one. Is she cute?" asked Bart, becoming intrigued.

"Pretty Miss Bea. That's what her students call her." Clancy shrugged. "I think she is, but I'm her cousin, so I'm biased." He grinned. "You could always tell her, 'Hey, I think you're pretty. I love you. Let's get married.' Then see what happens!" he said roaring with laughter, joined immediately by Bart.

218

Vic had listened to the two young men go on like this all night like long lost friends. When Vic saw Sheriff Havoc, he was going to make him wish he'd never told him to stay the night with the two troublemakers.

Chapter 11
Secrets

At dawn, Sheriff Havoc arrived at the jail house to let the two young men out as promised. Both sat slumped and droopy eyed on the bunk, and the bruises and swelling were showing up clearly in the dim lamplight.

"Good morning. Who's ready to get out of here?" he asked cheerfully as he entered the jail house. Vic sat up and rubbed his bloodshot eyes.

"I am!" Vic snapped. "These two were chewing the fat all night. Couldn't get a wink of sleep." Vic thrust on his boots and left, grabbing his hat in a huff. "See you later," he said, thick with sarcasm.

"See ya," Sheriff Havoc said, avoiding further discussion as Vic slammed the door behind him. He shrugged and retrieved the cell keys and unlocked the cell. "Okay, you're free to go. And no more fighting," he said, unlocking the rusty iron door. "Bart, you find the next train leaving for Missouri. You hear?" Sheriff Havoc pulled on the heavy metal door, swinging it wide and stood back, letting them pass.

"Sure," Bart said as he shuffled sleepily out of the cell, pulling on his suit coat, followed closely by Clancy. "Hey, Clancy! Can I buy you a cup of coffee before you head to work?" Bart cordially asked as he ran his fingers through his hair and put on his hat.

"You bet! I'd appreciate that. There's a place on the corner that serves coffee that'll put hair on your chest," Clancy said, slapping Bart agreeably on the back as he opened the front door and breathed in the crisp morning air.

Sheriff Havoc shook his head. "What in the world happened last night?" he wondered as they left.

"Hey Clancy, hold up! Give me a minute; I need to say something to the sheriff." Bart turned back and reentered the jail house. "Look, I'm still pretty mad at the fact that Cassie doesn't want me and she wants you." Bart shook his head in disbelief. "I don't get it, but if that's what she wants, there's nothing more I can do. Her mind is made up." Bart kept his eyes level with Sheriff Havoc's. "I messed up and missed my chance with her. Let me get one thing straight," Bart pointed his finger as he spoke with force, "you better treat her right. Cassie's a very special girl and I hope you realize what you've got and don't spoil it. I do want what's best for her…whatever that may be. I wish I had been able to tell her myself, but maybe you can tell her for me. I don't want her to feel bad. It's my fault, I never gave her a chance to tell me how she really felt. I just assumed that she would be happy and grow to love me. But you'll not get any more grief from me. I'll leave her alone." Bart looked at the floor and cleared his throat, carefully touching his swollen eye. "And thanks for not hitting me, I would have deserved it after the way I've behaved. You're clearly a better man than me." He looked up and reached his hand out towards the sheriff.

Sheriff Havoc was dumbfounded. Was this the same guy from last night? He'd wrongly judged this young man. Bart didn't seem all bad. Ed reached out and firmly shook Bart's hand, noting a stronger grip this time. "Hey, no hard feelings. All right? I understand. Stay in town for a day or two and have a good time, but no more fighting." Ed casually placed his hands in his pants pockets as his moustache

221

raised at the corners. "And I'll tell her what you said. Now get going, before I change my mind," he said, waving him off.

"Thanks! Maybe I will stay a day or two. You know, Clancy's a nice guy. We actually have a lot in common. I may do some looking around and see what Cassie likes so much about this place. Maybe even find me a girl of my own," Bart said, and went to join Clancy.

Sheriff Havoc scratched the back of his head, still amazed by the change. Cassie would be relieved to know Bart was doing fine.

Ed had some things to work out before he went to dinner at the Hartford's. He locked up, leaving a note on the door, and took a ride out of town to a friend's home. There wasn't much time before he had to be back for church.

***

Cassie woke a little before sunrise, turned over and reached for the biscuit on the bedside table that Aunt Mabel had placed. Eating slowly, she yawned and stretched as a feeling of dread settled over her. Cassie knew today she would have an unwanted conversation with her aunt and uncle. For now, she would focus on the words Ed had said to her last night. She smiled, hoping they would be publicly engaged by the end of the day. No more secrets.

Cassie was deeply in thought as she helped cook breakfast, feeling her anxiety and apprehension build. Uncle George came in from chores and sat at the kitchen table, opened the Bible and began reading silently as Cassie and Aunt Mabel plated breakfast.

"I asked Ed to supper tonight," Cassie blurted out as she brought over the plate of fluffy pancakes and strawberry preserves. "I hope you don't mind." Her hands were shaking as she set the pancakes down, waiting for their response.

"We're always happy to have Sheriff Havoc to supper," Aunt Mabel said as she carried the pan of fried eggs to the table, giving George a knowing look.

Cassie took a deep breath and rushed on, "Uncle George, Ed says he would like to talk to you later, and I have something I need to discuss with you both before he comes." She sat down before her shaky knees gave way.

"What is it, dear?" Aunt Mabel asked as she took her place beside Uncle George. "We've got time right now, don't we George?"

He closed the Bible and looked at Cassie. "Now is a very good time, Cassie. What's bothering you?" he asked sincerely.

"Well, it's very hard to say, but it has to do with why I have been so sick but should resolve in seven or eight months. It all started when…I…was taken…" her words trailed off, unable to continue as tears began rolling down her flushed cheeks.

Aunt Mabel arose and came to stand beside Cassie, putting her arm over her shoulders. Cassie impulsively wrapped her arms around Aunt Mabel's waist and laid her head on her aunt's chest and released the pent-up tears she'd been holding back.

"Cassie, my dear, we already guessed as much. I've been through many pregnancies, although never to full term, and I recognized the symptoms almost immediately. There's no need to feel ashamed. We know none of this was your fault. We want you to know we love you and will love the baby. Our hearts ache to think about all you've been through. But we're here for you now, and you don't need to suffer alone any longer." Aunt Mabel soothed

223

Cassie with her words and motherly touch.

Uncle George reached over and patted Cassie's hand, feeling a tightness in his throat. "We love you as our daughter, Cassie, and will love the baby as our own grandchild. You won't want for anything, and neither will your baby." Uncle George swept away a stray tear and cleared his throat. "We're glad you finally told us. We trusted you would when you were ready," he said understandingly.

Cassie lifted her head and sniffed. "What? They knew?" she thought in surprise and looked into her aunt's love-filled face. "You knew? I thought you would be ashamed of me and the situation I'd put you in." Frowning, she looked away.

Aunt Mabel stroked Cassie's hair and lifted her chin to look into her eyes. "Cassie, we could never be ashamed of you. This isn't something you've done; it was something that was done to you." Smiling warmly, Aunt Mabel continued, "And we're so proud of how strong you've been through it all, trying to manage this all alone. But you don't need to, not anymore. No more secrets, all right?"

Cassie took a deep breath of relief and embraced her again. "I love you both so much. Thank you for taking me in and loving me." Cassie was now crying out of relief.

Aunt Mabel nestled and soothed Cassie once more. "We can't help you if you won't tell us what's going on, Cassie. So please, if you ever need help, please talk to us," she said, loving their sweet girl.

"Okay, I will. Thank you," Cassie said pulling away and drying her tears as she gave them both a small smile.

Uncle George breathed a sigh of relief. "Now, let's eat before this gets cold. Mabel, would you say the blessing, please?"

Aunt Mabel took her place across from Cassie and bowed her head and prayed over the meal and then petitioned the Lord on behalf of Cassie. "We ask a special blessing on Cassie and the baby, that they will both be healthy and strong. Also, Heavenly Father, we are so thankful for the blessing she and her coming baby are to us; please bring her peace…"

Cassie let tears roll down her cheeks as she felt the love from her family and her Father in Heaven fill her heart. As Aunt Mabel finished the prayer, Cassie quickly wiped her tears away and smiled as she passed the food to her uncle.

"So, I wonder what Sheriff Havoc wants to talk to me about tonight?" Uncle George mused with an impish grin on his face.

"I really couldn't say." Cassie's face had a grin as she concentrated on dishing up and eating her breakfast, hopefully letting the question die.

"Mabel, do you know what Sheriff Havoc might want to discuss with me tonight?" Uncle George asked, teasing Cassie as he sipped his steaming cup of coffee.

"Hmm, not the slightest idea. I guess we'll have to wait and see, won't we, Cassie?" Aunt Mabel asked with a wink.

"I guess so," Cassie said, and quickly took another bite and chewed slowly so she wouldn't have to say any more on the subject as she tried to keep the smile off her face.

***

After cleaning up breakfast, Cassie changed into her Sunday dress as Aunt Mabel put a roast in the oven.

"Sorry to keep you waiting, I'm ready to go now," said Aunt Mabel as she hurried down the steps in her freshly pressed Sunday dress.

"I'd wait for you for as long as it takes; you're worth it," George said, as he kissed Mabel on the cheek and helped her into the rig.

Cassie smiled at the show of affection her aunt and uncle displayed for one another after all these years.

Arriving to church a little early, Cassie looked around to see if Ed was there. Sure enough, Ed was waiting for them near the steps of the white-steepled building, smiling broadly as he walked toward them.

"Good morning, Cass! Morning, George and Mabel! It's a fine day we're having," he said in a jovial voice as he took Cassie's white gloved hand and helped her down, admiring her soft flowing curls and flattering lavender dress, but most of all, her warm smile, just for him.

"Good morning, Sheriff! Yes, it is!" George said, smiling broadly as he thought of the evening ahead.

The worship service opened with an uplifting hymn sung by the congregation, accompanied by the deep rich sounds of the pipe organ. The invocation and inspirational sermon by Reverend Gather left them with a renewed conviction to do better. Cassie felt there was nothing quite like joining together with other believers each week to be reminded of what was important in life, and filling her with a bit more peace than when she entered. Recently she especially enjoyed services because she was sitting beside Ed, who placed his hand over hers and kept it there through the service, sending subtle messages with a gentle squeeze.

At the end of the service, Aunt Mabel and Cassie waited outside by the surrey, smiling and waving to friends and members of their church as they passed by, going to their rigs or walking back home as Ed and Uncle George walked slowly towards them.

Now alone with George, Ed cleared his throat. "Sir, I was wondering if I could speak to you tonight?" Ed felt very formal suddenly.

"That would be just fine. Come on out around six

o'clock, and we can talk before supper." George joined Mabel at the rig and winked at her as she smiled.

Cassie took the hand Ed offered her as she stepped into the surrey. "I'll see you later then," she said and then leaned in and whispered, "Good luck."

"Thanks," he whispered. Ed stepped back and waved goodbye as they drove off.

***

Ed returned to his room at the Railroad Boarding House, where he'd lived for the past two years. The boarding house was home to employees of the Union Pacific railroad, cooks and waitresses at the eating house, the ticket clerks, engineers, and conductors, as well as maintenance workers, and a few civil servants like himself. It was a great place for a bachelor; his meals were provided for by the county, if he wanted to eat at the boarding house. His laundry was sent out. And for the most part, all he needed was his bed, clothing, and a few belongings to survive. Even his horse boarded free at the local livery stables, one of the perks of being the sheriff. The boarding house had been a comfortable home for a single man who was rarely home. But in less than a week he was going to be married, and he needed a perfect home for his new bride.

The man Ed had just gone to see before church was a big part of his plan.

The afternoon flew by as Ed was busy making preparations. He called on his numerous friends in the community, calling in favors, but careful not to give away his secret. Many people in town felt a debt of gratitude and were more than happy to help out. After all, Ed had cleaned up the town and continued to keep them safe. They would do anything to help Sheriff Havoc.

As Ed rode out to the Hartford's, his heart was pounding recklessly and his hands were sweating. He would've felt more comfortable going up against a gunman than having to talk to George about his deepest feelings for Cass. More important than his discomfort, he felt it was the right thing to do. He wanted only the best for his Cass and that included the blessing from her uncle.

Ed arrived and knocked on the door. It seemed odd; usually they came out to greet him, long before he ever reached the steps. Everything about today felt very formal, as it should be, he figured. Friends or not, George was now seen as Cassie's father and showing him respect by asking him for her hand in marriage was proper.

The door opened; there stood Cassie with a bright smile, dressed in a simple blue flowered dress with a white lace collar and white pinafore. Her hair was twisted up into a knot held with pins and two combs at the sides. He'd never noticed how thin and pretty her neck was before. She usually wore her hair in a long braid or held partly back with a ribbon, the rest loose, tumbling over her shoulders. Pulled up this way made her look more mature, and elegant. His heart began beating even faster. "Hello, Cass!" His voice came out a little scratchy, his throat suddenly dry as a desert.

"Good evening, Ed, won't you come in?" Cassie asked as he stepped in and took off his hat, hanging it on a peg by the door.

"Hello, Sheriff Havoc. Good to see you this evening." Mabel looked up from her cooking, quickly drying her hands. "Glad you could join us for supper," she said, coming to shake his hand, as if he'd never eaten with them before.

"Thank you for having me." He looked around the

room for George. "Is George, er, Mr. Hartford here?" Ed asked nervously.

Aunt Mabel and Cassie tried to hold a straight face as Mabel directed him. "He said you could go out to the barn and talk with him there," she said, returning to her supper preparations. "And don't be too long, supper will be done in thirty minutes."

"I won't be long," Ed replied as he left the house. "Heaven sakes, I'll be as quick as possible. This is too nerve wracking."

Ed entered the barn to find George repairing a harness as he sat at his work bench. George turned. "Sheriff Havoc, good to see you tonight. What is it you wanted to talk to me about?" asked George as he left his work.

"Sir, I was wanting to talk to you about Cass." Ed shoved his sweating hands into his pants pockets and rushed on. "You see, I've been spending a lot of time with her and have grown to feel for her a great deal." George wasn't making this easy, keeping his face expressionless, giving Ed no clue as to how his revelation was being received. "I know it seems fast. But, when you know, you know." Ed chuckled nervously, smiling as he continued, "I love her very much and want to spend the rest of my life with her. I want to make her happy. With your permission, I would like to marry her." Ed let out a deep breath, relieved to finally get it out.

George's face broke into a wide grin, and he walked forward, taking Ed's hand in a hearty handshake. "Ed, I would be honored to have you as part of our family. I know you'll take good care of Cassie. Mabel and I can see plainly that you love each other very much." He became serious and the smile left. "I assume you know everything about her?"

"Yes, I know," Ed answered with sadness.

"Is that going to be a problem for you?" George's question was one of great concern to him. "I want to make sure that you understand what you're getting yourself into," George said, hoping Ed had seriously considered the ramifications.

"Sir, Cass told me everything a week ago." Ed's voice softened as he looked away, trying to keep his feelings under control. "I know she's pregnant with the Indian's baby. I fully realize the baby will be half Indian. I assure you I'm going to love the baby as if it was my own," Ed said with conviction.

"That's easy to say now. But not so easy to do once the baby's here," George said, pressing the issue.

Ed walked over to an empty stall and rested his arms against the board as he thought of how he could help George understand.

George waited patiently for his reply and took his seat at the work bench.

Ed started slowly, "I want to share something with you that no one knows here in Cheyenne, except Cass." Ed adjusted his hat as he stared down at the fresh straw strewn in the stall. "And I want it kept that way. I'm telling you because I want you to understand where my convictions lie," he added, becoming very serious.

"Go on, you have my word," George promised, unsure of where this was going.

"When the war was over, I came home to Kansas and married my childhood sweetheart." He swallowed. It wasn't as easy to tell George as it had been Cassie.

George raised his eyebrows. He would have never guessed Ed had been married before.

"I happened to be the deputy at the time and had been dealing with the local Indians that had been harassing the townspeople. I had encouraged my wife, who was pregnant, to stay with my mother and sisters at night while I was out patrolling. But she was strong-willed and insisted she would be fine. One night, I was out arresting a horse thief when Indians raided our farm. When I returned home the next morning, my wife was close to death and losing the baby. She was only six months along. I went for the doctor, but it was already too late, the baby was still-born, and my wife died soon after. It was the worst day of my life. I loved my wife dearly, and my baby daughter." Brushing away a tear Ed continued, "I came here to escape the memories that haunted me there. I wanted to never love again. I didn't think I could, my heart was broken. I was bitter and angry. But over time, I quit blaming God and came to accept that my wife and daughter had moved on from this world, and I could go on living. I worked hard and used my desire to protect people to ease my guilt. But I didn't ever expect to love again. That is until I saw Cass; immediately I felt drawn to her. I felt like we were being pulled together, and now it has become even stronger." He turned around to face him. "George, I love her more than life itself, and want nothing more than to have her as my wife and the child as my own, no matter how it came about. My heart's one desire is to be there for them both, to protect and provide for them in all their needs and wants. Maybe it's because Cass and I have suffered great losses and found love, understanding and acceptance in each oth-er. Whatever the reasons, I love her and will love the baby. I tell you this in hopes you now understand why I feel so strongly about Cass." Ed fell silent, waiting for a response as his heart drummed away, strong and steady. He'd bared his soul and hoped it had been enough to convince George his intentions were honorable and worthy of Cassie's hand in marriage.

"Ed, I'm at a loss for words," George said, clearing

his throat as emotion bubbled up from his heart. "Son, if I may call you that? You are a wonderful man, and God has sent you here for a purpose. You are just what Cassie needs, and now I see she is exactly what you need. Mabel and I couldn't be happier. Welcome to the family!" George said as he walked forward and embraced Ed with a hearty hug. Ed felt a weight lift off his shoulders and a peace settle over him as his eyes began to water. In that moment he felt he was being hugged by his own father. When George released him, they both quickly wiped away tears and cleared their throats, smiling self-consciously. "Ed? Can I call you that now since you'll be part of the family?"

"Sure! George, just one more thing. We want to get married as soon as possible so the baby will appear to be mine. This coming Saturday to be exact. We know it's fast, but there's no time. Cassie's already two months along," Ed tried to explain.

"Oh, I see, and where do you plan to live, then? Have you thought of that? It doesn't leave any time to build a house," George asked, seriously concerned. These were things that needed to be looked into before they rushed into marriage. George had assumed they would wait until the baby was born.

"I've already purchased the Crowley ranch." Ed smiled triumphantly. "My friend, Mr. Crowley, has been trying to sell his place for a while. He's wanted to move to California to be with his daughter ever since his wife died. He told me today he would give me a fair price and we shook on it. It's only a mile north of here. I'm sure you're familiar with the place. There's a small home and good-sized barn and he wants to include his herd and livestock in the sale as well. I've decided to resign as the sheriff and begin ranching as soon as they find my replacement. It's something I've been thinking about long before I even met Cass. I want to do what I love, and that's living and working on my own ranch. It's been convenient living in the city these past two years, but it's not my first choice. I'm ready to live my life again as I've always wanted, with the woman I love. I want to make a home and provide for her from the land," Ed expressed with building excitement.

"Well, it sounds like you know what you're doing. I'll not stand in your way. We'll help you get settled as quickly as possible. It sounds like we have some work ahead of us to get everything ready by Saturday. Let's go in and break the good news to the ladies." George put his arm around Ed's shoulder and together the two tall men, one young and one older, proudly walked towards the women they loved.

Straight faced, the two men entered the house as Mabel and Cassie looked on, waiting with anticipation for a hint of news.

Ed smiled at Cassie and walked to her, reached out and took her hand. "Cassie, darling, will you marry me?" Ed asked with all the feeling of his heart.

Cassie felt her heart pound and her stomach flutter in delight. With a joyful tear spilling over, she answered, "Yes! Oh, yes Ed. I will marry you."

As Ed took her into his arms and hugged her tightly, she wrapped her arms around his neck.

"Well, Cassie. It looks like you're engaged! Congratulations to you both!" Uncle George boomed in a jovial voice.

Aunt Mabel clapped her hands in delight. "Oh, my goodness! Congratulations!"

Cassie squealed with glee as Ed picked her up and spun her around. When he finally set her down, Mabel rushed over and hugged them both, adding to their embrace, as George patted Ed on the back, laughing with joy at the happiness in his home.

Cassie confessed, "I really wanted to tell you that we got engaged as of last week, but I thought I should tell you about the baby first. It about killed us with excitement to keep it to ourselves," Cassie said with a grin. "I hope you will forgive me?"

"Oh, we already guessed!" Aunt Mabel winked and hugged Uncle George. "The smiles on your faces didn't go unnoticed. You both thought you were being so sneaky, but we could tell something wonderful had happened when you came back from your picnic last week," she said with a broad smile.

"It was all we could do not to tease you both. Well, we did a little. But we knew you would tell us eventually. We are so relieved to finally know," said George. "Oh, tell Mabel the next part of your secret!"

"OH! Um, we plan to be married this coming Saturday," Cassie said cautiously, hoping not to shock her aunt too badly. "It's because of the baby, we can't really wait much longer," she added.

Aunt Mabel went and sat at the table without a word. Then she looked up at the three of them and said, "You know, there's a lot to plan if we're going to make this happen by Saturday. So, let's get eating and figure this out!" Aunt Mabel was all for jumping in and getting things done, and once she had a project there was no stopping her. "George, let's say the blessing and we can talk as we eat."

"Yes, Ma'am! You don't have to ask me twice!" Uncle George took his place at the head of the table with Cassie beside him and Ed next to her. The family supper table was all smiles that evening as they talked and made plans for the wedding.

Chapter 12
Wedding Plans

The two couples sat at the table by lamplight, working late into the evening, jotting down the list of things that needed to be accomplished before the wedding day. They needed to buy Cassie's dress and veil, bake the wedding cake and make refreshments, invite the guests and gather Cassie's bouquet, and visit with the pastor to plan the ceremony. The list seemed impossible to complete with the wedding just days away.

Cassie leaned forward and pointed to the first item on the list. "Aunt Mabel, don't worry about a wedding dress. I can wear my ballgown, the one I wore to the dance. All it needs is the green sash to be replaced with an ivory one. I can even turn my lace shawl into a veil, with a little sewing."

"Are you sure, Cassie? We could purchase a wedding dress, ready made from the dress shop," Aunt Mabel proposed. "This is your special day."

"Really, Aunt Mabel," she looked at Ed who smiled in approval, then back to her aunt. "I'm happy with my ivory gown. Unless you feel it isn't appropriate for a wedding."

"I think you'll look beautiful in any dress," Ed said, giving her hand a squeeze.

"Yes, you're right. Your gown will work splendidly. Tomorrow we can go into town and purchase the ribbon and thread we'll need to make the alterations." Aunt Mabel smiled and made a check mark beside the task listed:

Cassie's Dress and Veil.

"About the guests," Ed interjected. "My guest list is not long since none of my family will be able to make it on such short notice. That just leaves the few close friends I have here that I would like to invite, and I can get the word out to them personally. I would like to keep the wedding small and private, if that's all right with you, Cass?"

"That's fine with me." Cassie knew grand weddings only happened in fairytales. A small private wedding would suit her perfectly. "I really don't have anyone to invite that isn't already here." She paused and had a thought. "Although, I would like to send a telegram to Madeline and let her know the good news. Maybe she can come for the day." Cassie tried to think of the friends she left back in Missouri and couldn't think of anyone she would want to come to the wedding. Except for Mr. and Mrs. Smith. Cassie would write to them and tell them about the wedding and how well she was doing. They would be relieved to hear how happy she was here. "I need to write to my old neighbors back home, the ones who took care of me before I came here. They can spread the word. Really, the people that I truly want to come to the wedding are in this room," she said with a loving smile.

"Oh Cassie, we're so glad we could be here for you. We love you so much and will help make it a wonderful day," Aunt Mabel said as her eyes collected tears of joy.

"Thank you, Aunt Mabel." Cassie turned to George. "Uncle George, will you give me away? I know my father would want you to." Cassie's eyes glistened. Not having her family there was the one thing that made her sad. She was grateful her aunt and uncle would be there to support her.

Uncle George reached to take Cassie's hand. "My sweet Cassie, it would be an honor to give you away." He gave her hand a squeeze. Mabel wiped away a stray tear as she watched the exchange, never imagining her husband would be giving away a daughter on her wedding day.

"Thank you, Uncle George." Then Cassie turned to Mabel and asked, "Aunt Mabel, would you be my Matron of Honor? You are so like my mother. You're more than an aunt, you are my second mother." Cassie's face was now covered in tears.

Mabel let her own tears roll down her cheeks un-checked. She reached out and laid her hand on top of George and Cassie's. "It would be my pleasure to be your Matron of Honor, and a privilege to be your second moth-er." All those years that she had longed for a child to call her "mother" were fulfilled in that moment. "I know Mary would be happy knowing I'm here for you, when she couldn't be." Standing, Aunt Mabel moved around the ta-ble and was met by Cassie in an embrace. The two women cried tears of sadness over the loss of Mary and rejoiced in the bond they felt between one another.

Ed placed his hand on Cassie's back, wanting to soothe her. It broke his heart to see her like this. He knew her pain, having lost his own father and brothers. Ed knew how hard it was to be without family, especially on days like these. And then he had a brilliant idea.

"George? Would you mind being my Best Man? I would've had my father or one of my brothers stand in with me, if they were still alive. But since they aren't here, would you stand in their place?" Ed asked. "I would really appreciate it."

George tried to hide his tears, looking down at his hands encircling his warm coffee cup. Ed would be as close to a son as he would ever have. "Son, I would be pleased to be your Best Man." George stood to give Ed a hearty handshake, then thinking better of it, pulled him in for a tight hug.

Ed felt George's fatherly support again. Both the men struggled to hold their emotions in check, withdrew, then chuckled self-consciously, as Cassie and Mabel laughed too.

"All right, that's enough tears! Let's get this wedding planned!" Aunt Mabel said as she went to get a plate of shortbread and the kettle of hot coffee to bring back to the table.

"By the way, where are you two planning to live, Ed?" George smiled slyly, as he took a bite of shortbread, already knowing the answer.

Ed caught George's hint and turned to face Cassie. "Cass! I've bought us a place just a mile north of here." Ed took her hands and became excited as he shared his dream with her. "It's an established ranch, in a lovely, wooded area, with the Crow Creek running through it. It has a cottage and a barn and corral, with plenty of land for cattle to graze. The owner is going to sell me his herd. Then I'm going to resign as sheriff so I can be a full-time rancher like George," Ed said, smiling proudly.

"What!" exclaimed Cassie, caught completely by surprise. "That's wonderful news! I hadn't even thought about where we would live once married. When can we start moving in?" asked Cassie.

"We can start moving things in on Wednesday. Mr. Crowley, the owner, is moving to California right after the papers are signed. He told me he's only taking what little he can on the train, and leaving most of the furnishings behind, and what we don't want we are free to sell. I'm going to the cottage tomorrow to sign the papers, if you want to come with me and see it for yourself," Ed said excitedly.

Mabel looked at George and motioned toward the other side of the house. George nodded his head to Mabel, to answer her unspoken question. "Cassie, Ed, we want to give you the furnishings in Cassie's room. Everything is new and will be in better condition than what's in the cottage. It's our wedding gift to you," Aunt Mabel said smiling.

"Oh, Aunt Mabel and Uncle George, that's so generous." Cassie stood and gave them each a squeeze and kiss on the cheek. "We're so grateful, thank you so much. You've already done so much for me."

"Well, we did buy it for you, so it's only fitting they go with you," George said, blushing from her attention.

Cassie took Ed's hand and pulled him up. "Come on. Come and see."

"Sure, I'd love to," Ed said apprehensively, not sure he should be going into a young lady's bedroom. Holding back, he thanked George and Mabel for their generosity, then with a nod from George he let Cassie lead him by the hand to the front bedroom.

Cassie opened the door and lit the lamp on the bedside table. Ed appreciated the beautifully furnished room, noting the large oak bed, two bedside tables, a dressing table and mirror, as well as a bureau and wardrobe, all with intricately carved designs. He walked around the room admiring the fine craftsmanship, running his fingers over the smooth surface of the finished wood. Even the matching rugs and other accessories added to the splendor of the room. Ed had never owned anything so elaborate.

"Wow! It's lovely. Fit for a princess, like you." He watched as Cassie opened the window, letting in the cool night air that fluttered the curtains around her, and wondered what it would be like to be with her every night.

She turned back to him. "Not just for me, it'll be ours."

"I like the sound of that." Feeling the excitement of their future together, Ed pulled Cassie to him for a quick kiss.

Hearing the coffee kettle clank as Aunt Mabel put it back on the cast iron stove, they separated and quietly laughed. Blushing, they quickly regained their composure and returned to the kitchen.

"George and Mabel, thank you so much! It's more than generous of you. What a beautiful gift," Ed said seriously.

"You're very welcome," they said, pleased with Ed's acceptance of their gift.

Squeezing Cassie's hand, Ed picked up his hat off the peg by the door and put it on. "It's getting late, and I think I should get home. I have more things to follow up on tomorrow. The rest of the planning I think I can leave in your capable hands, Mabel." Ed tipped his hat to Mabel who nodded in agreement. "The only thing I'm particular about, is where I want to have the wedding." Looking at Cassie he continued, "I hope you don't mind. But I would like to have the wedding in the meadow by Clearwater Pond."

"I don't mind at all. It's a beautiful spot," Cassie said, understanding the deep meaning of the location.

"Cassie, will you join me outside for a moment?" Ed asked softly.

"Sure, Ed." Cassie looked back to her aunt and uncle. "I'll be right back."

"Good night, George and Mabel. Thanks again for everything!"

Once outside and a short distance from the house, Ed took Cassie into his arms, unable to control the overpowering affection he felt for her. "Cass, my love. I'm the happiest I've ever been. And it's your doing. I will love you forevermore." Cassie's dreamy eyes looked up at him as he wrapped his arms around her and kissed her passionately. "Goodnight, my love."

Breathless, Cassie whispered, "Goodnight, Prince Edward. I love you with all my heart." Her fingers slipped through his hands as he backed away.

Ed turned and strode to the fence, jumped up onto his horse and rode off into the night.

Cassie stood watching her handsome prince fade into the distance. The night breeze helped cool her hot cheeks as she gave herself a few minutes to catch her breath and let her pounding heart calm before she turned to go inside.

Closing the door quietly behind her, Cassie announced to her aunt and uncle, "I think I'll head to bed now. It's going to be a busy week and I am feeling exhausted. Thanks again for everything. Love you both," Cassie said as she gave them each a quick hug and kiss on the cheek. She retired to her room and closed the door and collapsed on her bed, smiling with a far away look. "Wow!" she thought. "What a day! So much has happened. So many things to think about. Aunt Mabel and Uncle George knew I was pregnant and were so understanding. And soon I'll be married and living with Ed in our own home." Cassie felt like she was floating on a cloud as her heart soared, all due to the miracle of love. She felt so much love from Uncle George and Aunt Mabel, more that she could have ever imagined, never guessing a month ago all the wonderful things that awaited her. In her wildest dreams she had never pictured a more perfect man than Ed.

***

The night air invigorated Ed as he galloped home on his trusty steed. His joy was giving him boundless energy. Cassie made him feel so carefree, and happy. With Cassie he felt stronger love than ever before. Perhaps it was because of the loss of his wife and daughter, that he felt love more deeply now. It was like walking through a desert on a scorching hot day, and finally taking a drink of cold water.

Ed never wanted to be without love ever again. Cassie was his sweet water, quenching his thirst, filling his soul with joy. As Ed continued to ponder on his feelings for Cassie, a song began to build in his mind and a desire to express his love for her. And that's what he would do, he would write her the song of his heart. Ed smiled as he rode, dreaming of serenading his beautiful wife on their wedding day.

When Ed got home, he set out to write a song to convey his deepest feelings for Cassie. He worked for hours into the night.

***

Monday morning came bright and warm, promising to be a hot day. Luckily a breeze always seemed to be blowing in Cheyenne.

Cassie and Mabel finished the morning chores and, changing into their nicest everyday dresses, they took the surrey into town. Their first stop was at the pastor's house to talk to him about the wedding ceremony.

"I know this is short notice, but Sheriff Havoc and Cassie would like to get married on Saturday," Mabel explained. "And they were wondering if you would perform the ceremony. And they want it at the Clearwater Pond, if that would be all right?"

"I'd be happy to conduct the ceremony for Sheriff Havoc and Cassie, anywhere they wish. Can you tell me your full names, so I can get it correct?" Reverend Gather asked Cassie as he took out a pen and paper.

"My full name is Cassandra Marie Black." Feeling a little embarrassed Cassie said, "I'm not sure of Ed's full name, all I know him by is Edward Havoc."

"That's all right, a small detail that can be remedied

right before the ceremony. Will you be exchanging rings?" asked the Reverend.

"Oh, I don't know that either. I'll find out and get back to you," Cassie said shyly.

Their next stop was the post office. Cassie sent a telegram to Madeline: Madeline MacRea: Getting Married Saturday July 3 6:30 pm. Come If You Can, Cassie.

Cassie had two letters to send as well. That morning before chores she'd written to Madeline detailing all the excitement at the church dance, including the surprise visit from Bart, which landed her unconscious in Ed's arms. Cassie voiced her frustration regarding Bart and how she firmly chastised him for coming to Cheyenne unannounced, and adamantly told Bart she was in love with Ed and planned on marrying him. Cassie included the part about Bart ending up in jail after getting drunk and brawling in the saloon. She confided her feelings about Ed and confessed how his kisses and tender words of affection had her floating on clouds. And how surprised she'd been when she told Aunt Mabel and Uncle George about the pregnancy, and how lovingly they accepted her and the coming baby. Lastly, Cassie included the wonderful news about the wedding and asked if she could try and be there for her, then signed the letter as her kindred spirit.

Cassie's second letter was to the Smith family.

June 28, 1869
Dear Mr. and Mrs. Smith,

I hope this letter finds you all well. I wanted to write and let you know how wonderful my life is in Cheyenne. I still miss my family and all of you, but I'm very happy here with my aunt and uncle. They're very good people and treat me like a daughter.

I have great news! I met a wonderful man, and we will be getting married this coming Saturday, July 3rd. My fiancé has purchased an established homestead and we plan to raise cattle there.

I want to thank you for sending Midnight back to me. It was a miracle he escaped and now brings me such happiness. Thank you again for all the love and kindness you showed me during that tragic time after the attack and death of my family. I appreciate all you did for me. I'm sure it brought my parents peace knowing you were there for me in my time of need. You are true friends.

Wishing you all the best,
Cassie Black

As Cassie handed the postmaster her letters, he found a letter addressed to her from Madeline. Thanking him, Cassie went outside to read the letter in the shade beside Aunt Mabel on the bench.

June 25, 1869
My Lovely Cassie,

I'm overjoyed to hear about your engagement! You're definitely a special young woman, and apparently, I'm not the only one to have noticed. He must be a special man to have caught your attention. You will make a wonderful wife. I am surprised to hear about your pregnancy, but do not despair, Cassie. From what you've told me, Ed loves you very much and I believe he speaks the truth and will love the baby as well. Go forward with joy. I will do what I can to get to your wedding. I would love to be there for you and share in your special day.

I have good news as well. My sister delivered on June 24th, a big and healthy baby boy. She's doing well. I plan to only stay a week or two more, then head home to Kansas. If your wedding is soon, I may still be around, otherwise I will be thinking of you on your special day. Please send word as soon as you know the date.

I think you should keep the blanket you were making for my sister. It should be for your baby. You never know, it might be a girl.

I can't wait to hear all about the dance that you're going to, be sure to tell me all the details. It's so romantic to hear about people falling in love. Reminds me of my courting years and makes me feel young and old at the same time.

Give my best to Ed and your aunt and uncle. Your sister in spirit,
Madeline

"Wonderful news! Madeline's sister had her baby and they're both doing well," Cassie said as she folded up the letter and placed it back into the envelope.

"Congratulations to Madeline and her family. That's great to hear." Aunt Mabel smiled and fanned herself with a letter. "Shall we go to the dress shop?" She squinted up at the rising sun and replaced her bonnet.

"May I stop by Ed's office before we go to the store?

I'd like to find out what time we are going to go out to our new place."

"That's a good idea. You go to Ed's office while I see about the cake. I can meet you at the dress shop in about an hour."

"That should be plenty of time." Cassie's mind was making a list of all the things she needed to get done today while in town. "I'll walk to Ed's office and see you in an hour." Putting her letter away in her drawstring purse, she headed eagerly towards the Sheriff's office.

***

Mabel had more plans to set in motion than she had let on to Cassie. Mabel needed to let her Sewing Bee Circle from church know about the wedding. As Cassie left the post office, Mabel turned the surrey towards the far end of town to visit a friend.

"Well Mabel, what a surprise. To what do I owe this pleasure?" Carole asked as she opened the screen door, dressed in her day dress and apron as her cheery smile and inviting eyes welcomed Mabel.

"Carole! I have wonderful news and a favor to ask," Mabel said in excitement.

"Come in. Come in," Carole said as she opened the door and invited Mabel into her kitchen. Carole started heating the kettle for tea while Mabel found a seat at the table. "What's the wonderful news?" Carole finally asked, anxious to hear.

Mabel's eyes twinkled with excitement as she removed her bonnet. "You remember my niece, Cassie? You met her when she first arrived about a month ago."

Carole set two teacups and spoons on the checkered

tablecloth. "Yes, yes. Such a sweet girl. She came here after her family was killed, poor thing. I remember well," Carole recalled. "How is she doing?"

"Oh, she struggled at first, still grieving for her home and family. George and I are all she's got now. Even though it's been hard for her to leave everything, she's doing much better now. Especially since Sheriff Havoc came along and took an interest in her. Maybe you've seen them together at church and the dance."

"Oh yes, I have noticed them. They're a very handsome couple. I never thought I'd live to see the day that Sheriff Havoc would be as smitten with a young woman as he has been with your Cassie. The eligible young ladies all resigned their efforts of catching his attention long ago, believing he was partial to bachelorhood, given his job and all. I see everyone was mistaken. It just took the right girl to come along," Carole speculated as she brought the cinnamon buns she had made that morning to the table. "Sherriff Havoc is such an upstanding man, and your niece is such a sweet young lady, it's a joy to watch their love blossom."

Mabel took a spoonful of sugar and slowly stirred it in her tea. "That's the reason I've come to see you. Sheriff Havoc has asked Cassie to marry him."

"Really! That is wonderful news! Congratulations, Mabel! How fantastic for them." Carole sat down and poured herself a cup of tea and added cream and sugar. "Tell them congratulations for me. When is the glorious occasion taking place?" Carole asked as she took a sip of tea.

"They're planning to be married this Saturday."

Carole looked up mid sip, in astonishment.

"I know it's short notice, but it's what they want." Mabel shrugged her shoulders and sipped her tea. "And

247

who am I to disagree? When you've found love, why wait?"

"I agree, if it hadn't been for my pa insisting on a six-month engagement, I would have been married to Gordon a month into our courtship. I know a short courtship is not always conventional, but out here in the West, nothing is. There's work to be done. And it's so much easier to do it together, as husband and wife," Carole said, nodding in approval.

Mabel was encouraged by her friend's response. "Do you think the church ladies would help me make them a Wedding Ring Quilt? If we got the women together from the Sewing Circle and anyone else who wants to, we could meet Thursday. We could have it quilted in a couple of days, I just know it," Mabel said with enthusiasm.

"I'm sure everyone would want to help. Certainly, we could get it done in time. And we can help with anything else you need. Do you want me to buy the fabric? Or do you have some you want to use?" asked Carole.

"I was thinking of using a couple of my old dresses to make the blocks. You know, like a hug from her aunt every time she uses it," Mabel said, grinning. "I can buy some backing from the store and we can cut out the blocks and piece them together on Thursday and quilt them Friday. I have an old worn-out blanket we can use for the batting. If we all work together, I think we could easily get it done in time for the wedding."

Carole agreed. "I'll get the word out to the women to meet Thursday morning, at nine o'clock. And I'm sure they'd want to help with other things as well. Would you mind if we had them each bring a small kitchen item for Cassie's new home? I know how hard it can be to start out with nothing. I'm sure we all have older things we aren't using; if we all pitch in, she'll be able to set up a functioning kitchen. After all, she hasn't had time to prepare her dowry," Carole said, taking a bite of her cinnamon bun.

"No, she lost all that in the fire. When the Indians attacked and killed the family, Cassie was left with nothing, no family and no possessions," Mabel frowned as she stirred her tea, deep in thought.

"Poor girl. We'll make sure she has everything she needs. It's the least we can do for Sheriff Havoc's wife. He's been a faithful member of our congregation and protector of our town for these past two years. If it wasn't for him, Cheyenne wouldn't have been safe enough for any woman to live here. I'm certain everyone will want to help."

"Thank you so much, Carole, I knew you would understand." She fiddled with her napkin before she looked up into her friend's kind eyes. "I have another favor to ask. They will need a wedding cake. With all we have to do, I won't have time to make her one. Sheriff Havoc bought a homestead, and we need to get it ready for them to move in. With all the cleaning and preparations, there just isn't time to bake and decorate a cake too," Mabel said, furrowing her brow. "I was hoping you'd be willing to make the wedding cake."

Carole's smile widened with delight. "Say no more! You know I make the prettiest cakes around. It would be a pleasure to make their wedding cake. It'll be my wedding present to them," she said, as she got up and pulled open a cabinet drawer to get out her recipe book. "I have just the cake." She sat down and turned to the middle of the notebook where her favorite cake recipe was. "This is the most exciting thing to happen in Cheyenne since that bull broke through the picture window in the dress shop last year," Carole said laughing. "Leave it to me! I'll have it ready to be delivered by Saturday morning. What time is the wedding?"

"It's at six-thirty Saturday evening at a secluded location. They want it to be a private ceremony. Sheriff Havoc knows nearly everyone here in town and figures they'll all want to attend. He's partial to keeping this one thing intimate. I agree, it should be. But I know everyone will still want to send their congratulations and wedding gifts," explained Mabel. "I can pick up the cake on our way to the reception after the wedding, around seven o'clock. If that's ok? I know they'll love the quilt and the cake. They'll be so surprised!" Mabel looked at Carole's grandfather clock and noticed the time. "Well, I'd better get back to town. I have so much to do. Thank you so much for your help. I really appreciate it and I know they'll love it too." Mabel emptied her cup and excused herself, walking to the door.

"Mabel, I'll see you Thursday morning. Don't worry about a thing. Just bring the materials and we'll do the rest," Carole said, giving her a tender hug. "I can't wait to spread the word! Everyone will be so excited!"

"Thanks again, Carole."

***

Cassie knocked on the sheriff's office door.

Ed opened the door. His delighted expression was Cassie's reward.

"Cass! I'm so glad you're here!" He led her in and shut the door, then wrapped his arms around her waist and gave her a kiss. "I'm so happy to see you! I was thinking I should have set a time to pick you up to go see the homestead," Ed said with excitement. "Mr. Crowley said he would be home all day to sign the papers. We can go any time you're able." He leaned in and kissed her soft cheek. "How in the world am I supposed to get anything done, when all I want to do is hold her and kiss her?" Ed asked himself.

Cassie gave him a sweet smile as she blushed. "Ed,

what if someone walks in?" she whispered as he continued to hold her close. She rested her hands on his shoulders, ready to push away at the first sound of someone opening the door.

"Fine, I'll behave. But the second we're married, no one is going to stop me from hugging and kissing you as much as I want," Ed said with a wide grin, teasing her.

"Ed!" was all she could say as she smiled and tried to change the subject. "I have to go to the dress shop. Oh, and the Reverend asked me if we were going to exchange rings. I didn't know what to tell him."

"I would like to give you a ring, but you don't have to worry about giving me one," he told her.

Cassie smiled, "But I want to get you a ring. It'll be your wedding present, please?" she pleaded.

Ed was touched. "I think that's very sweet of you. If that's what you want to do," he said taking her hands and squeezing them.

"Yes, that's what I want."

"I love a woman that knows what she wants," he said, causing Cassie to blush deeply.

Cassie regained her composure and smiled. "Also, the pastor wanted to know what our full names are. I was embarrassed to say I didn't know yours. Do you have a middle name?" Cassie asked inquisitively.

"Yes, it's Karl. Edward Karl Havoc. My parents let me pick my name when I was adopted. The name the orphanage called me not was not my given name. I was abandoned at the orphanage as an infant, they didn't know my name, so they just called me something they made up. I never liked it. So, when I was adopted, my ma and pa let me choose. We went through a book of names and I picked Edward Karl. They told me that Edward meant 'protector'. Which I liked since it was a fond nickname the children gave me at the orphanage. I was the one who protected the younger children from the older ones. After a while, the children started calling me Edward the Protector. They said I reminded them of the stories about Edward the Protector of England," he explained. "And I chose Karl because my parents told me it meant 'freeman' and that's how I felt when I was adopted, free." He smiled lovingly at her, feeling the same freedom he had felt as a child when he was finally free from the pain of a broken heart.

"Oh, Edward, how difficult that must have been for you to be left in an orphanage. I can understand why they called you Edward the Protector. That's how I feel when I'm with you. It's so fitting. I'm so glad your parents let you pick your name and that you were adopted by such wonderful parents." Cassie felt increased compassion and adoration for him. "I never would have guessed he'd been through so much and yet he's turned out to be such a wonderful man," she thought.

"And what's your middle name, Cass?" Ed led her to a chair and remained standing, leaning against his desk.

Cassie sat down, appreciating his thoughtfulness. "My full name is Cassandra Marie Black," she said with pride. "My parents named me after Princess Cassandra, the daughter of King Priam and Queen Hecuba of Troy from Greek mythology. I think it fascinating that Princess Cassandra had the gift of prophecy. I would love to have that gift; well, maybe not all the time," she said, thinking about it.

"Yes, maybe not all the time. Do you know what your name means? I like to know what a person's name means." Ed stretched his long legs out, sitting on the edge of the desk, relaxing as he crossed his arms over his chest, and waited for her response.

"Well, I was told once, Cassandra means 'one who

shines upon man,' or 'helper of mankind.' And Marie is the French form of Mary. My mother's name was Mary, which means 'beloved mother,' as in the mother of Jesus," Cassie said with realization. She'd never really thought about her name. It struck her as very significant now. She missed her beloved mother. Cassie was grateful she was named after her mother, so she could carry a piece of her with her always.

"That makes perfect sense! You have shined your light upon me and are definitely going to be a beloved mother," Ed said sweetly.

Cassie shook her head in delight and dismay. "Edward Karl Havoc! You are the most wonderful, sweet man. You certainly are Edward the Protector." She slowly stood and went to him, throwing her arms around his neck and kissed him tenderly. Pulling away, she let her hands slide down his neck, coming to rest against his chest.

Ed stood there in a daze, his heart pounding nearly out of his chest.

She slowly backed away. "I'd better go and run my errands. I'll see you back here in an hour. All right?"

Her smile grew as he blinked a few times, acting as if he was dazed. This was the first time she had initiated a kiss on the lips, and he smiled, realizing that she wanted him too. And wasn't too shy to show it.

"Sure. I'll be ready to go as soon as you come back," he said, then thought, "I'd follow you anywhere." His heart was hammering loudly in his chest. "Is it getting hot in here? Or is it just me?" he thought with a chuckle and exhaled deeply. Cassie's skirts swished as she turned and walked out the door. Looking over her shoulder she waved a little goodbye and closed the door. Ed shook his head slowly as he smiled after her. "What a gal!"

Swinging the door wide, Cassie entered the dress shop as the bell above the door announced her arrival. The shop was filled with extravagant dresses on shapely dress forms strategically placed around the store and in the window display.

"Welcome to Holden's Dress Shop; my name is Bea. How may I help you?" asked the young woman behind the counter.

Cassie approached her and smiled easily. "Hello, I'm Cassie," she said, shaking the tall woman's hand. "I'm looking to buy some ribbon for a gown I have. It needs to be ivory satin, about two inches wide and long enough to tie a bow. I plan to wear it in place of the green ribbon the dress has now. It'll be my wedding dress," she explained.

The strawberry blonde woman was dressed in a simple stylish pink frock and smiled kindly. "I think I have exactly what you're looking for. Just give me a few minutes to find it." Bea withdrew to the back room where her sewing supplies and creations happened.

The bell above the door rang again as Mabel arrived.

"Oh, Cassie, you're here already. Have you been here long?" she asked.

"No, I just got here a few minutes ago. Bea went to the back of the shop. She thinks she has what we need. I was also wondering if we could go to the jeweler. I would like to buy a ring for Ed."

"We can do that as soon as we're done here." Mabel said as she joined Cassie looking around the store at the dresses.

They admired each uniquely fashioned gown, appreciating the silk, satin, cotton and wool apparel embellished with lace and ribbon.

"I've never seen such beautiful dresses." Cassie's eyes sparkled with wonder.

"They do carry the best in town," Aunt Mabel said, admiring a dark brown two-piece wool ensemble. "When are you and Ed going to your place?"

"I need to meet him back at his office in about an hour," she said. "So hopefully we have enough time."

"The jeweler isn't far, I'm sure we'll have plenty of time," Aunt Mabel said as Bea returned.

"Will this work?" Bea asked, displaying the shiny cream-colored ribbon. "This two-inch satin ribbon should be just right for the sash. Let me measure around your waist and tie it in a bow, so I can cut it exactly where you want it." Bea came around the counter and placed the ribbon around Cassie's small waist and tied it in a big bow, leaving long tails about halfway to the floor. "I think this would be a lovely length, don't you?"

"Yes, it looks perfect!" said Cassie looking back. Mabel nodded in agreement.

"I also need a silver comb, maybe something with beading that I can sew my lace veil to. Do you think you might have something like that?" asked Cassie hopefully.

"I'm certain we do." Moments later, Bea came back. "What do you think of this?" She asked, setting on the counter a silver comb with ivory beads and scrolling that resembled flower buds.

"Oh, it's lovely! It'll be perfect!" Cassie held the comb momentarily and handed it back. "I'll take them both."

Bea smiled and began wrapping the two items to place them in a box. "Might I suggest an item for the bride-to-be? I have a beautiful nightdress with matching robe that would look lovely on you. Can I show them to you?" asked Bea.

Cassie looked at Aunt Mabel, who nodded her head in

approval. "Yes, I'd like that," said Cassie.

The nightdress was of lightweight cotton, white with long sleeves and little buttons down the gathered front, and lace trim that matched the robe. "They're lovely," Cassie said, delicately touching the soft fabric and lace. "It would be nice to have something new. I only have the one… that I had back in Missouri," Cassie said sadly, giving Mabel a knowing glance.

"Then you should have them, Cassie." Mabel looked at Bea. "Will you ring them up please." Looking at Cassie, she offered, "I'll buy them for you, and the comb and ribbon too. You'll have enough to buy after you're married."

Cassie hugged Mabel as Bea folded the night dress and robe and placed them in another box. "Thank you, Aunt Mabel."

"Congratulations on your wedding," Bea said pleasantly as she handed Cassie the boxes. "I'm sure you'll be a beautiful bride."

"Thank you, Bea, and thank you for all your help," Cassie said, taking the boxes.

Mabel paid and they left the shop, placing the boxes in the surrey out in front of the store.

***

Their next stop was the jewelry store. As they entered, the jeweler looked them up and down and sniffed snobbishly as he greeted them. His impeccable appearance and arrogant manner made Cassie reluctant to enter further. For the first time that day, she felt underdressed in her red calico dress and French braided hair.

Seeing her hesitation, Mabel took charge. "We'd like to see your wedding bands," she said with authority.

"Yes, Ma'am! Right this way." He strode smoothly across the floor around one of the three display cases that bordered the perimeter of the shop. Leaning down he unlocked the cupboard and withdrew a flat box which he ceremoniously opened with his white gloved hands, revealing dozens of rings of various precious metals nestled in the black velvet lining.

Cassie found a simple silver wedding band that she liked and held it out to the clerk. "I'd like this one, please."

Silently and with pursed lips he took the ring and placed it in a hand-carved box lined with red velvet. Cassie paid the jeweler, glad to be through with the transaction. As they were leaving, Mabel pointed out a lovely pair of silver chandelier earrings with an intricately etched design, and pearl tear drops, that would go perfect with her dress. There was a matching necklace as well.

"They're beautiful, but I don't need them. It's too much money," Cassie reasoned. "I have what I need. Let's go," she insisted, looking back at the scowling jeweler. Cassie did love them but didn't want to spend any more money and didn't want Aunt Mabel to, either.

Mabel finally agreed, and they left the store. But in the back of her mind, Mabel planned to come back to purchase them for Cassie, feeling a need to spoil her special daughter.

***

Meanwhile, Ed had gone to speak to the mayor, finding him seated in his plush office at the Town Hall.

"Mayor, I was wanting to talk to you," Ed said, peering around the doorway into the mayor's office.

"Sure, come on in and have a seat, Sheriff! So good to

see you. How are things going?" asked the mayor.

"Things are wonderful; that's why I've come to see you." Taking a seat across from the mayor, Ed announced, "I'm engaged!"

Mayor Hook's face showed surprise and then elation as he stood and reached over the desk to heartily shake Ed's hand. "Congratulations, my boy! Finally got some sweet gal to take you in!" he said jokingly. "Well, good for you!" They had been good friends through the war and naturally teased good-naturedly with each other.

"Well, the good men like you were taken, so she took the next best thing!" bantered Ed and they both laughed.

"True, true, my wife, bless her heart, used to think so. Just wait until you live with the poor gal a while, she'll come to realize her mistake." Mayor Hook laughed even harder.

"There's another matter. I've purchased a ranch and a small herd; well nearly, in an hour it'll be all legal." Seeing the Mayor's shocked look, he rushed on, "So, I'm giving you my resignation. I'm going into the cattle business. I know this comes as a surprise." Ed tried to smooth it over as quickly as he could. "But as you know, I took this job as a favor to you. I never intended to be the sheriff forever. My heart is set on living in the country and making a home with my new bride."

"Well, this does come as a surprise. But I heard a tale that you had a sweetheart. And now you want to settle down. So, how soon?" asked Mayor Hook.

"As soon as possible," Ed revealed with a twinkle in his eye. "I'm taking over the ranch on Wednesday. So, I'd like you to find my replacement soon."

"Oh! That is sudden." Mayor Hook scratched his head as he thought. "I guess I could call in another favor from a friend in Laramie. He's an experienced deputy there, maybe he'd like to take the job. I know Vic isn't interested.

I'll wire the man today." Mayor Hook smiled as the plan worked through his mind. "We can call an emergency town council meeting and vote on it tonight if he accepts. If all goes well, you can be retired on Wednesday." Slapping his hand on the desk, he exclaimed, "Yes! By golly, this could work. Vic can assist the new sheriff to get acquainted with the town. Come November, the city can vote him in officially, just like they did you two years ago. It'll give the city folk time to get to know him or they can submit another candidate if they wish. Sheriff, I'll handle it all. You just focus on your wedding and bride, and I'll let you know when it is official."

"That sounds great. Oh, and I'd like to invite you to the wedding. It's this Saturday at six-thirty at the Clearwater Pond," Ed announced.

"Count me in. I wouldn't miss it for the world," Mayor Havoc said, and shook Ed's hand as he stood to leave.

"Thanks, Hank!" Ed said, using his friend's given name as he hurried out the door.

"You bet! That's what friends are for, Ed!" he hollered after him.

Ed crossed the road in long even strides, making a quick trip to the bank to get a bank note needed for the down payment, and then rushed back to his office to wait for Cassie. He didn't have to wait very long. Ed spotted Mabel and Cassie through the window as Mabel pulled the surrey up in front of the office. Grabbing his hat, he hurried out.

"There you are. Hello, beautiful ladies." Tipping his hat, his smile was filled with knowledge of the dream he was about to make into reality.

Mabel and Cassie both smiled warmly at his compliment.

"Good to see you, Ed," Cassie said as Ed took her

hand and gave it a squeeze.

"Mabel, I was wondering if I could borrow your surrey to go to our new ranch. We could drop you off at your place and come back with it when we're done. I'll follow you out to your place and ride home afterwards."

"That sounds like a fine idea. Climb in and we'll drive you out to the livery stable," Mabel said.

"Thank you." Ed climbed into the back seat behind Cassie and sat next to a large flat box. "It looks like you have found what you wanted at the dress shop, Cass," Ed said with a smile.

"Yes, I did, and no peeking," Cassie teased as she looked over her shoulder at him just to make sure.

Ed teasingly moved his hand to the edge of the box, pretending he was going to open it.

Cassie saw him out of the corner of her eye. "Ed! No peeking!" she said as she laughed. Ed moved his hand back to his lap with an impish grin on his face. "You big tease," Cassie said, smiling back at him. As she watched the road ahead, she secretly opened her drawstring purse and slipped the ring box into it.

Mabel grinned as she listened to the two of them tease each other. Ed decided to tie Major to the back of the surrey and drive the women back to the ranch. He helped Mabel into the back seat and sat beside Cassie, while he drove the rest of the way.

When they arrived at the Hartford's ranch, Ed helped Mabel into the house, carrying the big box while Cassie waited for him to return.

"I see you were successful in getting some things for the wedding." George said coming out of the barn.

"Yes, we found quite a few things we were needing," Cassie said cheerfully.

Ed greeted George. "I've asked Mabel if we could borrow the surrey to go to the new homestead. She said it was fine, but only if it's all right with you."

"Sure, that's fine. You both have a good time and we'll see you back here for dinner," offered George.

"If I may, I'll be leaving Major here," Ed said, untying Major and then tying him to the corral fence. "We should only be gone an hour or so."

"Fine, fine. Take your time." George waved them off as he headed inside.

"Thank you, Uncle George. We'll see you in a little while!" Cassie said as they pulled away. She slipped her arm through Ed's and smiled up at him as the anticipation of seeing their new home filled her with excitement.

Chapter 13
A Place of Their Own

As soon as they were out of sight of Aunt Mabel and Uncle George, Ed wrapped his arm around Cassie's waist and pulled her close to him, holding the reins with one hand and her with the other. Cassie snuggled close and rested her head against his shoulder.

"This is so nice," she said with a contented sigh.

"Yes, it is. Did I ever tell you how much I love your voice?" asked Ed, glancing at Cassie's angelic face.

"No, I think I would have remembered," Cassie said, looking up to check and see if he was teasing her. He looked perfectly serious.

"I love the sound of your voice. It has a nice sweet tone, not grating or shrill, with a touch of southern accent, not much, but I can hear it. It makes it all the sweeter to listen to. You know it's been years since I'd heard my name spoken by a woman, so when I heard you say my name for the first time, it nearly melted my heart," he admitted with a smile. "And when you sang, my heart did melt." He turned and kissed the top of her head. "Cass, you've bewitched me with your silvery dulcet voice. All you had to do was speak, and I was yours," he said teasing, but felt it was truer than not. He'd fallen for her, all of her. He loved everything about her, the way she looked, the way she moved, the things she said and how she said them. She was his elixir and had cured what ailed him and he would never get enough of her.

Cassie blushed, "Oh Ed. You love to tease me. I talk just like every other woman," she reasoned. "I'm nothing special."

"Cass, I never want to hear you say that again. You hear me," Ed said, gently scolding her. "You're the most special person I've ever met. You don't think you are, but that's because you're humble. I know you don't see it, but everyone else does; you're amazing. And to me you're the most precious person in the world. You really are perfect for me. I love everything about you. If I keep telling you, one day you will believe you are special," he said, giving her a little squeeze.

Cassie laid her head back on his shoulder. "Ed, you're the dearest man. You are exactly what I need. I feel special when I'm around you because of the way you treat me. And speaking of great voices, Ed, you're one to talk," she said looking up at him; he smiled, causing his mustache to lift at the corners. "You have a smooth deep voice that melts women's hearts. When you sang to me, my heart was gone. I gave it to you, and you still have it," she confessed, giving him her sweetest smile.

Ed couldn't help it, that deserved a kiss. Looking down, he kissed her pretty little mouth for saying such wonderful things. As he pulled away, he grinned. "You keep saying things like that, and I'll never stop kissing you," he teased, as Cassie laughed. "And I will never tire of hearing your beautiful laugh. Your voice is like a melody I could listen to forever. I would do anything to keep you laughing. Probably why I tease you so much," he confessed.

"You can tease me all you like. I love when you make me laugh. Please keep me laughing for as long as I live, OK?" she teased.

"I'll do my best! I promise, as long as I live," he pledged.

263

"Oh Cass, I can't wait to show you our home. We're almost there." He pointed towards a thick forest to the west of the main road. "It's just through those trees. It is only about a mile north of your aunt and uncle's place. Close enough to walk or ride to in a few minutes, so you can visit as often as you please," he said happily.

Ed never wanted to live in town. His heart was in the country and he wanted Cass to be close to her family. Ed had heard that Jack Crowley was getting desperate to move to California and determined now was the time to act. Ed knew Mr. Crowley had lost his wife the year before and was lonely for his children. Mr. Crowley couldn't imagine spending another winter alone and wanted to leave as soon as the homestead sold.

A few years back, Jack's two girls had both married and moved to California. Then his wife had fallen ill. When she passed away, he lost all desire to stay in Cheyenne. He tried to sell the place a while ago, but no one was interested. Most of the ranches around Cheyenne preferred flat open grasslands, which made it easier to round up their cattle. Ed was the exception; he only wanted land if it came with plenty of trees, and once he heard that Mr. Crowley was reducing the price for his land, Ed went out to see him. Ed had worked roundups every spring and fall to earn extra money, saving it for an opportunity just like this.

Ed turned down a less traveled lane heading west with a slight incline. Cassie noticed the thick grass growing on either side of the wagon tracks, dispersed with sage brush and wildflowers. Soon the few small trees became a forest farther down the lane. She recognized some of the various trees, evergreens, quaking aspen, oak, and maples. Others she was not familiar with and would ask Ed about them later. In the open clearings, thick grass and small bushes grew, as did her excitement. This was by far the prettiest area she'd seen in Cheyenne, even prettier than Clearwater Pond.

The trees opened up to the grounds surrounding the cottage, where undergrowth covered everything except for the drive and paths to the outbuildings.

Cassie gasped, "Oh Ed! It's beautiful, I love it!" She couldn't believe this would be her new home. The cottage was small but quaint, painted white with green shutters. On either side of the front door were two large windows. Along the front of the cottage was a covered porch with a hanging swing on one side and a small table and chairs on the other. Cassie could imagine herself sitting outside, shelling peas from her garden as she enjoyed the beauty around her. And in the evening, she and Ed could sit together on the porch swing as Ed played the guitar.

"This is going to be ours? I can't believe it!" She could barely contain herself. Ed gave her a squeeze as he watched her eyes sparkle with excitement.

"Yes Cass, it'll be ours," he said, loving the sound of that. So many of his dreams were coming true, he wondered if he might be sleeping. But this was better than any dream he'd ever had.

As he stopped the rig in front of the cottage, Cassie wrapped her arms around his neck and gave him a big hug. "Oh Ed! It's wonderful, more than I could have ever hoped for."

Mr. Crowley met them on the front step. "Howdy, folks! Good of you to come out," the older gentleman said. "What do you think of the place?" he asked, as he walked down the front steps of the porch.

"I love it already!" said Cassie. "It is so beautiful here. You've done such a nice job with everything," she said, as Ed helped her down from the rig.

"Mr. Crowley, this is my fiancé, Cassie Black," Ed said

as he shook Mr. Crowley's hand.

Cassie shook Mr. Crowley's hand. "Mr. Crowley, it's so nice to meet you," she said, smiling at the kind-looking white-haired man.

"Pleasure is all mine," he said as he held hers with his work-worn hand. "I will sure miss the place. So many good memories here. But since my wife's passing, it just isn't the same. It makes me happy to see such a nice couple starting out here. I know you'll be happy here. This place has been good to us," he said, smiling. "Come on, let me show you around." He turned and walked up the porch steps with a little more effort than he had coming down and opened the front door. Cassie and Ed followed, grinning and holding hands as they went.

"This here is the front living area," Mr. Crowley said, pointing to the left of the open space.

Cassie's eyes were drawn to the rock fireplace against the far wall, where two slightly worn parlor chairs sat in front of it. Near them, a small writing table and chair sat under a window, where light filtered through the threadbare curtains. The house was dusty and had a musty smell, clearly lacking the touch of a woman. Cassie readily excused the middle-aged widower's housekeeping, knowing he probably had little time for cleaning when there was a ranch to run. She felt bad for him, thinking how lonely he must be in the cottage, with only his memories to keep him company. All the home needed was a bit of elbow grease and tender loving care, which Cassie was eager to do.

"And over here," he said pointing to the other side of the room, "is the kitchen area."

The large front window let in sunlight that flooded the kitchen. The kitchen had a large sink with a hand water pump and counter space, stacked with pans, dirty dishes, and crocks of food, with flies buzzing around them.

Beside the counter was a large rusty cook stove, in need of a good polishing, and in the far-right corner sat a hutch with its doors wide open. In the center of the kitchen sat a small table and chairs.

"Back behind this door is the storeroom," he said, walking towards to the door to the left of the stove. He opened it and allowed them to look inside. It was full of trunks, bottles, and baskets, stacked on the shelves and floor as well as a large tub for bathing. "It needs some cleaning out, but it's a good space. My wife always liked it." He turned to the door on the left along the back wall of the kitchen. "Here's the kids' bedroom."

He opened the door to the room, causing dust to stir and a strong musty smell wafted out, causing Cassie to hold her breath. The room was able to comfortably accommodate the two small beds and a chest of drawers beside the once pleasantly draped windows. The home's walls and ceiling were stained wood paneling, giving it a cabin feel, reminding Cassie of her home in Missouri. In spite of its need for a good cleaning, Cassie could see the house's potential and loved the home immediately.

"And this other room, over here," he said, leading them to the door in the back of the living area. "This is the larger bedroom where my wife and I slept." He opened the door to a spacious bedroom, sparsely furnished with a double bed, covered in a well-worn quilt lying beneath the sun-bleached curtains. A rocker sat in the far corner with a chest of drawers and a sewing machine cabinet beneath the back window. Cassie could see there was plenty of room to hold her bedroom furniture.

Cassie was becoming more and more nauseated the longer she was in the house with the strong odors. She was glad when Mr. Crowley suggested they go outside to see the rest of the property.

"The house needs some cleaning, I know, but I haven't had the time or energy to get to it," Mr. Crowley said apologetically. "Oh, I should mention there's a root cellar under the kitchen floor. It's quite large. Nice and cool down there, and never freezes," he explained as he walked. "When we moved here ten years ago, we lived in the cellar because the barn was built before the house. Before the war, we had a small herd and had the free range mostly to ourselves, but that has changed. During the war we made a good profit off the cattle we sold, and the homestead grew. Over the years my wife and I made many improvements." He pointed to each as he walked. "We have a well now. That's been a godsend. Before the well, we walked to Crow Creek," he said as he took them behind the house. "This here's rich soil, gets plenty of leaves in the fall and we add steer manure to it every spring." He reached down and took a handful of the dark brown earth and crumbled it in his hand. "We even set up an irrigation line from the stream to water the garden when needed," he said with pride.

"You have a beautiful garden," Cassie said, admiring the rich soil and straight rows of waist-high corn, potatoes, beans, peas, carrots and more. The garden was about as big as the house and would get sun a good part of the day. "How can you leave your garden, after all this hard work?" Cassie asked in amazement. She knew from experience all the hours he must have spent tending to the garden.

"I didn't know when I would get a buyer and had to prepare to eat for the winter if it didn't sell. It's just one of those things that happens to be in your favor, I guess. I hope you enjoy gardening; it was always a joy of my wife's," he said with a touch of sadness. "I took it over when she got too sick; she could still look out the window from her bed and watch it grow," he said, looking back toward the window where she would watch him work. "Evelyn always looked forward to each new growing season, preparing the soil, picking out her favorite seeds, watching the tender leaves pop through the dirt. And the harvest, always more than we could eat. Evelyn had the best garden around," he said, reminiscing.

Cassie looked at Ed and squeezed his hand. "We're very grateful for you and your hard work, Mr. Crowley. I promise I'll take good care of it, and honor what your wife started," Cassie said with emotion. She knew that they would have food for the rest of the year because of him; it was a great blessing.

"I can see why you want to marry this one," Mr. Crowley declared. "She's as sweet as a peach! It makes this old man happy to know that you'll be taking good care of it, dear," he said, beaming at her as she blushed.

"Yes, she is a peach!" Ed smiled down at her as he put his arm around her shoulders and gave her a squeeze. "Again, we're most thankful for your hard work. For what I'm paying for the homestead, I really feel you're getting the short end of the stick. I'm starting to feel guilty," Ed admitted.

Ed had told Cassie the sale included the homestead, farm equipment, and the animals at a good price. Mr. Crowley was only taking two of the four horses and the rest were theirs to do with as they saw fit.

"No, no! Don't feel guilty. You're doing me a favor. I've wanted to sell for over a year. Now I'm free to take my money and go live with my children. I'll get to enjoy the next years living with my grandchildren. It is an added bonus to know the old place went to a sweet young couple who will raise a family here. I'd much rather sell to you two, than one of those land grabbers from back East, just making more money off the back of an old man," he said with conviction, patting Ed's arm.

"We love the place and can't wait to raise our family here. Right, Cass?" Ed asked as Cassie nodded enthusiastically. "We'll do our best to take good care of the homestead." Ed gave her another squeeze as she agreed.

"I appreciate that," Mr. Crowley said, a little misty-eyed, then motioned to the barn. "I know I've already shown you, Sheriff, but Cassie, that's the barn, and henhouse, and further back are the smokehouse, and icehouse," he said, indicating each in their general area. "I can take you back out to see them after we sign the papers and have some coffee."

Cassie declined the offer, stating she was too hot already and secretly didn't think she could handle the smells inside the house. "If you don't mind, I would like to look around on my own for a bit while you men take care of business," she said smiling.

Mr. Crowley nodded in approval and the men excused themselves and went inside to work out the legal formalities.

Cassie took a stroll through the barn's large double doors, noting the sturdy hay loft above and clean straw that carpeted each of the stalls. Chickens pecked and scratched around in the fenced chicken coop on the far side of the barn, and out back, the brown Jersey milk cow was grazing contentedly. The corral attached to the barn was big enough for the additional horses, milk cow, and other animals as they needed. She turned around and looked back toward the house, noticing the clothesline for the first time. Mr. Crowley and his wife had put a lot of thought into the layout of the homestead, making it quite homey. Smiling to herself she thought, "This is going to be my home now."

She wandered further along a path until she found the smokehouse, nestled deep in the trees. It was smaller than an outhouse but had a vent at the top that had blackened from the smoke over the years. Its tight-fitting door had a latch, and a rock floor to keep out hungry predators.

Roaming deeper into the tree line was the icehouse. It was well concealed, being built into a small hill, mostly underground. It was camouflaged by the vegetation growing over it. The front was covered with mossy stones surrounding the heavy wooden door and shaded by the thick trees. "I'll look inside later," she thought, "I want to find the stream first."

She walked until she heard the sound of rushing water and left the path to meander through the thick underbrush towards the sound. Finally finding the stream, she followed its path with her eyes as it traveled south, back towards the house.

Although it had been named Crow Creek, it was much wider and deeper than a creek. The stream was clear enough that she could see the smooth rocks below. Downstream it bubbled and churned, moving faster as it wound through narrowed passages and over large rocks. From where she stood the stream appeared calm and smooth, about knee high and as wide as a wagon bed was long. She wondered if there were fish in the stream and sat down on a large log and removed her shoes and stockings. The damp grassy bank gradually declined into the soft wet sand as she walked to the creek. Lifting her red skirt and petticoat to her knees, she gingerly stuck her toes into the icy cold water, gasping as it hit her hot skin. Gradually she became more accustomed to the cold water and waded further in. Cassie stood, calmly taking in deep breaths as she closed her eyes and enjoyed the cool water rushing past her legs. She loved their new homestead and all its wonders. This would be their private paradise.

Cassie heard a branch snap and turned to see Ed standing there. She gasped. "Oh, you scared me! I didn't hear you coming." Standing there holding her skirts up and her feet in the water, she laughed. "What are you looking at, hmm?" she teased.

"I'm looking at the prettiest woman I've ever seen," he said smiling. "And enjoying the look of those legs, too," he thought as a wide grin spread across his face.

Cassie blushed as she walked out of the water, letting the hem of the calico skirt drop back to her ankles. Sitting on the log, she pulled on her stockings as quickly as she could. "I couldn't help it," she explained. "The water looked so refreshing in this heat," she said as she pulled on her shoes and tied the laces.

"You didn't have to get out just because I'm here. I enjoyed watching you. You looked so happy and carefree." He took a few steps closer. "…and beautiful," he said slowly as he closed the distance between him and Cassie and lifted her chin to kiss her sweet inviting lips.

Cassie enjoyed the intensity of his kiss and didn't want it to end. But he was a gentleman and pulled away to gaze at her as she smiled dreamily up at him.

Ed felt he was looking at an angel, her radiant face and sparkling green eyes made his heart swell until he thought it might burst. "I love you, Cass," was all he could say.

"I love you too, Ed," she said in her sweetest voice, leaving a mark on his heart.

Slowly pulling out of what felt like a trance, Ed offered his hand to Cassie and helped her stand. Keeping hold of his hand, she followed him back to the house through the brush.

Looking back, he declared, "Well, the place is ours. We signed all the papers, and I gave him the down payment. We'll be able to start moving in on Wednesday." Ed pulled her to him and held her tight as he kissed her. "I can't believe it. It's ours, all ours," he whispered. His dreams were coming true, and he found it unbelievable.

"I can't believe it either! This is ours!" She held him firmly around his waist, resting her head on his chest, and breathed in deeply.

With his arm around her shoulders, they walked the rest of the way back. "He'll pack up tomorrow, then leave bright and early on the Wednesday morning train."

"That's wonderful," she said with excitement. "It's all happening so fast. Maybe you are taking on too much. Won't it be hard taking care of the animals and the ranch with your job as Sheriff?"

"I forgot to tell you. I talked to the mayor and gave him my resignation; day after tomorrow I won't be the sheriff of Cheyenne anymore," he explained with some excitement and a little sadness. He hadn't hated the job, but it was a good time to be moving on to what he really wanted in the future with his new wife.

"Oh Ed," she exclaimed, giving him a squeeze around his waist. It was wonderful news, knowing he would be on the ranch with her full-time. It immediately settled some of her anxiety about living so far from town. "I'll bet you're excited to start working this place. I know I am," she added, thinking of all the cleaning she would like to get done before the wedding. "What do you think of the house?"

"I can see it needs some work. But I have no doubt you'll make it a beautiful home for our family," Ed said, hoping she caught his meaning.

"Yes, I'll make it our home. The list of things to do is already filling my head. If it's all right, I want to come by Wednesday morning and begin cleaning. I want it to be perfect before our first night together," she said innocently, then blushed as she realized what that meant.

"I'm sure our first night here will be perfect," Ed said,

not thinking about the house at all. He smiled as Cassie's face reddened deeper as she looked away. He loved to tease her and watch her cheeks turn rosy.

"Oh Ed!" she chuckled as she realized he was teasing her.

By the time they returned from the walk it was time to get back for dinner. Mr. Crowley came out to say good-bye to them, walked over and shook Ed's hand. "Thanks again, Sheriff, for giving me peace of mind. I'll see you on Wednesday morning. Cassie, it was very nice to meet you," he said, shaking her hand. "You're a sweet girl. I'm happy for you both." He untied the horses as Ed helped Cassie into the rig.

Cassie had a thought and put her hand on Ed's arm. "Just a minute, Ed, I need to ask him something," she said. "Mr. Crowley, I know you're leaving most of the furniture, but what about the sewing machine? You should take that with you, so your daughter can use it. It must be fairly new." She'd noticed it in the bedroom and knew it was valuable.

"Dear, I want you to have it. I got it for my wife a few years ago. Evelyn loved to sew. Made most of our clothes with it, she cherished it so much. Neither one of my girls sews, and I think it should stay here with the house. I'm sure you could get good use out of it," he said with a smile.

Cassie's heart filled with compassion for the older man, who clearly adored his belated wife. "Can I at least pay you for it? I don't think it's right just to give it away with every-thing else," Cassie offered. She'd only seen a few sewing machines before, and only in the dressmaker shops. This sewing machine was a Singer. Using the foot-treadle she could keep sewing without stopping, effortlessly stitching fabric together. "No, really, I have money. I insist on paying you for it."

"I have an idea. I want to give it to you as a wedding

present," he said smiling. "Now you can put your mind at ease. It's a gift for your wedding. Congratulations to you both. Now get going before you're late for your dinner," he said, waving goodbye. He turned and walked back into the house, but not before Cassie got one more chance to say thank you.

Ed drove the team out of the yard as Cassie sat there, baffled. "Ed, do you realize what a wonderful gift that is? I can use that for years to make everything we need. I can sew in minutes what would normally take hours to sew by hand," she exclaimed.

Ed looked at her and grinned. "I love it when you get excited, you're so adorable," he said, meaning every word. Cassie was definitely the one for him. Every day he knew it more and more.

Cassie tried not to smile at him, but it was no use. She was too excited and couldn't help but let it show. "How does he do it? Always making me feel so wonderful. Even about things like getting excited about a sewing machine." It felt amazing to be around someone who thought everything she did was special. "You make me that way all the time. And I can't help it!" she said laughing.

"I love it. I love it when you're being yourself, bubbling about some new experience. Everyone can feel your enthusiasm. That's why you're so endearing to people, especially me. I want to scoop you up and swing you around every time I see you that way," he said honestly.

"There you go again, making me feel marvelous." She grinned. "What about you, Ed? You're constantly surprising me with your talents and ideas. I keep thinking, 'Wow, how did I get so lucky? How is the most incredible man in the world in love with me?'" Cassie gave his arm a squeeze as the rig bounced along the dusty road. "You're remarkable, handsome, strong, honorable, intelligent, witty, musical, and romantic…just to name a few of your traits. I can go on if you would like me to," Cassie said, smiling as she noticed Ed become self-conscious and blush. He looked away, pretending to be interested in a hawk circling over the open range, hoping she hadn't noticed his embarrassment, but she had.

"Nah, I'm nothing special. Just an ordinary man in love with an extraordinary woman," he said, trying to dismiss what she'd said. Ed loved giving compliments, but he never felt comfortable getting them. He didn't like being the center of attention. He felt more comfortable being the man behind the scenes, the strong silent type. But for Cassie, he had pushed himself to dance and sing or share his feelings. He felt safe with her, he trusted her with anything, especially his heart. He had only done that with a handful of people in his life.

Cassie smiled and then she realized something she hadn't before. Ed didn't see himself as she saw him. Well, maybe he knew his talents but didn't see himself as special or unique. "Where does this self-doubt come from?" She was puzzled. "Ed, you are anything but ordinary. Don't you believe me when I tell you how wonderful you are?"

"I believe you think I'm wonderful, because you see what you want to see. Not everyone feels the way you do," he said solemnly. "When I was growing up at the orphanage, I was told I was nothing and no one wanted me or would ever want me. They said that's why I was left there as a baby. It took a long time for me to finally trust my adopted parents. Eventually I did learn to trust them and accept their love. But it's still hard to trust most people and feel that I'm truly wanted or loved," Ed explained as he opened himself up to her.

"Oh Ed, I'm so sorry. No child should ever have to feel unwanted or unloved." Her heart was breaking for him.

She could imagine the cute toe-headed boy, little Eddie, tall and wiry, putting on a tough exterior defending the smaller children, when inside he felt so lonely and unloved. Maybe that is what helped him feel loved and wanted; to become someone's hero. "Oh Ed, I'm sorry you've felt this way. I hope you know that you're special in every way, and not just to me, but to most people. Don't you see it? You're amazing at so many things. You're honest, and hard working. You care for people before your own needs. You put your life on the line for this whole town for years." He looked at her and bowed his head humbly. "You don't think people notice, Ed, but they love and respect you. I was a perfect stranger and noticed it right away. And rarely have I heard a more beautiful singing voice or talented musician as you. You melted my heart when you sang and played for me."

Ed got misty-eyed from her sincere compliments and looked away again. When he could finally speak, he said, "Now look what you've done. You've gone and made me speechless. And that's hard to do," he joked, trying to side-step the emotion he was feeling. Again, his heart was swelling with love for her.

"That's all right, I'm sure you'll recover," Cassie said, and they both laughed.

Ed turned the rig onto the lane toward the Hartford's homestead. It'd been a busy and eventful day so far, and there was still so much to talk about. They had bought themselves a new home and things were falling into place.

When they arrived, they were welcomed by George. "How'd it go?" he asked, as he held the horses so they could climb out of the rig.

"We're the proud owners of a wonderful homestead." Ed smiled as he helped Cassie down.

"It is so beautiful, Uncle. I can't wait to tell you all about it. There's still some work to do to fix it up before

277

we move in. But it won't take much," Cassie said as she hurried in to tell Aunt Mabel the good news.

They had dinner and talked about the new homestead, making plans for the next four days, in hopes to have everything ready for the wedding.

Tomorrow Cassie planned to spend time fixing her veil and sash. Sometime during the week she would need to go into town to check the mail, hoping to receive a letter from Madeline, saying that she was coming to the wedding. The rest of the time, she was determined to work on their new home in order to have it ready to move into by Friday.

Aunt Mabel offered to help Cassie clean on Wednesday and then would make some excuse to slip into town without Cassie on Thursday and Friday in order to keep the quilt a surprise.

George said he would be able to help with the new place, moving furniture in and out between his work on the ranch.

Ed had secret plans to buy the wedding ring for Cassie later that afternoon and work on his song for her, but shared with the group that Tuesday would be his last day as Sheriff and he would spend it working. He was looking forward to his new adventure as a cattle rancher. Early Wednesday morning, he would go out to the homestead and walk through the routine with Mr. Crowley, wanting to be familiar with everything, down to the small details, hoping he would figure it out quickly for the sake of the animals. Then he could help Cassie with the house preparations, not wanting Cassie to overwork herself, keeping her strong and healthy for the baby.

There were so many things to do, but for now everyone just wanted to sit back and enjoy their dinner as they relished the many blessings the good Lord had afforded them during this exciting time.

Chapter 14
Bart and Bea

Meanwhile, Bart spent Sunday sleeping late, trying to rid himself of a splitting headache. In the early afternoon he pulled himself out of bed, washed up, dressed, and went out to see the town.

The city of Cheyenne didn't seem as bad as he had first thought. Clearly, it was a growing city that seemed to never stop moving, and with a renewed interest, he found it quite appealing. Deciding to stay far away from the saloons and dance halls, he explored shop after shop to examine the type of wares they were selling. He was surprised at the variety of goods available this far out West. As he walked through town, he started to wonder if his father would be interested in opening a mercantile in Cheyenne. Certainly, they could do well.

Prices for the same goods were higher than they were in Missouri, but nothing sat long enough to gather dust, as he learned from speaking to the shop owners he visited with. It was evident that business was booming since the opening of the railroad. One shop owner explained to Bart how much of an increase in demand the railroad had on most supplies, and how dependent they were on the continuous shipments from the East on those same trains. The new territory was a fast-growing market, fed by the constant flow of travelers through Cheyenne on their way to California and Utah, as well as the cowboys and railroad workers coming into town to spend their paychecks. The number of employees working for the railroad alone was into the hundreds. Bart knew the town was a goldmine for merchants; all he needed was a chance.

After finishing work that afternoon, Clancy showed Bart around the area, as promised, pointing out the best places to eat and where to get the best shave and haircut. Clancy took Bart to the outfitters shop where he could buy a cowboy hat and proper cowboy duds, wanting Bart to feel a part of the real Wild West. Later, he took Bart riding out into the hills to see the open prairie, where cattle grazed on waving fields of green as the sun set in the horizon. Bart was actually impressed at how beautiful the countryside was.

Clancy even tried to get Bart to go to the Opera House where the dance hall girls were performing, but Bart declined, his eye still stinging from last night's mistakes. Instead, Bart suggested that Clancy introduce him to his cousin Bea. Clancy had an even better idea; he would have his cousin meet them for supper, in the Rollins House hotel dining room, on Monday. By then, Bart hoped his swollen eye would be better so he could make a proper first impression.

Thankfully, by Monday evening Bart's eye was much better, and he looked almost normal except for a tint of blackish purple around his eye. A little before six, Monday evening, Bart walked across the street from his room at the Cheyenne Hotel, to meet Clancy and his cousin outside the Rollins House. Bart paused to watch Clancy as he drove up in a buggy and helped his cousin out. She was a tall young woman with strawberry blonde hair pulled back into a knot at the nape of her neck. Her dress was a modest dark blue satin with matching buttons down the front, and lacked any other frills, which suited her perfectly. The only accessory she wore was a small ivory cameo at her throat. To complete her look, she had placed a stylish dark blue felt hat slightly forward on her head. Bart was hypnotized by her deep blue eyes as she glided towards him.

"Bart, this is my cousin, Beatrice Holden," Clancy formally introduced her, as if he was a perfect gentleman, then added, "but we call her Bea, for short," earning himself a sideways glance from his cousin, which he shrugged off. "Well—we do," he said under his breath.

Bart ignored the exchange and reached out to shake her hand, noticing how gracefully she moved. She offered just the fingertips of her white gloved hand, which he took gently.

"Nice to meet you, Miss Beatrice Holden. Or would you rather I called you Bea?" he asked, with a twinkle in his pale blue eyes and a modest smile.

"Pleased to meet you too, Bart, and yes, you may call me Bea," she said with perfect diction.

"Thank you, Bea. And actually, it's Bartholomew, but my buddies call me Bart, for short," he said, and then laughed when he realized he sounded like he was making a joke.

"Bea, Beatrice, Bart, Bartholomew. Oh, that is funny," she said, laughing lightly. "Clancy, you didn't tell me he was funny, too." She looked at Clancy with amazement and then back to Bart with a pleased smile.

"That's because he isn't," remarked Clancy dully. Which made Bart and Bea laugh harder.

"You're one to talk, Clancy; your idea of funny was to give me this black eye," Bart replied sarcastically. And they all broke out laughing again.

"You should have seen this guy, Bea! He tried to take on five of us Saturday night. He was giving us grief for smelling like cows—him straight from Missouri in his nice city suit, drunker than a skunk. Still, he never backed down, not even after I gave him a wallop to the breadbasket." Clancy punched the air, demonstrating how he'd done it. "But he sure gave me a couple of good ones that rang my bell. And that's hard to do!" Clancy exclaimed, rubbing his head under his cowboy hat, feeling the tender lump.

"If that's true, Clancy, first you'd have to have a bell to ring!" Bea teased, and they laughed again.

"All right, all right! Let's get inside and get some supper, I'm starving. Even a guy without a brain knows when it's time to eat," joked Clancy as he strode across the board-walk in his freshly polished cowboy boots.

Bea was starting to wonder if accepting this invitation was a good idea. She was never impressed with the rough unrefined cowboys Clancy introduced her to. But lately, that seemed to be all there was here in Cheyenne, at least among men her age. Ever since her family moved out West, she'd wondered if she would ever find someone suited for her. And now to hear of Bart fighting in a saloon, gave her worry. "Maybe this city fellow will be just like all the others. Although, he is pretty funny, and quite good looking," she thought. Determined not to get her hopes up, Bea decided to try and enjoy herself and the evening ahead.

Bart was already having the best time he'd ever had in the company of a woman. For some unexplained rea-son, he felt at ease with Bea; she had already made a huge impression on him. Bea's classy appearance, cultured de-meanor and good sense of humor were very attractive to him. As they approached the restaurant, Bart offered his arm to the lovely lady, and she placed her hand around it, allowing him to lead her.

"I don't usually pick fights with strangers," Bart whis-pered to her as they walked arm in arm through the crowd-ed dining room. "My first night in Cheyenne was a pretty rough one," he explained, not wanting to give her the wrong impression. "I'd never been to a saloon before, and don't plan to ever go back. It's too rowdy for me. I'm typically very well-behaved," he said with a grin.

They were taken to a table and Bart helped Bea with her seat, then took the chair beside her. As Bart surveyed the grandeur of the dining room, he was thankful he'd worn his best dark suit and hat for the occasion.

A black-tie and white-gloved waiter handed them each a menu and excused himself, saying he would be back to get their order shortly. As Bart scanned the menu, looking for his favorite food, Bea periodically glanced over at him to get a closer look. She first noticed his hands as he held his menu, smooth yet manly, with evenly trimmed nails that were cleaner than most around Cheyenne. He appeared polite and cultured, as he displayed impeccable, gentlemanly manners. Maybe she had passed judgement too quickly.

The waiter came back and asked if they were ready to order. Clancy jumped in and gave his order first, then the waiter turned to Bart.

Bart immediately turned to Bea. "Ladies first." When Bea hesitated, he asked politely, "Bea, what are you having?"

Clancy realized he had probably been rude, and decided he had some things to learn about how to treat a woman and was taking notice of Bart's good manners.

Bea placed her order. "I'll have the pork with mashed potatoes and gravy, please."

"I'll have what she's having. It sounds delicious," he said as he handed the waiter the menu, then smiled at Bea. "I'm sure you know what's good here."

Bea was flattered, noticing how polite Bart was in comparison to her cousin and his usual crowd. Clancy was a little rough around the edges, but she still loved him. He was her favorite cousin and excused his behavior as part of his charm. However, Bart was making her feel like a proper lady and needed no excuses.

As they waited for their supper to arrive, Bea commented on the room's décor, then inconspicuously studied Bart's loose auburn curls while he turned to see what she was referring to. Being redheaded herself, she automatically compared his thick dark locks to her sleek gingery blonde hair. Once she'd read a book about a red-headed woman who was described as plain with a congenial personality. That was how she would describe herself. But she had qualities that some girls didn't have, and she felt that was more substantial than looks. Most of her life she'd been told she had a pleasant personality and was able to make friends easily, possibly because they felt no competition. But what she lacked in looks she made up for in humor and wit. And those were the things she found most notable in men as well.

"So, Bea. Clancy tells me you're a teacher," Bart said, eager to learn more about the lovely young lady sitting beside him.

"Yes, I teach school here. And when school isn't in session, I work as a seamstress at my family's business. Working as a seamstress is how I paid my way through college," Bea explained, appreciating his interest.

"Sounds like you're a woman of many talents," Bart said, intrigued with her range of accomplishments. "She's independent, ambitious, and intelligent," he thought to himself.

Bea smiled and changed the subject. "Clancy says you work at your father's mercantile," Bea said as the waiter came with their food.

Placing their plates in front of them, the waiter refilled

their coffee, then excused himself. All the while Bart and Bea continued to talk uninterrupted.

Clancy smiled as he watched the two of them hitting it off. He'd been right, Bart was a great match for his cousin. Two of a kind, they were. He began eating as they kept talking, not even caring that their food was getting cold.

"I've worked in my father's mercantile since I was little. I've learned the business inside and out, and I had planned to take over managing it someday, but I'm beginning to have second thoughts."

"Oh, and why's that?" Bea asked.

Bart thought for a moment. "I don't really have any desire to take over what my father built. It's not mine, it's his," Bart said, realizing for the first time what he really wanted.

"What is it you want to do then, Bart?" asked Bea, sincerely curious to know.

Bart was flattered that Bea was interested in what he wanted and spoke his dream for the first time out loud. "I want to make my own way. I want to build my own business. I've seen what this city has to offer, and at first, I'll admit, I wasn't impressed. But now that I've had a chance to look around, I think I would actually like it here. I'm thinking of opening my own shop. I know how to run a business and have money from working all those years for my father," Bart explained.

"You would do well here, especially if you have the know-how. New businesses are always opening up, and most who know what they're doing, have been successful. My pa opened his dress shop here two years ago, and we can barely keep up with all the orders. As a matter of fact, we're looking for help. My father wants to open a shop specifically for men's tailor-made suits. There are many wealthy men here who order their suits from back East, but often need them tailored once they arrive. So, he decided, why not just have them tailor made here?" Suddenly Bea had a brilliant idea. "You should talk to him, maybe you two could work out a partnership. His only delay with opening the shop has been finding someone he trusts to manage it for him. Bart, I'm sure you would do well," she said with enthusiasm.

"Now, that's an interesting proposal. I will definitely have to think about that," Bart said, contemplating the possibilities. "A partnership, in a men's clothing store. Hmm. Intriguing," he thought.

The two were oblivious to Clancy, who was content to just enjoy his meal. Clancy found it amusing that his cousin appeared to be enjoying herself with his new found friend. Usually when he set her up with his friends it ended with her swearing she would never do it again. But tonight was different—she seemed captivated with Bart. And from the looks of it, Bart was equally pleased with her company.

"I notice you have good taste in clothing and know how to dress as a proper gentleman," Bea admitted. "I'm sure you could assist in outfitting other men in the latest styles as well."

Bart blushed over the compliment Bea had given him. "That's very kind of you to say," and he needlessly straightened his tie. "I will give your idea some thought. But first I want to know what you enjoy doing. I know what you do for work, so what do you do for fun?" he asked, deflecting the attention away from himself.

Bea noticed the color rising in his cheeks and was touched at how modest he was, as he turned the focus of the conversation back to her. "Oh, you'll think it's dull. I don't want to say."

"Try me!" Bart encouraged.

"She's a bookworm!" Clancy interjected. "Good grief! Bea, it's not that bad. We all like to do things other people find odd," he said, trying to make her feel better.

Bea knew Clancy meant well, but all he'd done was make her feel uncomfortable.

"Really?" asked Bart in astonishment. "I love to read! It's my favorite pastime." He couldn't believe it, but then again, she was a teacher. It did make sense. "What's your favorite book?" He leaned closer, completely enthralled with her.

"'Little Women'! It's my most recent favorite. I loved it." Her eyes sparkled as she talked about the characters and story line. "Have you heard of it?"

"This is a little embarrassing, but yes. I've heard of it and read it," Bart admitted. "My father always stocks the most recent publications, and I read everything as soon as it comes in. And that one, I couldn't put down. I loved it!" He shared in her delight and tried to think of another she might enjoy. "Have you read 'The Last of the Mohicans'? That's one of my favorites."

"Yes, that's a great one, as is 'Moby Dick'." Bea loved having someone to talk about books with.

"My list of favorites is extensive. All of which I'm sure you've read. What other hobbies do you have?" Bart was beginning to think they might have even more in common.

"I also love to play the piano. It's what I do to express how I'm feeling. I know that sounds silly, but I don't know how else to explain it," she said shyly, and put the napkin on her lap and took her first bite of her supper.

"Amazing! I have always loved the piano. I find it one of the most beautiful sounding instruments, especially when accompanying the violin. I play the violin. It was my mother's wish that I learn to play. I would love to hear you play the piano sometime. If that's possible," Bart wondered aloud as he began eating his meal. Glancing at her hand as she lifted her fork, he noticed her long elegant fingers and imagined them gliding gracefully over the keys, playing one of his favorite songs.

Bea smiled. "I would be happy to play for you anytime. And I would love to hear you play the violin; it's one of my favorite instruments as well. Maybe sometime before you go back to Missouri, we could play together," she suggested.

"I would love that! You know, I may not be going back. I think I may have found a few good reasons to stay here," he paused as he beamed back at Bea. "And then you can play for me all the time."

Bea blushed and looked down, wondering if he was counting her as a reason to stay. "We shall see," she said demurely as she looked into his blue-grey eyes.

Clancy didn't miss the looks between the two and figured this was a good time to leave and let the lovebirds continue getting to know each other. "Well, I hate to be a stick in the mud, but I need to get going. I must say goodnight; I have an early day tomorrow," Clancy announced as he stood. "Let me get the bill," he offered, taking out his cash.

"No, no! Put that away, I insist. I owe you for introducing me to Bea. It's the least I can do."

Bea looked down bashfully, trying to keep her face expressionless.

"OK, then we're even and I get to pay next time." Clancy tipped his hat to Bea and gave her an amused smile as she glanced up and returned in kind.

Clancy walked home, grinning to himself as he mused over what had transpired. "I'm a matchmaker," he thought and laughed out loud, clearly pleased with himself.

Bea and Bart continued their discussion about music as they finished their meal, sharing their favorite songs and composers. And as they talked, Bart was silently thanking his mother for making him take all those violin lessons. Maybe, they would be of some use besides the yearly Christmas program at church.

They concluded their meal with pie and coffee, then Bart settled the bill and helped Bea out of her chair. "Bea, that was a very nice meal. But I must admit, the company was even better," he said as he offered his arm to lead her out of the restaurant.

"I agree, it's been very enjoyable." Bea took his arm as they left the restaurant. She laughed lightly. "I must admit something as well. I was a little worried at first. Clancy has introduced me to a few of his friends, and all of them have proven to be greatly disappointing. So, I want to thank you for a wonderful time," Bea graciously said as she stopped in front of her buggy.

"I had a great time too. I was wondering—it's still early. Would you walk with me for a spell? I would love to see your father's business and learn more about you."

Bea was flattered. "I'd like that. It's up the street a few blocks." She slipped her hand through Bart's arm again and together they walked north up Main Street, passing saloons, a bakery, the bank, and other establishments along the way. She felt confident on his arm as he instinctively positioned himself to keep her away from the road and rowdy men as they passed the dance hall and saloons.

Walking silently for a while, Bea had a question that continued to riddle her mind, and decided she needed to ask Bart before things went any further. "I have a personal question to ask you and I hope I'm not overstepping by asking it. So, don't answer if you don't want to." She paused and waited for his response.

Bart was pretty sure he knew what her question was. "Sure, you can ask me anything," he said, feeling completely at ease with her. It was an unfamiliar feeling for him but one he was enjoying.

"I'm curious as to what brought you to Cheyenne. Clancy said it should come from you. So I was wondering if you would tell me." Bea hoped she wasn't going to upset him. She'd already concluded that he'd come from Missouri on the train, gotten drunk and picked a fight all because he was having a bad day. But why, and why was he here? That part she didn't know. He didn't seem the type to act so recklessly and imagined there was more to the story.

Bart thought for a minute. "What if I tell her the truth and she wants nothing to do with me? But she may eventually find out anyways, and if I stay here I would rather her hear it from me." Resolved to tell her the truth, he took a deep breath and began. "I was engaged about two months ago."

Bea caught the word "was" and held her tongue as she nodded and let him explain.

"We had planned to be married next spring, that is, until everything changed," Bart said, and proceeded to tell her what had happened to Cassie and her family. "I was at a loss as to what to do. When I found out she was moving, I suggested we call off the engagement; I felt it was the right thing to do at the time, and she even seemed relieved. But as time went on, I realized I had been a fool, and took the coward's way out. So, that's what I was doing. I came here to make things right." He stopped on the boardwalk in front of a closed mercantile and looked at Bea for her reaction.

Being thoughtful and a good listener, Bea asked, "And when you got here, what happened?"

Bart looked away, collecting his thoughts. There was understanding in her big blue eyes, so he continued. "At first, I sent her a letter explaining my regrets and my intentions to make it right. But instead of waiting for her response, I acted impulsively. Strangely, I felt an urgency to come and get her before it was too late. I didn't heed my parents' warning that I was making a grave mistake, and instead I got a ticket that very same day and hopped the train in hopes to find her when I arrived." He took his hat off and ran his long fingers through his wavy locks. "I've always been one to think things through, make a plan and stick to it. But this time, I acted rashly. As soon as I arrived, I went looking for her." Pausing again, he gathered his thoughts. This was the hardest part to tell.

Bea encouraged him to continue. "And did you find her?" She was starting to put the rest of the pieces together.

"Yes, I did, and it appeared I was too late. When I found her, she was with another man—and they were kissing." He took a deep breath and went on. "When I saw them, I felt my heart drop into the pit of my stomach. But at that point, I had to follow through. I'd come all this way to see her, so I approached them. Maybe my timing could have been better. Because I definitely startled her. When she saw me, she went pale as a ghost and fainted." He shrugged and smiled weakly. "I must have been the last person she expected to see in Cheyenne."

Bea nodded, feeling she understood.

"I felt terrible for frightening her." Bart relayed to Bea his conversation with Cassie and her revelation that she'd never had those kinds of feelings for him. Looking down, he rubbed the back of his neck, surprised that he could say those things without the hurt he had felt a few days ago. "The man she was with just so happened to be the sheriff. I was crushed and angry. I'd acted foolishly and was humiliated," he said, baring his soul. Why was he telling her his feelings? Maybe because he felt safe with her. And now he was revealing his deepest feelings to her.

"I'm sure it was a hard blow to find out the way you did. It must have hurt tremendously," she said sympathetically.

"It did. And to make matters worse, I handled it poorly. I've never had a drink before, much less been in a saloon. I'll admit that whole evening wasn't pleasant. Alcohol is awful tasting stuff. But it helped numb the disappointment. And the more I drank the more it fueled my anger. I ached to get back at the man who had taken away my future." Bart admitted how he'd goaded the cowboys in the saloon until Clancy took the bait, ultimately resulting in blows. "I wanted the physical pain to take away the emotional pain in my heart. I reacted to the situation in anger and ended up with this black eye and a night in jail," he said, looking at her as she looked deeper into his sad eyes.

"I can see why you did what you did. It's understandable." She felt compassion for him. "I'm so sorry you had to go through that."

"I'm better now that I've had a few days to think about it. I won't deny I was greatly disappointed when things didn't go as I had expected. But I think now, things may have worked out for the best," weakly smiling as he regained his composure. "I guess sometimes you have to let go and let God take over. I was trying too hard, even from the beginning with her. I see now, she was never right for me. These past few days I've had a lot of time to think and learned so much about myself." He looked into the distance, deep in thought. "It took me getting away from my family and home to discover who I am and what kind of life I want to have."

"The hardest experiences in life teach us the best lessons," Bea mused, thinking of all the hard lessons she'd had to learn over the years.

"I believe you're right. When I was young, I was mercilessly teased for my red hair and I eventually learned how to stand up for myself, and that was sometimes with my fists," he said, admitting his biggest trial up until recently. "It's been a long time since I've had to stand up for myself, but when Cassie refused me, I was hurt and embarrassed, more than ever before. And I reverted back to the one tactic that I had used, all those years ago. I fought back, only this time, I couldn't fight Cassie or the sheriff. So, I chose the next best thing," he admitted.

Bea stared at him in disbelief. "You say her name is Cassie, and her beau is the sheriff?" she asked as the puzzle pieces came together, and the picture was complete.

"Yes, her name is Cassie, and she says she is going to marry the sheriff. I'm sure you must know him."

"I can't believe it! It really is a small world. I do know the sheriff, and I also know your Cassie. I met her in our dress shop. I remember when she first came here, she bought a riding dress from us, and then I saw her at church. I'd heard about the loss of her family. It's tragic, the poor girl. We all feel so badly for her. And then one Sunday, I watched how Sheriff Havoc took an interest in her at the church picnic. I noticed a change had come over both of them when I saw them dancing together at the church dance. They were so happy and radiant, and obviously in love. I know you don't want to hear this, but they are getting married this Saturday," she said with reluctance. "I'm truly sorry."

Bart let out a deep sigh. "It's okay. She already told me. I just didn't realize it was going to be so soon. It was my fault for coming here before knowing Cassie's wishes. After all she's been through, she deserves to be happy. And if I'm not the one to do that for her, then I hope the sheriff is. I'd be relieved just knowing she's happy." He smiled weakly. "Now that I think about it, I don't suppose

293

we would have ever truly made each other happy. I would have never been enough for her. I pursued the engagement even though she was never really interested in me that way. But I'd hoped she would grow to love me in time. And now, I'm not sure I really loved her, or just loved the idea of her being my wife. I understand now, there should be more than that," he said, as he spoke out loud what he was realizing for the first time—that he wanted a woman that would love him for who he was. That's what he was looking for now, a woman that was equally yoked with him.

"You are very interesting to me, Bart," Bea said seriously.

"You are very interesting to me too, Bea. I've never met anyone like you. No woman ever put me at such ease before. I usually keep my thoughts to myself. But with you I am different. I feel I can tell you anything and you understand." Bart felt his heart race as he said the words, then placed his free hand on top of hers as they began walking arm-in-arm again.

Bea flushed as she felt his hand on hers and smiled. "I'm glad you feel that way. Thank you for trusting me enough to share your thoughts. I enjoy hearing what you think. I'm learning so much about you. And so far, I like what I know." Her cheeks pinked a deeper shade as she admitted her feelings. "Oh, here's our place," she said as they arrived in front of the shop. "The Holden Dress Shop," Bea announced and stood back as Bart evaluated her family's business.

Bart objectively assessed the white store front, appreciating the elegantly scrolled lettering on the large picture window, with magnificent dresses displayed inside. "This is a fine-looking store. I'm impressed. It's in a good location, with plenty of foot traffic, and such an eye-catching display in the window. I'd definitely shop here if I was a young woman in need of a gown. You must be doing very well. And these aren't just any dresses," he said, peering through the window at the stylish gowns. "These are just as splendid as the ones I've seen from the big cities back East. I like how you've even added a little western influence as well. You do marvelous work," he said, looking back at her in admiration.

Bea smiled, pleased that he liked her family's work. She knew they made the best dresses in Cheyenne, but she was happy to hear it from someone else, especially a businessman. "Thank you. We work hard. And like I said, we are looking for help. I really am serious about you talking to my father about opening a men's clothing shop," she said with excitement. She was becoming more and more impressed with Bart and knew her father would definitely approve of him. "Could you come by the store tomorrow and meet him? I'll be here all day and could introduce you."

"I'll be available." He smiled. "I'm not doing anything tomorrow except sitting around deciding my future." Bart chuckled at his joke as Bea joined him. He continued in a less sarcastic tone, "My pa will expect me home soon, and it will come as a great blow to him if I decide to stay. It will change all his future plans for me and his mercantile. But, yes, I'll come by and meet your father tomorrow morning," he said with certainty. He knew the gravity of his decision would greatly impact the life of his whole family as well as his own. "Thank you for the introduction. I should get you back to your buggy. I don't want to get off on the wrong foot with your father. I want him to know I'm a gentleman and will take good care of his daughter," he said, and then realized what that might imply and blushed.

Bea caught the slip and smiled to herself as she imagined the possibility, then responded, "He will be impressed. As am I," she said as Bart returned her smile.

They walked back towards the hotel in comfortable silence. Periodically she looked over at Bart, trying to figure out how she happened to meet such a charming man, all the way from Missouri. It reminded her of a book she'd read a long time ago, about a dashing young man in pursuit of his lost love, traveling across the country only to be scorned once he found her, and as a result, ended up finding his true love. The title of the book escaped her at the moment, but she recalled it was a marvelous love story with the perfect ending.

Bart caught her glancing at him and gave her his sweetest smile. "You're something else, Bea, truly one of a kind. Intelligent, ambitious, talented, and such a lovely personality. And pretty, too," he added, wanting her to know he thought she was pretty.

"Oh, Bart! You don't need to say that. I know I'm not. But I appreciate the generous compliment," she said modestly, blushing.

"Well, you are! And I will fight any man that says otherwise," he said grinning, "and you know I will," he added, thinking she was beautiful in every way.

Bea laughed. "No more fighting! You stay in one piece. I would hate to think of what Clancy would look like if you two hadn't been drunk. You don't need to defend me. And yes, I believe you would," she said, feeling flattered.

"Bea, you're worth fighting for." Impulsively he leaned forward and ever so lightly kissed her silky soft cheek. Slowly withdrawing, he stared back at her in a daze. "Thank you for a wonderful night, Bea," he said, as she flushed from his public affections.

"Thank you, Bart, for everything. I had a delightful time. I'll see you tomorrow," she said, still collecting herself from the kiss.

Bart led her the final steps to her buggy and assisted her inside, untied the horse, and watched as she drove away, as the last of the evening light faded.

Bart stood there for a while, thinking about how marvelous the evening had been. Slowly he crossed the bustling street to his hotel. He had a lot to think about and expected it would be long into the night before he would fall asleep.

Bea slowly drove home, wanting to collect herself before arriving. She was unfamiliar with the feelings she was having, and it amazed her. Never had a man showed so much sincere interest in her, and she felt the same attraction for him. It was like a dream. Bea had wondered if this day would ever come, having waited for what seemed like forever for love. "Is that what I'm already feeling for Bart?" she wondered. She had to admit, from his shy smile, to his fiery ambition, to the way he pursued love with courage, her feelings for him were undeniable. She was sympathetic to his plight; he'd suffered great disappointment and humiliation, and she admired his resilience. Surprisingly, he seemed to be regaining his optimism. Bea felt certain she had a part in that. She delighted in their shared interests, similar talents, and even their red hair that others had ridiculed. Tonight with Bart, she didn't feel like an old schoolmarm spinster. Bea felt like a woman, one that a gentleman appreciated for her uniqueness and beauty; he'd confessed genuine interest in her, and from his spontaneous kiss, she believed him. Delighting in the memory of his kiss, she thought of his tender lips pressing to her cheek, causing her heart to flutter once more. "I need to calm down. I can't let Mother and Father see me this way," she thought, and could feel the heat in her cheeks even as she tried to slow her breathing. "Oh, how I wish this feeling would never end. I feel like a bluebird soaring through the sky and I never want to land." She wondered, "Is this what romantic love is like? It certainly feels the way it's described in books. No wonder people do crazy things for love; this feeling is stronger than I could have ever imagined."

By the time Bea arrived home, she had collected herself and entered as poised and reserved as usual. As she talked to her parents, it was a struggle to keep the excitement out of her voice, describing the young businessman she'd gotten to know, working hard not to give away her true feelings for him. Father agreed, Bart sounded promising for the job and thought it would be a good idea to meet and talk to the young man. When her younger sisters asked about her evening out, she simply said she'd had a good time, then excused herself to go to bed. Once alone in her room, she sat at her writing desk and recorded her thoughts and feelings in her diary, daydreaming about the glorious evening again.

That night Bart thanked God for bringing him to Cheyenne. As he reflected on the tough lessons he'd learned in such a short time, he pondered on the wondrous path that God was leading him on. Unexpectedly he'd met Bea, an amazing young woman, all the way in this god-forsaken place, a woman who was capturing his heart and he couldn't wait to see again.

He would write to his pa tomorrow and tell him the news if things turned out the way he hoped. As the night drifted on, he continued to wonder about a future with Bea. One thing he knew; he was staying whether it worked out with Bea's father or not. He was determined to make his own way, be his own man. God had led him here and he was going to do his best to follow His promptings. Finally, he drifted off to sleep and dreamed about Bea.

Chapter 15
Getting Ready and Making Plans

Tuesday morning, Cassie awoke suddenly to a clap of thunder and flash of lightning. From the bedside clock, she saw it was still too early to start chores, but didn't mind staying in bed listening to the thunderstorm until it was time to get up.

Reaching over to her bedside table, she took a biscuit off the plate and nibbled on it as she watched the storm from under the warm blanket and waited for the nausea to pass. Still early, but feeling better, she ventured out of bed into the chill of her dark bedroom and dressed for the day.

"Today will be a perfect day to sew my veil. Maybe I can get an early start on it. There's still so much to get done before the wedding," Cassie thought with excitement as she brushed and braided her hair.

Leaving her bedroom as quietly as she could, Cassie went to the kitchen. A loud boom of thunder shook the house and dazzling light burst through the windows, lighting her way to the kitchen. Feeling her way in the darkness, she found the matches and lit the lamp on the table. She shivered as she started the fire in the stove and prepared the kettles for tea and coffee. "I can't wait to get up in the morning and prepare Ed's coffee in our own kitchen. Edward, my husband. Oh, I love the sound of that," she thought as she warmed herself by the stove and began daydreaming of being a wife.

"Good morning, Cassie," Mabel said, startling her.

"Oh!" Cassie turned around and happily greeted Mabel.

"You're up early." Mabel returned Cassie's smile as she entered the kitchen and put on her apron.

"The thunderstorm woke me up, so I decided to get a head start on the day. I put the kettles on. They should be ready in a few minutes." Cassie walked to the front window, pushed back the lace curtains, and peeked out at the storm.

"That sounds wonderful." Mabel set spoons and cream and sugar on the table then sat down to wait for the coffee to boil. "There's a lot to get done before the wedding. I'll bet you're getting excited; I know I am," Mabel said, suddenly feeling a little sad. Cassie had been with her and George only a short while and she knew the house would be quiet without her. Of course, they would see her often, but would miss waking up to her sweet smile and receiving her nightly hugs and kisses.

"Yes, I've been thinking about the wedding, and also about being a wife in my own home. I've imagined being a wife and mother ever since I was a little girl. I used to play 'house' and pretend my doll was my real baby. I made mud pies for her to eat and sewed her clothes and blankets from scraps of material. It was so much fun pretending—but soon I won't be pretending. Soon, I'll be doing all those things for my own family. Well—all except the mud pies." Cassie lightly laughed and joined Mabel at the table.

Mabel chuckled and then became more serious. "You'll be a wonderful wife and mother, Cassie. To be a mother is a glorious blessing, one of which I was finally able to experience with you." "And it will end all too quickly," Mabel thought, and rose from the table to hide her tears. She waited until her emotions were in control before she returned to the table, bringing a cup of tea for Cassie and coffee for herself.

Cassie looked up at her aunt as she set the teacups down and saw the sadness in her eyes. "Aunt Mabel, just because I'm getting married doesn't mean I'll stop needing you. I'll depend on your wisdom even more after I'm married. There is so much I don't know, and when the baby comes—I'll need your motherly advice for that too." Cassie smiled warmly as Aunt Mabel sat beside her. "Don't you worry, I plan to see you every day, or at least try to," reassured Cassie. "I just don't want to become a bother by constantly dropping in."

"Cassie, you could never be a bother. Our time with you is always cherished. You're like a daughter to us." She gave Cassie's shoulder a gentle squeeze. "I would love nothing more than to see you every day. As a matter of fact, George and I were wondering if you two would like to come over for Sunday supper, each week. It could become our new family tradition." Mabel blew on her cup of coffee.

"Of course, we would love Sunday suppers with you, too. And you could come over to our place for supper as well." Cassie added cream and sugar to her tea and gave it a stir.

Mabel smiled at the thought. "You're welcome to drop in whenever." Her mind raced ahead in time. "It'll be so much fun keeping each other company during the long winter and making baby things together. Oh, and when the baby comes, the fun will never end. I can hardly wait." Mabel looked forward to the days ahead. "What a blessing you've been to us, Cassie. You've brought so much love into our home. I just know it will grow even more with your baby," Mabel said, giving Cassie's hand a squeeze. "We love you so much."

Cassie felt the tears spill onto her cheeks; her emotions were so close to the surface lately. "I love you too,

Aunt Mabel. Both you and Uncle George have been such a Godsend to me. I don't know what I would have done without you." Cassie smiled through her tears as she returned the squeeze. She felt so loved and cherished living with them and would miss the routines that had become so familiar to her. This house felt like home to her. She too felt a touch of sadness along with the joy, as she prepared to move into her own home. Determined not to let too much time pass between visits, she made a silent promise to keep the bond strong between them. "You're welcome to visit Ed and I anytime, no invitation needed. We will always be glad to see you."

They sat quietly listening to the storm as they enjoyed just being together.

"What's all this?" George asked as he came out of his bedroom. "Having coffee without me?" he teased, breathing in the strong aroma. "Thank you for making it, dear," he said, leaning down and giving Mabel a kiss on the cheek.

"It wasn't me, George. It was Cassie. She had it going before I got up," Mabel said, sipping her coffee as the rain tapped steadily on the roof overhead.

"Well, bless your heart, Cassie. We're sure going to miss having you around," said George, filling himself a cup from the kettle on the stove.

"I'll miss you, too. Even though I'm excited for Ed and me to have our own place, you've made this feel like home, and I'm grateful to you," Cassie said, beginning to get emotional again.

George was getting a little choked up as well and cleared his throat. "You know it won't be that easy to get rid of us. We plan on dropping in without notice, eating your food and drinking your coffee," he said, forcing a smile, trying to lighten the mood.

Cassie loved the way Uncle George teased to hide his

emotions and smiled at him lovingly. "I think I can deal with that."

Clearing his throat again, he announced, "I have plans to go into town today, if either of you are interested in joining me." George gulped down his cup of coffee as he stood by the stove.

"I think I'll be staying home all day. I have sewing and ironing to get done. And I'm sure Ed will drop in at some point, so I want to be here when he comes," Cassie said as she stood to take her cup to the sink.

"I'll go in with you, George. I have some things to follow up on in town," said Mabel vaguely.

"All right, then it's settled. I'll head out and get the chores done and we can leave right after breakfast. Hopefully the weather will clear up a little by then." George put down his cup and went to the door, put on his hat and jacket, and stepped out into the dark blustery morning.

***

Bart was startled awake as thunder rumbled outside the window of his hotel room. He flung back the covers and sprang out of bed. "I can't wait to see Bea!" he thought as he lifted off his nightshirt and tossed it aside. The cold water in the basin felt invigorating as he washed up and wet his hair down. He ran his hand over his chin and decided he needed a shave. "And maybe a haircut won't hurt either," he thought, as he tried to tame his unruly curls with his comb. Bart carefully dressed in his dark blue suit, starched shirt, and black ribbon tie, and checked his reflection in the mirror to make sure everything was impeccable before he left. With a spring in his long stride, he headed down to the hotel dining room. After eating breakfast, he set out to Clancy's favorite barber shop.

The rain started pouring as Bart reached the shop, and he hurried to get inside. A bell above the door tinkled and announced his arrival.

"Welcome!" came a holler from the back. A slightly rotund man came through the curtain covered door in back, carrying a cup of coffee. "Come in, come in! I'm open. Just having my morning cup o'joe. Would you like one?" he asked as his grin lifted his well-manicured greying moustache.

"No, thank you. I've already had mine but thanks for the offer," Bart said graciously. "I just need a shave and a trim, please." Bart took off his hat and suit coat and hung them on the coatrack.

"Sure thing. Name's Bill," he said, shaking Bart's hand.

"Name's Bartholomew Clark," Bart said, feeling right at home.

"At your service, right this way." Bill put down his coffee and walked with Bart to the barber's chair.

"Thank you very much." Bart was impressed with the small orderly shop. Two large mirrors hung on adjacent walls and a built-in cabinet that held the barber's tools.

"You must be from out of town. I can tell. You have a slightly different look about you," Bill said as Bart sat in the barber's chair.

"Yes, I'm from Missouri," said Bart, as Bill wrapped a cape around his neck.

"Ah, yes, I recognize the accent now. Very faint but I can hear it," Bill said, reclining the chair back. Retrieving a hot wet towel, he placed it on Bart's face. "So, what brings you all the way to Cheyenne?"

"I came to visit a friend," Bart said from under the towel.

"Well, I hope you enjoy yourself while you're visiting.

There's usually something going on here day and night. Especially for a young lad, such as yourself." Bill removed the towel and with the brush he began applying the shaving lather he had mixed, covering Bart's upper lip and lower half of his face with the white foam. Bill began to shave Bart's face with the straight edged blade, removing the stubble from his face. When he finished, he placed another warm wet towel on Bart's face for a moment to clean and soften the skin, and with a few pats of shaving lotion, the shave was complete.

Bart rubbed his fingers over his smooth face. "My friend Clancy was right; you do give a great shave."

"Oh, you're friends with Clancy. What a character that lad is. Not a bad bone in his body, but constantly getting into scrapes," he said, adjusting the chair so he could cut Bart's hair.

"Yes, so I found out the hard way. It wasn't completely his fault though." Bart explained how he and Clancy had met, as Bill combed and snipped.

"Oh, I guess that's what these are from," he said, motioning to Bart's fading bruises.

"Yah, I had it coming. I was drunk and in a rotten mood. I said some pretty bad things and got him fired up," Bart said, trying to defend his new friend. "Then he crossed the line by making fun of my red hair; that's when it came to blows."

"I see," Bill said, understanding how sensitive people were about their hair. "Well, you have nice hair," Bill said, trying to make Bart feel better. "The curl isn't too tight either. If you use this here pomade," he said, holding up a jar of waxy cream, "it'll help it stay in place, so it doesn't look so unkempt." He finished the cut then applied a small amount of pomade and combed it through.

Bill handed Bart a hand mirror to take a look. Turning

from side to side, he inspected Bill's handiwork. Bart thought he looked distinguished, almost handsome. "Thanks, Bill. Looks great. I'm wondering if I could buy some of that hair pomade from you."

"Look son, I'd be happy to give you a small jar, free of charge." He scooped up some and put it in a smaller jar and handed it to Bart.

"Thank you, that's very kind of you," Bart said, taking the jar.

"It's my own concoction, maybe one day when I'm too old to cut hair I'll make enough to sell," Bill said, chuckling as he smoothed his moustache.

"You know, you could sell it now. It works perfect for guys like me." Bart handed him money for the cut and shave, adding a nice tip as well. "Thanks for everything." Bart carefully put on his hat and suit jacket and placed the small jar of pomade in his pocket as he left the shop.

Bill looked down, examining the generous tip. He was impressed with Bart; most young lads didn't even leave a tip. He slipped the money into his vest pocket, hoping to see Bart again soon.

***

Sheriff Havoc left the boarding house, hastening to his office as the gusting wind blew hard against him, threatening to rip the hat off his head as he held it in place. As he jumped and dodged puddles across the street, the clouds let loose a sheet of rain, drenching Cheyenne and those unlucky enough to be outside. He was thankful for his last-minute decision to wear his oilskin slicker; it helped keep him relatively dry and protected his sidearm holstered low on his hip. He picked up his pace, as puddles gathered on the boardwalk, splashing up his boots and trousers with each step.

Sheriff Havoc didn't mind summer rainstorms. They were one of his favorite things. He loved God's display of power in the elements; the spectacular lightning tore across the heavens as a roar of thunder shook the earth. The summer rain smelled fragrant and earthy. Smiling, he dodged other pedestrians seeking shelter under awnings and store fronts, and thought of his own place, in the wide-open countryside.

Bursting into his office, he shook the rain off his hat and jacket before hanging them up on the peg by the door. He dropped his gloves onto the desk along with his office keys. Finding his silver star on his desk, he pinned it to his leather vest, as he did every day. Looking around the office, he took note of the two rusty cells in the back, thankfully devoid of prisoners. On the far wall was a heavy cabinet full of hundreds of warrants and reports he'd filed over the years. Near the front of the office sat the black stove where he'd stood as he listened to countless confessions and allegations, stewing over what the proper course of action should be. The weight of the town rested on his shoulders to do the right thing. He was the law, the enforcer, their protector. He'd been given a challenge, something to focus on besides his grief-filled past. Being sheriff had given him purpose and time to work through his sorrow. Ed often reflected on how much things had changed in those past two years, and he thanked the Lord for His guiding hand along the way. Fondly, he ran his fingers over the edge of the desk, remembering when he and Vic had moved it in. It seemed like eons ago, and yet here he was, ready to hang up his badge.

Ed started the fire in the little pot-bellied stove and put a fresh pot of coffee on and settled in at his desk to finish up some paperwork. As he sat at his desk shuffling through files, he began humming the song he had written, when a fresh verse came to him. He quickly pulled open the desk drawer, found a pencil, and jotted down the new lyrics, feeling pleased with the song's progress. "Darn, I wish I had my guitar with me so I could practice. Oh well, guess I'll practice tonight."

Just then a hasty knock brought his head up and Bart burst through the door. Ed couldn't have been more surprised.

"Sorry to barge in, but it was coming down pretty hard," Bart explained as he shut the door and took off his hat.

"Couldn't keep away, I see," said Ed sarcastically. "Well, now that you're here, you might as well have a seat." Standing, he pointed to the chair across from the desk.

"Thank you," Bart said, attempting to brush off the water that had beaded up on the shoulders of his wool suit. "I'll just wait a little bit to see if the storm passes. Then I'll be on my way." He really hadn't intended to drop in, but he didn't want to get his nice suit soaked before meeting with Bea's father. Maybe it was fate that the rain came pouring down at just the moment he was passing by.

"Can I get you a cup of coffee? I think I'll have one." Ed walked to the stove and poured a cup for each of them and handed one to Bart.

"You know, I appreciate what you did for me the other night." Bart glanced over at the cell where he and Clancy had spent the night. "I didn't deserve it. But thanks." Bart took a long sip of his coffee, feeling it burn all the way down, warming him immediately.

"Well, I think you learned your lesson—maybe the hard way. I see your bruises are healing nicely," Ed said with a touch of amusement, as he sat down and put his boots up on the corner of the desk, also noting Bart's new haircut. There was something different about him, more than just bruises and hair, and Ed couldn't quite put his finger on it.

Bart ignored the comment as the lyrics on the tablet caught his attention and looked up as the sheriff flipped it over abruptly. Bart cleared his throat, swallowed, and smiled uneasily. "I hear you're getting married this Saturday. Congratulations. I'm happy for you and Cassie," he said humbly as he lifted his cup, toasting, and took a drink.

"Oh, you heard. I'm surprised you're happy. What's changed?" asked Ed dryly, surprised by the sentiment.

"That night locked in here with Clancy gave me the opportunity to think about some things. I will admit it wasn't easy at first to accept Cassie's words. But in time I realized she was right." Looking out the rain-streaked window, a touch of sadness crossed Bart's face. "I was never the one for her. She said yes to my proposal out of respect for her father. Truthfully, she never really showed any interest in me beyond that of friendship. If she would have married me, we would have never been truly happy. Although, I could see she was happy when she talked about you," Bart said, looking at the sheriff. "I really do want Cassie to be happy and have everything she deserves. I thought I was in love with her, but now I believe it was more of an infatuation. It was what I wanted, but not what was right for either of us," Bart said, trying to explain his change of heart. "So, what I'm trying to say is, I won't be causing any more trouble for you or Cassie." He rushed on, "And I'd like to stay here in Cheyenne."

Sheriff Havoc swung his feet off the desk and sat upright with his mouth open wide, appalled at the prospect.

Before the sheriff could interrupt him, Bart blurted out, "It has something to do with a girl that I've met, as well as a possible business opportunity, not Cassie. So, what I'm asking is, if it would be all right with you if I stayed here in Cheyenne. I know you said, 'stay a few days.' But I want to stay much longer." Bart waited anxiously for an answer as the sheriff slowly drank his coffee.

"Hmm, this is an interesting change. You've met a girl." He rubbed his cleft chin with his thumb and forefinger. "I see," he mused. "I guess I can understand," he said, with a small smile. "A man will do crazy things for a woman. Especially one he loves." Ed stood to refill his coffee before turning back to give his final verdict. "You're welcome to stay as long as you like," he proclaimed. "I won't be the sheriff much longer and could care less what you do." Sitting down in his chair again, leaning forward, resting his forearms on the desk, he gave Bart a warning. "As long as you're in Cheyenne, I want to be sure you won't upset Cassie again. She's felt bad enough about this whole sordid experience," Ed admonished.

Bart sat there looking ashamed. "I'm really sorry for the way I've behaved. I give you my solemn word, I will not cause her any more grief. And I would also like to apologize to her. If only she would let me talk to her," Bart pleaded, seeking forgiveness.

Ed felt compassion for the young man, realizing he would have probably acted the same way, had the shoe been on the other foot. "Let me talk to her and see what I can work out. She has our wedding to get ready for and I don't know when she'll have time." He stood and went to the window, seeing the clouds were breaking up. "You know, it actually might be good for her to see you're moving on, and in a new direction," Ed said, as he turned back with a grin. "So, who's this lucky girl you're pining after?" Ed was curious who he could have met in just a few days.

Bart felt a wave of relief and excitement at the chance he'd just been given. "Her name is Beatrice Holden. She's the teacher here and works at her father's dress shop," Bart explained with a pleased smile.

"Yes, I know her. A fine young lady. Good for you. I hope it works out." Ed liked Bea; she was a dignified, well-respected woman in the community, although he had assumed she would be a spinster, and teach all her life.

"Thank you, really. It means a lot to know you're all right with me staying, even if you aren't the sheriff anymore. Out of respect for Cassie, I would like her approval as well." He could see the sun breaking through outside and stood and put on his hat. "I think the rain has let up, so I'll be going now. I need to talk to Mr. Holden this morning about a business proposal. Thanks again for the coffee. And if you would please talk to Cassie for me. I would like to apologize as soon as possible." He offered his hand. "I'm glad that Cassie fell in love with a good man, even if it wasn't me."

Ed graciously took Bart's hand and gave it a hearty shake. "Thank you. It's nice of you to say. Good luck with your pursuits," he said sincerely.

***

Bart walked across the muddy road, careful to avoid the larger puddles and the spray from passing wagons as he walked down the boardwalk toward the Holden Dress Shop. Talking to Sheriff Havoc had eased his conscience some. He felt taller and lighter, knowing he had cleared the tension between him and the sheriff, and hoped Cassie would allow him to do the same with her. This meeting with Mr. Holden would determine whether he went into business for himself or as a partner. Either way, he was going to stay in Cheyenne and would soon have to break the news to his father.

Bart arrived at the Holden Dress Shop, took a deep breath and opened the door. Bea was standing behind the counter and looked up to see who had walked in. The pretty pink dress she wore was simple and elegant, like her, and flattered her tall slender figure. Her hair was pulled neatly into a twist at the back of her head with only a few small wisps falling softly around her face. As she met his gaze, he smiled and watched her expression brighten.

"Good morning, Bea," Bart said cheerfully as he closed the door behind him.

"Good morning, Bart," Bea replied, noticing how handsome he looked in his blue suit that seemed to brighten his eyes. As he removed his hat, she saw he had done something different with his hair, making him look very debonair. "How are you this morning?" Bea asked as Bart approached the counter, setting off butterflies in her stomach.

"I'm much better now that I'm here with you," he said, smiling even bigger as he watched her blush from his flirting.

Feeling a little breathless, she quickly announced, "My father's in the back, let me go get him. I'll be just a moment." "Good grief, I can hardly keep from shaking. What's happening to me?" Bashfully, she turned to retreat behind the curtain to the back of the store.

"I'll be right here when you get back," Bart said smiling at her as she rushed out. He felt on top of the world, so sure of himself, and his heart felt so full.

A few minutes passed before Bea came back, followed by Mr. Holden, who was dressed in a dark grey vest and trousers.

"Father, this is the man I was telling you about. Bart…" Bea paused, looking from Bart to her father, suddenly realizing she didn't know Bart's last name.

Bart jumped in and saved her the embarrassment. "Bartholomew Clark, but you can call me Bart. It's a pleasure to finally meet you, Mr. Holden," Bart said confidently shaking Mr. Holden's hand. Bart could see some resemblance between father and daughter; Mr. Holden was nearly as tall as Bea, of average build, with dark auburn hair and a kind, fatherly face. The wrinkles at the corners of his blue eyes deepened as he smiled.

"Nice to meet you, Bart," said Mr. Holden, noting Bart's impeccable appearance and manners, as well as his red hair.

"Bea tells me you're busier than ever. I must say, you have a splendid shop here, and the dresses are magnificent," added Bart, looking around the room at the different colors, fabrics and styles of gowns.

"Thank you for saying so," Mr. Holden said, beaming with pride. "Now Bart, why don't you tell me about yourself," getting straight to the point.

"I'm from Missouri, Jackson County, to be exact. I've been working in my father's mercantile since I was just a lad. I'm now an apprentice merchant and know his business inside and out. I do the books as well as the purchasing of stock and most of the daily operations and I was planning on taking over the business completely in a few years. But since I've been in Cheyenne, I see there are wonderful opportunities to be had here. I was considering going into business for myself, maybe a branch of my father's store, or one completely of my own. I mentioned my plans to Bea last night at dinner, and she thought I should talk to you first." He looked at Bea who smiled in encouragement, and back to Mr. Holden. "She wondered if you might be interested in a possible partnership with me for your men's clothing business. So here I am," said

313

Bart, smiling hopefully.

"Well, that's a very interesting idea. Let's go to my office to talk some more about this idea of yours. Bea, will you bring us some coffee, please? I would like to talk to Mr. Clark for a while in private." Smiling at Bea, he motioned for Bart to follow him. "Right this way, Bart," he said, parting the curtain as he led the way.

"I'll be right back with coffee," Bea said, smiling gleefully at Bart as she followed behind them. She knew having her father invite Bart into the office was a good sign; her father was not one for beating around the bush. If he didn't like something he said so right away; it was in his Irish blood.

Bart followed Mr. Holden to the back of the store, past sewing machines, bolts of fabric, dress forms, and large tables. The women working at the sewing tables looked up, curious to see who was coming through. Bart tipped his head, smiling at each one.

Not losing a beat, Bart did what he did best, and began to get to know the customer, or Mr. Holden in this instance. "So, Mr. Holden, where are you from? I detect an accent of some sort. Possibly Scottish or Irish?"

"I'm Irish and so is my wife. Our parents came to America from Ireland when we were very young. We both grew up in Massachusetts, where we met and fell in love. We moved here a few years ago. Apparently, my accent has not been completely lost," said Mr. Holden with a smile.

"I like your accent," Bart said honestly.

"Thank you. And are your ancestors from Ireland or Scotland?" Mr. Holden asked.

"Neither. My ancestors are Old English. I'm the only one of my siblings that got my mother's red hair," Bart added as he touched the sides of his newly cropped hair.

"Hmm, me too," Mr. Holden said as they entered his

314

office at the back of the store. A small desk, two chairs and a wooden cabinet barely fit into the cramped space. The lightless window facing the alley only made the office seem more confining. A hanging kerosene lamp filled the space with enough light to do the daily tasks.

"Shut the door, will you, Bart?" asked Mr. Holden as he sat down behind the desk. "Have a seat, please."

Bart shut the door and took a seat as he looked around. Scribbled notes were tacked to the wall, catalogues and accounts were scattered on the desk, and piles of order forms were stacked on top of the cabinet, with fabric scraps pinned to them. The clutter appeared to be overtaking the office.

"As you can see, I have more business than I can manage," Mr. Holden said, pushing the piles to one side to clear a spot to rest his arms as he leaned forward. "I can't keep up with filing and the bookkeeping when I'm also needed out there." Motioning with his head toward the work room. "On top of everything, we need two more seamstresses. With all the work coming in, we have been putting in extra-long days just to meet our customers' expectations. You see, we provide the ladies of Cheyenne with the highest quality dresses to their exact measurements and their individual specifications. I also see an untapped market for men's finer clothing in Cheyenne as well."

Bart nodded in agreement.

"Only a few shops in town sell a basic suit, ready-to-buy off the rack, and most of them fit poorly. If you want an expensive suit it has to be ordercd from shops back East and it still needs to be tailored. To be honest, I'm tired of making alterations on someone else's suit. I want to take out the middleman. My plan is to open a shop specifically for men's custom-fit evening and formal wear, here in Cheyenne. I want to capitalize on the opportunity before someone else does. But there's no way I can keep up with two stores. I would need a partner; someone I could trust and count on," Mr. Holden explained, drumming his fingers on a stack of papers, anxious to get back to work. "What do you think?"

"It sounds like a wonderful idea. From what I've seen these past three days I can agree, there's nothing like that here, and ample opportunity for it. As you said, very few places sell men's clothing, and even fewer sell suits. I didn't see any evening wear or formal clothing in the shops I explored," Bart said. "From what I can see, about half the men in Cheyenne wear suits." He straightened his suit coat subconsciously as he added, "But all men in Cheyenne, at some point in the week, require a suit for church, a town dance or other entertainment. I see this to be a big business opportunity, but also a big undertaking. If it isn't executed properly, the idea will be stolen and taken over by someone else."

"That is exactly why I've held off. I've had the idea for quite some time now but have yet to find someone I trust that would be capable of such a venture. I'm looking for a partner that can pull his weight, someone full of energy and determination. I would have to depend on him to keep up with the demands, make orders, hire seamstresses, and do the fittings. Do you think you're ready for that kind of challenge?" asked Mr. Holden, sizing up Bart.

"Sir, I'm sure I can. I'm a hard worker, with good business sense. I'd like a chance to earn your trust and show you what I can do for your business. I could work here for a while and learn the ropes while I help with the books and orders. After a trial period, you can see how I've done before you decide to make me a partner. And as an added insurance, I give you my word that I will keep your secret." He smiled, hoping he'd be given the chance to prove himself. "How does that sound?"

"I like the way you think, Bart." Mr. Holden was impressed with the young man's tenacity. "All right, I'll hire you. You can start back here in the office, and we can discuss the finer details about the men's shop over the next few weeks. I think we'll know whether it's working or not by then." Mr. Holden pulled out his pocket watch from his vest and checked the time; momentarily, a slight frown crossed his face as he clicked it shut and put it back. "I could sure use your help. Every minute is crucial. I just hope you're able to convince your father that you are not returning. He may talk you into coming back. I know I wouldn't let you leave so easily," he said as his face brightened, hoping he wouldn't lose the young prospect he'd just discovered.

Bart smiled, noting the compliment. "I was going to send a letter to him today, but wanted to talk to you first. If you're serious about hiring me and a possible partnership in the future, I will tell him I am staying. But either way, I'm staying in Cheyenne, with or without this job. My mind is made up. There's nothing he can say that would change my decision," Bart said, determined to make his own way.

"Then Mr. Clark, you have a job. And if this works out as well as I think it will, you will soon be a partner in the finest men's clothing business in Cheyenne." Mr. Holden reached across the desk to shake Bart's hand. "We work ten-hour days, six days a week. I'll pay you thirty cents an hour. That's eighteen dollars a week. You can keep the books while you learn the business. It's up to you. What do you say? Do we have a deal?" asked Mr. Holden with anticipation.

"Yes, Sir! That sounds very fair. Thank you, Sir. You won't regret it," Bart exclaimed, shifting excitedly, wanting to leap from his chair and shout for joy.

"Ok, I'll put it in writing. You come back and sign the papers after you've notified your father. I can have Bea start training you today if you have time; I'll pay you, of course," Mr. Holden said as he scratched some figures down on a piece of paper.

"I sure can, Sir. I'd like to start as soon as possible. Although, I'm going to need some time to go post that letter to my father, possibly over my lunch break," Bart said, standing as Mr. Holden opened the office door.

"Bea, is the coffee ready?" he asked, spotting her beside the potbellied stove.

"Yes Father, sorry it took so long. I had to make a fresh kettle." Bea turned to fill two mugs with hot coffee.

"And can you work with Mr. Clark and show him how we run things? He's starting today. Oh, except for around noon, he needs to go post a letter, but until then he would like to get acquainted with things," he said, smiling as Bea handed him his coffee.

"I'd be happy to, Father. Give me one minute to hand my garment over to Shirley so she can finish the buttons I've started, and then I'll be free to show Bart around." Bea handed Bart a cup of coffee and gave him a warm smile.

"Thank you, Bea. I appreciate you taking the time," Bart said, returning her smile.

"You're welcome, Bart. I'll be just a minute," she said, and went to her sewing station and took the partially completed dress to Shirley. Talking in hushed tones, Bea explained what needed to be done and then returned to Bart. "All right, let's get started," she said with enthusiasm. Excitedly, she took Bart around to each area of the office, explaining to him who each person was, what they did, and how each task was carried out.

As she talked, Bart followed and asked questions, wanting to know all the details. It was hard to keep the smile off his face as he watched her graceful movements and listened to her voice, loving every minute he spent with her.

At noon, Bart excused himself to return to his hotel room, then ran to the post office with his freshly penned letter. It was pouring rain again as he entered the post office and posted the letter and sent a telegram that read, "Pa, I'm not returning. Letter will explain. Please send my things care of the Cheyenne Hotel. Love Bart."

In his letter he explained his desire to stay in Cheyenne, his new job, and his possible partnership with Mr. Holden in his men's clothing shop. He also told them about Bea and his interest in her. Hoping to soften his father's disappointment, he suggested that John, his younger brother, might want to take over the business in the future. In closing, he emphasized how he never intended to disappoint them and hoped they understood his strong feelings about making his own way.

Bart then dashed to a corner bakery to grab something for lunch and ordered sweet buns for the workers. If he was going to be a partner in a flourishing business, he was determined to make sure it was a pleasant place to work. Bart intended to be the best manager he could be. Full of enthusiasm, he ran the two blocks to the dress shop, protecting his bag of pastries from the drizzling rain.

"I brought back treats!" Bart announced as he came through the curtain into the back room. He set the sack down on the cupboard by the potbelly stove where the aroma of brewing coffee filled the room. The seamstresses gathered around, thanking him for his thoughtfulness as he smiled and tried to learn their names as they each took a sweet bun and a mug of coffee back to their stations.

Mr. Holden smiled appreciatively. "Good job," he whispered as he passed by Bart and took a treat to the office and closed the door.

"Thank you, Bart, that was very kind of you," Bea said with a sweet smile. Then leaning forward, she whispered, "You keep this up and he will force you to marry me," Bea teased, then blushed at being so presumptuous.

Bart didn't even flinch. "He won't have to force me," he whispered back with a sly smile as she blushed further.

Smiling, she turned away so no one could see her reddened face and took her coffee and sweet bun back to her sewing machine. Try as she might, she couldn't keep the smile off her face. Taking turns with her father, she helped teach Bart the ropes of the business. She showed him the different fabrics, where to place the orders when new customers came in, and all the products they sold. The day flew by as they worked together.

***

Later that afternoon, the rains slowed, and the sun broke through the clouds, opening up to a bright blue sky as Vic came into the sheriff's office with a wide grin. "The mayor wants to see you; he has some news for you."

"Finally!" Ed jumped up and grabbed his hat as he passed, giving a friendly pat to his deputy's shoulder. "Thanks, Vic," Ed said as he left. Walking briskly to the Town Hall, he looked up at the expanding blue and inhaled deeply. "I hope today is the day I get to start my new journey," he thought as he leapt up the Town Hall steps two at a time.

As Ed entered the mayor's office, a shout went up, "Surprise!" Before him was gathered a group of city council members, the mayor, and Vic followed right behind him. Ed stood there in a daze, as a slow smile spread across his face.

Mayor Hook was the first to shake his hand. "Congratulations, old boy! Your replacement has arrived. You can turn in your badge!"

Ed's heart swelled as well-wishers congratulated him on his retirement. "It's over, today is my last day as sheriff!" he thought as his smile lit his whole face.

"Did you think we were going to let you get away without a proper goodbye?" Mayor Hook smiled at Sheriff Havoc and squeezed his shoulder. "We wanted you to know how much we appreciate all you've done for us and this town. And as a way of saying thank you we want to let you use the Town Hall for your wedding reception. We know. We know. You want to keep the wedding private, but you can't deprive the public from celebrating in your good fortune. We won't take no for an answer," the jovial Mayor insisted.

"All right, I can see you have your mind made up. I will comply," Ed teased. "Really though, thank you all for the support. I couldn't have done it without the backup of the city council and the good citizens of this community," he said, looking around the room at the dedicated leaders he'd come to admire. "I'm ready to pass on the badge to someone else and I hope he's as lucky as I've been to have such wonderful friends. It makes a man proud to know you." Ed shifted nervously. "So, when does this new sheriff get into town?"

"He's already here!" Mayor Hook announced, "Sheriff Havoc, I want you to meet your replacement, Patrick O'Malley," motioning behind Ed.

A tall broad-shouldered man with thick brown hair and mustache stepped forward from the back corner where he'd been standing quietly. He gave Ed a firm handshake.

"Congratulations, Sheriff Havoc. I've heard great things about you. I hope I can live up to the high standards you've set. And congratulations on your upcoming wedding. She's a lucky lass," said Patrick in his slight Scottish accent.

Ed was impressed with the new sheriff. He appeared strong and capable. The town needed someone who could command respect and also socialize well with the good citizens of Cheyenne. "It's a tough job, but you have my support as well as these good people. And there's no finer deputy than Vic. He's covered my back more times than I can count," he said, smiling at Vic. "I have a feeling you will do just fine," Ed said, patting Patrick's sturdy shoulder.

"Good to know. And thanks for the vote of confidence," Patrick said modestly.

Mayor Hook interrupted their exchange with an announcement. "We have a gift for you. Follow me." Heading out of his office and down the steps, he led Ed and the others to the street where a buggy sat. It was painted shiny black with cushioned leather seats, and a canopy for protection from the weather. Everyone stood back, letting Ed approach the rig.

"It's yours! You need something to take your bride home in. So, we found a used buggy and with a little work, made it good as new. It's our wedding gift to you," Mayor Hook said, patting a stunned Ed on the back.

"My goodness! You are all being so generous. Thank you. I love it, and I'm sure Cassie will too." Ed ran his hand over the smooth frame. "Wow! She's a beauty. I can't wait to take it for a ride," looking around at his comrades who'd gone above and beyond to make his day.

"Vic, go get Major from the livery and hitch him up," Mayor Hook directed. "Come on, Sheriff, let's get some cake. We'll get it all hitched up, and then you can take a ride out to see your fiancé and surprise her! Tell her congratulations from all of us." He put his arm across Ed's back as he turned to walk with him back into the Town Hall. "You know, Ed, this is the best reason to lose a good sheriff. Please, tell that sweet girl we bear her no ill will," Mayor Hook said, laughing at his own joke.

"Thanks, Hank, I will." Looking back at the gift, he could barely contain his emotions. He hadn't realized how much he would miss the job. Well, not so much the job really, but the people he served with. He hoped he could continue to stay close to them, maybe even serve on the city council in the future.

As Ed said his farewells, he removed his badge and set it in Mayor Hook's palm. "Thanks again for getting my replacement so quickly. From the looks of it, we'll be in good hands. And thanks again for the buggy and the Town Hall for the reception, it's more than generous. I gotta go share the good news with my fiancé. She'll be thrilled. Goodbye, Hank, my good friend," Ed said with an ache in his throat. "It's been an interesting ride."

"That it has, that it has," said Mayor Hook, pressing his lips together to control the quiver in his chin.

"Thanks again for everything, everyone." He was feeling a little strange, realizing he wouldn't be in charge of the law and order in Cheyenne anymore.

Mayor Hook replied, "No, thank you. I'll see you at the wedding, friend. Good luck."

Ed stepped out of the Town Hall to see Major hitched up to the beautiful new buggy. It looked grand. "You look pretty fancy, Major," he said, smiling as his horse looked back at him as he stepped into the buggy. Taking the reins, he waved at the mayor and the council members who were standing on the Town Hall steps, waving back at him shouting, "Good luck!"

"Let's go, Major. Let's go get our gal."

The buggy moved smoothly over the damp hard-packed road. Avoiding the few remaining puddles, Ed steered the buggy onto the grass, hoping to keep it as clean as possible. He pulled into the Hartford's yard and jumped out of the buggy and tied the reins to the railing. Cassie came out as Ed came up the front steps.

"Ed!" Cassie exclaimed. "I'm so happy to see you." She met him on the steps, standing eye to eye, wrapping her arms easily around his neck.

He hugged her tightly around the waist. "Cassie! Today I handed in my badge. I'm officially no longer the sheriff. When I went to see the mayor, he surprised me with a party, and I met my replacement. And look what the mayor and city council members gave us for our wedding!" Ed loosened his hold and motioned behind him.

"Oh, my goodness! I can't believe it! That's wonderful news!" Overwhelmed with excitement, she hugged him again.

"Do you want to go for a ride?" asked Ed, smiling at her.

"Yes! Let's go right now. Let me just grab my shawl and leave a note for my aunt and uncle. They're in town and I don't want them to worry." She ran inside.

"Are you ready?" Ed asked with a light chuckle as Cassie hurried to the buggy, her hair flying loose in the breeze.

"Yes, I'm ready now," she said as he helped her up.

Ed easily maneuvered the buggy out of the yard and down the tree-covered lane.

"I still can't believe it! What in the world made them think of getting us a buggy?" asked Cassie in astonishment.

"They said, every proper lady needs a buggy. And they're right. It's the first time I've needed a rig in Cheyenne," said Ed, as they rode toward their future home. "Even though we'll have a wagon to haul feed and equipment, you'll need something to take into town. Besides, I've been thinking, I don't think it'll be safe for you to ride a horse much longer. I don't want you to risk hurting the baby or yourself."

"I was actually wondering about that myself," she said.

"It's my job to make sure you stay safe." Ed put his arm around her shoulders and pulled her close. "As I've told you before, I want you and the baby healthy. So, tomorrow morning I'm coming to get you so we can work on the house together. I want to make sure you don't over-do it or do any heavy lifting."

"Oh Ed, I'm so excited. Things are falling into place so nicely. It means so much to me to get the house cleaned before we move in. I'll have enough work to do with the regular chores. Thank heavens Aunt Mabel is coming to help as well. With all three of us, it shouldn't take long," Cassie said with relief as she smiled up at him. "Thank you," she said, knowing he had more important things he could be doing besides housework.

"My pleasure," he said, kissing her forehead, then turned onto their road and drove under the shade of the trees to their homestead. As they pulled into the yard, Mr. Crowley stepped out from the cottage to greet them.

"Howdy, folks!" he said, waving. "That's a fine rig you have there!" He ambled over and reached out and shook Ed's hand and then Cassie's. "Came to see the place again, did ya'?" he asked cheerfully.

"We were just taking a drive, trying out the new rig. Is there anything we can do to help you, Mr. Crowley?" asked Ed. "Any boxes that need lifted?" Ed wondered how the older man had managed the property alone all those years.

"No, I think I have everything packed that I'm going to take to the train. Oh wait, yes!" he declared, suddenly thinking of something. "There is one thing you could help me with. I need a ride to the train station. If you came in the morning, we could load up my trunks on the wagon and then drive into town. Everything will be yours after that, the wagon, the herd, the cottage and the homestead," Mr. Crowley said resolutely.

"I'd be happy to. I'll be here at seven o'clock to get you. Your train leaves at eight, right?" asked Ed.

"Yes, that'll be plenty of time to load up the wagon and get it on the freight car. I really appreciate your help. It was lucky for me that you stopped by."

"Yes, it was. Well, I'll see you in the morning then."

"Thank you so much. See you in the morning. Goodbye, Missy."

"Goodbye, Mr. Crowley. And thanks again for your generosity. God speed and safe travels," Cassie said.

"You're welcome, little Missy. And thank you, God bless you."

***

Arriving back at the Hartford's, Ed exclaimed, "Oh, I almost forgot to tell you! The mayor and city council insisted we use the Town Hall for our reception, free of charge. I hope that's all right with you," Ed asked, as he stopped the buggy at the porch steps.

"It's fine with me. I'm sure everyone wants to thank you for your service and congratulate us. And as soon as I'm married to you, I don't care what we do after that as long as you're with me," Cassie said, as Ed helped her out of the buggy.

"I feel the same way," Ed said, kissing her lightly on the cheek.

"Would you like to come inside for a refreshment?" Cassie asked, as she pulled the shawl tighter around her shoulders as the breeze picked up.

"Not today. I still haven't packed up my things for the move tomorrow. But I'll be here bright and early in the morning to pick you and Mabel up. Until then, my love," he said, giving Cassie a soft kiss before he got back into buggy and drove away.

"Until then," she said waving. "I love you." She turned and hurried up the steps. "Tomorrow the homestead will be ours! Our own home!"

Chapter 16
Cleaning House

Wednesday morning dawned as Ed finished loading his clothes, guitar, and other belongings into the back of the buggy. As he turned in his key, he said goodbye to the Union Pacific Boarding House manager. He had now fully moved out, just in time for the new sheriff who needed a place to live. Ed drove the buggy out to the homestead where Mr. Crowley was waiting with the wagon harnessed and his bags ready. Helping him load the heavy trunks into the back, Ed then climbed in and drove Mr. Crowley to the train station, thanked him again for everything, and wished him God's speed on his journey.

***

Cassie awoke with excitement, and a smile spread over her face. Today she would be working in her own home and the idea of it seemed almost too good to be true. She ate her morning biscuit, then dressed in one of Aunt Mabel's oldest dresses and an old apron. Looking in the mirror as she twisted her hair into a tight knot, she tied a clean white cloth over it, covering every dark strand. She felt self-conscious, dressed in faded thread-bare rags with her hair hidden under a dishtowel. "Oh well," she reasoned, "It's better than getting dust and spiders in my hair and ruining one of my new dresses."

Mabel and Cassie ate breakfast together and cleaned up the dishes well before Ed arrived.

When Cassie heard the wagon coming into the yard, she grabbed the bucket full of rags and soap and headed out the door. Ed pulled to a stop and put the brake on when he saw her coming.

"Good morning, Cass," Ed said, jumping down from the wagon as she wished him good morning. "I got Mr. Crowley off to the train. The homestead is ours now, darling," he said, grinning broadly as he walked towards her. "What can I help you with?" he asked, seeing Cassie with a bucket full of supplies, wondering if there was more.

Cassie descended the steps, meeting him at the bottom. "I think we have it all, but thanks," she said, holding the bucket with both arms until he took it from her.

Ed noticed Cassie's worn-out clothes and dishtowel scarf. "You can dress in your oldest gown and hide your hair, 'Cinderella,' but I still think you're beautiful," pronounced Ed, giving her a hug around the shoulders and a kiss on her forehead as she smiled up at him.

Cassie decided to stop worrying about how she looked. "If Ed thinks I'm still beautiful, regardless of what I'm wearing, then what does it matter," she thought as they walked together to the wagon.

"Up you go, my little princess in disguise," he said, helping her over the wheel and then handing her the bucket while smiling at his little rag princess.

"Oh, Ed, you're such a tease. You always make me feel pretty, even in this old thing." Cassie smiled demurely at him as she rolled up the loose-fitting sleeves.

Mabel emerged from the house, dressed in an equally worn dress, cheerfully swinging a bucket of cleaning supplies from one hand. "Good morning, Ed," she said as he greeted her and asked how she was. "Wonderful! It's a wonderful day for cleaning. I think we're all ready to go. George is checking on the herd this morning, so he'll be along later," Mabel said as she handed him the bucket and climbed into the wagon with his help.

Sitting beside Cassie, Ed clucked to the horses and headed to their new home as the sun rose on a dewy morning. The birds were chirping, and insects were busy buzzing in the warm sunlight, and a subtle breeze rustled the leaves overhead as they neared their final destination.

The homestead was incredibly picturesque in the morning sunlight as it shone on the white cottage—like a beacon amidst the wooded grove. Dewy blades of grass sparkled as if dressed in diamonds as flowers tipped their colorful heads toward the bright rays, smelling like a freshly picked bouquet. The rich soil was still wet from rain among the thicker grove of trees, giving off a clean earthy aroma. Cassie placed her hand on Ed's arm and squeezed it. Her face radiated with joy as he reflected her sentiment.

The milk cow mooed from the corral, signaling their arrival to the other animals.

Cassie smiled. "Our home," she whispered with emotion, leaning her head against Ed's arm.

"Yes, our home," he said proudly as he pulled the wagon to a stop and gave her a quick squeeze.

As Ed began unhitching the horses, Cassie and Mabel took their cleaning supplies into the cottage.

Mabel used to call on Mrs. Crowley regularly, since they were close neighbors. Once Mrs. Crowley fell ill, Mabel visited more frequently, bringing food and helping with housework when she could. It had been over a year since her passing, and Mabel hadn't been inside the house since. Oh, she had tried, but Mr. Crowley was too proud to let her come in and clean, insisting he was doing well enough.

So, Mabel did what she could to help Mr. Crowley by dropping off bread or baked goods when making her neighborly rounds. Mabel expected the place would need some work, but when she opened the front door, she was taken aback by its magnitude. The once immaculate home now appeared to be decaying. As she walked around the rooms, pulling back the shabby curtains, she noticed a layer of grime covering the panes of glass. Then, running her fingers along the hearth and windowsill, she disturbed a thick layer of dust that had settled there. As she approached the kitchen, an overwhelming odor assaulted her senses and she held her finger to her nose.

"Well, Cassie, we have our work cut out for us. The first thing to do is open all the windows and let some fresh air in. Then we can remove all the curtains and wash them later. I doubt we will be able to hang them again. Maybe they could be used as rags if they survive," Mabel said.

Cassie grinned. "I'll get the bedroom curtains," she said, setting her bucket down on the kitchen floor. "Let's take the rugs outside and beat them on the line while we're at it," she suggested, seeing how dingy they looked, caked with dirt and grime.

"That's a great idea," said Mabel. "You might as well pull off the bedding too. Then, we can boil everything in the large kettle outside. I'll have Ed start a fire," she said as she opened the front room and kitchen windows and left to find Ed. She could tell this was going to take a few days. There was a lot to get done before the newlyweds could move in.

Cassie took down the curtains in the master bedroom, seeing they were paper thin, almost nonexistent, noting they were worse than rags as she piled them on the bed. She opened the windows and breathed in the scent of damp, woody pine and spruce that surrounded the property. In the garden behind the house, she could see flourishing green plants of various sizes amidst the damp mounds of dirt, and noticed the weeding would need to be done soon. Returning to her inside work, she gathered the two rag rugs from the bedroom floor and took them outside to hang on the clothesline.

Ed was already gathering the wood to start the fire for the boiling kettle when she passed. He smiled up at her as he crouched down to light the kindling. As she tried to lift the heavy rugs up and over the ropes on the clothesline, Cassie struggled, not quite managing to get them high enough to clear the line. Ed, seeing her predicament, came rushing over to lift them for her, quickly swinging them up and over.

"There you go," Ed said, winking at her.

"Thanks, Ed. What would I do without my 'Prince Charming'?" Cassie teased with a twinkle in her eye. It was such fun to be working with him.

"It's my pleasure to reach the high places for you, 'Cinderella.' No need to struggle," Ed said, teasing her right back as she strolled back into the house. He loved helping her, and even more, he enjoyed watching her, even if it was just doing chores.

Back inside, Cassie pulled the blankets and sheets off the sagging bed, noting Mr. Crowley had taken his wife's quilt with him. Piling the bedding on the floor, Cassie began tugging at the mattress ticking, trying to get it off the bed; unfortunately, it was too large and heavy for her. Before she could go for help, Ed was standing beside her, taking it out of her hands.

"I wondered if you might need my help. This is too big for you to manage alone. Here, I'll take it," he said, smiling. He lifted it easily and carried it outside, emptying the insides of the thick canvas shell into the fire that was now roaring and quickly consumed the dry straw.

They carried out the old furniture to be cleaned with Ed's help; the two red parlor chairs, the small writing table under the front window, and its chair. After beating out the dust from the cushions, scrubbing the upholstery, and polishing the wood until it glowed, they were satisfied to let them air out in the sunshine. Next, the rest of the rugs were taken up and beaten on the line, while the floors were swept and scrubbed with lye soap until they gleamed. Finally, inside and out, they washed the windows to sparkling, saving the curtains for washing later, piling them in baskets with the bedding.

Next, Cassie moved on to the smaller bedroom. The frames and mattress ticking of the two beds were dismantled and placed in the barn for later use. In the master bedroom, the ropes were removed from the frame and placed in boiling water, to be restrung later in the day. Finally, the mattress cover was washed with lye in the kettle of boiling water outside and hung on the line to dry and bleach in the sun.

While Cassie worked in the bedrooms, Aunt Mabel began scouring the kitchen, emptying the cupboards and wiping them down inside and out, disposing of old food and broken dishes she found inside. The smell was greatly improved when she removed the rubbish bin from under the sink, full of rotten left-over food. Finally, Ed took the old bucket out far from the house and buried its contents.

By dinner time they were all ready for a break. Climbing into the wagon, they rode back to the ranch to eat. They had made significant progress that morning. The washed things were drying, and the house was slowly becoming bright and clean. When they'd finished their dinner of cold sandwiches and milk, they returned to the cottage to resume cleaning the kitchen.

Mabel started on the cast-iron stove, which badly needed scraped, scrubbed, and polished. It was rusting in spots, and burnt food and grease coated everything. Mabel sanded down the rust, then scoured the grime away until it was smooth and clean, then polished it until the outside shined like ebony.

Once the cupboards were clean, Cassie began working in the pantry, taking out the old boxes and baskets so they could wash the shelves. Suddenly, Cassie let out a blood-curdling scream and came running out of the pantry. She was jumping around in a frantic state, shaking her skirts as she continued to scream.

"What is it!" yelled Mabel. "What's happened?" she shouted in alarm as she turned from the stove.

Ed came running in from outside. "Cassie! What's wrong?" he hollered. Cassie was white as a ghost as she ran to him. He took her in his arms and held her trembling frame as he tried to understand what had happened. "What's the matter?" he asked again.

"Mice! Everywhere! In the pantry!" exclaimed Cassie, pointing back towards the pantry door. A mouse ran into the kitchen, and then another and another, scurrying along with his friends. Cassie let out another terrified scream. She tried to run out of the house, but Ed held her snugly. Then, as she pushed against him, he let her go, and she ran outside.

Thinking impulsively, Ed grabbed the broom by the door and began swatting at them. Mabel jumped up on a kitchen chair and started yelling. "It went that way! Get it, Ed!" Every once in a while, she screamed when a mouse came running past. "It's right there! Get it!" she shrieked.

Ed did his best to stomp or hit the mice, but they were quick little devils. Every once in a while, they would squeak when he attempted to beat them. Ed finally exterminated the three mice, but it took quite a bit of effort, and he was breathing hard from the exertion. They were speedy critters, darting under furniture, hiding behind the stove and cupboards. It was chaos for a while, never knowing when one would pop out and make a run for it.

Cassie remained outside, holding her arms around herself, shaking and jumping every time she heard Aunt Mabel scream. Jolts of fear continued to surge through her as she imagined what was happening inside. She listened to the bumps and bangs, squeezing her eyes shut as she grimaced, imagining the squished rodents. She was disgusted; she had never seen so many mice in one place and it set her nerves on edge.

Triumphantly, Ed came outside to try and console Cassie, taking her into his arms and holding her as she trembled. "I got them, Cass. It's ok, they're all gone. The mice are dead. I got all three," he said proudly. "You can come inside now," he said, trying to reassure her.

"No! I can't go back in there," she said adamantly, shaking her head. "There aren't three, Ed. There's more than that. There was a nest of them. I pulled out a basket, and it was full of them; they were lying in a pile of rags in a huge nest," she said with disgust. "Ed, there are still more!" she insisted as she looked towards the house and began to cry. "I saw the mice and dropped the basket. Some of them scattered right at my feet. So, I ran. I was afraid they would run up my skirt. They were everywhere! I can't go back in there! I won't!" she declared, standing her ground, shaking and pale. Her heart was pounding, and she felt creepy-crawly all over.

"Ok, ok, I'll go see." Ed relented and turned to go back inside to check the pantry. He hoped there weren't more. He was exhausted from chasing the first three all over the kitchen, and his back was aching from hunching over for so long. "Those little buggers sure are fast," he thought, and stretched his back before he went inside.

Mabel stepped down off the chair and tried to calm herself. She wasn't afraid of a mouse, but three mice at once tended to rattle a person's nerves. Cassie's terrified screams had shaken her, then to see the mice come running towards her was an even bigger fright. Not knowing which way they were going and if they would run up under her skirts didn't help her either. She started laughing at herself as she realized how silly she must have looked to Ed, standing on the chair squealing and yelling at him to, "get 'em."

"I thought when you had the one pinned under the stove, and the other one ran under your legs, you were going to crack your head on the edge of it; you jumped up so fast," laughed Mabel. They both cracked up as Ed acted out some funnier moves he'd made, trying to kill them.

"The one in the corner behind the cupboard…I was about to smash him, and his little friend decided to jump on my boot." Ed reenacted, shaking his foot to get the mouse off before it could scamper up his pant leg. They both laughed heartily, easing some of the tension.

They finally stopped laughing, and Ed suggested, "Maybe you should go check on Cassie; she's distraught. She believes there are more in the pantry." Truthfully, he wanted her out of the house just in case more mice came running out of the pantry. He'd heard enough screaming for one day.

Mabel was more than happy to comply.

Ed went to the pantry door and looked into the small, poorly lit room. Finding the outside door into the pantry, he opened it to let in more light. The clutter of old bottles, boxes, and baskets full of odds and ends filled the shelves and floor of the room. The basket of rags Cassie had taken down and dropped was in the middle of the floor. Sure enough, it was full of shredded fabric and stuffing, making a giant nest. On closer inspection, he could see pink baby mice inside, about a dozen of them squirming. Two full-grown mice scurried into a corner behind a box as he moved the basket. He was disgusted; their new home was infested with mice. Picking up the basket full of mice, he carried it outside to the fire and tossed it in. He hated to kill anything, but this was their home, and he wouldn't allow Cassie and the baby to get sick from vermin. He knew where plagues came from, and already, he was worried about Cassie being exposed to the mice droppings and their possible fleas from handling the basket.

As soon as he had the basket burning, he told Cassie to wash up for fear of her getting sick. He filled a bucket with well water, brought out soap and a clean towel for her, and told her and Aunt Mabel not to come into the house for a while. Ed worked for hours, catching and killing the mice as he pulled out boxes and trunks and took them into the yard. Some of the mice left of their own accord, frightened by the moving of their homes; the others he willingly exterminated.

The women stayed outside and worked, boiling linens and wiping down everything with lye soap and scalding water. Once the pantry had been emptied, everything was mopped and wiped down. The lye wash water was very strong but effectively sanitized the room. Cassie stayed outside, not wanting to go back into the house for a few reasons. By afternoon everyone was exhausted. The bed ticking was dry, as was the rope for the bed. Ed took the rope into the bedroom and restrung the bed, tightening the rope so as it dried, it would shrink even more, keeping the mattress firm. Cassie and Mabel filled the mattress with fresh straw, plumping it up nice and thick. Once the rope was completely dry, Ed brought in the ticking and placed it on the restrung bed that no longer sagged. Aunt Mabel came in and made the bed with the fresh, clean sheets and blankets. Ed would be living here now and needed to have a place to sleep. Even though there weren't curtains on the windows, Ed didn't mind; he was a long way out of town and secluded in the woods. To make sure all the mice were gone, he decided to leave the boxes and things outside for the night and close all the doors. It was getting late, and soon he would need to feed the animals and milk the cow.

Cassie and Mabel decided to head back to make supper while Ed finished the chores. George had stopped by briefly in the afternoon and saw there wasn't much for him to do. Then saying he had an idea, he left them, informing them he would be back by supper time.

Back at Aunt Mabel's house, Cassie changed out of her dirty clothes and removed the towel from off her hair, which she was extremely grateful for. Then, washing thoroughly to get all the dust off, she changed into one of her day dresses and apron. Next, Aunt Mabel took her turn washing up and changing out of her dirty clothes while Cassie started cooking. Cassie was still feeling jumpy and kept looking down in the corners of the kitchen and shadows, expecting to see tiny creatures there. By the time Ed arrived, supper was on the table. Soon after, they heard George drive into the yard.

"I have a surprise for you, Cassie!" hollered George as he pulled up to the house.

Cassie and the others came outside to see what he was yelling about.

"I have a surprise for you, Cassie," he said excitedly as they came out to the wagon. "It's here in this crate." George jumped down from the wagon seat, reached into the wagon bed, and lifted a wooden crate with a cat inside.

It meowed, wanting to be let out.

"A cat!" Cassie cheered, clasping her hands together. "What a wonderful idea!" She loved cats, and this was a pretty one, a light orange short hair with yellow eyes and a cute little face.

"Mr. Tucker said she's a good mouser and will lend her to you until you get the mice problem under control. He even offered to let you keep one of the kittens she'll be having soon," he said excitedly.

"That's very nice of Mr. Tucker, but won't he want her back long before that?" she asked as she stuck her fingers through the slit in the crate to pet the cat's soft fur.

"Mr. Tucker also has a tomcat that keeps his mice away, so he can let you have her for a while," he said.

"Oh, thank you, Uncle George!" Cassie wrapped her arms around George's neck and gave him a quick hug. "Thank you, Mr. Tucker!" she said, bubbling with glee. "She's so pretty. Let's take her inside and give her some milk. We don't want her to be scared of us."

Ed delighted in Cassie's enthusiasm as she ran ahead to get the milk ready. Then, as he walked with George into the house, he thanked him for making Cassie so happy.

"It's my pleasure," George said, still blushing from Cassie's affection.

Once inside, George slowly opened the crate, letting Cassie take the cat out very carefully. At first, the cat was frightened, but then calmed as Cassie stroked her and sat her in front of the bowl of milk on the floor. The cat looked around at the people standing there staring at her, and then crouched down and drank the milk hungrily.

Leaving the cat, they went to the table and sat down to eat their supper as they talked about the day's events, which centered around the mice. With each telling, the stories became more and more animated, laughter erupting around the room, with Cassie joining in. It did settle her nerves a little, knowing that a cat was coming to live with them.

"Getting a cat was a great idea, George," Ed said, as relieved as Cassie about having a cat in the house. It would take care of the mice he'd missed and keep more from coming in. He planned to take the cat home and keep her inside to stalk and catch mice through the night.

Once they finished supper and cleaned up the dishes, Cassie packed Ed a loaf of bread, butter, bacon, cheese, and coffee grounds for breakfast. There were chickens and the milk cow at the cottage, and the old pans and dishes had all been washed and placed back into the cupboards, ready for him to use. Ed was grateful for Cassie's thoughtfulness; now he would be able to make himself something to eat.

George put the cat back into the crate and took it out to the buggy, then came back into the house and said goodnight to Ed, who was carrying out the box of food to the buggy. Cassie followed with a jar of preserves and pickles that Aunt Mabel insisted he take. Ed loaded the box and jars carefully into the buggy and turned to hug Cassie before he left.

"Goodnight, my love. Sleep well, and no more worries about the house. By the time you get back tomorrow, all will be safe and sound," Ed said as he kissed her forehead. "I'll be by to pick you up at eight," he said, and jumped into the buggy.

"Goodnight, my Prince Edward. I will see you in the morning, my love." Cassie stepped back, letting Ed drive away as she smiled contentedly.

***

Ed came to the house the following morning to pick up Cassie and Mabel for another cleaning day. To his surprise, Mabel apologized and said she had to go to town and finish up some preparations for the wedding reception. Now that they were having it at the Town Hall, she had more to do and wanted to ask friends to help with refreshments. She was also going to help make the wedding quilt that Cassie didn't know about and make a few surprise purchases for Cassie.

Cassie didn't mind cleaning the cottage without Aunt Mabel. There were only a few things left to do, and Ed would be there to help her if any problems arose.

As Ed and Cassie drove to the cottage, Ed told Cassie that the cat had been active all night and cleared out the last of the mice. That eased Cassie's mind, but she was still a little leery.

From a distance, the cottage looked cleaner as the windows reflected sunlight brightly back at them. The boxes and trunks from the day before still sat outside, and the cat was sunning herself on the porch. Cassie smiled at the welcome sight. As she entered the cottage with a bit of apprehension, she was greeted with the familiar smell of coffee, bacon, and only a hint of lye. The rooms were bright with sunlight. She smiled as she sat her bucket down and put her hands on her hips and surveyed the home with new determination. This was her home, and nothing was going to keep her from feeling safe and comfortable in it, not even pesky mice.

Ed and Cassie spent the day sorting through what was left in the house and kept only the bare essentials. The unwanted, they stored in trunks in the barn, with the idea of fewer hiding places for mice to make nests.

That afternoon while Cassie was busy doing a final scrubbing of the kitchen floor, she discovered the root cellar door. She stopped scrubbing to lift the rug in the middle of the room when she saw the latch and hinges of the trapdoor. She'd forgotten all about it and wondered what it was like and what she would find. Cassie was not about to go down there without Ed checking it out first. She finished scrubbing the floor and took her bucket of water outside to dump when she saw Ed coming back from the barn.

"Ed, I found the door to the root cellar. Do you want to come and see what's down there? I'm afraid to look," she said, smiling hopefully.

"Sure, Cass, I'll come and check it out. Give me a minute to get the lantern. I'm going to need to see down there." Ed went back into the barn and brought out the metal can of kerosene.

As he came through the side door, Ed found a lantern hanging on a nail in the pantry. He took the lantern to the kitchen table and carefully filled it with kerosene. The odor was pungent. Placing the can of kerosene back outside to keep the fumes out of the house, he then lit the lantern and lifted the trapdoor of the root cellar as Cassie stood back. Ed carried the lantern and ducked as he descended below the kitchen floor. Once he reached the bottom of the steps, Ed noticed how cold it was, close to forty degrees, he guessed. The cellar was pretty large, ten feet deep and ten-foot square. The floor was hard-packed dirt, and the walls were covered with planks running floor to ceiling. The planks were yellow orange in color, and as he brought the light closer, he was amazed at what he was looking at.

"Cass, come on down. I have to show you something. It's amazing!" Ed exclaimed. "Don't worry, it's safe; there aren't any mice down here," he said as he walked to the steps and shined the lantern so she could see to come down safely.

Cassie bent over, looking down through the hole. She could see Ed and the steps and the dirt floor, but nothing else. "Ok, but you better be sure," she said, cautiously coming down the first few steps. Ed moved a few steps up and took her hand and walked down with her so she wouldn't fall. It was surprisingly cold and damp and felt wonderful compared to the increasing summer heat. She took a deep breath; it smelled fresh and earthy.

The walls were clean and smooth, with bright wood planking. There were wooden shelves built behind the stairs along the back wall with jars of canned food neatly lined up. Another group of shelves had baskets of vegetables; potatoes, carrots, turnips, and beets packed loosely in sand. Hanging from the ceiling rafters were bunches of herbs tied together, and braided ropes of onions and garlic that were kept dry for future use.

"My goodness, what an amazing cellar," Cassie said, investigating further. Along the walls she opened barrels of dried corn, beans, and wheat.

"Look at this!" Ed pointed to the paneling. "Do you know what this is?" he asked with excitement.

"No, I'm not sure what you mean."

"It's called Osage Orange or bow wood. It's what the Osage Indians used to make their bows with. It's known for its hardness and resistance to moisture and is believed to repel rodents and insects. They don't like the smell." Ed leaned forward and took a sniff. "But it smells nice to me. It smells like citrus. And look, it's on the ceiling as well—what a wonderful idea. Mr. Crowley is a genius. This is a perfect place for storing the vegetables during the winter and all sorts of other things." Becoming even more excited, he said, "Cass, you can put your milk, cream, cheese, and meats down here to keep from spoiling. It will save you from going to the icehouse so often."

Cassie was amazed. "I remember he said they lived in the root cellar for a while when they first moved here. Building the barn first, then later building on top of this. Can you imagine living down here? Look how nice they've kept it," Cassie said in awe.

The cellar was one of the cleanest places in the cottage. They were both excited and continued to explore its contents. There was a crock of lard and one of butter she found on another set of shelves. The jars on the back shelves were dated two years ago, and Cassie supposed they were probably still good. Among the jars of fruit and vegetables were peaches and pickles. She smiled, loving both, and silently thanked Mrs. Crowley for her hard work.

"Shall we go back up?" asked Ed as he took the lantern off the hook he'd hung it from. "I don't want to let all the cold air out."

Cassie went up the steps in front of Ed and moved aside as he came through the opening, ducking a little, then he closed the trapdoor and smiled at Cassie.

"Well, that's a little pot of gold. What luck!" Ed exclaimed in amazement.

"It's wonderful. I'm so looking forward to living here with you. This has been such an adventure, and I'm excited for it to continue," she said, hugging and smiling up at him.

"Oh yes, my dear. The adventure is just beginning. There is so much more to come," Ed said, and kissed her softly on the lips.

Cassie pulled away gently after a few seconds, feeling breathless and needing to redirect the situation. "Um, I need to clean out the fireplace," she said, quickly thinking of another chore. "Can you use lantern to check up inside the flue to make sure it is free of debris?"

He grinned as he released her, understanding her unspoken meaning. She was a virtuous woman, and he would not do anything to make her feel uncomfortable. Stepping back, he squeezed her hand. "You know, I would do anything for you. Even get covered in soot." Taking the lantern to the fireplace, he kneeled and held it up as he looked up inside. "It looks good; Mr. Crowley's kept it clean. So, we'll be safe lighting a fire when we need to."

Cassie sighed a breath of relief. The house finally seemed to be in order. After they finished cleaning for the day, they packed up and drove back to Cassie's aunt and uncle's place for supper.

***

Friday was the last day for wedding preparations, and Aunt Mabel needed to go to town again, refusing to let Cassie come along this time, asking instead if Cassie would stay and bake cookies for the wedding reception.

Cassie was happy to help and especially enjoyed baking. And while she baked, her mind was busy thinking of all the things happening on Saturday. However, Cassie did ask a favor from Aunt Mabel, wondering if she would stop at the post office and see if she had any letters, hoping that Madeline would have replied about coming to the wedding.

Mabel was busy helping with the wedding quilt that morning, but as soon as she was done, she stopped at the post office to check for mail. Sure enough, the postmaster had two letters for Cassie. One was from the Smiths and the other from Madeline.

"Oh, there's also a telegram here for a Cassie Black. She's your niece, correct? Maybe you can take it to her. It came yesterday," he said as he handed it to Mabel when she confirmed she was a relative.

Cassie Black. I will be on the Friday train at 1 pm, arriving for your wedding, Madeline MacRea.

Mabel read the telegram. "Oh goodness!" she thought, "that's in an hour. That'll be a wonderful surprise for Cassie. I'd better hurry and finish my errands so I can go meet her at the train station." "Thank you very much," she said as she took the letters and left.

Mabel hurried to the general store and purchased some simple white lace yardage for curtains she wanted to make for the cottage. She had planned to sew them in secret and put them up Saturday while Cassie was busy getting ready, adding to her purchase some checkered linen for the kitchen table. She wanted the little cottage to be perfect for Cassie's wedding day.

***

Ed was also in town that Friday. He'd just finished having his hair cut and mustache trimmed when he left the barbershop and almost ran into Bart.

"Bart!" exclaimed Ed with excitement. "How are you?" he asked, shaking Bart's hand like they were old friends.

"Sheriff Havoc!" Bart smiled broadly. "Good to see you," he said, and really meant it.

"You know you can call me Ed now. I'm not the sheriff anymore," Ed said, smiling. "How are things going? You said you had a business opportunity you were getting into. How'd that work out?" asked Ed.

"Yes, it's going very well. I met with Bea's father, and I have a job at the dress shop, doing bookkeeping for now, and soon plan to open another store as partners. I love the business," Bart said excitedly, happy to share the good news with someone he knew. "And how are the wedding plans coming?" asked Bart. "Are you getting nervous yet?"

He grinned as he waggled his eyebrows.

Ed chuckled lightly. "I'm more excited than nervous. The house we bought is coming along, as are the wedding preparations. Honestly, I think I'm the happiest I've ever been," Ed said. "I have a thought—I wonder if you'd be willing to come to the wedding? I know Cassie would want you there as a guest once she knows how things have changed, with you and Bea. You and Cassie have known each other for a long time, and I think she needs a few more friendly faces at the wedding," Ed rushed on, hoping he would convince him. "You can bring Bea if you want as well."

"Well, only if you think Cassie would be happy about it. I don't want to ruin her wedding day." Bart was sincerely concerned about how she would feel seeing him there.

"I'm certain she will want you there. It's at the Clearwater Pond at six-thirty p.m. Bea can get you there, she knows where it is. And please come to the reception afterward. It will be held at the Town Hall; you already know where that is," Ed said with a mischievous grin.

"Yeah, I do," said Bart sarcastically and then laughed. "How could I forget?" he thought. "Ok, I'd be happy to come, and I'll ask Bea if she will join me. And thank you for the invitation, you really are a good guy. I can see why Cassie's so happy with you." Bart shook his hand again and excused himself, getting back to work.

***

It was one fifteen when Madeline's train pulled into the station. She stood and lifted down her bag from the overhead rack as the train stopped. Madeline was unsure if

Cassie had gotten her telegram and wondered if she would be able to find her aunt and uncle's place. Either way, she decided she could stay at the hotel and get someone to drive her out to the Clearwater Pond on Saturday. It would be a wonderful surprise. So, as she disembarked the train with the other passengers, she scanned the platform for the ticket master and went to ask directions to the nearest hotel.

Mabel was standing nearby and overheard a brunette woman in her late thirties asking the teller if he knew where the Hartford's lived, and before he could answer, Mabel stepped forward.

"You must be Madeline MacRea," Mabel bubbled as she approached the woman clothed in a dark green traveling dress and hat.

"Yes. Who wants to know?" Madeline asked, questioning the jovial middle-aged woman.

"I'm Cassie's aunt, Mabel Hartford." Her cheeks lifted as her smile broadened. "I got your telegram today, and it was very lucky that I did. Cassie will be so excited to see you!" Mabel reached out a hand and gave Madeline's hand a squeeze, immediately seeing why Cassie had been drawn to the kind-looking woman.

"Oh, I'm so glad you got my telegram. I wasn't sure if you would. I sent a letter but wasn't sure it would get here in time to let her know when I was arriving. Either way, I decided I would be able to find the wedding location by Saturday and surprise her," smiled Madeline.

"You don't have to worry about that anymore. I want you to come home with me right away and see Cassie. I know she'll want to visit with you as long as possible. She's told me so much about you," Mabel said as she picked up Madeline's bag and put her arm through Madeline's as if they were best friends instead of new acquaintances. "I feel like I already know you," she said, feeling a strong bond with the woman who had cared for Cassie on her journey to Cheyenne.

Madeline smiled warmly at the gesture. "She's such a kindred spirit, so much like a sister. I couldn't go home to Missouri without supporting Cassie on her wedding day," she said, walking with Mabel across the train station platform. "She's a special young lady."

"That she is. Well, you can stay with us until you go back home. You and Cassie can share her bed; it's big enough for the two of you. I can't wait for her to see you," Mabel said excitedly as they walked down the steps towards her rig.

"Thank you so much for the hospitality. But I hope I'm not a bother. I'll do anything to help get things ready for the wedding; just tell me what needs done," said Madeline politely, not wanting to intrude or make more work for Mabel.

"It's not a bother. She'll be thrilled and could use the extra set of hands. But we can worry about wedding plans in a bit. First, let's get you to the house, and we can go from there. Here's my wagon," she said as she loaded Madeline's bag and climbed in with Madeline following.

Chapter 17
Unexpected

It was a little after one o'clock when Cassie finished baking the cookies for the wedding reception, and with nothing pressing and no one home, she decided to make good use of her time alone. She had a lot on her mind and could use a ride in the countryside to think. Leaving the cookies cool, she wrote a short note and left it on the table, telling her aunt and uncle that she was going for a ride and would be back in time to help with supper.

Not wanting to miss her opportunity, Cassie hurried to get Midnight from the corral. He met her at the fence and whinnied, seeing her in her riding clothes and hat. She stroked his forehead as he nodded his head up and down in excitement. "Shall we go for a ride, Midnight?" she asked with a smile, and he whinnied again. "It's the last day Miss Cassie Black will be riding you. Tomorrow I'll be Mrs. Cassandra Havoc, a married woman," she said as she saddled him. She climbed up and settled in the saddle, then rode out of the yard and down the lane. Right away she noticed the afternoon was heating up, with no breeze or cloud in sight. At the end of the lane, she turned north on the main road and headed away from town out to the open range, where she knew she could be alone.

As she rode, Midnight picked up his pace into a trot. The air moving across her face cooled her some, and she relaxed the reins, letting him take the lead. As her mind wandered, she found herself missing her family with a deep ache in her heart. Today was her last day as Cassandra Black. And with a pang of sadness, she realized once she was married, there would be no one to carry on the family name. The Black name would cease to exist. If only one of her brothers had lived, but it was not to be. She worried if she was enough to represent their family's legacy? She had a child on the way, and although she would not pass on the name, the Black lineage would continue in flesh and blood. Was she not part of her father and mother, and this child she carried part of her? She would pass on the best parts of herself and her parents and their parents, she prayed as she placed a hand on her stomach.

Cassie felt the tears spill over as she gave way to the lump in her throat. She was happy, happier than she'd ever been, yet she was sad. She wished her mother was there to do her hair and make sure she looked perfect on her wedding day. Her throat ached, and a sob escaped as she wished Charlotte was there to stay up late with her, talking and giggling on her last night as a single woman. She missed her family so much.

"Father in Heaven," she prayed silently as she stared without seeing across the horizon of fields and sky. "I miss my family so much; my heart is breaking. I'm so lonely for my ma and pa and brothers and sisters today. Please let them know how much I love them. Let them know I still think of them every day and miss them. I wish Pa were here to give me away. And I wish they could meet Ed." She looked heavenward as the tears continued. "I know they would love him. He's such a wonderful man. He's been through so much heartache, yet Lord, You helped him love again. I feel like he understands me better than anyone else because of his loss. We cherish each other because we know what it's like to lose someone you love. I trust him completely, Father. With him, I feel like my past can be healed and a new start created. It's a glorious feeling to be in love. I never knew what love felt like between a man and a woman. Loving a man like Ed makes me want to be a better person. I want to make him happy and spend forever with him. Please bless our marriage. Let it be good and holy, filled with love and joy. We will be a family soon. Please help us love the baby for the miracle that it is. I know You love each one of us infinitely. Help me love this baby. Father, please grant us this miracle of a long life of love and happiness. In the name of my Savior, Jesus Christ, Amen."

Closing her prayer, she wiped away the tears as she pondered the feelings and words she had shared with her Father in Heaven. Her mind was open, and her heart was listening when an overwhelming feeling of comfort came over her. Breathing deeply, she looked heavenward again with tears of joy and praised God for the peace she felt as her heart swelled with love, the love of God.

Cassie continued to ride aimlessly for a long time, contemplating. When Midnight finally stopped to eat a tall bunch of grass, she suddenly became aware of her surroundings. Being lost in thought, she hadn't realized how far they'd wandered. Startled, she looked around for landmarks and recognized the area was near Horse Creek, seeing the tree line about a mile away that ran beside the stream. The sun was lower in the sky than when they'd left, and she guessed she'd been gone about an hour or two. It was getting hotter, and she knew she should get home, but Midnight needed water soon, and she was feeling very hot and thirsty herself. Turning Midnight toward the creek, she cut across the prairie, careful not to push him too hard. She noticed the grass was drier than when she'd been there last. The summer heat was drying out the prairie quickly, even with the rain they'd had a few days ago. The dust billowed up with each hoof step. Everywhere she turned, the grasses appeared tannish brown and the sage grey-green. But as they approached the creek, the grass looked almost as lush as before. Climbing off Midnight, she led him down to the creek bed through the thick willows and shady poplar trees. The stream was a little lower today, but was still cool and refreshing as she put her hand into the rushing water to scoop up a drink. Midnight lowered his head downstream and drank as he stood ankle-deep in the clear, flowing pool. He shook his head and blew playfully as she smiled back at him. She let him drink his fill and then took the reins and led him back up the creek's bank and through the trees. "You're such a good horse," she said, looking over her shoulder at Midnight, and gave thanks to God for returning her long-time friend.

Suddenly she heard rattling. Turning towards the sound, she saw coiled up a few feet away, a rattlesnake. Cassie froze, but Midnight reared up on his hind legs and jerked the reins out of Cassie's hand as he let out a scream and bolted to the side. It all happened in a blurry instant as the rattler sprang through the air towards Midnight, striking but thankfully missing by mere inches. Adrenaline shot through Cassie's veins, and she dashed in the opposite direction. When she was at a safe distance away, she stopped running, leaning over with her hands on her knees, trying to catch her breath. Her heart was pounding loud in her ears and hard against her chest.

"Oh, my heavens! That snake nearly scared me to death," she thought. She placed trembling hands on her cheeks and felt her shaking legs go suddenly weak, nearly collapsing under her. Cassie took a deep breath and blew it out slowly, trying to calm herself down, not wanting to pass out in the scorching heat. She looked around, trying

353

to see Midnight, but he was just a speck in the distance, heading in the direction of home, leaving a cloud of dust behind him. Perplexed, she cupped her hands around her mouth and shouted with all her might, "Midnight! Come back, Midnight! Midnight!" she yelled, then sighed, "Good grief." Frustrated, she started walking towards the main road, through a mile of dried grass and sagebrush. Midnight was long gone, nowhere in sight. So, exasperated, she kept on walking. If she didn't find Midnight soon, she would have an eight-mile walk home.

Yelling for him would be futile at this point, so she didn't even try, but hoped and prayed he would stop running and come back for her. With no other choice, she kept on walking in the blinding sunlight that now burned her cheeks as it lowered. Calculating the distance, she guessed it would take two or three hours to get home. Her feet were already hot and beginning to blister from walking the dusty road as the heat radiated from it. "It must be close to one hundred degrees today," she thought, then huffed and shook her head in dismay. "Of all things…"

It didn't take long before her neck and temples were dripping with sweat from her thick black hair under her hat, soon soaking her back and neckline with moisture. Trying to cool herself, she removed her vest and unbuttoned the top buttons of her blouse. It only gave her temporary relief while the moisture evaporated. But soon, her shirt was dry and felt hot against her skin, and she wondered if she was being baked. Taking off her wide-brimmed hat, she began fanning her face. "That darn horse! Where is he?" she fumed in frustration. Cassie trudged on and on, growing weary as she squinted, looking for any sign of movement. All she could see for miles was dry prairie grass and sagebrush. Further down the road, heat waves shimmered in the distance as a hawk circled in the sky above her, looking for its next meal.

"Just another couple of miles to go, I think," she told herself as she began to feel dizzy and extremely nauseous. "I don't feel very good. Maybe I should…" she thought as darkness closed in on her vision and she collapsed on the hot, dusty road.

***

Meanwhile, completely unaware of her situation, Ed was in town picking up Cassie's wedding ring at the jeweler's shop.

"Thank heavens you got it done in time," Ed said as he examined the exquisite gold ring with the emerald stone, similar to the color of Cassie's eyes. "It's beautiful," he said, handing it back to the jeweler, who placed it in a tiny red velvet-lined box for Ed to take home. Then, tucking the ring box into his vest pocket, he thanked the jeweler again as he left the shop.

As he walked down the street, he passed by a boy selling newspapers and stopped to buy one, tucking it under his arm as he went on his way. Ed always enjoyed reading the paper in the morning with his first cup of coffee. Arriving back at the mercantile where he'd left Major, he untied him and swung up, turning towards home, when Vic spotted him from down the block.

"Hey! Sheriff!" hollered Vic, waving as he strolled along, spitting a stream of tobacco juice into the street.

"Hi, Vic!" Ed waved back, pulling up on the reins and stopping Major to let him approach. "You know I'm not the sheriff anymore. You can call me Ed now," he said with a grin.

"Yeah, I know. I know," Vic said, waving it off. "Hey,

I can't wait to see you all dressed up at your wedding to-morrow. I saw the announcement in the paper. It sounds like a great party," said Vic, as he put his thumbs in his belt and shifted his weight to one leg. "I don't think anyone will miss it." He smiled wryly as he lifted his hat to see his friend's expression at the news.

"Wait, what did you say?" asked Ed, confused.

"I said, I'll see you at your wedding and then the recep-tion at the Town Hall. It says it all right there in the paper; 'Come and celebrate our former sheriff's union with Miss Cassandra Black', or something like that. You have a paper, read it for yourself," he said, punctuated with a stream of spit. "Well, see you tomorrow," Vic said with a wave and continued on his way.

"We're in the paper," Ed said to himself. Still sitting in the road, he opened up the newspaper, scanning each page, until he got to the middle section titled "Announcements," in bold letters. Then, running his finger down the columns, he came to a smaller heading titled "Events." That's where he found the write-up. "Former Sheriff Edward Havoc will be tying the knot with Miss Cassandra Black, niece of George and Mabel Hartford, on Saturday, July 3rd, 1869, at 6:30 pm, at a private ceremony, in an undisclosed loca-tion. A celebration of their union will be held at the Town Hall from 7:30-9:00 pm. Music and dancing are planned; refreshments will be served. Come and wish the newly-weds, Mr. and Mrs. Havoc, congratulations," he read aloud. "Well, there it is, in black and white. It must have been the mayor. Who else would have posted it?" He wasn't upset, just surprised. Wanting to show Cassie her name in the paper, he tucked it into his saddlebag and headed out to the Hartford's.

356

***

Mabel and Madeline were disappointed that Cassie wasn't home when they arrived but used the time to work on the curtains. As they sewed and talked, the time passed quickly, but when supper time approached, they became concerned. It was nearly five o'clock, and Cassie still wasn't back. Checking out the window, again and again, they continued sewing as they listened for Cassie to ride up, expecting her any minute. Then, suddenly, they heard a horse ride into the yard and breathed a sigh of relief. They jumped up and giggled as they gathered up the almost finished curtains and ran into Mabel's bedroom to hide them.

They anticipated Cassie to come in any moment but were surprised to hear a knock at the door. Mabel shared a perplexed look with Madeline as she went to open it, wondering who it could be.

Her eyes widened, and her jaw dropped when she opened the door and saw who was on the other side.

"Ed! We thought you were Cassie," Mabel said, furrowing her brow, now more concerned. "What in the world! Where's Cassie?" thought Mabel as she stood in a panicked daze, imagining the worst. Madeline came forward and put her hand on Mabel's shoulder, bringing her attention back to the room. "Oh, Ed, I would like to introduce you to Madeline MacRea, Cassie's friend. They traveled cross country by train when they became good friends," explained Mabel, trying to remain calm.

"It's so nice to meet you, Ed. Cassie's told me all about you in her letters," Madeline said as she shook his hand, congratulating him on the upcoming wedding. It was clear that he was the handsome man Cassie had accurately depicted in her letters.

357

"Thank you, it's nice to meet you," said Ed politely, then got right to the point. "I was hoping to see Cass," he said, looking around for some clue of her whereabouts. "It'll be the last time I'll see her before we get married tomorrow."

"I'm sorry, Ed, she's not here," Madeline said with disappointment.

"Do you know when you will be expecting her?" he asked, wondering where Cassie could be the evening before her wedding if she wasn't home.

"We were expecting her back by now. She went riding hours ago, possibly longer. She left a note. When we got home around two o'clock, she was already gone. Her note said she would be home to help with supper. I don't know what's keeping her, but I'm worried. She's never been gone this long," Mabel said as she covered her mouth, holding back her next thought. "What if something's happened to her?"

"Maybe she went to our cottage to do some more housework and lost track of time. I'll go look for her and bring her right home." He turned away, putting his hat back on. "Don't you worry. You go ahead and start supper, and I'll be back with her soon," said Ed, as he tipped his hat and forced a smile.

Ed had tried to reassure Mabel, but he didn't feel reassured. He was worried. It wasn't like Cass to be gone alone for so long. A hundred scenarios started to run through Ed's mind. He had no idea where she might be but had to start at their cottage. He kicked Major into a gallop and arrived at their place within minutes. There was no sign of Cass anywhere on the homestead. Now he was seriously concerned. He jumped back on his horse and wondered which way he should go. "Did she go to Clearwater Pond? Or is she on the prairie riding out into the middle of God knows where?" he wondered. As he reached the main road, he saw a movement out of the corner of his eye. It was a black speck on the north road moving towards him. "Oh, thank heavens, there she is," he thought and galloped out to meet her. As he got closer, he felt a jolt of panic. It was only Midnight. He rode up to the horse slowly, careful not to spook him. Cass was nowhere in sight. "Oh no, what's happened?" he anguished, feeling as if he'd been kicked in the gut. He began to panic, his heart beat wildly, and his hands shook uncontrollably. Without hesitation, he tied Midnight onto his saddle and galloped in the direction Midnight had come from, heading north on the road towards Horse Creek. He squinted in the glaring sun, trying to see any movement of life. His head was swiveling, looking for a sign, but all he saw and heard were lowing cattle and a circling hawk that screeched ominously overhead. He'd gone about a mile more when he spotted something in the distance. Something or someone was lying in the middle of the road. As he drew closer, he recognized the dark hair and small figure as Cass. "It's her!" he thought in horror as his stomach did a nasty flip. He pushed the horses to gallop faster. "Dear God, let her be all right!" he prayed desperately.

Cassie took a deep breath and blinked her eyes in the bright sunlight as she tried to lift her head, but it resisted her efforts. Looking back, she saw a dark, blurry image moving toward her. She blinked and tried to focus. It was getting closer and bigger until she could tell it was two horses. "Midnight, you came back," she thought, "and you brought Ed."

Cassie tried harder to lift her head as Ed pulled the horses to a hard stop, sending a cloud of dust in their wake. Ed jumped off and ran to her side.

"Are you all right? What happened? Did you get bucked

359

off? Does anything hurt?" he asked rapidly, lifting her head gently, feeling for lumps and looking for blood or broken skin.

Her eyelids fluttered as she tried to open them. "I'm fine. 'm just really hot and thirsty. I must have passed out," she muttered in a raspy whisper, trying to sit up with his help. Her body felt stiff and heavy.

"Stay here," he said, gently laying her back on the ground, then jumped up and ran to his horse, bringing the canteen back to her. Then, lifting her head, he brought the canteen to her lips. "Here, drink some water," he said, lifting it, allowing the water to run into her mouth as she took a few hard swallows.

Her dry lips and sandpaper tongue welcomed the moisture that almost choked her as it burned down her throat. She coughed and sputtered and tried again. This time her throat didn't fight the movement and allowed the tepid water to course down its path. A few more swallows, and she lifted her chin to stop the flow. Then she cleared her throat and whispered, "That's enough for now."

"What were you doing out here?" he asked, when he could see there was nothing broken or bleeding.

Cassie squeezed her eyes shut, trying to think of what had happened, and then it returned to her. "I went on a ride and made it to Horse Creek. Midnight and I were walking out of the creek bed, and a rattler spooked him. He took off and left me." She paused and tried to think past the headache behind her eyes. "So, I was walking home. I'm so glad you found me," Cassie said with relief as she looked up at him, trying to focus as she blinked. She felt Ed shaking as he supported her head and shoulders. As her eyes cleared, she saw the look of terror on his pale and drawn face, his eyes wild with fright.

"I'm glad I found you, too," he said, his deep voice

sounding strained. "Now, let's get you home and out of this heat. Do you think you can ride?" he asked as he helped her sit upright.

"I think so," she said as he slowly stood her up, supporting her under her arms. "I'm sorry I scared you," Cassie said groggily, trying to soothe his nerves. "I'll be fine. I just need to cool down." She put her arm loosely around his waist as he walked beside her, holding her up.

"It's just if anything ever happened to you…" His mustache pulled downward at the corners, and his chin shook. "I would never forgive myself," he said with a tear rolling down his cheek. He pulled her into his chest and buried his face in her hair and held her, trying hard not to lose control as he held her tight.

"Ed, I'll be all right," Cassie said in a muffled voice, hugging Ed. She felt him relax his hold a little as she tried to comfort him.

"I should get you back. You're burning hot," he said, releasing her a little. "Let's get you onto my horse. Then I can hold you up," he said, walking her the last few steps to Major and, helping her put her foot in the stirrup, he lifted her. While he grabbed her vest and hat, she settled in the saddle. Stuffing her vest in his saddlebag and placing her hat on her head, he climbed on behind and wrapped his arms around her. Taking the reins, he kicked Major into a trot, wanting to get Cassie home, and fast. With Midnight trailing close behind and dust billowing, he headed south with his precious cargo.

As they reached the turnoff to their homestead, Cassie swayed as her head fell back onto Ed's chest. "Cass, we're here!" he said, trying to rouse her. He knew it was imperative to get her cooled down as fast as possible. So, he pulled up to the house, jumped down and slid Cassie off into his arms, and carried her into the house.

"I'm so thirsty," she muttered as he kicked the door open and placed her on a kitchen chair.

"I know, dear; I'll get you some water." Ed turned to the sink, pumped water into a cup, and quickly brought it to her, holding it for her as she drank it up. "We need to get you cooled down." He went to the middle of the room, threw back the rug, and pulled open the root cellar door. "Let's get you down there where it's cool," he said, lifting Cassie easily and carrying her carefully down the steps.

They welcomed the cold air, feeling like winter bliss on a scorching hot July day. Ed set her down on the bottom step, ran back up, pulled a blanket off the bed, and brought it back. Laying the blanket on the floor, he helped Cassie ease down. She took a deep breath of light, crisp air, feeling the coolness of the dirt floor seep through her clothes to her back. Her head was pounding, and her eyes burned as she closed her eyes and tried to relax, letting the coolness soothe her.

"My feet are burning hot," she whispered. "Will you take my shoes off, please?" Cassie asked as she lay there feeling better, bit by bit.

Ed unlaced her shoes, carefully removing them along with her stockings. Her feet were red and swollen with a few small blisters forming. "Oh, Cass. I'll go get you some water," he said and went to fill a pan. This time he also grabbed a pillow from off the bed and brought it down. Propping her head up a little, he placed her feet in the dishpan of cool water.

"Oh, thank you, Ed." The water eased the burning in her feet immediately. "I'm feeling much better," said Cassie, as she rested her head on the pillow, looking up at him in the dim light from above. "I'm so sorry. I didn't mean to worry anyone. I just needed to be alone. I was thinking and lost track of time before realizing how far I'd gone.

We were almost to Horse Creek, and we both needed water badly." She closed her eyes, still seeing the awful snake raise up to strike, and decided to tell him everything. "After our drink, I was leading Midnight out of the creek bottom when a rattler spooked him." She heard him inhale sharply and hurried on as he squeezed her hand and muttered her name. "I was lucky. If I'd been riding him, I would have been bucked off. Instead, he reared up and pulled free of the reins. The snake struck out towards him, giving me time to go the other way. Midnight probably saved my life. But he was so scared he kept on running towards home," Cassie explained as her chin quivered. "I was hoping he would eventually come back for me…but he didn't," her voice shook, remembering the despair she had felt. "If it hadn't been so hot, I would've been fine. I'm so sorry," she apologized as tears ran down her cheeks. She felt so bad about the panic she'd caused Ed and the worry Aunt Mabel must be feeling by now.

Ed wiped her tears away. "Look, darling. I'm just happy you're not seriously injured. You have heat sickness, which could have been worse if you'd been out there any longer. But thank heavens I found you. You should start feeling better soon. But you must promise me, no more horse rides until after the baby's born. And even then, no more going off alone. Please, for my sake and the baby's, if not for your own. I need to know you're safe. It about killed me today to see you laying there. I thought…" Ed paused, his mouth frowning and brow furrowed, unable to finish. He swallowed and tried again, "It was too painful. I couldn't stand to lose you, too. Please," Ed pleaded, brushing the dusty hair away from her tear-streaked face as he tried to force a smile.

Cassie's heart was aching as she reached up and placed her hands on his cheeks. "Yes, my dear, anything for you.

I can't cause you pain. It hurts me too badly. I'll be more careful. I promise," Cassie said, lifting up and kissing him softly on the lips. "I'll be a good wife; I won't make you worry unnecessarily," she promised with a loving smile.

Ed held her right hand against his cheek, then turned and kissed the palm. "Love, I will always worry about you. It's what people do when they love each other. And I know you'll be a wonderful wife because I know you love me," he said, releasing her hand, sitting back and smiling. "If you're feeling better, we should get you to your aunt and uncle's before they send out a search party," he said, trying to joke, but it fell flat. There was too much truth in it.

"Yes, I'm feeling much better. I don't feel hot anymore, and my headache is almost gone. Thanks to you, I think I'll be OK," she said, and thought with adoration, "My hero!"

Ed helped her dry her feet and put her shoes and stockings back on, noting the redness and blisters had improved greatly. Moving slowly, she stood up with his help. At first, her head felt a little dizzy but then cleared. Carrying the things he'd brought down, he followed behind her, ensuring she didn't fall.

"You need to wash up before we go," he suggested as she reached the top. "You have some dust on your face and in your hair. They'll wonder what happened to you, and we don't need to worry the others any more than they have," Ed said as he closed the trap door and threw the rug back over it.

Cassie went to the kitchen sink, pumped some water into her hands, and scrubbed her face as Ed handed her a clean towel. Dusting off her clothes and brushing through her hair, with the help of Ed, she quickly braided it again and gave him a reassuring smile. "That good enough?"

"That's much better," he said, winking at her. "We can take the buggy. I'll go hitch it up while you get another drink of water. I'll be ready in just a minute," he said, rushing out to the horses. First, he put Midnight in the corral to get some food and water, then he took Major to the barn and hitched him to the buggy.

While Ed was away, Cassie took a minute to look around the cottage and smiled contentedly. Tomorrow she would begin living here with Ed, as his wife, for the rest of her life. A wave of excitement made butterflies flutter in her stomach as she thought of what that meant. Closing the door behind her, she left the cottage for the last time as Cassie Black. Tomorrow she would enter their lovely home as Mrs. Cassandra Havoc.

***

Ed drove the buggy as fast as he dared back to the Hartford's place. It was close to six thirty when they arrived. He'd already been gone an hour and knew they'd be worried. As they pulled up, Mabel and George ran out of the house, followed by another woman close behind. Cassie waved at them to show that she was all right. As they reached the buggy, they observed her rosy cheeks and crimson lips, and decided she looked whole and well.

"I'm fine, I'm fine," she said to her aunt and uncle and then suddenly recognized the woman with them. "Madeline!" she called out in a hoarse voice. Madeline came rushing up to Cassie, hugging her while still inside the buggy.

"Cassie!" Madeline exclaimed with excitement and relief. "We were so worried. I'm so relieved to see you're OK," she said, helping Cassie out of the buggy and hugging her tightly. She laughed cheerfully. "Let me look at you." Taking Cassie by the shoulders, she held her back to

365

look at her more closely. She'd changed; there was a sparkle in her eyes and a radiance about her that only love could put there. "You look happy." Madeline smiled broadly and laughed. "Surprise! I came in time for the wedding!" she announced as she gave her another squeeze.

"I'm so glad you could make it!" Cassie said with her cheek against Madeline's, her heart feeling so much love for her dear friend.

"I want to hear everything!" Madeline said as she let her go.

Mabel hated to break up the reunion but couldn't stand it any longer. She wanted an explanation. "Cassie, where were you? Why were you gone so long?" she quizzed as she took a turn, hugging Cassie and kissing her on the cheek. "We were so worried."

"We almost sent out a search party for you, Cassie," teased George, trying to ease the tension. Although, truthfully, he had been very worried and had almost gone out to look for her himself if Ed hadn't produced her soon.

"I'm fine now. I just took a long ride, and when we stopped for a drink at the stream, Midnight got spooked and ran off, leaving me stranded. It was just annoying more than anything. Sorry to worry you all. Lucky for me, Ed happened to find me before the vultures started circling," Cassie joked, causing everyone to chuckle. Everyone except Ed; he just smiled and lagged behind as Madeline, Cassie, and Mabel walked into the house with their arms around each other.

"Ed, you certainly are a knight in shining armor," Madeline said over her shoulder. "Thanks for bringing our Cassie back safe and sound."

"It was my honor and pleasure to do so," said Ed with a bow and a forced smile, as he and George followed close behind the women into the house.

366

"I believe this is the biggest bunch of jokers in Cheyenne," George teased. "And I think the title for best jester goes to Cassie," he said, chuckling with the ladies as he imagined buzzards circling, as he'd seen in a cartoon drawing. Ed didn't laugh, and George could see the strain on his face. George became serious again. He didn't believe that Cassie had been fine when Ed found her, not in the least. "Sheriff Havoc doesn't get upset over nothing. Whatever really happened to Cassie has him shaken up," he thought as he put his hand on Ed's shoulder, giving it a friendly squeeze. "My good man. We're lucky to have you to look out for our Cassie. Heaven knows she needs watching over," he wanted to say, but instead gave him a nod and a grateful smile.

"Who's hungry?" Mabel asked cheerfully as they entered the kitchen, smelling chicken pot pie with new peas and potatoes. "It's time for supper." Overjoyed that Cassie was back and no worse for wear, she determined to enjoy their last evening together before the wedding.

Supper was delightful, as everyone filled up on the delicious food and enjoyed the added company. Madeline was a pleasant guest, complimentary as well as amiable. She quickly gained their favor as she shared her humorous experiences of caring for her mischievous nieces and nephews. One story led to another as they reminisced about their growing-up years and laughed and joked around the table. As they finished their meal with apple pie and coffee, the stories continued, and George noticed the joy slowly coming back into Ed's face.

On the other hand, Ed watched Cassie as she talked animatedly, telling Madeline all about her adventures since she came to Cheyenne. Cassie seemed full of joy, even after all she'd been through that day. She was a strong woman; it was a fact he already knew and was again reaffirmed in his mind. He eventually relaxed and joined the conversation wholeheartedly, telling jokes and teasing as usual.

Cassie was happy to see the worry leaving Ed's face. However, she still felt bad for upsetting him. She really would try not to get into a pickle again. It was a close call; she knew she could have been hurt in so many ways and felt she had been protected. "Thank you, Father in Heaven," Cassie said in her mind as she realized how blessed she'd been. "And thank you for Ed, Father," she prayed as she watched Ed's smile, this time reaching his eyes. Subtly, she reached under the table, took his hand, and squeezed it. That brought an even bigger smile, and his eyes twinkled as he squeezed her hand back.

Supper was cleaned up, and the dishes were done while they continued to catch up on everything. It was getting late, and Ed decided he should be going. He thanked them for the delicious meal and mentioned how happy he was to finally meet Madeline. Cassie was sad to see him go and offered to walk him out. The rest of them stayed inside and continued to chat, allowing the love birds their privacy to say goodnight before the "big day." Ed took his hat off the hook by the door and, with a final "goodbye," walked out, followed by Cassie.

Together they walked with their arms around each other to the buggy. Ed stopped before he got into the rig and took Cassie in his arms, looking down at her moonlit face. "You know, I love you more than life itself. I learn it more every day. I can't wait to make you my wife, Cassandra Black. In less than twenty-four hours, you will be mine forever, and I will never let you go," he said and leaned down, kissing her softly on the lips. He withdrew slowly and smiled at her.

Cassie felt her heart overflowing with love for Ed. It almost brought her to tears, she loved him so much.

Her feeling of connection with Ed was so strong she was having a hard time imagining ever being without him. She loved him so completely, it made her heart ache to have him leave her even for one more night. "Ed, I don't ever want to let you go. I'm yours forever," she said and laid her head on his chest, listening to his heart beat strong and steady as she held onto him tightly. Tears rolled down her cheeks, wetting his shirt. "I love you with all my heart," she whispered. "And I thank God for you every day. You make me the happiest woman alive. I can't wait to be Mrs. Edward Havoc," she said, looking up at him beneath her long dark lashes.

Ed kissed her on the forehead and released her before he couldn't. "Sleep well, my 'Sleeping Beauty.' When I see you tomorrow, you will become Mrs. Havoc, and I will be the happiest man alive. Goodnight, my love," he said, and jumped into the buggy and drove away.

Cassie stood there, loving him and feeling her heart pull as the distance grew between them in the moonlit night. Cassie looked up at the stars in the giant universe and again thanked the Almighty for her many blessings. Her heart was swelling with so many reasons to be thankful and joyful. Three of them were inside the house, and she needed to go and let them know it. She slowly turned and walked back to the house.

***

Ed arrived at the cottage feeling drained. He walked up the steps and sat outside on the porch in the cool night air. He finally had a minute to consider what had happened that day. "Dear God, I almost lost her," he thought as he leaned forward, resting his elbows on his thighs and putting his hands over his face. "Not again, dear Lord. I can't lose her too." His shoulders rolled forward, and he finally let out the tears he had held back for hours. When he had spent them, he calmly straightened up, looked heavenward, and prayed again. "Father in Heaven, I know You have a plan for us. I'm trusting in You that You know what's best. I only want to love and cherish her forever. Please give me the chance to do that. I love her so much, Father. Please don't take her away from me. Allow me to be the baby's father. I will raise and love it as my own. Please, let Cass grow old with me, and I will do my best to deserve her love." He closed his prayer with tears streaming. "Amen."

***

Back inside the house, Cassie hugged and kissed her aunt and uncle goodnight. And again, she apologized for causing them to worry. They reassured her that they only worried because they loved her so much.

"I love you too," she said, then headed off to her room where Madeline had gone to change for bed.

Cassie knocked quietly and entered her room at Madeline's acceptance. Madeline was already in bed, reading a book. Cassie changed into her nightdress, then sat at her dressing table and let her hair out of its braid.

Madeline sat up and asked, "May I?" Madeline missed doing her daughter's hair.

Cassie smiled. "Sure." It had been so long since she'd had her hair brushed. She and Charlotte used to take turns doing each other's hair every night. Cassie came to the bed and handed the brush to Madeline. Sitting on the edge of bed beside her, she closed her eyes as Madeline brushed her long black hair, smooth and shiny.

"Well, tomorrow will soon be here. I bet you're excited," said Madeline. "I know I am. I think your story is like a fairy tale. You're the damsel in distress, and Prince Edward comes to rescue the fair maiden. It is a beautiful story. Cassie, the beautiful princess, marries Edward, the handsome prince, and goes to live in a cottage in the woods. It couldn't be more romantic," Madeline said with a far-off look in her eyes.

Cassie smiled at the extent of Madeline's imagination. It did sound like a wonderful story. And she had to admit, "I do feel like a princess. Every day I feel like I'm in love with a prince. But I don't feel like I deserve such a happy ending. I feel like it's all too unbelievable. How can I be so lucky? But here I am, getting married tomorrow to Edward, the most charming, handsome, gallant man I've ever met," Cassie said as her brow furrowed, and she turned to face Madeline.

"Cassie, why wouldn't you deserve a happy ending? You deserve it as much as anyone. Believe it!" Madeline said, taking her by the shoulders and looking into her eyes. "You are worth all the joy and happiness that life can give. You are a survivor," she said, leaning in. "You lived and should live life to the fullest, because you can. That's what your family would want you to do. It's OK to be sad sometimes, but you don't have to be sad forever. Let yourself be happy, Cassie." Tears filled Madeline's eyes as she felt a great love for her. "Let go of the things you can't control and trust in the Lord. He has a plan for you, a glorious plan. He wants you to be happy in this life and to feel joy. And you will." She nodded as Cassie tilted her head, listening as tears filled her eyes. "You will have more happiness and joy than you can ever imagine. Marriage and children are some of the most wonderful blessings on earth. But if not, then it will still be a wonderful life because it's meant

371

to be that way. There is a joy to be found in every little thing life offers. Even in the darkest nights, the sun rises in the morning. Let its light fill you," Madeline said with a quivering voice, and leaned forward and embraced her. "My dear Cassie, I love you so much," she said, as tears ran down her cheeks and she smiled at Cassie. The love she felt for this sweet girl was so strong and had grown even more in such a short time. Her bond with Cassie felt so much more than friends.

"Oh, Madeline, I feel the same way. You are so much like a big sister. And I needed one today," she said as she let the tears flow. "When I went for a ride today, it was because I was missing my family so much. I needed time alone to think. And then you show up and fill my heart with so much sisterly love. I'm thankful you could come. The Lord must have known I would need you here. Thank you for coming to support me," Cassie said, sitting back and wiping the tears away from her cheeks as she smiled.

Madeline chuckled, "Are you kidding? And miss the biggest event of the century? I can't wait to see you in your wedding dress. Tomorrow it will be my pleasure to be your 'Fairy Godmother.' I will be here to help you with anything; dress, hair, jewels, whatever you need," she said, beaming. "I'll work my magic on you. I've done my daughter's hair her whole life. I will make you the most beautiful bride ever; you just wait and see," Madeline promised. "But first, you must get your beauty sleep." Madeline leaned over and blew out the lamp on her bedside table.

Cassie sniffed and smiled again. "You're right. I'd better get to sleep. I don't want circles under my eyes tomorrow." She climbed into her side of the bed and blew out her lamp. Taking a deep breath in the darkness, she added, "Thank you, Madeline, for being here for me. Goodnight, 'Fairy Godmother,'" Cassie said with a little laugh, closed her eyes, turned over, and fell asleep within minutes.

***

As George and Mabel said their nightly prayers, they thanked the Lord for bringing Cassie safely home to them again. Their greatest joy had given them quite a scare, and they were reminded again of how precious each day was with the ones you love. Tomorrow would be a busy and joyful day, and they looked forward to it with mixed feelings.

Chapter 18
Wedding Day

Cassie awoke with a smile on her face. She'd slept so soundly that she hadn't even heard Madeline get up. Her room was illuminated with early morning sunlight filtered through the lace curtains. Sliding up in bed, she pulled her knees to her chest, wrapped her arms around them, and took a moment to take a mental picture, wanting to remember every detail of the room. She would miss the special room her aunt and uncle had created just for her. This was home when she had none, where she had cried herself to sleep many a night and woke with renewed hope. It was where she had dreamed of Ed and written letters to Madeline, telling her she'd fallen in love. In a short time, she had grown to love this special place of her own, and now she would be leaving it.

As she sat thinking, she could hear the others in the kitchen talking in hushed tones and the smell of breakfast cooking. Suddenly, she felt a surge of energy to start the day. Cassie jumped out of bed, slipped on her robe, and opened the bedroom door to find everyone at the table with breakfast ready.

Cassie squealed. "I'm getting married today!" she said with glee and rushed to give them each a kiss on the cheek.

"You must have slept well," guessed Madeline with a chuckle. "You didn't move an inch when I got up this morning."

"I slept great," she said with enthusiasm and sat down beside Madeline.

"You've plumb worn yourself out these last few days. All that cleaning at the cottage and then your long walk yesterday. You deserved a good night's sleep," reasoned Mabel. "I hope you're feeling better today," she said, still worried about Cassie's ordeal.

"I'm feeling full of health. Better than I have in months," said Cassie cheerfully.

"Well, that's good to hear," said George. "Now, let's pray before this gets cold."

Immediately following, everyone hungrily passed the steaming pancakes, bacon, and eggs around the table as they talked about the day ahead.

Cassie had to remind herself to eat slowly even though she felt like rushing. It wouldn't do to make herself sick on her wedding day.

"What's your plan for today, Cassie?" asked Madeline as she poured warm maple syrup on her stack of fluffy pancakes with melted butter running down the sides.

"I think I'll bathe right after breakfast. I'll need all the time I can get to allow my hair to dry before it's curled," Cassie said as she took a bite of her scrambled eggs and washed it down with milk. "This is the last time I'll ever have to wear this old nightdress. I'll wear my new one from now on," she thought.

"That sounds like a great idea. You've planned your day, it sounds like. I can help you with your hair once it's dry," offered Madeline. "And anything else that needs to be done today. As I said, I'm your 'Fairy Godmother.'"

"I'll be out of your hair…so to speak," George said impishly. "I'm going to load up your bedroom furniture this morning and take it to the cottage." Pushing back his chair, he went to the stove for more coffee.

"That's a lot of work, Uncle George. Are you sure you can't wait until I'm done bathing so I can help too?" Cassie asked, feeling bad about her uncle doing all that work, because of her.

"No, no. You'll be busy enough getting ready for the wedding. Don't you worry, Ed will be over there to help me set it up," said George, refilling his coffee mug. "Then I'll bring back the other bed for Madeline to sleep in tonight," he said, nodding to Madeline.

"Madeline and I can come with you," suggested Mabel. "We can help set up the bedroom so it looks pretty," she said, slyly winking at him. "And get the new curtains hung and put the new quilt on the bed," she thought with excitement.

"I would love the help. A woman's eye is always welcome when setting up a new home," said George, catching the hint.

***

Bart arrived a little before eight, wanting to be at the dress shop before it opened. As soon as he walked into the store, he was greeted by Bea and responded cheerfully, feeling the happiest he'd ever been.

"We'll have to hurry and get changed as soon as we get off. We want to have plenty of time to get there if it takes as long as you say it does," said Bart with excitement. He was thrilled that she had agreed to go with him to the wedding. Yesterday he even bought a black suit with matching trousers and a gold and black vest for the occasion. He had a standard to set for his future business, and more importantly, he wanted to look his best for Bea.

"I think I can talk Father into letting us off early. He's

very sentimental about things like this." Bea leaned in and whispered, "Especially weddings." Knowing for sure, he would insist on it.

Together they headed to the back room, talking excitedly about the evening to come. Bea excused herself and went straight to her father's office, coming out a few minutes later with a smile.

Bart entered the office and found Mr. Holden busy working on an account. "I'm going to go to the post office to mail these orders for the next shipment of fabric," he said as he took the letter from off the top of the file cabinet. "I'll be back in a few minutes. Unless you need me to do something else first," Bart asked as Mr. Holden looked up momentarily from his project.

"No, go ahead," he said and remembered. "Oh, I told Bea you could both leave at five o'clock to get ready for the wedding. I don't want you to be late and hold it up," Mr. Holden said. His approval of Bart was increasing, not only with respect to becoming his partner but also as his daughter's suitor. Bea had been lonely for so long that he had wondered if he should have arranged a marriage for her long ago. But now, it seemed she had found a match on her own.

***

Bart handed the thick letter full of fabric orders to the postmaster, paid the postage, then hesitated before he left.

"Is there something else?" asked the postmaster, sensing his reluctance.

"Umm, yes. Might you have a letter for Bartholomew Clark?" Bart asked with mixed feelings. He wanted to know what his father thought, and then again, maybe not.

The postmaster turned and looked through a stack of letters behind the counter, shuffling the stiff envelopes of various sizes. "Bartholomew Clark, you say. Oh, yes! Here's one," he said and pulled one out of the bunch and handed it to him.

Suddenly Bart's heart was pounding in his throat; it was from his father. He immediately began to sweat. "Thank you," he said as he headed outside and sat on the bench in front of the building and tore open the letter.

July 1, 1869

Bartholomew,

I tried to understand your reasoning when you left to bring Cassie back to marry her. But now, I can't imagine what you think you are doing.

You say you're not coming home and have a plan for the future. How could you disappoint us like this? After all we've done for you. I taught you everything you know, all my planning and training over the years, are now wasted. I practically handed you the mercantile, and now you throw it back in my face. I expected better from you. But, I see you have made up your mind, and I will respect your wishes. And I hope you will respect mine.

You have broken your mother's heart, and that is unforgivable. No son of mine would do that to his parents. You are no son of ours. Do not contact us any further. If you want to be your own man, then be one. Don't come crawling back when things don't work out. You have your path

*to follow. You've made your choice. I will pass
the business on to your brother, John. I will not
support you in this endeavor of yours, financially
or otherwise. You will reap what you sow.*

*Your things have been sent by train; they
should arrive on Saturday afternoon.*
Mr. Clark

Bart's heart sank with deep disappointment. He had
assumed his father would feel this way, but to read it in ink,
engraved it in stone. "Well, that's it, I guess. My path is set.
No going back now," thought Bart with a twinge of uneasiness. Resting his arms on his knees, he leaned forward and
stared at the letter, swallowing back the tears that threatened to come. Then, taking a deep breath, he covered his
face with his hands; he closed his eyes and offered a silent
prayer.

"Dear God, please help to guide me. I know You have
a plan for me. Help me be strong enough to follow it.
Forgive me for causing my mother heartache and for disappointing my father. I never intended to cause them pain
in doing what I thought was right. I have always tried to
love and honor my parents, as the commandments say. I
don't know how to do what I know is right and reconcile it
with my parents. Help me, Father in Heaven. Soften their
hearts so that they may one day forgive me. In Thy Son's
Holy Name, Jesus Christ, Amen." Resolutely, he stood to
go back to work. "Disowned…I will show him. I will be a
success, and I will do it on my own! Maybe then he will be
proud of me," he thought.

***

379

Ed rode through town as the bustling Saturday crowd arrived. Shopkeepers opening their doors for business greeted and welcomed customers in. Stopping at the post office as he jumped down and tied Major to the hitching rail, he looked up and saw a familiar face.

"Bart, how are you today?" he asked excitedly.

"Oh! Hi, Sheriff…I mean Mr. Havoc. I should be asking how you are doing," Bart said, teasing. "You're the groom!"

"I'm doing great. I just had a last-minute thing or two to get done in town before the wedding. I want to look my best, so I came in to get a shave," said Ed, rubbing the stubble on his chin.

"What are you planning to wear for the wedding?" asked Bart.

"Just my brown Sunday suit," Ed said, wondering why Bart would care. "Why?"

"I am only asking because it's my new business venture. Mr. Holden and I plan to open a men's clothing shop soon. It's still in the early stages, so please don't say anything to anyone. We want to be the first to open a shop for tailor-made suits here in Cheyenne," Bart explained as an idea suddenly came to him.

"That sounds nice. You should do very well. I know there's a need for one." Ed was impressed with Bart, and it sounded like he would do well in Cheyenne. "What does your father think about you staying here?" Ed asked as he saw the letter in Bart's hand.

"He's very disappointed in me. As a matter of fact, he told me not to come home. So, I guess I'm on my own now," he said. "He's essentially told me I'm disowned."

"Well, that's too bad. I'm sorry he feels that way. Are you going to be OK?" Ed asked, tilting his head with concern.

"Yeah, I'll be OK. With or without his blessing, I was going to stay anyways. I finally feel passionate about something for the first time in my life," Bart said with a sad smile. "I just wish he could be supportive of me."

"I'm glad you're doing what you feel passionate about. I know how that feels. I resigned as sheriff to follow my passion," Ed confessed with a grin. "And I will follow her till the end of time."

Bart chuckled at that, understanding completely what he meant, knowing he would follow Bea anywhere. "I'm wondering, Mr. Havoc, if you would do me a favor? I know this is not what you had planned, but I would like to outfit you with a new suit—an advertisement of sorts. We would give it to you free of charge, just for wearing it. You know how people talk; it would only take one person to say you had your suit tailor-made here in Cheyenne. What do you say?" asked Bart. "And who better than one of the most well-known people in the community. We couldn't ask for a better subject to model our first creation."

"Well, I don't know what to say. Is there even time to make one?" asked Ed, bewildered by the request. "A new suit for the wedding, just to be their first display. Sounds like an amazing deal."

"You could come to the shop right away, and we'll get started on it. I'm sure we could have it ready for you by five o'clock," Bart said with enthusiasm.

"All right then! You have a model," said Ed, chuckling lightly. "Wonders never cease."

"As soon as you can then, come by the dress shop. We'll be waiting for you," Bart said, and ran off down the block to get the word to Mr. Holden and the seamstresses. Of course, they would all have to work together to get it done, but they could do it, and it would look fantastic.

381

Ed shook his head in astonishment. "What just happened?" he wondered as he entered the post office.

The postmaster greeted him by name and quickly retrieved a letter for him. It was from his mother. He had written his mother and sisters back in Kansas about his engagement and upcoming wedding. Due to limited funds, since his father and brothers had died in the war, Ed assumed they wouldn't be able to come, but hoped by some miracle they could. Opening the letter, he began reading as he walked outside to his horse.

July 1, 1869
Eddie, My Dearest Son,

We were surprised and delighted when we read of your upcoming wedding. I'm sure Cassie's a lovely young lady. The way you described her, she sounds perfect for you. The poor girl deserves all your love after hearing about what she has lost. We know you both will take comfort in each other. You have grieved a long time, and it pleases me that you found someone to make you smile again. We are so happy for you. Our prayers have been answered.

We wish we could be there for you both, but you know how tight things have been for us since the war. There is always something that needs replaced or fixed on the farm. Even if we had the means right now, there isn't the time either. There's too much that needs to be done here. The dress shop in town keeps sending us more and more work, and we can't turn down the money. And when we aren't sewing, there is the farm to run. I don't tell you this to worry you. It is hard work, but we can manage well with your sisters and me. Perhaps we could come for a visit later in the year when things slow down.

We miss you terribly and wish we could be closer to you. We love you very much. Tell Cassie we love her too, for making you happy again. And tell her we can't wait to meet her. We send our congratulations and blessings to you and Cassie.

We love you and wish you all the happiness you deserve.
Love,
Ma, Beth, and Joy

It was just as he had suspected. He would miss having them here, but he understood. He folded the letter, placed it in his vest pocket, and checked the time. It was eight-thirty. "Still plenty of time to get a shave. Then home to help move the furniture. That should still give me enough time to bathe and to come back here to dress for the wedding," he thought. Suddenly his nerves kicked in. His hands felt a little shaky, not because he was apprehensive but because he was so excited. He wanted it to be the perfect day. Jumping on Major, he rode down the street to the dress shop. Looking up and down the boardwalk, he tipped his hat further down on his head and ducked inside, feeling a bit awkward walking into a women's dress shop.

Having arrived a few minutes earlier, Bart had rushed to the back office and announced his idea to Mr. Holden.

"Bart! I'm impressed. That's a brilliant idea," he said, slapping his hand on the desk as he stood. "By George! I know we can get it done in time," exclaimed Mr. Holden as he went to the office door. "Attention, everyone! I have an announcement to make. Today we're going to work together on an important project. We have a suit to make for our former Sheriff Havoc. He's getting married today, and we will make him the best suit in town. It's part of our newest venture in opening a new store just for men's suits and formal wear. Currently, this has to stay a secret about the shop opening, but not the secret that we can provide men in town with the best suits west of the Mississippi. Bart here, had the genius idea to create this suit and have our well-renowned sheriff model it for us. Nearly the whole town will be at the reception tonight and see it firsthand," announced Mr. Holden to his seamstresses.

The women looked at each other in awe. "How exciting!" they whispered and nodded in agreement.

Ed reluctantly came into the store and closed the door behind him, looking out the front window to see if anyone had witnessed him entering. Bart heard the bell and hurried out to the front counter to find him there.

"Come right this way, Mr. Havoc," he said as he led him back to the office.

As Bart and Ed passed, the seamstresses stopped their work, looking shyly up at them, hiding excited smiles and giggles from the handsome sheriff.

"We'll get your measurements, and then you can be on your way. The suit should be ready for fitting by four o'clock with enough time to make any final adjustments. That will leave you plenty of time to get home and change for the wedding," said Bart as he closed the office door.

With the help of Mr. Holden, who took the measurements as Bart recorded them, they could get started quickly.

"All right, you're free to go and leave the rest to us,"

said Mr. Holden, slapping Ed on the back. "We'll make sure you are the most dashing man in Cheyenne," he grinned.

Grabbing the book of swatches from the cabinet, he flipped to the fabric he had in mind for the jacket and trousers, a charcoal grey tweed. For the vest, he chose silk with narrow black and white stripes. Next, he chose black silk for the puff tie and white linen for the high-collared shirt. Out at the cutting table, he called the women to gather around. Making a quick sketch of the suit, Mr. Holden assigned the articles of clothing to the seamstresses to make. From the patterns he'd been designing for months, he selected the ones he wanted that would set his dream in motion. He laid out the fabrics and began pinning the patterns as the ladies joined in. As soon as the patterns were affixed, they began cutting the material with expertise. Mr. Holden then selected buttons and thread, matching each fabric, and sent them with the ladies to their machines to start sewing.

***

With breakfast out of the way, Cassie began to heat water on the stove for her bath. Together, George, Mabel, and Madeline loaded up the wagon with Cassie's belongings and some lighter furniture from her bedroom. Once the wagon was full, Cassie gathered her clean clothes, toiletries, and scented oils for her bath and set them beside the tub. With the help of Uncle George, she was able to fill the large cast iron tub with the steaming hot water in the room behind the kitchen.

George was the last to climb into the wagon as he, Mabel, and Madeline waved goodbye to Cassie, telling her they would be back in an hour or so. Mabel and Madeline smiled at each other as they shared the secret of having just snuck the curtains and wedding quilt past Cassie without her seeing.

***

When they arrived at the cottage, they found Ed had gone to town. It was just as well. This way, they could surprise them both. George began taking the old bed apart as the women took off the bedding and set it aside. Unloading the wagon of all the smaller furniture, they then helped George load the old ticking into the back of the wagon. Careful to keep the bedding and ticking clean, they laid the bed frame on top, protecting it from getting scratched. All of the other pieces of furniture, including the sewing machine, were moved into the smaller bedroom and organized into a cozy sewing room. Next, they brought in Cassie's furniture and set up the nightstands, lamps, and rugs. Then, working together, they hung the curtains on all the windows, brightening the look of the unstained wood walls of the cottage. Lastly, Mabel lay the blue checkered tablecloth she'd made on the table and set the lamp in the middle, making the kitchen look cheery.

Mabel and Madeline stood surveying their handiwork and smiled with satisfaction. The cottage was coming together nicely.

***

As Ed neared the Hartford's, he hoped he wasn't too late to help move the furniture. His shave at the barbershop had set him back a little, unexpectedly having to wait for the person in front of him to be finished. Arriving at the homestead, he tied up Major, looking around for someone to come out, and when they didn't, he decided to knock on the door.

Having finished her bath, Cassie, then dressed, and was brushing her damp hair at Mabel's dressing table when she heard the knock at the door. She wondered who it could be.

"Is anyone home?" called Ed. "Maybe they're all busy inside moving things and can't hear me," he thought.

"Ed!" Cassie exclaimed from the other side of the door. "You can't come in. It's bad luck to see the bride before the wedding," she warned as she put her hands on the door to brace against it if he should happen to try to push it open. "Everyone's gone to our house."

Ed smiled; he was tickled that he had found her home alone. He wanted to see her so bad, but he would wait. "OK, Cass, I'll stay outside," he said with his hands on the door. "Love, there's something I've been meaning to talk to you about," he said through the barrier between them. "I've invited Bart to the wedding. And before you say anything, there is something you should know."

"OK, go ahead. I'm listening," said Cassie, wondering why Ed would have invited Bart to the wedding when they had been rivals just days ago.

"Bart's come to realize some things. He agrees, you weren't right for him." Ed smiled, leaning against the door. "Good thing, because you're perfect for me."

Cassie smiled and moved closer, wanting to be nearer to Ed.

Ed rushed on, "He's decided he wants to stay in Cheyenne and pursue a business venture… and a lady he's met. Her name's Bea, and she works at the dress shop," Ed explained.

"Oh, yes, Bea's lovely. I met her the other day. So that's

who he's staying for?" she puzzled. "How interesting." She recalled the tall, kind seamstress with strawberry blonde hair. "What business venture? I thought he would go back to Missouri to take over his father's mercantile."

"He's going to go into business with the dressmaker, Mr. Holden, who also happens to be Bea's father. They're going to open a men's clothing store as partners. As a matter of fact, just today, I ran into Bart, and he's offered to make me a new suit for the wedding, free of charge. As a sort-of advertisement of what they are capable of doing at their new shop," Ed said excitedly.

"That's incredible. What a nice gesture. It makes sense to me, since you're the most handsome man in Cheyenne," Cassie said with a grin.

Ed chuckled at that. "Well, I'm glad at least you think so. I'm not sure everyone would agree with you. But yes, it's very generous of them." He grinned, thinking of the beautiful woman just inside the door, and became more serious. "You see, Cass, Bart just wants you to be happy. He really would like to apologize in person and be someone from home supporting you. I felt it would be a good idea. You might get some peace of mind if you talk to him. I also offered for him to bring Bea. I hope you are all right with that," Ed said. He'd invited Bart on the assumption she wouldn't mind, hoping he wasn't wrong, pacing nervously as he waited for her response.

After some thought, Cassie finally answered, "Yes, Ed, it's all right. You did the right thing by inviting him. If he's set on staying, then I should talk to him and put it behind us once and for all. I bear him no ill will, and I know we'll both feel better if we do. I'd love to see him with someone that makes him as happy as you make me," Cassie said sweetly as she leaned her head against the only thing standing between them.

388

Mabel, George, and Madeline saw Ed standing on the porch outside the door as the wagon pulled into the yard.

"Ed! Don't go inside. Cassie's in there!" Mabel hollered with an excited voice and a smile on her face.

Ed waved and came down the steps to greet them. "Not to worry, Mabel, I know the tradition all too well. I've stayed outside the whole time. I just came to help move the furniture with George," said Ed. "And good day to you all. How's the moving coming?"

"It's coming along, and with your help, it will go even faster. Help me get the frame and ticking out of here, and then we can take Cassie's bed apart," said George as he jumped down.

Mabel spoke up, "I'll go inside and have Cassie hide in my bedroom. Madeline and I can keep her busy while you men work in her room." She walked up the porch steps and hollered through the door, "Cassie, dear, it is just Madeline and me. We're coming in." Slowly, she opened the door, and Cassie giggled as they slipped in and closed it quickly behind them.

"We're coming in!" announced George, sending the women squealing and scurrying into Mabel's bedroom. Giggles escaped the bedroom as George and Ed entered the house, laughing at the antics.

The men made haste as they took apart Cassie's oak bed and stacked the covers on top of her trunk. They brought in the other bed from the wagon and set it up, tightened the ropes, and laid the ticking. Carefully they loaded up the bed, dressing table, and chest of drawers, planning to come back for the bureau and trunk on the next trip. Slowly, they drove down the road, careful not to scratch up the beautiful new furniture.

The women came out when the coast was clear, giggling as they peeked out the front window.

389

"OK, they're gone," said Madeline. "Let's get to work."

The three women had the older bed made up with new sheets and blankets in practically no time, talking and laughing as they worked. Next, Mabel took the wedding dress from Cassie's bureau and placed it in her own bureau, while Madeline and Cassie gathered up all the things she would need for the wedding and placed them neatly on Mabel's bed and dressing table. Finally, the rest of Cassie's items were taken from the bureau and neatly packed in her empty trunk, ready to be taken to the cottage.

It was around noon when the men returned. Dinner was prepared and served. Cassie ate in George and Mabel's bedroom, joined by Madeline to keep her company. While Cassie ate, she got caught up on Madeline's family news and all the fun she had had with her sister's new baby. Then Cassie told of their cleaning adventures with the mice and had a good laugh when Madeline was finally able to see the humor in it. It was fun to share her stories with Madeline. Although she'd written her letters, it was better to tell her thoughts, feelings, and experiences in person. It was exciting seeing Madeline's reactions and sincere interest as she shared her feelings about her betrothed, exhausting every detail to the fullest. It had been a long time since she'd had a friend to talk to, and she missed it immensely.

As soon as dinner was done, the men hefted the large bedroom furniture through the house and down the steps and loaded it into the wagon. Meanwhile, Mabel and Madeline cleaned up the dishes, and Cassie paced in the bedroom. All this waiting was making her anxious, checking the clock repeatedly. It felt like she was a little girl again on Christmas Eve, excited for the big Christmas day.

"OK, that's the last of it," George said, wiping his brow with his bandana hanging around his neck. "Let's go, Ed. The afternoon's heatin' up."

The two men helped themselves to a drink of water from the pump at the sink before they left. They drank it down, quenching their thirst as the sweat ran down their temples and stained their shirts.

"George, I'm coming with you," Mabel announced. "I want to make sure it's all put in the right place," she said, grabbing her bonnet off the peg by the door and tying it on.

"That's fine. We could use your expertise," George said, winking at her.

"If you don't mind, I'd like to stay and help style Cassie's hair for the wedding," offered Madeline. "I'm her 'Fairy Godmother,' after all. And I've got to work my magic," she said, smiling as she waved her imaginary wand. "And with her 'Fairy Godmother's' help, Cassie will be the most beautiful princess of all," she thought with excitement. It was fun to be a part of their story. She was a romantic at heart and always loved a good fairytale.

Cassie's voice filtered through the bedroom door, "That's right, me and my 'Fairy Godmother' have some work to get done before 'Cinderella' is ready for the ball."

Her muffled giggles got them all laughing at her game of make-believe. Then wishing Cassie and Madeline good luck, George and Mabel headed out to the wagon.

Ed approached the bedroom door for a final farewell. "Goodbye, 'Cinderella.' I'll see you at six-thirty. I can't wait to marry you," he said softly through the door. "Then I'll whisk you away in my magical carriage to our cottage on the hill," Ed said to Cassie.

Cassie's heart fluttered with excitement. "Goodbye, Prince Edward," Cassie said breathlessly, loud enough for him to hear.

"Goodbye, my queen," Ed said in his deep soothing voice, then turned to leave, tipping his hat to Madeline as he smiled and closed the door behind him.

As soon as he was gone, Madeline went to the bedroom and began to work on Cassie's hair. Sitting at Aunt Mabel's dressing table, Cassie applied some pomade to help set the curls that Madeline would make with the curling tongs. Once the pomade was evenly through her hair, Madeline took the tongs and heated them over the lamp. Carefully she took a small section of Cassie's hair and wrapped it around the long wand, held it there for a few seconds, and then released the hair, forming a perfect springy curl. She repeated this process over and over, layering curl upon curl. An hour later, they were nearly half done and continued even after Mabel and George had returned.

***

Now that the bedroom furniture was moved in and situated to Mabel's specifications, Ed was able to finally bathe and rid himself of the day's sweat and grime. Squeaky clean, he dressed in his brown Sunday trousers, starched white shirt, and vest. Taking special care, he combed his newly trimmed mustache and applied shaving lotion to his stubble-free jaw and neck, leaving a mild sandalwood scent. Repeatedly he parted and re-parted his hair, combing it back on the sides, until he finally gave in and added a small amount of pomade to hold it in place. He'd never really liked the greasy-feeling stuff, but today was his wedding, and he would do whatever it took to look his best.

Once he was satisfied with the reflection in the mirror, he started in on his sable boots, polishing them to a like-new shine. Then, with a little time to spare, he settled down with his guitar and began practicing the song he'd written for Cassie, finally committing the words to memory. They were the deepest feelings of his heart and almost brought him to tears as he sang the ballad. This was his wedding gift to her.

***

Back at the Hartford's, Cassie's hair was now full of long shiny spiral curls that flowed down her back. Once the curling was completed, Madeline began fashioning the hair into the final look. Parting Cassie's hair in the middle, Madeline took small locks of hair from the sides and twisted them, securing them up off her face and ears with hairpins. From high on the crown of her head and halfway down her back, trailed satin ebony curls. She appeared regal even without the lacy gown and veil. Cassie's "Fairy Godmother" had worked her magic.

"Thank you, Madeline. I look just like a princess," Cassie said as she turned her head side to side, appreciating the reflection of Madeline's handiwork.

"You are, dear." She stood behind her, appraising Cassie's beautiful reflection in the mirror, and gave her shoulders a reassuring squeeze.

Cassie looked beautiful, with her shiny dark hair framing her angelic face. Her rosy lips, still sun-kissed from the day before, turned up in a serene smile. Even her eyes were deeper emerald than usual, contrasted by her pink cheeks, and sparkling from the noticeable happiness on her face. Cassie was glowing.

"Thanks to you, 'Fairy Godmother,'" said Cassie appreciatively.

They both turned as Mabel entered the room, bubbling with excitement. "It's almost time!" Seeing Cassie, she exclaimed, "Oh my goodness! Don't you look as lovely as a princess," she said, complimenting Cassie's natural beauty.

"Thank you, Aunt Mabel," Cassie said, blushing.

"Just being honest," Mabel said as she squeezed Cassie's hand. "Now, let's get you in your gown and see the whole effect." Then, opening her bureau, she removed the ivory gown.

Cassie undressed down to just her camisole, bloomers, and ivory stockings. Stepping into the corset, she pulled it up around her waist and rib cage, holding it up in front while Madeline adjusted the strings in the back and tied them off. Next, Cassie stepped into her crinoline hoops that would hold the skirt out wide and smooth. Madeline tied a double knot securing it at her now smaller corseted waist. One at a time, Mabel helped her slip the two petticoats over her head, one plain and the other trimmed with lace, careful not to ruin her hair. Madeline and Mabel lifted the ivory-laced wedding gown over her head. Next, they straightened the layers, moved her camisole sleeves off her shoulders, and tucked them under the small lace sleeves of the dress. Holding the bodice to her front, they buttoned up the back, perfectly fitting her tiny waist and hourglass shape. Lastly, they added the ivory sash that was tied in back into a big bow, leaving long tails. Continuously they straightened and smoothed the dress until it laid perfectly.

"Oh no, I forgot about my shoes. I'm so sorry," said Cassie. "They're over there on the floor. I'm sorry. I should have remembered to put them on before everything else," she said, pointing to the ivory shoes.

"It's not a problem," said Madeline as she brought them over while Cassie situated herself carefully on the edge of the bed. "And for good luck," she said, placing a sixpence from her pocket into one of the shoes. "It's supposed to bring you good fortune," explained Madeline as she slipped the shoe on Cassie's foot and buttoned the

394

small buttons along the sides above her ankles.

Cassie stood and smiled, swishing her full ivory skirt back and forth to let the layers settle back into place.

"And now the veil," said Mabel, allowing Madeline to do the honors.

The ivory lace veil was carefully secured with the silver beaded comb to the crown of Cassie's head. It fell elegantly over her hair and fanned out halfway down the dress. Cassie walked over to the mirror and twirled around as Mabel and Madeline looked on with pride. She was so pleased with the effect, hardly able to believe it was her in the reflection, truly feeling like royalty.

"I think you're missing a couple of things," said Madeline. "What's the saying? 'Something old, something new, something borrowed, something blue, and sixpence in your shoe.' You have the sixpence in your shoe, but what about the rest?" asked Madeline, smiling at Cassie and Mabel.

"I have something new for you, Cassie," Mabel said with excitement as she opened a drawer from the dressing table, removed a small wooden box, and handed it to Cassie.

"What's this?" Cassie asked with astonishment as she opened the box. In the black velvet lined box, there were the earrings and the necklace she'd admired at the jeweler's. She carefully touched the silver chandelier-shaped earrings with the pearl teardrops and matching necklace.

"Just a little something I thought you could use," said Mabel modestly.

"Aunt Mabel!" Cassie said, "You shouldn't have! Oh, I do love them!" She took the earrings out of the box, put them on, and then asked Aunt Mabel to help with the necklace. A tear collected in Cassie's eye, which she quickly brushed away. The chain lay close to her throat when the clasp was done, cascading down in a waterfall of silver and teardrop pearls. She looked in the mirror, eyes glistening, face beaming.

"They look beautiful on you, Cassie!" Madeline said, admiring the effect with the dress, hair, and veil. "You're more beautiful than ever."

"Oh, thank you! Thank you so much, Aunt Mabel," said Cassie as she hugged her and kissed her on the cheek.

"One more thing, I have the something borrowed, and it's blue," Madeline said as she went to the other room. She brought an elegant wooden fan with light blue lace and a tassel. "It will help when it gets hot," she said, handing it to Cassie.

Cassie took the fan and opened it. "It's so beautiful. I promise I'll be very careful with it," she said and hugged Madeline. "Thank you both so much for everything. I'm the luckiest bride ever. You're both so wonderful," she said, now the tears spilled faster than she could catch them.

"Only tears of joy today," said Mabel as she brushed tears from her eyes. "Oh, and one more thing. 'Something old.'" She opened her chest of drawers and took out a pair of long ivory gloves. "These are old but have only been worn once…on my wedding day. I think they will complete the look of a perfect lady," she said, handing them to Cassie. "I want you to have them now," she said.

Cassie was speechless as she hugged Mabel tight. This wonderful second mother was touching her heart with all the sentiments. More tears of joy were spilled between the women.

"OK, you two. We have to get this princess to the ball," Madeline sniffed as she wiped away a few tears of her own. "It's nearly time to go. We'd better get dressed so we can get her there on time," she said, smiling. As she hugged Cassie, she whispered, "You are the most beautiful bride

I've ever seen. Thank you for letting me be part of your special day, Cassie," she said and kissed her cheek.

"Thank you for coming to be a part of this day with me. It means the world to me. I needed a sister to help me today. Thank you for that," whispered Cassie as she hugged her back and kissed her on the cheek.

Madeline excused herself and went to the other room to change into her gown and Mabel into hers, while Cassie waited in the front room. Pacing the floor, Cassie fidgeted as she tried her best to remain calm as she waited for Mabel and Madeline.

"Bless my lucky stars! I believe I've died and gone to heaven because I'm seeing an angel," George said in astonishment as he walked through the door. He was already dressed in his brown Sunday suit, hair slicked back, and shoes polished and ready to go.

Cassie blushed at the compliment. "Thank you, Uncle George. You always know how to make me feel special," she said as she went up to him and kissed him on the cheek. And then it was his turn to blush.

"I think we should leave as soon as the others are ready," he said quickly to change the subject. "Maybe we should have a bite to eat before we go. It'll be a long night. How about I make us all a sandwich. You sit down while I make them. We can eat, and then we should leave," he said, going to the kitchen to prepare sandwiches.

***

Ed drove the buggy as calmly as possible into town, wanting to slap the reins and speed across the prairie to release his pent-up excitement. But instead, he restrained himself, knowing it wouldn't do to have him and the buggy, not to mention his guitar, covered in dust. "The ring!" he thought with a gasp. Panicked, he felt his suit coat pocket for the ring box. "Goodness! That was a close one. I can't wait!" he thought with anticipation and relief.

Tying up the buggy in front of the Holden Dress Shop, Ed entered for the second time that day and was met by Bart.

"We're ready for you. Come back, and you can try it on," said Bart, leading Ed behind the counter and through the curtains to where the suit coat, shirt, trousers, and vest hung on the male dress form.

"Here you are. What do you think?" asked Bart as the seamstresses and Mr. Holden stood by, waiting for his answer.

The charcoal grey suit and striped vest were very handsome. "I'm impressed. It looks like it came from back East. I can't wait to try it on," Ed said, feeling the sleeve of the elegant suit jacket. "I'll look quite the gentleman tonight."

"Well, let's see how it fits," said Bart. "You can change in the office." He carried the suit to the small room.

Moments later, Ed peeked his head out, wearing the new trousers, white shirt and boots, and the new vest.

"Excuse me, Bart, could you help me get this tie on, please? I have no way of seeing what I'm doing." Ed said with a chuckle, holding the puffy tie.

"My pleasure," said Bart as he came to assist. Standing behind Ed, he cinched and hooked the strap of the puffy necktie against the stand-up collar of his shirt, then fluffed the black fabric evenly, tucking the edges under the lapel of the striped vest. "There, now, just one more thing," he said, placing a pearl tie pin in the center of the tie as Ed raised his chin to give him room. "Mr. Holden, he's ready for you," Bart said, thinking Ed looked dapper.

Mr. Holden entered and nodded his head in silent approval, then began to circle Ed, examining the fit of the vest and length and cut of the trousers. "How does it feel?" he asked.

"Very comfortable," Ed said, moving his arms back and forth and squatting down to check. "Yup, they fit great," he said, straightening up.

"Wonderful, now let's try the jacket," Mr. Holden said as he helped Ed slip the coat up his arms. Smoothing the padding over his square shoulders, he checked the fit, ensuring the sleeves hung straight. Then moving to the front, Mr. Holden made sure the collar sat against his neck without a gap, and the single breast pocket was positioned correctly. Looking closely, he ensured the wide notched lapel lay smoothly across Ed's broad chest. Ed buttoned the jacket at the fitted waist, and Mr. Holden pulled it forward to see how much room there was. Not too snug, with just enough room to move and still give him a V-shape look. It was tailored to be long, ending just above his knees with one pleated vent in the back for a formal look. Mr. Holden ensured the length of the jacket sleeves ended just above his wrists and the white shirt hung a half-inch below that. The black and white striped vest showed only a few inches between the lapels of the jacket, giving it an eye-catching contrast. The completed suit looked very striking. Mr. Holden smiled after making his assessment. "I think it fits magnificently, and you look quite exquisite in it," he said with pride, as Ed agreed.

"One more thing. It wouldn't be complete without the hat," Mr. Holden said as he brought out a hatbox and opened it, taking out a black felt Western-style hat with a four-inch crown and black silk ribbon at the base. Handing it to Ed, he watched him place it on his head and smiled in appreciation. "Now you're ready," he declared.

Ed confidently emerged from the office and was immediately given a standing ovation as the seamstresses stood from their sewing machines and clapped ecstatically. Their hard work had paid off. He looked as dashing as the most refined gentlemen in New York, "or maybe even Paris," someone whispered.

Ed swept his hat off and bowed before his audience, then stood and tucked it under his arm. "Thank you, everyone," he said, looking around the room at the beaming faces, including Bea. "You've all worked so hard today. I must say, you're excellent at your jobs." He smoothed down the jacket front and tugged gently on each sleeve. "I'll be sure to spread the word that the best seamstresses and tailors work here," he said smiling, and turned to Mr. Holden and Bart. "Thank you both very much." He reached out and shook their hands. "I hate to run, but I need to get going. I can't be late for my wedding. Oh, I almost forgot the ring," he said, suddenly turning and rushing back into the office. Finding the ring, he carefully placed it into his new vest pocket along with his silver pocket watch in the other one, stringing the chain through the buttonhole and buttoning it back up. "There! Now I'm ready!"

He gathered his old suit and hat and went to leave, stopping to talk to Bart. "Thank you, again! This is very generous of you. I know you could have picked anyone, and I appreciate you thinking of me. I'll do my best to spread the word. And I wanted to tell you that I talked to Cassie today about your request. She would like to speak to you tonight before the ceremony," Ed said, giving Bart a pat on the back. "Good luck to you."

"And good luck to you as well. I am happy for you both," Bart said sincerely.

Ed passed through the curtained door and stopped momentarily to look in the long mirror out front, turning back and forth. It was an impressive suit, and he felt quite dashing in it.

Placing the new hat on his head, he jumped into the buggy and drove to Reverend Gather's home as fast as he dared. Together, they would go out to Clearwater Pond to rehearse the vows and ceremony before the guests arrived.

Reverend Gather was waiting when Ed arrived, already dressed in his robes to officiate. Holding his Bible and the marriage certificate, he got into the buggy with Ed, and they set off.

The sun's orange glow rested low in the western sky as they arrived, casting beautiful long shadows through the grove. Cool shade spread across the meadow and the crystal-clear water. The summer flowers still in bloom stood tall among the grassland and saplings. Ed pulled the buggy to a stop and tied Major to a tree just off the trail where he would whisk his bride away.

***

It was after five o'clock when Bart ran back to his rented room to get dressed. His trunk had been delivered to the Union Pacific Boarding House, where he now lived.

***

Bea could have walked the distance home, but her father was waiting with the buggy to drive her so she would have more time to get ready. She wondered if her father was as excited for her as she was to be escorted by Bart today.

With expertise, she fashioned her hair into a braided bun high on her head, held in place with a silver comb and pins, then changed into her hunter green gown. The off-the-shoulder dress was edged with lighter green lace outlining the neckline of the fitted bodice. The three skirts of draping satin were trimmed with the same light green lace, held full by her crinoline hoops. Tying on her favorite broach with a black ribbon, she adjusted it to lay just below her throat. Quickly she buttoned her polished black shoes and checked her reflection one last time in the mirror. Her cheeks were rosy from the heat, and her eyes were sparkling bluer next to the dark green of the dress. Then, pinning on her green felt hat to sit tilted forward on her head, she was ready to go. She was grateful to her father for leaving the buggy hitched and ready for her to pick up Bart at the hotel.

***

Bart dressed in his black suit with the black and gold paisley vest and secured his black puffy tie with a pearl pin. Hastily, he combed his hair using the pomade and put on his black bowler hat. Finally, he was satisfied with his reflection, and he rushed down the stairs to wait for Bea's arrival.

"Good evening, Bea!" said Bart, tipping his hat as Bea arrived.

Bea smiled, thinking Bart looked dashing in his black double-breasted suit. "Good evening, Bart," she said and slid over to give him room.

Bart climbed into the buggy beside her, admiring how lovely she looked in her green gown, her eyes even more striking blue. "You look beautiful, Bea."

"Thank you, Bart," Bea said, feeling her cheeks flush. "You look very nice as well."

"May I have the honor of driving you to the wedding?" he asked, reaching for the reins. His heart raced as his fingers brushed against her gloved hands.

"You most certainly may." Bea was flattered by Bart's gentlemanly gesture. "Thank you for asking me to accompany you," Bea said as she observed his handsome profile while he snapped the reins. "He looks quite debonair tonight," she thought as her stomach fluttered.

"It's my pleasure, believe me. I appreciate you saying yes," Bart said, grinning at her.

***

Cassie couldn't believe the time had finally arrived to get married. The trip from home to the pond seemed to take no time at all. She could feel her heart racing as they pulled up behind the line of rigs along the path. Up ahead, she could see wedding guests standing beside the pond, looking back, awaiting her arrival. With hands trembling, she pulled the veil over her face and handed the ring to Aunt Mabel. "I guess this is it," she said with a nervous grin.

Madeline squeezed her hand with a reassuring smile. "Your handsome prince awaits."

Mabel and Madeline went ahead as George helped Cassie out of the carriage and walked with her on his arm, leading her towards the assembled guests.

Reverend Gather and Ed were standing at the front of the gathering, and the pond was the backdrop of the shaded stage, built by God's hand. No better setting could have ever been constructed for this special day. In this very spot was where they had professed their love for one another and where they would seal it with their vows, with God's promise.

As Cassie and George neared the open meadow, she spotted Bart and motioned for him to come join her.

Looking up at her uncle, she explained, "Uncle George, I need to talk to Bart. It's important. It'll just take a minute." Patting his hand and leaving him, she met Bart near the trees.

Bart bowed his head and took his hat in his hand as she drew near. "Cassie, thank you for agreeing to talk to me. Especially on your wedding day," he said with appreciation.

"Ed said you had something you wanted to tell me," she said behind her veil, anxious to get this over with and on with her wedding.

"Yes…by the way, you look lovely," he said, gathering his courage as he looked over at Bea, who nodded her head and smiled. "Ed's a lucky man. I just… wanted to tell you how sorry I am for the way I behaved, and I hope you can forgive me," Bart said sincerely with a weak smile.

"Bart, I do understand, and I forgive you. I have no problem with you staying here in Cheyenne. Ed told me you've met a girl. I believe I know her. I met her in the dress shop. Bea seems very nice, and I'm happy for you," Cassie said and reached out and took his hand. "And thank you for what you've done for Ed. He said it was your idea to make him a new suit for the wedding. Even though it was for advertising your new business, it was still very generous of you. So thank you."

"It was my pleasure. In a way, I felt like I owed him. But, things seem to have worked out just as they should have," he said, squeezing her hand before releasing it. "Now, don't make Ed wait any longer. He's a very good man. Congratulations, Cassie," Bart said, tipping his head and leaving her.

Cassie breathed a sigh of relief and smiled as she returned to Uncle George and took his arm. "I'm ready," she said with a radiant smile.

Mabel and Madeline were already standing at the front of the group opposite Ed and the reverend. The wedding guests parted, making a path leading to Edward. Cassie and George slowly walked forward. Her gaze was fixed upon Ed, looking so tall and handsome in his new suit. She smiled lovingly at him through her veil. Her heart burst with joy as she neared the love of her life.

Ed watched as Cassie came gliding gracefully towards him, looking more beautiful than he could've ever imagined possible, a vision to behold. Her petite feminine figure, flowing ivory dress, and black curls that framed her angelic face mesmerized him, so much so that he couldn't take his eyes off of her. It felt like a dream, and he was alone with her in their private world. He was oblivious to the others observing the glorious occasion. In a moment of déjà vu, he recalled the day they first came to the pond. He had proposed here and imagined her becoming his wife, and now his dream was coming true in the blink of an eye. His heart swelled with overwhelming love for Cassie as she neared.

George brought Cassie to the front, then turned and faced her, lifting the lace veil. Bending down, he kissed her on the cheek.

"I love you, Uncle George. Thank you for giving me away," Cassie said, grateful for this good man standing in her father's place.

"I love you, Cassie, dear. Thank you for allowing me the honor," George whispered in a shaky voice, loving this girl as his own daughter. Gently he took Cassie's hand and placed it in Ed's, then took his place beside him as Best Man.

Cassie, now unveiled, looked up through fluttering

405

dark lashes with sparkling emerald eyes and smiled lovingly at Edward. She looked even more angelic close up, with
the lace flowing over her silky onyx curls, smooth skin, and
pink rosebud cheeks and lips. Ed could hardly breathe from
the beauty he beheld, affecting him so profoundly it created a memory he would never forget. His throat tightened
as tears threatened to emerge, laying just under the surface.
Ed beheld her with pure love and joy. Cassie was the one
who had captured and healed his heart. He loved her more
than life itself. Ed took both her gloved hands and rubbed
the backs of them with his thumbs, softly communicating
his love for her as his eyes shimmered with tears.

Cassie's heart was overflowing with love for Edward.
Feeling the intensity of his love for her, she blinked to
keep the tears of joy from running down her cheeks. He
was such a strong man, yet so gentle, as he protected and
comforted her at the same time. Edward was her hero. He
had rescued her from her loneliness, a broken heart, and
troubled spirit. Cassie knew that God had chosen Ed for
her and placed him in her path at just the right time. It
was miraculous how he understood her needs, wants, and
feelings and continually surprised her, knowing exactly the
right thing to say and do to help her. She trusted him completely with everything, especially her heart.

Reverend Gather began the proceedings. "Friends, we
are gathered here in the sight of God to witness the blessed
union of Edward Karl Havoc and Cassandra Marie Black
in holy matrimony. Marriage is a contract not to be entered
into lightly, but thoughtfully and seriously, and with a deep
realization of the obligations and responsibilities. Marriage
is the moment where your hearts and souls are joined together for eternity," he said, looking around at the group
of loved ones and friends and then at Cassie and Edward.

Mabel wiped a tear from her face, as did Madeline.

Finally, Bart gathered his courage and took Bea's hand. His heart was pounding in his chest as he felt her curl her fingers around his.

Bea was delighted with his boldness. She glanced at him and made eye contact for just a second before she looked away, blushing. He squeezed her hand, reassuring her as she smiled.

The reverend looked at Ed and said quietly, "Repeat after me. I, Edward Karl Havoc, take you, Cassandra Marie Black, to be my wife."

Ed kept his eyes on Cassie and said loud enough for all to hear, "I, Edward Karl Havoc, take you, Cassandra Marie Black, to be my wife."

"To have and to hold, from this day forward, for better, for worse, for richer, for poorer," said Reverend Gather for Ed to repeat.

Ed continued in his deep bass voice, "To have and hold, from this day forward, for better, worse, richer, and poorer." He squeezed her hands gently.

"In sickness and in health, to love, honor, and cherish, for as long as we both shall live," said Reverend Gather.

Ed finished the lines, "In sickness and in health, to love, honor and cherish, for as long as we both shall live." A lump tightened in his throat at the last word. He wanted to say, "and forever and evermore." Ed never wanted to part from Cass, even in death. He believed with all his heart he would be with her one day in heaven, for their love was eternal to him.

The reverend looked at Cassie quietly, saying, "Repeat after me. I, Cassandra Marie Black, take you, Edward Karl Havoc, to be my husband."

Cassie said with deep feeling, "I, Cassandra Marie Black, take you, Edward Karl Havoc, to be my husband." She tried to control the quivering of her chin and steadied her voice.

"To have and to hold, from this day forward, for better, for worse, for richer, for poorer," he prompted Cassie.

Cassie repeated clearly and confidently, "To have and hold, from this day forward, for better, worse, richer, and poorer."

"In sickness and in health, to love, honor, and cherish, for as long as we both shall live," continued Reverend Gather quietly.

Cassie smiled as she thought of all they had been through so far and repeated the words, "In sickness and in health, to love, honor and cherish, for as long as we both shall live." Cassie believed their love was eternal and squeezed Ed's hands to signal that she was his forever, in this life and the next.

"May we now have the rings?" asked Reverend Gather.

Ed took Cassie's ring out of his pocket, and Cassie pulled off her long gloves and handed them to Aunt Mabel, as she then took the ring from her in her right hand.

"You may now exchange your rings," Reverend Gather instructed.

Ed took Cassie by the left hand, looked into her eyes, and said, "Cassandra Marie Black, I give you this ring as a symbol of my love, that I am choosing to share my life's journey with you. I pledge to love you today, tomorrow, and always; in the name of the Father, the Son, and the Holy Spirit."

Cassie looked down and watched as he placed a beautiful gold ring with an emerald stone onto her finger. Ed lifted her hand and kissed it gently. Cassie smiled as a tear rolled down her cheek, unchecked. Her emotions were spilling over with joyful tears.

Cassie then took Ed's left hand, looked into his eyes, and said in her sweet harmonious voice, "Edward Karl

Havoc, I give you this ring as a symbol of my love, that I am choosing to share my life's journey with you. I pledge to love you today, tomorrow, and always; in the name of the Father, the Son, and the Holy Spirit." And she slid the silver band onto his finger, squeezing his hand as more tears flowed.

They continued to look into each other's eyes, smiling as the reverend went on with the ceremony. "Now that Cassandra and Edward have given themselves to each other by solemn vows, with the joining of hands and the giving and receiving of rings, I pronounce to you that they are husband and wife; in the name of the Father and the Son and the Holy Spirit. Those whom God has joined together, let no one put asunder. Amen," he said with a smile. "You may now kiss the bride."

Ed released her hands and placed his hands on her waist, and gently pulled her towards him, leaning in. Cassie wrapped her arms around his neck as he bent down and kissed her soft lips. Her heart was pounding, and her head was swimming. She couldn't believe she was married. Ed had accepted and loved her entirely as she was; it was a miracle of love. At that moment, it was as if time stood still and everyone around them had disappeared. It was not that long ago they had been here alone, sharing their first kiss. Ed wrapped his arms around her and pulled her in closer. His heart was whole again and filled with pure love for this beautiful woman. His joy was overflowing as he lifted her and spun her around. They both began laughing as the crowd of guests clapped and cheered for them.

Ed never wanted to let go of Cass for as long as he lived. Finally, he set her down only long enough to sweep her off her feet and into his arms. She wrapped her arm around his neck and giggled as he carried her towards the buggy, followed by the guests throwing wheat, symbolizing fertility. Cheers went up as he placed her in the buggy and kissed her again. He quickly untied the horse and climbed in beside her as the group of friends and family followed them. Ed snapped the reins, prompting Major to get going, and they dashed away. The sun was lowering on the prairie as they drove down the road back to town. Colors of yellow, orange, pink, and purple glowed on the horizon as sunbursts shot out across the scattered clouds in the darkening sky, as it set on the couple's glorious wedding day.

Chapter 19
Wedding Reception

Ed was laughing as they traveled down the road, feeling that this was the best day of his life. As soon as they were out of sight, Ed put the reins in one hand, wrapped his arm around Cassie's shoulders, and pulled her close to him.

Cassie smiled and nestled into him, looking up at his face with a twinkle in her eyes. "I love you, Edward," she whispered, her heart swelled with joy.

"I love you too, Cass," he replied, and leaned in for a kiss, pressing firmly into her lips. "To have and to hold, and that's what I'm going to do. For as long as she'll let me," he thought, and kissed her again with all the joy and passion he felt.

Cassie was breathless when Edward pulled away. Her heart raced, and her stomach was full of butterflies. "Wow, being married is fantastic," she thought. "I could stay like this forever. I wish we could go straight home and start our lives as Mr. and Mrs. Havoc," she thought with a smile as she rested her head against his sturdy shoulder.

As they entered town and drove up Main Street towards the Town Hall, they noticed a large crowd of finely dressed people gathered outside. Someone at the church must have gotten word of their arrival, for the church bells rang as they came to a stop. A joyous cheer went up from the crowd as the newlyweds smiled modestly and waved at their welcoming party. The rest of the wedding guests rolled up behind them, having driven quickly, so as to not miss out on the festivities.

Ed climbed out of the buggy and helped Cassie down, adjusting her wedding dress and veil, so it lay perfectly before they entered. As they were paraded up the sidewalk towards the Town Hall, the group parted, letting them through, applauding and cheering as they passed. Today was a deeply touching show of support from those Ed had worked and served with during his time as sheriff.

Cassie was overwhelmed with the amount of attention they were attracting and tipped her head down shyly as she tried to focus on the path ahead. Ed, seeing her reaction and understanding her feelings, leaned over and whispered, "Chin up, dear. They are here for both of us. You are mine now, and we are in this together," he said with pride.

Ed beamed down at his new bride as she accepted his words and lifted her gaze, radiating love and adoration back to him.

Half-way up the walk a tall, middle-aged woman with red hair stepped into their path, momentarily halting their progress.

"These are for you, my dear," she said, presenting Cassie with a bouquet of small white roses. "Mabel asked me to have them ready for when you arrived."

"Oh, they're beautiful," declared Cassie, as she accepted the bouquet of white roses tied with pink ribbon, and paused to enjoy their heavenly scent. It had been a long time since she had seen roses. She assumed they had come from the woman's personal garden. "Thank you, so much," she said sweetly. "I adore roses."

"You're welcome and congratulations to you," said the pleased woman. "You both look so elegant," she said, giving Cassie's hand a squeeze. "I think they did a marvelous job on your suit, Sheriff Havoc," she said, appraising his fashionable attire.

"Thank you very much, Mrs. Holden. Your husband had a lot to do with it," Ed said, shaking her hand. "I'd like to introduce you to my wife, Cassandra Havoc," he said proudly, smiling at Mrs. Holden before turning to Cassie and explaining, "Cass, this is Mr. Holden's wife and Bea's mother."

"Oh, so nice to meet you, Mrs. Holden. Your daughter, Bea, was a wonderful help with my dress and veil," said Cassie as she made the connection.

"You look beautiful in it, dear," Mrs. Holden said with a smile.

"Thank you," Cassie said modestly, immediately taking a liking to Mrs. Holden. "And thank you again. It was very kind of you to offer your flowers for my wedding. I greatly appreciate it. They've made a perfect bridal bouquet," Cassie said, gingerly touching the silky soft pedals. "And please, thank your husband for Ed's suit. He did an amazing job."

"He had help, but I'll be sure to tell him and the others at the shop," she said, smiling appreciatively, and stepped aside so they could continue on their way to the reception.

"Those look lovely, Cass," Ed said, nodding toward the roses. "Just like you, my dear," he said, smiling down at her.

Starting up the walk again, he tipped his hat to the excited well-wishers who waved and shook hands with him as they passed. Cassie smiled and replied politely to the many giving congratulations, as she kept one hand around Ed's steady arm and held her bouquet in the other.

Together, they ascended the wide steps of the Town Hall. Once inside they climbed the staircase to the upper room where they had danced only a week earlier.

The large room was filled with familiar faces, including Cassie's aunt and uncle, Madeline, and Bart and Bea. Ed nodded to Vic, who was standing against the wall, and received a nod in return as well as wagging eyebrows. Ed chuckled at his old partner, as he fully understood the sentiment of "well done," with regards to Cassie.

Mayor Hook approached from the far side of the room, his cheery smile and open arms drawing everyone into the center of room.

The billowing white curtains had been drawn open and tied back with pink bows, allowing the cool evening air into the room. Sunlight spilled through the many windows as it moved lower in the sky, wishing them a final farewell on their glorious day, before it dipped below the horizon. The chatter softened as some spotted the newlyweds entering, and soon halted altogether as they entered the center of the room.

Mayor Hook announced, "I would like to present, Mr. and Mrs. Edward Havoc!"

The room filled with applause, whistles, and cheers, as Edward and Cassie stood glowing from their friends and family's show of affection.

The newlyweds were ushered by Mayor Hook to the back of the room. Along the wall were three tables decorated with white tablecloths and pink bows. On the table to the left was a large crystal punch bowl with filled glasses of red punch and platters of tasty cookies. On the other end of the table were bottles of champagne and stemware. On the center table was a three-tier cake, decorated with white frosting and tiny pink rose buds. And the other table was stacked with wedding gifts.

Cassie and Ed were led to the table to the left, where graciously, the mayor and some of Ed's wealthier friends had supplied many bottles of champagne for the wedding toast. George began opening a few bottles of champagne to serve the guests. Two of the prettiest crystal glasses were filled and handed to Cassie and Ed. George then poured his own. The room hushed and all stood still to hear what he was going to say.

George cleared his throat. "I want to thank everyone for coming tonight, to support our lovely niece Cassandra and her husband Edward on their very special day. Today, Cassandra and Edward made a holy covenant with each other and with God. We honor them for their desire to join together on their journey and to start a family. We wish them all the happiness and joy their love will bring them," he said, lifting his glass. "To Mr. and Mrs. Havoc! Cheers!"

The guests exuberantly exclaimed, "Cheers!" and clinked glasses.

Cassie and Ed entwined their arms before drinking their champagne. This custom proved to be a little tricky since Ed was so tall. They laughed as they struggled. Everyone clapped as they watched.

"It's time for Ed and Cassie to have their first dance as husband and wife!" announced Mayor Hook, helping the couple to the dance floor.

The musicians stood poised on the corner platform. Cassie and Edward walked to the center of the room to the cheers of everyone. Ed turned and faced Cassie and took her by the right hand and wrapped his left arm around her back. Cassie's beautiful dress and veil with her dark hair and Ed in his new handsome charcoal suit, looked the picture-perfect bride and groom. The band started to play the couple's favorite song, "Beautiful Dreamer." Ed and Cassie kept their eyes on each other as they began to dance the waltz. Cassie's dress swished slightly as they moved back and forth and side to side. Both felt like they were dancing on clouds, lost in a shared dream. To them, it seemed the room full of people had vanished and left them alone in their own world of music under the glowing lamplight.

Ed began to sing along in his rich deep voice.

> *"Beautiful dreamer, awake unto me,*
> *Starlight and dew drops, waiting for thee,*
> *Sounds of the rude world, heard in the day,*
> *Lulled by the moonlight, have all passed-away,*
> *Beautiful dreamer, queen of my song,*
> *List' while I woo thee, with soft melody,*
> *Gone are the cares of, life's busy throng,*
> *Beautiful dreamer, awake unto me.*
> *Beautiful dreamer, awake unto me."*

Cassie's eyes glistened and sparkled; his words touched her heart.

> *"Beautiful dreamer, out on the sea,*
> *Mermaids are chanting, the wild Lorelei,*
> *Over the streamlet, vapors are born,*
> *Waiting to fade, at the bright coming morn',*
> *Beautiful dreamer, beam on my heart,*
> *Even as the morn', on the streamlet and sea,*
> *Then all the clouds, of sorrow depart,*
> *Beautiful dreamer, awake unto me*
> *Beautiful dreamer, awake unto me."*

Whispered comments passed through the room about how elegantly dressed the couple was. Some speculated on how they'd met, and others wondered where she'd come from. Some whispered about how lucky Cassie was to have captured the highly sought-after Sheriff. While others said he was the lucky one and how such a beautiful young woman would be treasured by any man. Regardless, everyone was happy for the couple.

Those observing their joy were either filled with hope or renewed feelings of commitment. Seeing the two of them lost in each other's eyes as they glided around the dance floor, reminded them that weddings were a celebration of life, where two souls came together in love, unity, and purpose, to begin building a family of their own.

Mabel and Madeline stood close to one another, wiping away their tears with their handkerchiefs as George put his arm around Mabel's shoulders and gave her a hug.

"There's our girl," George said. "I think she did really well for herself, and I think Ed is pretty lucky too. But not as lucky as me," he remarked, as he smiled at his lovely wife and kissed her on the forehead. Mabel may be a little older now, but she looked as beautiful as the day he married her. George felt he was, most definitely, the luckiest man alive.

Mabel put her arm around his waist and looked up at her dearly beloved. "You silly man. You really are adorable. Always making me feel like the prettiest woman in the room," she said as she leaned her head against him. George was her rock, her best friend and companion. Every day he made her proud. Proud of the good man that he was, always kind and generous. His tenderness was endearing to her, and the way he put her needs above his own let her know how special she was to him. Even when he had every right to complain, he never did. She guessed it was the give and take in marriage that kept them humble and forgiving of each other's faults.

The song came to a close and Edward leaned down and kissed Cassie. The room erupted in a hearty applause. The band paused for a moment, allowing George to come to Cassie, and Edward to bring Mabel to the floor for the next dance, and the music struck up again.

"Mabel, I really am grateful for all your hard work.

You've organized such a beautiful reception. It seems everyone is having a great time," Ed said graciously as he looked around the room at the decorations, food, drinks, and cake she had somehow organized in such a short time.

"It's been my pleasure. I can't think of two more deserving people to celebrate," Mabel said with a smile as the two of them danced.

Soon, the four of them were joined on the dance floor by other couples. Colorful skirts swished and swayed as boots glided across the highly polished floor. Couples moved in the now lamp-lit room, spinning and twirling, weaving along an imaginary path, crisscrossing this way and that way. For an onlooker it may have seemed to be perfectly orchestrated, except for the occasional divergent couple, joining or leaving the group.

"Cassie, you look so lovely tonight," said George. "It was a very beautiful ceremony today and made me think of when I got married. That was a glorious day. We thought we loved each other then, but it was just the beginning. Our love has grown so much since. You'll see."

"I believe I will, Uncle George," she said with a soft smile. "I know Ed and I were meant for each other. I feel it when I'm with him. I'm at peace," she confided. "Little did either of us know what God had planned for us, long before we met. I believe our paths were leading us directly to each other. God knew what we each needed. Ed's heart was ready for me to come along when I needed him most."

George nodded in understanding.

"We've both suffered from heartache, but I think it makes us cherish each other even more," Cassie mused, as she glanced over to Ed, watching him lead Aunt Mabel effortlessly in the waltz.

"That it does, that it does," George confirmed, as he thought of all they had been through. "It's been so hard, losing baby after baby, over and over, year after year. Mabel has borne it all graciously, without becoming bitter. She's found a way to serve and love others as if they were her own. And just when we thought our chances for a family were gone, Cassie came along and brought so much joy," George thought, smiling down at Cassie with overflowing love in his heart. "We cherish you, my dear," he said, with eyes glistening.

***

On the other side of the room, Bart took Bea's hand and led her to the edge of the dance floor. Gently, taking her into his arms, he waltzed her around the room. Their steps were in perfect unison. Bea blushed as the warm light and music swept her away like her favorite romance novel. Bart smiled, for Bea appeared to be enjoying herself by the look of her cheeks and dreamy eyes. As the song ended, he spun her around, then bowed to her as she curtsied, both smiling broadly.

On and on, the music and dancing continued as couples traded partners. As the evening wore on, they danced a couple of reels and the two-step as well as a polka and a jig. During the square dances, bystanders clapped and toe-tapped exuberantly as the caller instructed the more-lively dancers to do-si-do, promenade and sashay back and forth across the floor. The waltzes brought out the lovers, and those wishing to be, as couples paired up to dreamily dance the romantic night away. All the while, Cassie and Edward stayed close together, unwilling to part, even when they weren't dancing, clasping hands, and even sneaking a kiss when they thought no one was watching.

Only once did Ed ever leave her side that evening. "I'll

be right back," he said as he went to the musicians and asked them if he could take a moment.

Thankful for a break, the band put down their instruments and left the stage to seek refreshment.

"I would like to sing Cass a song that I wrote for her." Ed looked lovingly at her as he spoke, "You mean the world to me, and I want you to know how much I love you. So, Cass, this song's for you. It's titled, 'Be My Wife'." Ed reached out and took his guitar from George and slung the strap over his shoulder. Ed played the opening chords, as the room fell silent. In his smooth deep voice, he began to sing to his sweetheart.

"After all these years, suddenly you were here.
When I first saw you, on that summer's day.
There was no stopping, once you came my way.
Our hearts pulled us together, come what may.
Like two broken pieces, bound together to stay.

(chorus)
To have and to hold, forever and ever,
These happy moments, we spend together,
I will love you, all my life,
If you will just, be my wife.

I wanted to rescue you, but you rescued me.
I knelt at your feet, and you looked at me so sweet.
We were meant to be. Can't you see?
I wanted you to be mine,
Not for just a day, but for all time.

(chorus)
To have and to hold, forever and ever
These happy days, we'll spend together,
I will love you, all my life,

If you will just, be my wife.

You don't have to be afraid, I'm here, I'll stay.
So, lay your head on my shoulder,
And I'll dry your tears and quiet all your fears.
When you're having a bad day,
I'll make you laugh and kiss your blues away.

(chorus)
To have and to hold, forever and ever
These happy months we spend together,
I will love you, all my life,
If you will just, be my wife.

I know you are the woman for me,
And I'm the man you want me to be.
Maybe we should start a family?
I'll be your king if you'll be my queen.
And together, we'll reign in majesty.

(chorus)
To have and to hold, forever and ever
These happy years, we'll spend together,
I will love you, all my life,
If you will just, be my wife.

So, let me stay by your side, if I may.
And hold your hand when we're old and grey.
I'll keep you warm when you are cold.
And hold you tight and keep you safe.
And together we'll fly, when that joyous day arrives.

(chorus)
To have and to hold, forever and ever
This happy life, we'll spend together,
I will love you, all my life,

421

Because today, I made you my wife.

Today, God gave you to me, to love, honor and cherish,
We'll fly like angels to the stars.
Happiness and joy will be ours.
Together we'll travel throughout time,
Now that you've chosen to be mine.

(chorus)
To have and to hold, forever and ever
A glorious eternity, we'll spend together,
I will love you, all my life,
Because today, I made you my wife."

Tears rolled down Cassie's face as he held out the last note and smiled at her. As he strummed the last chord, Cassie rushed forward and was caught in his arms.

"Oh Ed, I love you so much," Cassie said softly through her tears, standing on tip toe hugging him, then boldly kissed him on the lips. Realizing what she had just done in front of everyone she blushed, hiding her face in his neck. For a moment the room fell silent as women dabbed their tears and men cleared their throats and made dreamy eyes at their own sweethearts.

Ed tipped his head down. "I love you forever and ever, Cass," Ed whispered against her hair, getting choked up and wiping away a tear from his eye before anyone could see. He lifted her chin and kissed her again, earning them a warm applause and a few cheers.

"That was beautiful," Madeline said to Mabel. She smiled as a tear ran down her cheek as she watched the two share an intimate moment. "It makes me miss my husband something fierce. I'll be glad to get home to my family. But I wouldn't have missed this for anything," she said sincerely.

"It sure has meant a lot to Cassie to have you here. We've all enjoyed your company and will miss you when you go," Mabel said, giving Madeline a squeeze around the shoulders. "We should get this party moving towards a close, so the two lovebirds can head home," she said with a grin.

"You'd better make it hasty, Mabel," said George with a wink and chuckle.

Mabel raised her voice as she stepped forward, "I think it's about time to cut the cake, if you two can stop kissing long enough." Mabel laughed as clapping, whistling, and cheering erupted again. "Come over here, you two."

Together they walked with their arms around each other to the cake table, where Aunt Mabel handed them a long knife. Cassie stood nearest to the cake with Ed standing close behind her. Taking the knife in her right hand and Ed placing his gently over hers, she positioned the knife over the cake. Pressing down together, they cut through the thick bottom layer of white frosting and cake. With Ed holding the plate, Cassie carefully lifted the piece of cake away and laid it on the plate.

Each of them broke off a piece, careful not to spill on each other's clothes. Ed was the first to feed Cassie. Her eyes sparkled, and she laughed as she closed her mouth over his fingers holding the cake.

Ed smiled and as he withdrew, feigned being bitten, vigorously shaking his hand as he jokingly grimaced. The group roared with laughter. Cassie laughed even harder and wished she had bitten him, just a little, for pulling such a trick.

Next, it was Cassie's turn to feed Ed. Reaching up, she placed the piece of cake into his mouth. Quick as a wink and smiling with delight, he took hold of her wrist and held it there so he could lick the frosting from her fingers as she giggled. The guests clapped and whistled; they loved the teasing.

Laughing heartily, they attempted to clean each other's hands and faces with a napkin. While Mabel and Madeline worked together to cut the cake for the gathered guests, the band announced a waltz and guests scrambled looking for their next partner. Music filled the room as the band played a familiar ballad.

"May I?" Bart asked Bea as he took her hand and led her out to the floor again.

"That was a beautiful song Ed sang to Cassie, wasn't it?" Bea asked as they waltzed in the flickering lamplight.

"It was very romantic. It made me think of someone very special," he said with a smile. "Someone I met one summer's day." Bart had been very touched by the song; the words were ones he could relate to. "If only she would be my wife."

Bea blushed. "Oh, who's that?" she asked, feeling the recurrent flutter of excitement in her stomach. "Could this be true? Is he talking about me?" she wondered. "What if I'm mistaken and there's someone else?"

"Well, she has beautiful blue eyes, and strawberry blonde hair, and just a few freckles on her pretty little nose." He grinned. "She's very smart, talented, and hard working. And I want to know everything about her," Bart said with a wink.

"Oh, Bart, she sounds lovely. You'll have to introduce me to her some time," Bea said, trying to remain calm, still not believing what she had just heard. "He's just teasing me," she thought. "Or is it true? Is that what he really thinks?" she wondered. "After all, he was engaged to Cassie once, and she's beautiful and perfect in every way."

"I could, but you already know her. All you have to do

is look in the mirror and she'll be right in front of you," he said, giving her hand a gentle squeeze. He couldn't believe how bold he was acting. Bea seemed to have that effect on him. He felt he could be himself with her, safe to tell her anything, feeling she would find whatever he said interesting or amusing, and it was exhilarating.

"Really? You think of me that way?" she asked seriously, with a catch of emotion in her voice.

Bart was endeared by her modesty. "Yes Bea, is that so hard to believe? I really like you. And to be honest, you're the reason I'm staying here."

Bea was stunned, her breath caught in her throat. She blinked a few times to keep the tears of joy from spilling over and smiled shyly when the music ended. Leaning in close, she whispered, "I'm so glad you're staying, for whatever reason." Her heart was pounding, and she was breathing fast. She wanted to say so much more. But didn't feel it was proper.

Mayor Hook loudly announced, "This is the last dance, everyone." He looked around the room and spotted Ed and Cassie. "And then we'll send the newlyweds off, to begin their new life."

Edward and Cassie took the floor as did George and Mabel, and Bart and Bea, along with many others. The band began playing a classical waltz, as lamps cast an amber glow overhead, setting the stage for romance. Couples held each other, moving as one, swaying back and forth to the rhythm. Eyes sparkled and smoldered as they held each other's gaze as hearts raced and pounded with exhilaration.

Bart wanted nothing more than to dance like this forever with Bea. Holding her in his arm, touching her back, and watching her gracefully move was the best feeling he had ever had. The pink glow in her cheeks and the shine in her eyes transfixed him. He couldn't think to speak, the

425

feeling in his heart was too big. When she turned her head slightly, he followed her long, graceful neck to where her soft red hair had been pulled up, neatly weaving in and out of the braid. He wished he could touch her cheek, sure it was as smooth as silk, and soft as velvet.

Bea caught him studying her and smiled demurely, trying to hold his gaze. She blushed as her heart skipped a beat. She was shaking with excitement. All reasonable thoughts left her as Bart swept her effortlessly around the room. Everything around her faded; her only focus was on feeling the moment with him.

Nearby, the blushing bride and grinning groom found themselves lost in the splendor of love. Ed watched as Cassie floated with the music like an angel. She was his angel, guiding him along the happiest path of his life, uplifting him to heights he had never experienced. How was this possible, he wondered? He was just an ordinary man. Not particularly special. And yet she was here with him, and now his wife. His heart was bursting with love. He made a solemn promise to her today and he would die keeping it. He wanted only her happiness, above all else. He would give her all she wanted and needed; most of all, he would give her his complete love and devotion. He vowed she would have all that and more. Ed's heart ached to pull her close and hold her tight, smell her hair and run his fingers through it, something he had wanted to do for as long as he had known her. Today, finally, within God's laws, he was blessed to make Cassie his, completely.

Cassie was feeling the heat in the room, or was it coming from inside her? She felt such a strong connection with Ed. She felt as comfortable in his arms as she did in her own body, as they moved around the dance floor as one. His strength supporting and lifting her, she seemed to hardly touch the floor.

426

The song faded out as it ended and couples reluctantly released each other, not wanting the moment to end. As the musicians bowed to their appreciative listeners, those gathered eagerly let them know that they had outdone themselves.

Cassie fanned herself with the blue fan as she stood catching her breath, holding onto Ed's arm to clear her spinning head and steady her trembling legs.

Mayor Hook took front stage as the band stood, instruments by their sides. "I want to thank these talented musicians, for providing us with such wonderful music. We greatly appreciate your gift to each of us tonight, and a special thank you to the happy newlyweds, for letting us celebrate with them." As the applause faded out, he made the final announcement. "Edward and Cassandra Havoc!" The floor cleared around them as they stood in the center of the room. "We want to wish you a very happy life and prosperous future. Cassandra, you just need to toss your bouquet and then Edward can take you away." He motioned for her to join him on the stage. "Come on up."

Cassie smiled with eyes twinkling at Ed and left his side to join Mayor Hook.

"Single women, gather up. The one who catches the bouquet will be the next to wed!" shouted Mayor Hook, getting into the excitement.

Excitedly, girls of marrying age gathered, giggling, and clutching each other's hands in glee. Aunt Mabel brought Cassie her bouquet as Cassie smilcd at the excited girls.

Bart gently pushed Bea forward. "You too, Bea," he said, smiling impishly.

Bea reluctantly moved toward the back of the group of squealing girls and bubbling young women, feeling embarrassed to be one of the oldest of the bunch. Only weeks before, she had assumed she would be a spinster for the rest of her life. She felt foolish even bothering with such a silly tradition. Glancing back towards Bart, she gave him a pleading look, wishing he hadn't made her join the group. But he waved her on and gave her an encouraging smile and nodded his head in approval.

Words of support were hollered from the side-lines by hopeful gentlemen, wishing their sweethearts good luck. Fingers were crossed, and silent prayers uttered, in hopes they were the next ones to wed.

Cassie smelled the ivory roses one last time. Turning around, she held the bouquet in her outstretched arm, and in one fluid motion, flung it over her head. The bouquet spun in the air end over end, arching high above young giddy girls and came down right in front of Bea. Instinctively, Bea reacted, and caught the bouquet in her hands. Everyone spun around to see where it had landed. There was Bea, in her lovely green gown, holding the bouquet with an expression of astonishment. She blushed as the other girls rushed up to her and cheered in excitement. They were clearly glad for her. As custom had it, they believed that she would be the next to marry.

Cassie turned to see who had caught the bouquet and could see Bea, surrounded by giggling ladies. Bea looked up at Cassie and lifted the bouquet in triumph, feeling it was the right way to react in the situation. Cassie clapped, then clasped her hands together, bringing them to her heart as she smiled broadly at Bea, hoping it was going to come true. Bea had been so sweet to her in the dress shop, and now knowing that she was Bart's reason for staying, made her even happier for her.

Mabel and Madeline joined Cassie, helping her down from the stage.

"You did that wonderfully, my dear," said Mabel giving her a hug. "It's getting late, you'd better get going. We'll stay here and gather your presents and take them home for you. You go home with your husband. You've had a big day. We'll catch up with you tomorrow."

Ed came over and put his arm around Cassie's waist and leaned down to her. "It's time to go, sweetheart," he whispered in her ear.

Cassie felt an excited shudder run through her body and looked up at him, smiling. "I'm just going to say good-bye to Madeline, and then I'm ready."

Madeline stepped forward and gave Cassie a hug. "Congratulations, my dear. I'm so happy for you. And I'm so glad I was able to be here for you," Madeline said with tears in her eyes.

Cassie's heart was full. She didn't want to say goodbye to Madeline, who was leaving on the morning train, knowing she would possibly never see her again. "I love you, my sweet friend. Thank you for being such a wonderful support and for all you've done for me. Oh, and here's your fan back. Thank you so much for letting me borrow it." She reached for the fan on her wrist, to remove and give back to Madeline.

Madeline put out her hand and gently stopped her. "No, I want you to keep it. I want you to remember me whenever you use it," Madeline said with tears running down her cheeks. "I love you, my dearest sister. God is with you, and you have every reason to trust that this is where you're meant to be. You deserve all the happiness that is in store for you," she said, squeezing Cassie's hand. Then looking to Ed, she said, "Ed, I know you will take good care of her, and give her an extra hug for me every day. Thank you for making her so happy. Congratulations to you both." She reached out and squeezed Ed's hand in appreciation and farewell.

"You don't have to worry; I'll give her plenty of hugs

429

for you. Thanks again for coming and helping, it means a lot to both of us. Travel safely," Ed said.

"I'll write. I promise," Madeline said, leaning forward and kissing Cassie on the cheek one last time. Then she whispered, "Good luck with the baby when the time comes. I know you will do wonderfully. You are stronger than you know." And with that she gave her one last hug. "Now go, start your life together," she said, smiling as tears continued down her face.

Uncle George stepped forward and kissed Cassie on the cheek. "Congratulations my darling, and congratulations, Ed," he said, shaking Ed's hand. "We'll see you both tomorrow at church," George said, smiling with a wink.

"And for supper, don't forget. Supper at our house on Sundays," reminded Aunt Mabel as she came forward and gave Cassie one last hug and kiss and a quick hug for Ed.

"Yes, Aunt Mabel, we'll be there. I love you both so much. Thank you for everything. Goodbye, Madeline, thank you again. Travel safe," she said, smiling at her beloved family and friend.

Then Ed took her by the hand. "It's time to go, sweetheart," he said, smiling as he gently guided her away.

The group of wedding guests and townsfolk followed Ed and Cassie to the door to see them off.

***

Bart approached Bea as soon as all the girls had dispersed. Bea turned around and smiled as soon as she saw his huge grin.

"Well, you're the lucky one. Providence has spoken. Seems you will be the next to be married," said Bart, with mischievousness in his voice. Although he teased her, he hoped she would be the next to be married, and that it would be to him.

Bea held the bouquet in her hand, looking down at the beautiful white rose buds. She smiled at his teasing but felt her heart jump inside her chest as she imagined marrying him. She looked up at Bart, as his teasing smile turned to one of love.

"You never know. If the right man was to ask, I just might be inclined to say yes," she said shyly, as the heat rose in her cheeks.

Bart's heart was pounding now. It was clear she was alluding to him, and he felt his own cheeks blush. Soon they were the only ones standing in the room. Bart didn't know what possessed him, the words just spilled out. "I would love to be the right man for you," he said as his heart nearly burst with emotion. He hoped he hadn't been too forward and scared her away.

Bea's mind was trying to grasp the words, as she replayed them over and over in her head. It was too unbelievable. "Is this really happening?" She could hardly believe what she had heard. Then Bart moved forward, standing close to her, and placed his hand over the one holding the bouquet. He stroked the back of her wrist softly, keeping his eyes on the flowers. She could feel him shaking slightly and then he took a step closer still. Tenderly, he took her chin and lifted it, causing her to look up at him. She had a tear on her cheek. He took his thumb and gently swept it away. Then, leaned forward and kissed her sweetly. Her soft lips welcomed his. She sighed softly as he slowly pulled away. Smiles slowly spread across their faces.

Bea looked down and spoke breathlessly, "You are the right man for me, Bart."

He wrapped his arms around her waist and gently pulled her closer; her arms moved to rest on his shoulders, as he waited for her to look up at him.

"Bea, I want to marry you. When the time is right, that is exactly what I will do. I have nothing to offer you right now. But someday soon, I'll be able to provide for you. And then I'll ask for your hand in marriage," promised Bart, feeling his heart burst with the words. "You are everything to me. 'If you will, just be my wife,'" Bart said, quoting the song Ed had sung to Cassie.

Bea looked up into his blue eyes. "Wild horses couldn't stop me from being your wife. It's all I've dreamed about since I first met you," she confessed. "I've been waiting for you, all my life. I didn't think you would ever come. And now you're here, and I can hardly believe it's real," Bea said, spilling her heart's deepest secret.

Bart was reeling from her soulful words. "Believe me, I'm real and I'm here to stay. And I will make you my wife," he vowed as he kissed her again. His arms tightened slightly as he held her close, desperately wanting to hold onto her forever.

She wrapped her arms around his neck and held him as her heart swelled with love for this wonderful man of her dreams.

***

Ed and Cassie pulled away from the Town Hall in their buggy as the throng of well-wishers cheered on. Finally, alone. The dark cool night welcomed them. Hidden in the dark, they held each other and kissed, both of them anxious to begin their journey as husband and wife.

The drive passed quickly in the dark. By now Major knew the way. Ed couldn't keep his eyes off Cassie's face; it shone in the moonlight silhouetted by her dark hair and white veil. Cassie shivered in the cool air, and Ed moved his arm around her shoulders, pulling her next to him to keep her warm and safe, just as he had promised to do. She rested her head on his chest and listened to his heartbeat faster. Ed gently stroked her bare shoulder with his thumb, her soft skin glinting like porcelain in the moonlight.

Pulling to a stop in front of their cottage, Ed said, "Wait here, I'll be right back." He kissed her quickly and jumped down and ran up the steps and into the cottage. Within minutes the home had lights glowing inside the curtained windows that splashed yellow across the yard. Ed was setting the stage for Cassie to see her beautiful new home for the first time as his wife.

Ed came rushing out and reached his hand out to take hers. Cassie stepped down from the buggy. As soon as she was down, he wrapped his arm around her waist, and lifted her effortlessly. She wrapped her arm around his shoulder and smiled at him as he looked at her, grinning. "Home at last," she thought as she rested her head on his neck. Ed carried her up the steps and gently kicked the unlatched door open. Carrying her across the threshold of their home, he set her gently down on her feet once inside.

"Welcome home, my love," Ed said, pulling her to him for a sweet kiss.

Cassie returned his kiss, holding his face. She had never felt so completely happy and in love. "Welcome home, darling," Cassie said, wrapping her hands behind his neck. "I'm so happy. Today has been the most wonderful day of my life." She kissed him again, leaving them both breathless.

"I need to go put Major in the corral. Will you be here when I get back?" Ed asked mischievously and gave her a quick kiss again.

"I'll be here. Anxiously awaiting your return," Cassie

said grinning, letting his fingers slip through her hand as he turned and left the room.

Cassie's heart was rejoicing from all the happenings of the day. She looked around the room, finally registering all the changes. There were new white lace curtains on the windows and a tablecloth on the kitchen table. The home was warm and cozy-looking now. Their bedroom door was open, and a light shone from inside. Cassie walked into the room. It was her bedroom furniture but more beautiful than she had ever seen it. On the bed was a magnificent new patchwork quilt, pieced together with pink, blue and sage green fabrics fashioned into interlocking rings. She counted forty-two interlocking rings, representing wedding rings, set against the white background. Walking to the bed, Cassie touched the quilt lovingly. She was certain that her aunt had something to do with this special gift. Cassie walked to the back window and opened it a crack, letting in the cool night air. The new white curtains billowed in the breeze. She sat down at her dressing table and looked at her reflection. She looked so happy and at peace. Her emerald eyes were sparkling brilliantly, and her face was glowing in the lamplight. Carefully, Cassie removed the veil and draped it over the table, then removed the earrings and necklace and laid them inside the top drawer. Realizing she would need help getting her dress unbuttoned, she blushed at the thought. She couldn't even reach her shoes with her dress and crinoline on. She would have to wait for Ed's help. Standing, she pulled the curtains closed.

Ed came into the cottage and saw Cassie through the bedroom door, standing at the window. He had never seen such a beautiful woman. Her white dress and black curls down her back, with slender arms and smooth shoulders were so beautiful. Ed removed his jacket and hung it on the back of the kitchen chair, then slowly entered the bedroom.

"Can I help you with something?" he said gently, not wanting to startle her. "I know I don't look like it, but I am pretty handy at a lot of things." Smiling, as he unhooked his tie pin and unclasped the tie, he laid it down on the dressing table next to Cassie's veil. Ed unbuttoned the top button of his shirt and took a deep breath.

Cassie flushed. "I just realized I can't reach my shoes. Would you be so kind to help me take them off?" Cassie asked, moving to sit in the chair in front of Ed. "My feet are killing me. I can't wait to get them off," she said as she sat down.

"It would be my pleasure, my queen." Ed knelt down in front of her and lifted one foot and unbuttoned the tricky little buttons, finally slipping one shoe off and laying it down. Then the other one. But this time he didn't put her foot down. Instead, he began to rub her foot, gently massaging her heels and arches, covering every inch. Then he moved to the other foot to repeat the process.

"Oh, that feels wonderful," she said relaxing with his touch. "My feet have been hurting for hours. Thank you so much." Ed continued working out the soreness. Cassie watched as he worked with his strong fingers, touching her gently but firmly, careful to not hurt her.

"Anything else?" he asked, as he gently set her foot down and stood up. Ed began unbuttoning his vest and removed the pocket watch and laid it on the table.

"Umm," Cassie hesitated. "I will need a little help with the buttons on the dress." Shyly she stood and turned around, looking over her shoulder.

Ed felt his pulse quicken. He came close behind her and gently swept her hair away from her back. Carefully he unbuttoned the small buttons down the back of the dress.

She stood holding the dress over her front, frozen in

place.

"I'm going to go make some coffee," Ed said. "I'll let you change. It'll be ready when you're done, if you want some." Ed leaned down and kissed the back of her neck before he left her.

"That would be lovely. Thank you, darling," Cassie said in relief.

Ed left the room, closing the door behind him. He removed his vest and placed it on another chair back and opened the kitchen window to cool the stuffy kitchen before he made a small fire in the stove and started the coffee. As he sat at the kitchen table waiting, he removed his boots and socks. His feet were hot and tired, and the cool floor felt good. Sitting back against the chair, he looked toward the bedroom door. Ed was patient, like Job. It was one of his virtues. He had waited years for Cassie to come along, and he could wait a few minutes more. Ed understood her more than she probably realized. Knowing what she had been through, he in no way wanted her to be apprehensive or uncomfortable with intimacy. He loved her too much to pressure her.

It took Cassie a minute to get undressed and place the gown in the wardrobe, hang up petticoats and pack the crinoline into the trunk. Removing the corset, she placed it into one of the drawers and took out the new nightdress and put it on, leaving the robe draped over the chair. The room was too hot to put it on. Finally, dressed, Cassie slowly opened the bedroom door to see Ed sitting in the parlor chair with his coffee cup in hand. He smiled as she emerged.

"Well, that looks just about as pretty as your wedding dress," Ed said, grinning at her.

Cassie smiled at his teasing. "It's new," she said, blushing.

"Come sit here," he said, patting his leg. "I have your coffee right here." Ed smiled. Opening his arms, he wrapped one around her as she sat across his lap. Ed handed her the cup of coffee, and she took a sip and set it back down on the table beside the chair.

"It's too hot for me. I'll let it cool," Cassie said softly, not really wanting coffee anyways.

She started rubbing his back a little and then his neck. Ed closed his eyes, enjoying the feeling. Her hands were working their magic, releasing all the tension in his muscles. His breathing deepened and he pulled her closer. Setting his cup down, he closed his eyes again. Ed could stay like this forever. Cassie moved her hand to the back of his head and ran her fingers through his hair, enjoying the soft short hair as it slipped between her fingers. She rested her forehead against his temple, closing her eyes as she gently kissed his cheek.

"I love you, Ed, my one and only," Cassie whispered as she placed her other hand on his cheek and turned his face towards hers.

Ed opened his eyes to look at her. "Cass, I love you forever and ever. I'm so glad you're my wife." He moved the few inches to her and kissed her softly and then more intensely.

When Ed reluctantly released her lips she said, "I think it's time to go to bed." Cassie was ready. It had been a long day. And finally, she was home where she wanted to be.

Ed slipped his arm under her legs and lifted her as he stood. "Yes, my queen," he said and carried her to the bedroom, softly closing the door with his foot, and gently put his wife to bed.

About The Author

For as long as I can remember I have had a love for the American frontier and the idea of living in a time period where people lived off the land with determination and true grit. Growing up I, like other little girls, read the *Little House on the Prairie* books and watched the television series over and over, imagining I was Laura Ingalls.

Series like *Grizzly Adams* and *My Side of the Mountain* helped shape my imagination. I couldn't get enough of adventure stories set in the Wild West; especially stories of the tough women who braved the untamed land alongside their husbands.

I discovered books by Janette Oke, Gerald Lund and Lauraine Snelling, whose stories rang true with me. Their faith filled stories set in the late 1800's gave me hope for a better world and found myself imagining stories of my own.

Telling stories and writing them down has been a passion of mine since my childhood. Now in my later years, I have the time to devote to writing my stories. What started as a short story has become a full-length historical romance called *Cassie's Miracle*. In the past three and a half years I have written a four-book series about Cassie's legacy. I have loved every step of the journey, researching for hundreds of hours about the time period that I already loved was fuel for my imagination. I learned about the history of the transcontinental railroad, steam engines, the clothing worn during the Victorian Era, their customs, phrases used, common recipes, religious practices, and even old-fashioned weddings during that era and couldn't get enough.

As I reread my favorite books and re-watched *Doctor Quinn Medicine Woman* and many other Native American documentaries and movies, I completely immersed myself in the world of the past. I've worked as a nurse for the last thirty years in labor and delivery and other branches of nursing, and found it easy to describe childbirth and add vital details to my story from my personal experiences and those of others I cared for. My study of herbs and natural healing also add to my story as they were used to practice old medicine. Other details that I was unsure of, I consulted doctors to keep medically accurate, wanting every detail to be right. As part of my research, I interviewed numerous Native American members of the Shoshone tribe and studied their customs and language so that I could use it correctly in my story. As part of my love for the frontier, my children and I have participated in dressing as pioneers in the Pioneer Days celebration held in Utah and Idaho.

Thousands of followers on my professional Yvette Blake Author Facebook page are daily entertained by stories and history of the olden days, country themed photos or humorous writing jokes. Social media is a small distraction from my passion of writing, but I feel a loyalty to my followers. It's a personal goal to be present daily for them through my Instagram, Twitter and Facebook posts.

My love of the past has shaped who I am. I love crocheting, sewing, canning, gardening, baking bread from scratch, fishing, camping, horses, nature and all the simple pleasures of life. As well as my talents, they are my passions

as much as writing is. Clean romance in historical fiction

has been my favorite genre all my life and, as I've gotten older, I've found the world lacking the good wholesome entertainment with real love stories and Christian themes. So, I started writing what I would want to read, and in the process wrote my favorite type of story.

Tragedy comes along to all of us and as I experienced it in my own life, I felt a type of therapy as I wrote about the strong female protagonist. As I wrote about Cassie's tragedy and loss, I looked inside myself for the strength that it would take for her to go on. Her journey is as much mine as hers and many other women. Cassie does hard things and perseveres as she finds hope and strength through love of family and true love of her own. My goal is not only to entertain, but to give hope and inspire those who read my novels to have faith in themselves and in God.

Made in the USA
Thornton, CO
02/03/23 03:22:57

aafa60ef-1c98-4344-bea0-ef59bfc760f3R01